# Praise for the Works of Bruce Campbell

## *Make Love the Bruce Campbell Way*

"Campbell knows of what he writes, and this endless barrage of extreme silliness obviously spoofs (and quite possibly mirrors) a frenzied acting career made up of equal parts exasperation and hilarity."

— *Publishers Weekly*

"A wholly entertaining read, peppered with numerous comical photos and graphics, which alone are worth the price of the book. B movie virus or not, Campbell definitely has buckets of talent as a writer. . . . A must-read for fans."

— *Fangoria* Book of the Month Club

"Sharp, satirical, and savvy, *Make Love the Bruce Campbell Way* is a must-have not only for the author's diehards, but for anyone who enjoys a rollicking Tinsel Town tale."

— *Horror.com*

## *If Chins Could Kill*

"This book is indispensible to anyone aspiring to a career as an actor, director, producer, or just about any other aspect of moviemaking . . . a fast, enjoyable read and is sure to garner Campbell even more of a following."

— *Fangoria*

"In his first book, Campbell forgoes Hollywood anecdotes for more entertaining tales of struggling to break into the biz. With a quirky assortment of rants, as well as self-deprecating chapter titles like "The Higher the Budget, the Lower the Part," he's like the dinner guest you wish would never leave. A-."

— *Entertainment Weekly*

"An insightful and rant-filled guide to being almost famous."

— *GQ*

"This entertaining and witty Hollywood memoir combines [Campbell's] life story with how-to guidance on making independent films and becoming a pop culture cult hero. Has enough insights and smarts to appeal to readers with a serious interest in popular culture"

— *Publishers Weekly*

"Fun to read, filled with amusing anecdotes and black-and-white snapshots, and written with boyish charm and wit. Campbell's casual, chatty style and intelligent but modest insights make this a great book for anyone interested in pop movie culture."

—*The Oakland Press*

Also by Bruce Campbell

*If Chins Could Kill: Confessions of a B Movie Actor*

make Love!*

*the bruce campbell way

STARRING

# BRUCE CAMPBELL

PIXEL WRANGLING & GRAPHIC SARCASM BY
## CRAIG "KIF" SANBORN

AND FEATURING THE PHOTOGRAPHY OF
## MIKE DITZ

THOMAS DUNNE BOOKS
ST. MARTIN'S GRIFFIN ⚭ NEW YORK

THOMAS DUNNE BOOKS.
An imprint of St. Martin's Press.

www.stmartins.com


Library of Congress Cataloging-in-Publication Data

Campbell, Bruce, 1958–
    Make love!—the Bruce Campbell way / starring Bruce Campbell ; pixel wrangling &
graphic sarcasm by Craig "Kif" Sanborn ; and featuring the photography of Mike Ditz.
    p. cm.
    ISBN-13: 978-0-312-31261-9
    ISBN-10: 0-312-3126-1-X
    1. Motion picture actors and actresses—Fiction. 2. Motion picture industry—Fiction. 3.
Hollywood (Los Angeles, Calif.)—Fiction. I. Title.

PS3603.A465 M35 2005
813'.6—dc22

                                                                                    2005045508


First St. Martin's Griffin Edition: August 2006

10 9 8 7 6 5 4 3 2 1

*For Chook*

# Prologue

Making B movies can be exhilarating. The pace is usually brisk and ideas, forced to the surface by a sheer lack of money, are kicked back and forth with the energy usually reserved for a World Cup soccer match.

Directors of these movies (referred to variously as genre, low-budget, or schlock) are usually inexperienced, callow, and unrealistic, but they are also enthusiastic, daring, and indefatigable. The writers, typically working on their first screenplay, have something to prove, and while they revel in their awkward dialogue and stupid (or missing) plot, you'll occasionally find a spark of genius — fanned by simply not knowing what the rules are.

Fellow actors in these second-tier films are often very green, with careers on the rise, and it's fun to watch them deliver every line of dialogue like it's their last. Mostly, they'll suck, but there is a certain truth in early work that isn't always displayed by the other type of actor found in B movies (and I must insert myself into this category) who are very experienced, with careers more prone to gravity, and are excited just to remember dialogue.

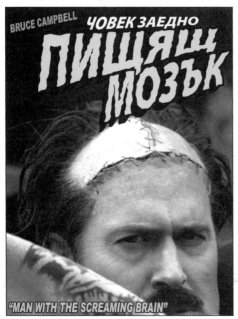

BRUCE CAMPBELL ЧОВЕК ЗАЕДНО ПИЩЯЩ МОЗЪК

"MAN WITH THE SCREAMING BRAIN"

But in the midst of the exhilaration, making B movies can also be a pain in the ass. For starters, there is never enough money to make the vision floating in your head translate to the silver screen. The latest B movie I made was *Man with the Screaming Brain*. I'm embarrassed to say that it took eighteen years to scrape the money together to make this on-again-off-again pseudo pet-project, and even at that, production was diverted to Eastern Europe.

What worked in Bulgaria's favor, aside from a wicked Shopska salad and vodka for sale on every corner, was how cheap everything was. A roomy apartment would set you back about $3,000 (to buy, not rent), a two-story house in the nearby foothills sold for $50,000, and the average Bulgarian made $110 a month. You can see, economically, why films, particularly those destined for the Sci-Fi Channel, are made in strange, distant lands.

In retrospect, would I say that the former Eastern Bloc is a good place to make a movie? Yes and no. Yes, if you like a charming, hardworking society, struggling to emerge from communism. No, if you are disturbed by roaming packs of wild dogs and a language that is spoken like the person is permanently annoyed. But after eighteen years of kissing everyone's ass in sight to direct my first feature film, Bulgaria was good enough for me.

What comes with shooting in countries with far greater needs than those of an American film is what I call "the Bulgarian Box of Chocolates," whereby you never really know, day to day, what you are going to get.

A key scene in the film revolved around a Vespa. I'll spare you the narrative details of why it was critical, but the Vespa had to be painted pink, with streamers from the handlebars and, by the time we were done, was going to be destroyed.

At the time, I felt that my first meeting with the transportation department had gone well. Since only a small handful of crew members spoke English, my translator, Assia, was there as well. We discussed the alleged Vespa with Uri, the head of the transportation department.

"Now look," I remember saying, "I'm assuming that when I say a Vespa, we're all talking about the same type of machine."

I brought this up because of the array of odd vehicles I had seen on the Bulgarian roads — old Soviet SUVs, two-cylinder German cars with a pressed paper shell, and lots of horse-drawn carts, driven by mysterious Romas.

"Of course," Uri, the transportation captain, assured me, with Assia's assistance. "No problem."

"And I can paint it pink, right?"

"Of course," Uri said, rolling his head from side to side in the Bulgarian way of expressing, "Understood."

About a week later, I passed Uri in the hallway of the production office and I couldn't help but follow up on the Vespa. Through Assia, who was continually at my side, I asked, "Hey, Uri, are we good on the Vespa?"

Uri thrust a thumb in the air and smiled confidently. "Of course."

"And we can paint it pink and wreck it, right?"

Uri responded simply by rolling his head in that strange way.

A week after that, with no Vespa news, I began to get nervous — we were only a few days away from needing it. I insisted that Uri bring me an actual picture of the Vespa he intended to use.

He did, in fact, produce a picture — of a *blue* Vespa.

"This is fine, Uri, but it's blue. You can paint it pink, right?"

Through translation, Uri assured me again that it wasn't a problem.

"Okay," I said, chewing on my lower lip. "We shoot with that in two days. Good luck."

Forty-eight hours later, the second unit was preparing for the shot of the Vespa careening out of control, sans rider, and smashing into the side of a parked car. I was filming in a laboratory set across the street, but peeked out when I had a chance and was relieved to see a perfectly pink Vespa with cute girlie tassels fluttering from the handlebars.

A few minutes later, the ill-fated machine was rolled to its doom. Bouncing off the parked car, it smashed to the ground and let out a final gasp, courtesy of a cheesy spark effect. The crew applauded politely, as is usually the case after a "stunt" is performed, but as I glanced at Assia, I was shocked to see tears streaming down her face. This was very unusual, because Assia had always been very calm and professional. I looked to Joel, the first assistant director.

"Joel, why is Assia crying?"

"Oh, that's her Vespa," he said, glancing at the smoldering wreck. "It was a gift from her father on her birthday. I guess they never told her they were going to wreck it."

"But she is the fucking translator. She was *there*. How could she not know?"

Joel shrugged. "Welcome to Bulgaria."

After an almost physical altercation with Uri, the lying bastard "transportation" captain, I stepped away to cool down. We had converted an old military complex into a back lot, so there was plenty of room to wander and ruminate about my lot in life.

*For Chrissakes, I'm a middle-aged man. I shouldn't be dicking around Eastern Europe, wrecking the personal property of poor people just to make a movie about a brain transplant! Grown men don't glue prosthetic appliances to their faces and run around in silly costumes, fighting digital creatures that aren't even there. Actors my age should be doing Shakespeare in the Park, or at the very least headlining some innocuous Neil Simon comedy in Branson, Missouri.*

Instead, I was halfway around the world, wearing a disco shirt, bleached blue jeans, a rubber skull appliance, and limping because of ill-fitting, white clown shoes. On top of that, I was fighting off a nasty infection, courtesy of a rusty hunk of metal, left behind by our departing Russian friends.

This, I thought to myself, is the point in every movie where someone — usually an unlikely minor character, like the hero's eccentric grandfather who's never had a kind word for anyone, or the wisecracking Hispanic maid who worships Elvis — interrupts the hero's self-pitying depression with a firm but loving lecture that leaves them with a renewed sense of self-worth and purpose. Ideally, this moment would be accompanied by some soft rock or a Motown classic.

But there was no cantankerous grandfather or wisecracking housekeeper in sight — that was just an A list movie cliché. Deep down, I identified far more with the grizzled-on-the-verge-of-retirement- B-movie-cop cliché, where the guy follows up every car explosion, crackhead smackdown, and serial killer confrontation with the time-honored "I'm too old for this shit."

My body had been spattered, bruised and battered in B movies for twenty-five years. A steady diet of craft services have made my lower intestine a Superfund site, my lower back gets tight after standing on marks all day, and whatever I did to my right ankle during *Evil Dead* has been coming back to haunt me.

*Maybe it's time to hang up the chainsaw and ride into the celluloid sunset.*

But there was still time for a graceful exit — before the horror convention circuit, before the heroin possession charges, before the reality show with other B movie actors all living together in one house — I would simply fall back on my budding writing career. My first two books were *New York Times* bestsellers, and a third was sitting on my editor's desk, so transitioning beyond the silver screen would be a cakewalk.

As I stood in the rank Bulgarian air, seasoned by a nearby brick factory, I dreamed of sauntering out to my office in Oregon, steaming cup of Chai tea in one hand, a pipe filled with sticky, black cherry tobacco in the other — ready to write the great American novel. But as my fantasy played out, as I began to get a fix on that groundbreaking work, I heard shouting in the distance.

It was Joel, from across the base. "Hey Bruce, the car gag is ready to go!"

"Okay, be right there."

The glamour of show business beckoned, so I hiked up my bleached jeans and clown-shoe-shuffled back to work.

Mailbox    File    Edit    Options    Help

Search Address Book

Inbox

| From | Subject | Date Received |
|---|---|---|
| AshFan12678 | Where were u in Quick and Dead? | Monday, March 8th, 6:04 AM |
| ChinKiller45 | I'm Watching You!! | Monday, March 8th, 9:32 AM |
| **Barry Neville** | **Introduction** | **Monday, March 8th, 11:14 AM** |
| Kiffington | RE: moola | Monday, March 8th, 1:00 PM |

From: Barry Neville
Subject: Introduction
Date: Monday, March 8th, 11:14 AM
To: Bruce Campbell

Dear Bruce,

Hello. Hope you are well. Sorry for the delay in
responding to your book, *Walk This Way*. At St. Martin's
Press, we're very thorough, and we wanted to get feedback
from a wide variety of people within the company before
we made our decision.

You know, travel books are tricky. If there isn't a
special twist, we find that they tend to rot on shelves.
While we all got a kick out of the graphics, particularly
the shots of your feet walking on different surfaces, we
don't feel that there is any room for another book of
this type in our release schedule.

As always, we wish you the very best on this project, and
any writings with other publishers. You'll always get a
look here.

Yours truly,

Barry Neville

p.s. But please call me, I have another idea.

# 1

# Let's Make Love!

I read the e-mail out loud and wrinkled my nose when I got to the "another book of this type" part. "What kind of horseshit is that?" I wondered aloud.

I dialed Barry's office in New York, stabbing at the numbers on my phone.

Pat, Barry's loyal secretary, answered: "Barry Neville's office."

"Pat, how the heck are you? This is Bruce Campbell."

"Oh, hello, Bruce, I'll see if Barry is in."

That's one of my favorite phrases in the "get past the secretary" game: "I'll see if he's in." Pat knew whether Barry was in or not — he was only twelve feet away in his ten-by-ten cubicle. I was expecting to hear "he just slipped out," or maybe "he's tied up in a conference call," but suddenly, she jumped back on the line.

"I'll put you right through, Bruce."

Getting an editor on the line first try made me instantly suspicious — that meant Barry had either good news...or the opposite.

"Hello, Bruce," Barry said, sounding reasonably happy to hear from me.

I decided to get right into it. "Okay, so you don't want to do the book."

"Well, no," Barry replied. "We kicked it around, but we couldn't make it work."

"I understand that, but what's with 'another book of this type'? You told me that travel books were hot stuff."

"That's true, but I said they *could* be — if they were done right."

"And what's so wrong with *Walk This Way*?"

"Honestly?"

"I guess, yeah."

"This book made me feel like I was walking."

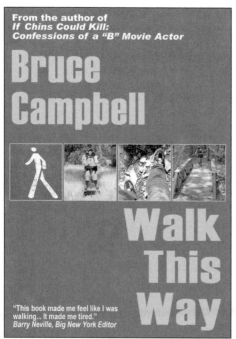

From the author of
*If Chins Could Kill:
Confessions of a "B" Movie Actor*

**Bruce Campbell**

**Walk This Way**

"This book made me feel like I was walking... It made me tired."
*Barry Neville, Big New York Editor*

"Good. You felt in the moment — what's wrong with that?"

"I'm referring to the pace," Barry clarified. "It made me tired."

"Oh."

"And how many suburban walks can a person take? I know you were filming on location a lot, but I'm not so sure a book about the routes you took to keep from being bored would be a big seller. Call me crazy."

"Okay, you're crazy."

"Look, Bruce, I hope I am. As your friend, I hope you go and sell a million copies. We've been wrong before. But look, this doesn't have to end here. I want to pitch a book to *you*. I think you're a great match for the material."

"What is it?"

"A relationship book."

The intensity of my laugh startled Barry, but he pressed on.

"I'm serious. I can get that book approved," he assured me.

"Well, yeah, but, wow, that's a whole new deal."

"Relationship books are huge. If you win with one of these, you win big."

"I dunno," I hemmed. "I'd have to think about that and call you back — I'd have to see if I could get my head around it."

"Okay, sure, I understand. Take your time. The offer stands."

As I hung up, I pitied Barry. *Poor bastard.* My editor still remembered me from the TV show *The Adventures of Brisco County Jr.,* where I successfully managed a new girlfriend almost every week. He couldn't shake the images of my character Ash from the film *Army of Darkness*, where I coolly manhandle my leading lady with lines like, "Gimme some sugar, baby."

He'd seen me up close and personal with some damn sexy women, the likes of Vanessa Angel, Alyssa Milano, and Elizabeth Hurley, so in the world according to Barry, I was the living embodiment of a chick magnet — the perfect choice to write a relationship book. Barry is a nice guy, but he's also a fool. What he fails to realize is that the Bruce Campbell who romanced his way through a succession of beautiful leading women bears no resemblance to the Bruce Campbell who forgets anniversaries and hoards Victoria's Secret catalogs. In the real world, none of what he sees on the silver screen relates to me, the actor — or any actor, for that matter.

Let me walk you through a few of the key differences. For starters, love scenes are never the result of an actor's romantic prowess, or insistence. These are obligatory elements of any cinematic romance story, and actors in leading roles are often confronted with them. In reality, shooting a love scene is about as exciting as groping my sister – and thankfully, I don't have one.

Actors don't make up all that clever dialogue. I'll throw in a quip or two, sure, but I'm mainly hired to say words that are written for me. And when it comes to scenes about relationships, I'm happy to have the help of a clever writer who is, at the end of the day, manipulating a given situation into how it *could* play out, not necessarily how it *would*.

As an actor, I don't have any say in how the relationship will go, or even who my romantic partner will be. The writer has determined my on-screen fate far in advance — and that's a really scary thought, because the only people who have *worse* relationships than actors are writers, because they spend most of their time alone, never talking to anyone, staring at a computer screen.

Hollywood is successful at portraying relationships because it manages to bring our fantasies to life; it presents a "what if" world in which we can lose ourselves for a few hours. In movies, when it comes to men and women, everything happens at the speed of light. Couples fall in love at first glance. Later, during sex (which happens on the first date), men get instant erections and can make love for hours. Women achieve orgasm in record time, some going for three in a row. The sex will always be good, and it must always be in some imaginative place, like a freight elevator or a nuclear submarine. Poor Barry, I can see why he was so confused — like all of us, he had been brainwashed for years.

Aside from all that, what the hell does a guy who lost his virginity at age twenty-three know about the opposite sex? Jack shit, that's what. When it comes to women, I don't know my ass from a hole in the ground. I learned about sex through the mass marketing of the early 1960s, when Fred Flintstone was doing cigarette ads and products like Space Food sticks, Tang, and leaded gasoline were the order of the day. Sex back then meant sleeping in separate beds, closed mouth kissing, wearing PJs to bed (even adults), and no sex before marriage. No wonder I had such a bogus view of the world.

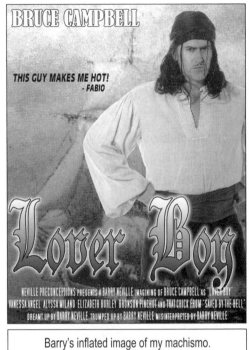

Barry's inflated image of my machismo.

As my "female awareness" sprang to life in the late sixties, the sexy babes on television at that time were Anita Bryant, a conservative singer selling orange juice; Julie Newmar, who played Cat Woman in the TV show *Batman*; and Marta Kristen, the teenage daughter on *Lost in Space*. I didn't know right from left, but I can tell you this: it wasn't the intricate plots, or the acting that held my attention, it was the way these foxy women filled out their skintight costumes week after week.

Women didn't seem like people who had sex; they just wore lots of makeup and smelled funny. Sears catalogues, and later my dad's *Playboy*s, helped straighten a few things out, but there were more questions than answers.

Motion pictures often wind up being an early, vital source of insight into the sexual dynamics between men and women. The problem was, I couldn't get into any movie that might have been of use to me (the cursed M rating, for Mature Audiences Only) so my model for intergender relationships came primarily from John Wayne westerns between 1962 and 1973. My mother was a huge western fan, and since my father couldn't have cared less, she'd drag me along instead.

Given my prolonged exposure to the bizarre, archetypal behavior of cowboys, I shouldn't have been surprised by an incident on the playground when I was nine. I "rescued" a girl who was being harassed by a bully (a cattle rustler, as I saw it) by socking him once in the jaw (that's all Duke ever needed) and down he went. I grabbed the girl (the feed store owner's daughter, Sue), whipped her around, and kissed her but good — closed mouthed, because we did such things proper then. To my shock and horror, Sally Sue Jenkins slapped me across the face.

"Lower and to the left, missy."

"Get out of here, you weirdo. My brother was just trying to give me lunch money...."

"Sorry, ma'am," I said, nodding. "Didn't mean to cause no fuss."

Dating? I was too busy making amateur films in high school to take advantage of those prime years. Relationships? That's a good one. The "relationships" in my civilian life can be counted on one hand, minus the use of my thumb. Don't come knocking here, brother, I married the first woman who ever came on to me. The weight of hypocrisy would be too much to bear if I wrote a book about a subject on which I was essentially retarded.

The phone rang.

"Hello."

"Hi, it's Barry."

"Dude, c'mon, I don't have an answer for you yet."

"What are you talking about? I haven't called you in a month."

"Who is this?" I asked.

"This is the *other* Barry. Your *acting* agent."

"Oh, *that* Barry. Hi, what's up?"

"I have a possible gig for you."

"Let me guess — something for the Sci-Fi Channel?"

"No."

"A convention in Butt Crack, Kansas?"

"Nope," Barry said with a smile in his voice. "A romantic comedy."

"Get out of town."

"It's a green-lit, A-list romantic comedy starring Richard Gere, Renée Zellweger, produced by Robert Evans, directed by Mike Nichols — shooting in New York in the fall."

"Don't mess with me, Barry. I'm going through some shit right now."

"Bruce, I'm not that kind of a guy," he assured me.

"So, I would play the what, chauffeur? Bus boy?"

"The wise-cracking doorman — he's like the comic muse to Gere. It's the best role in the film. He tells jokes, he gives advice on relationships. You get the idea."

"What's it called?"

"*Let's Make Love!*"

It sounded good — *too* good, as they say. "Do I have to audition?"

"Well, yes, unfortunately. I sent them your demo reel, but they still need you to read in New York. But as a little FYI, Mike asked for you specifically."

"Bullshit," I shot back immediately. "Mike Nichols doesn't even know I exist, and his casting people sure as hell don't."

"Hey, don't shoot the messenger, Bruce. I'm just passing the information along so you can make an informed decision."

I sighed loudly. "Barry, you know how much I hate auditions. In twenty-five years I've gotten exactly *three* acting jobs from auditioning, and I must have had, what, a hundred of them?"

"Two hundred and nine," Barry corrected.

"You keep track of things like that?" I asked, incredulous.

"Yeah, the head of the agency likes charts and graphs."

"What a dismal record."

"That aside, this is a great opportunity, Bruce. Movies don't get any bigger, or *better* than this."

I glanced in my Frequent Flyer file — America West was looking good for a free ticket. "What the hell...set it up."

I hung up and stared at the phone. This would be a worthless cause, but at least it was a chance to meet Mike Nichols, a truly big shot director.

New York City in May was beautiful — trees were starting to bloom, the sky was a freshly laundered blue, and aside from the stench of decomposing trash, I felt positively invigorated. I walked with a spring in my step all the way up West 26th Street, to an old brownstone where Mike Nichols keeps his office.

The first thing an actor does at an audition is sign in. I always take my time with the sign-in sheet, because it's a chance to see the competition. The list tells me who else is or was there, what time, for what role, and who represents them.

The sign-in list for *Let's Make Love!* made my jaw drop: *Bill* Campbell, for starters, a namesake nemesis if there ever was one, Ben Affleck, Adam Sandler, John Turturro, Liam Neeson, Chevy Chase, and on, and on.

*Everyone on the goddamn planet is auditioning for this role. What am I doing here?*

I scanned the room and my hopes were further dashed: Gary Sinise was sitting next to John Malkovich, who was telling a bawdy joke to John Cusack, who was trying to study his lines.

SIGN-IN SHEET

PROJECT: LET'S MAKE LOVE

| NAME | REPRESENTATION | TIME | ROLE | AUTOGRAPH |
|------|----------------|------|------|-----------|
| Bill Campbell | A.I.A.Ltd | 9AM | Foyl the Doorman | |
| Ben Affleck | M. Damon | 9:15A | Fowl | |
| Adam Sandler | RHTS | 9:30 | door guy | |
| John Turturro | Fink/Coen | 9:45am | Foyl | |
| LIAM NEESON | "OSCAR" | 10:00 | Doorau Doorman | |
| Chevy Chase | N/A | 10:15 | anything, please | |
| Sir Antony Hopkins | HRH | 10:30 an | Mr. Foyl | |
| Gary Sinise | C/S/N/Y | 10:45 | Foyc | |
| Carrot Top | Satan | 11 | Ghost of Xmas Past | |
| Robert Patrick | A#PA | 11:15 | Fox | |
| J Malkovh | PUJ Agency | 11:30 | Foyl | |
| Edward Norton | Joe | 11:45 | Foyl | |
| Robin Williams | My agent | noon | door guy | |

The "competition."

I was seriously considering feigning a strange illness and making an early departure, when I became drawn into what I feared most at auditions: a conversation.

"So, we meet again."

The husky voice belonged to tough-guy actor Robert Patrick, who stiffed me out of an *X-Files* role.

"Yeah, I guess so," I said. "You won the last round."

Robert smiled confidently. "I did, didn't I? Good gig, that *X-Files*."

"Yeah, but long hours, I'm sure," I managed, trying to make it sound like I didn't want the part anyway.

"The pain goes away on payday," he said, smiling. "Hey, you been working much?"

The issue of employment is always an Achilles heel for an actor who hasn't worked in a long time, and Robert wasted no time in going for it.

"Well, not really," I admitted.

Robert raised his eyebrows and whistled silently to himself — the "Oh, I see" expression.

"I was writing for a while," I tried to clarify. "So, then I did a couple conventions, and then...." I stopped myself before it got embarrassing. There wasn't anything to brag about in the conventional sense. I knew it, and now he knew it too.

"Hell, I wish I had your problem sometimes," Robert said, possibly trying to make me feel better. "I can barely get back to my Montana ranch, I work so much. I may have to sell it and move to the Palisades."

I smiled and excused myself, feeling a sudden need to use the bathroom. During tense audition situations, the only sanctuary is the men's toilet. Under the right conditions, I can kill an hour or more, reading stall graffiti and making sure my hair is just right. It's a great place to gather yourself, get centered, and have one last frantic look at your lines.

A moment from my audition.

Once inside the tile-and-porcelain sanctuary, I gave myself a pep talk. *Okay, chump, you're here, get over it. Do your thing and move on. Enjoy the moment.*

As I stepped back into the waiting room full of famous actors, my name was being called.

*Go time.*

I followed the secretary down a long hallway and wiped the

sweat from the palm of my clammy right hand one last time.

I entered the room and couldn't help but gasp. Richard Gere was there, smiling and shaking hands with an exiting Johnny Depp. As Johnny passed, he winked. "Hey man, have fun."

*Have a coronary, that's what I'll have.*

The secretary introduced me to Mike Nichols, a very serene man with a wicked handshake.

"Damn nice to meet you, Bruce. Been a big fan for a long time. Hey, nice turn in *Icebreaker* — convincing stuff."

*He didn't actually see that piece of shit, did he?* "Well, there's one folks don't usually mention," I said, incredulous.

"Oh, the indies are my favorite," he said, nodding. "That's all I watch, really. It's where the new ideas are."

"From your lips to God's ears, Mike."

Mike gestured to a lit area across the room. "Why don't you go on over there, Bruce, and we'll have a go at this."

"Okay, sure."

"Have you met Richard?" Mike asked, nonchalant.

I turned to see Richard Gere offering his hand, and smiling.

"Hi, Bruce, loved your stuff on *Xena*."

I stammered a response, losing my train of thought.

"Any questions?" Mike asked.

"Yeah, actually. How 'Southern' should the guy be?"

Mike shrugged. "Why don't we just have a look at one?"

I shrugged too, having only asked the question so I wouldn't appear as terrified as I was. My Southern accent was merely passable anyway, so it was an irrelevant exchange.

"Let's do the first scene," Mike said, nodding to the video technician, who began taping.

I had prepared two scenes for the audition. This first one was snappy, back-and-forth patter between the lead character, Harry Grayson, and the doorman, Foyl Whipple. The second scene

— only done if asked — was an eloquent speech from Foyl, to Harry, about true love.

The first scene began like this:

```
Foyl holds the door open.

                 FOYL
            (with a smile)
        How are you tonight, Mr.
        Grayson?

Harry stops on his way out.

                HARRY
        Foyl, how is it that every day,
        you manage to have a smile on
        your face?

                 FOYL
            (holding his
             grin)
        Just another day in paradise,
        Mr. Grayson.

                HARRY
            (starting to
             walk)
        If you only knew about the real
        world, Foyl.

                 FOYL
        I know a little something about
                 (CONT'D)
```

>           FOYL (CONT'D)
>   the real world, Mr. Grayson.
>   I'm holding a door in the dead
>   of winter for a man who doesn't
>   know how to treat a woman.

Harry stops in his tracks and turns back to
Foyl.

>           HARRY
>   I beg your pardon?

>           FOYL
>   Personally, I treat women like
>   royalty.

>           HARRY
>   I don't treat anyone like
>   anything, Foyl. I'm just me.
>   I just am. And how is it, a
>   doorman has all the answers?

>           FOYL
>   A doorman takes the pulse of
>   humanity. Every day, he hears
>   the talk, he watches behavior,
>   he knows what there is to know
>   about people.

>           HARRY
>   Tell me one thing about me that
>   I don't know.

```
                    FOYL
       You're in love more than you'll
       ever let yourself be.


                   HARRY
                  (pegged)
       That's what I like about you,
       Foyl. You always give it to me
       straight.


                    FOYL
                (with a wry
                  smile)
       It's the only way, Mr. Grayson.
       Well, you have a great day.
                 (then, after
                  Harry leaves)
       You should be holding the door
       for me....
```

The group around Mike Nichols chuckled politely, and the scene was over. There is always an awkward moment between reading the first scene and the second scene. But before I could even get anxious about it, Mike stood up.

"Thanks, Bruce. Thanks for coming in. I think we've seen all we need to."

The words were: "Thanks for coming in. I think we've seen all we need to." The meaning was: "Thanks for wasting our time, Bruce, I think that's all we can stand."

Richard Gere offered his hand again. "That was fun, Bruce."

"That was fun": actor-speak for "that sucked ass."

Symbolism was everywhere. Richard's sincere handshake was the kind you give to someone after a death in the family.

Something was dead all right — my ability to audition. Barry can now raise the "failed auditions" tally to 210. Knowing not to linger after a mediocre offering, I thanked my way out of the room and grabbed the elevator straight down.

Outside, I walked aimlessly down the street, repeating the words of the first scene verbatim, nailing the delivery each time. Actors are always at their very best on the way home.

Oh, well, I thought. *At least I tried.*

During the multiple flights home, I was comforted by thoughts of the long fun summer ahead — river rafting, hiking, and all-around fun in the Oregon sun. The previous winter had been a wet one, and that usually resulted in a kick-ass summer.

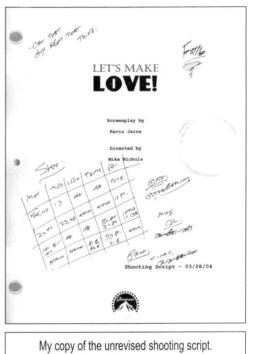

My copy of the unrevised shooting script.

But when I arrived home, three new phone messages waited on my machine. I only get multiple messages when someone either dies or needs money, both of which were cause for dread. The first message, while somewhat cryptic, changed my mood immediately:

*Beep* — "Hey, Bruce, it's Barry — call me!"

The second was from my manager, Robert. He's always more subdued, but I could tell he was giddy:

*Beep* — "Bruce, Robert here. Something good...."

The third message was strictly business, but the most definitive of all:

*Beep* — "This is Dale, your lawyer."

When Dale calls, it means I'm either going to spend money defending myself in a lawsuit, or I'm going to spend money negotiating a film deal, but either way, I'm going to spend money.

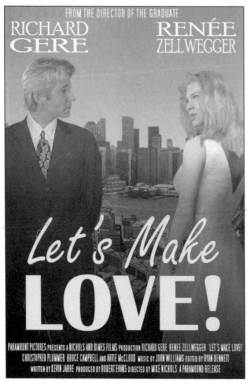

I didn't check any more messages because I was too busy dancing a victory jig around my office.

But before I could say, *Holy shit, I got the part*, the phone rang.

"Hello?"

"Bruce? Mike...."

"Mike Nichols?"

"Yeah. Listen, welcome aboard. I'm really pleased," he said with genuine warmth.

"This is insane. I feel like you're Ed McMahon and I just won that Publishers Clearinghouse thing."

"We both won on this one."

"Mike, I don't want this to sound weird, but why?"

"Why what?"

"Why was I cast instead of every name actor in Hollywood? Was my audition that good?"

"Actually, I cast you *despite* the audition," Mike clarified. "I wanted you in *Let's Make Love!* because you're ready for the next step. You've paid your dues, Bruce. Those other actors who auditioned — and Sean Penn was astounding — have all gotten their shot in the A leagues. I've always wanted to put you in a role that can feature the depth you showed in *Tornado!* I have to tell you, the scene in the field with that guy's daughter blew me away."

Is Mike messing with me? I wondered.

"And while *McHale's Navy* sank like an anchor, the pathos you brought to an average navy guy was heartbreaking."

I never thought I would live long enough to hear the words "heartbreaking" and "*McHale's Navy*" in the same sentence, but it was heartening nonetheless, especially from an icon like Mike Nichols.

"You've been playing below your game," Mike said politely, "and it's time to change all that. I'm happy to be in a position to finally make it happen."

"Jesus, Mike, what can I say? Thanks...."

"But you can't let me down," he warned. "I fought for you over the objections of the Paramount guys. Your character is the emotional linchpin of this movie. If he doesn't work, the movie doesn't work — simple as that. Kid, this is the kind of role the Best Supporting Actor award was created for, but you'll have to work your ass off."

Before responding, I took a moment to catch my breath. "I'm... I'm up for it, Mike — and thanks for the —"

But Mike had hung up already.

As I ran both hands through my sweaty hair, I noticed that they were trembling. As an actor, it was a sensation that happens once every five years — the sensation of elation and panic at the same time — otherwise known as The Butterflies. Every time I got butterflies in my stomach previously, the acting experience had been a good one.

Mike was right. This role was going to be special.

# 2

# Doorman for a Day

I got the part — now all I had to do was pull it off. It was one thing to work on a cheeseball, straight-to-DVD horror film for two weeks in Vancouver, where the only challenge is finding new ways to express fear or pain. But to act in a Mike Nichols film is to exist on another plane, with no "B" anything in sight. Working with the likes of Mike Nichols and Richard Gere, my input would not only be welcomed, it would be *expected*.

Prior to *Let's Make Love!,* my method of preparing for a role was making sure I had enough razor blades and a fresh container of dental floss. But this time I would need more than just a close shave and healthy gums. To meet the challenge, I had to prepare with a new level of intensity. If I was going to make a favorable impression in a legitimate Hollywood production, I couldn't drag my feet. This time, I had to invest and go the distance. If I was going to *play* a wisecracking doorman relationship expert, then by God I was going to *become* one!

I rifled through the shelves in my office, digging out every acting book I had either ignored or derided over the years, and began to read them anew for the next forty-eight hours. I hadn't read as much or as intensively since my six months of college, but it was a liberating experience. In recent years, my sense of acting had devolved to hitting marks, catnaps in my trailer, and free haircuts. But after tearing through books like *An Actor Is* and *The Id of Acting*, I began to see my craft in a new light. Acting is more than tailored clothing, it's an expression of truth, a liberating exploration of the soul, a deeply personal journey that is shared with the entire world.

The books were a marvelous inspiration. While serving up a hodgepodge of theories, each one left me with the desire to take my craft to new heights. I realized that to prepare, an actor must seek, ask, study, ponder, and most importantly: learn.

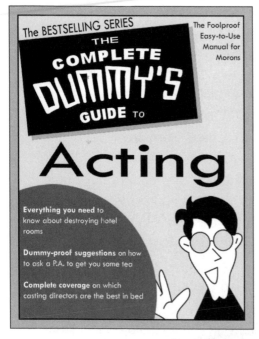

The BESTSELLING SERIES

The Foolproof Easy-to-Use Manual for Morons

THE COMPLETE DUMMY'S GUIDE TO

Acting

**Everything you need** to know about destroying hotel rooms

**Dummy-proof suggestions** on how to ask a P.A. to get you some tea

**Complete coverage** on which casting directors are the best in bed

One of the tricks I learned in *Acting for Dummies* was to write a "back story," or biography, of the character I was portraying. They're helpful because nine times out of ten, even the writer hasn't gone to this length to create a character, and it's up to the actor to fill in the blanks. I decided to take a whack at it:

## The Back Story of Foyl Whipple
### by
### Foyl Whipple

I was born outside of Savannah, Georgia, in 1958. My daddy, Dwight, was a pea farmer, but mostly he made ends meet by selling "shine" off the back porch. Mother Beulah was a housewife, but there was always extra money to be made by disappearing into the back room with strange men during Friday night poker games.

My two older sisters, Joyce and Eunice, took off when I was three. There was a lot of shouting when it happened. Growing up as the youngest of three poor children, I didn't have nothin' to call my own.

I landed a job as a dishwasher at the Savannah Gentlemen's Club, but because of my family background, I couldn't get beyond bus boy. I knew if I was going to make something of myself, I had to go to a place where it didn't matter who I was, or where I came from. I decided to try New York City, mainly because it was too busy runnin' itself to give a hoot about me. The thought terrified me so, but I never looked back.

After bein' a bricklayer, cab driver, and dishwasher, I got me a job as doorman at the Park Avenue Arms. Not long after that, I met my future wife, Trudy, waitin' tables at a local deli. After chasin' her down for two years, we tied the knot in nineteen eighty-three, and kicked out a couple of cute kids, Rhett and his older sister Lottie, named after my gramma. We live in Brooklyn, just a spit away from Prospect Park, where most week-ends we're out there playing ball, or hunting coon in the restricted areas with my bird dog, Yeller.

I'm happy at the Park Avenue Arms. I been there for twenty years, and worked my way up to head doorman. I know everyone by name, their apartment number, how long they've been there, their extended families, and the name of their damn pets. I even know who's doin' who, but I don't gossip about it. I love collard greens, Budweiser, and sleepin' in on Sundays.

Pappy

One of the joys of being an actor is occasionally doing what is known as a "tagalong." Journalists do it all the time — they ride with an undercover crime unit, or "embed" themselves in a military operation to get the inside scoop. Actors do the same thing — they shadow FBI agents, observe operating room procedures, or interview real-life characters so they can faithfully portray a given role. I'd played working stiffs before — a mechanic, a custodian, a cab driver — but never a doorman.

Hoping to receive a crash course in this ancient art, I offered to join the curbside staff of the prestigious Waldorf-Astoria Hotel in New York City, and was fairly shocked when they took me up on it. To be honest, I already had my eye on a sweet gig at the Garden City Marriott, and was simply using the Waldorf as a test run. Later, I found out that someone in upper management had given the go-ahead as long as I signed an *Army of Darkness* poster for her son.

Actors get to learn a new craft with almost each role. Some skills are fun to pick up, like sword fighting or horse riding, yet others, like line dancing, aren't worth the pay. In this case, I was about to get a crash course in baggage handling, cab calling, door holding, hat tipping, and generally intuitive, cheery behavior.

My day started Monday, June 2nd, at exactly six o'clock in the morning. The first challenge was to find the employee locker room, deep within the bowels of this 1893 behemoth. It wasn't hard — I just kept heading down.

Eventually, I arrived at the main locker room. Tiled and elegant, but well worn from the hundred years of Waldorf employee use, it could easily double as a bomb shelter. The lockers were large and had plenty of hooks. Inside one of them hung my uniform, neatly pressed and ready to wear.

Personally, I have always loved wearing uniforms. Nothing motivates me more as an actor than a crisp, well-tailored outfit.

The Waldorf doormen looked particularly nice, I thought, with their brown pants starched stiff, and a golden stripe down the outer seam. The jacket was a well-molded, padded-shoulder affair with epaulets. White gloves, a snappy hat, and a referee's whistle rounded out the look. I felt like a cross between a dictator and a band leader.

Shortly after I finished dressing, at 6:15 A.M. sharp, the Door Chief, an imposing fellow named Eldridge, called us together.

"Listen up, door people: This is the start of a new week. We're going to face today's challenges with the enthusiasm, grace, and dignity that the Waldorf establishment demands. We're going to service our clients. As door persons, you provide the first impression of this hotel, and often the last — make it a good one. Okay, be smart, be safe — lift with your legs."

As seen on TV: The landmark Waldorf-Astoria hotel.

With that, the doormen and doorwomen clapped enthusiastically, and poured up the numerous flights of stairs to our posts outside the Waldorf.

I took my place as "curb monkey." Initially, the job description included opening car doors and helping folks with their luggage. From my acting perspective, however, this was a chance to hear stories, and more importantly, ad-lib some sage advice about relationships.

Before you could say "Bellman!" a black Lincoln town car rolled up. I opened the rear door and escorted a very elegant older woman to the curb. Her tiny dog was stuffed under one arm. She looked back in disgust at her wealthy but disheveled husband doddering along.

"Hurry up, Wallace," she hissed. "We'll miss the buffet."

"Then go ahead, go," he grumbled, stepping up on the curb. "I'll be there in good goddamn time enough."

Don't I look a-door-able?

His wife did exactly that — she left him alone, next to me, searching for tip money.

"A word of advice, son," Wallace offered.

"Sir?"

"Never get married. I've done it four times now, and each one is worse than the last."

"Do you have poor choice in women, sir, or are you just a poor husband?"

"Ha! I'm the best husband she ever had. I give that dried-up old prune everything she wants," he said, still fishing in his pockets.

"But do you give her what she *needs*?" I pressed.

"You're an impudent little prick, aren't you?" the old geezer said, not finding any tip money. "I'll have to catch you on the way out."

"Sure, sir. You have yourself a great day."

I watched him waddle after his long-gone wife, and felt sad

that they had basically given up on each other. They were beyond even the formality and polite deference of a relationship in decline — their marriage had devolved into guerrilla warfare.

Before I could ask "How does that happen?" a cab pulled up to the corner. The door opened and a burly man about my age got out.

"I got it, pal, thanks," he said, in a way that told me not to expect any tip.

I could tell he was one of those self-described "players" who hated staying at a fancy hotel — or at least hated *paying* for it.

Stepping out of the cab after him was a much younger woman, who was clearly impressed to be at the Waldorf.

"Do you have any luggage, Mr...?"

"Peterson. John Peterson. Uh, no, I —"

The cab driver popped the trunk to reveal two overnight bags.

I reached for the luggage, getting a good look at the I.D. tags, none of which said Peterson. But before I could grab a handle, my tightwad friend waved me off again. "I've got those bags, pal. Don't worry about it."

As "John" grabbed the bags, I could see the exposed skin on his ring finger — the circle of pasty skin caused by the prolonged wearing of a wedding ring (now missing). Sensing that he was up to no good, I stepped back and let him carry his own goddamn bags.

Mr. "Peterson" paid off his cab driver as if he had lost a bet, slowly and agonizingly. I was able to make eye contact with the young vamp participating in this fling. Maybe twenty-three, the woman was certainly insecure, but mostly just naEFve.

As Money Bags walked past me, I couldn't help but chime in — I was, after all, doing research.

"A word of advice, Mr. Peterson," I said, deftly blocking his path. "Or should I say, *Mr. Walter?*"

"Is there something you want from me, buddy?" the cheating man demanded.

"No. I want to give you some advice: there is still time to save your marriage."

"What the fuck are you trying to say?" he asked, becoming very agitated.

"I'm referring to the, ahem, *affair* you're having. The highs aren't worth the —"

Whack!

"You little punk," the mug added, shaking out the pain in his right hand.

I had been knocked semi-unconscious only once before, and that was courtesy of a nine-iron to the bridge of my nose when I was a kid. I awoke to the fuzzy image of Eldridge, the Door Chief.

"Hey, Bruce, you with me? Come on, man, talk to me."

I rallied myself enough to sit up on the sidewalk, on one elbow at least. "I'm here, chief, I'm just not *here,* here."

"Do you want me to call a paramedic?"

"No, I'm good," I said, trying to stand.

"You want me to call the cops?"

"No. I just need to walk it off."

"What the hell happened, man?" Eldridge asked. "Rodriguez said some guy really clocked you."

"Rodriguez was right," I assured him. "Sorry, chief, I was trying to help a guy out, and he just blew up."

"You didn't give him advice, did you?"

I looked at Eldridge and tried to focus. He was a hard guy to lie to. "Well, yeah, sorta."

Eldridge shook his head, like I was his wayward son. "No, man, you don't ever do that. You take their bags, you hail a cab, you hold the door, but more than anything, you hold your tongue. Be *pro*-fessional, not *con*-fessional."

"Okay, chief," I nodded. "Will do."

Eldridge fished out a handkerchief. "You might want to wipe your nose. Now, be careful, Bruce. Don't be gettin' killed on your first and last damn day."

As I paced around the plaza, breathing deeply and nursing my near-broken nose, a cab full of upscale women were making their last stop of a very late evening — the *Sex and the City* express.

As I held the door for each of the three women, I tried to access the uncanny, soul-penetrating X-ray vision that my character, Foyl, possessed. I knew that somehow he'd connect with each of them and divine their personalities and problems with alarming accuracy.

"Goob bordig, ladies," I offered, through a damaged nasal passage. "Welcome to the Waldordh."

The first woman, a stunning blonde, completely ignored me. I surmised that she was used to having doors held open. She looked like a Karen to me.

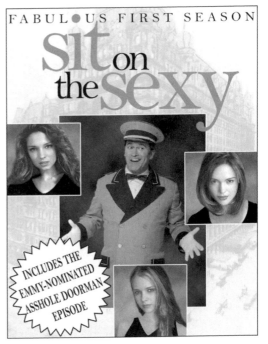

"Karen, right?" I guessed, snapping a finger as she passed.

The woman spun back to me, alarmed at the question. "No," she barked, and turned away.

Behind "Karen" was a hot African-American woman with an ultra-fitted business suit. She at least made eye contact.

"Thank you," she said with a smile that also said "not in your wildest dreams, Jack."

*Foyl would know what she did for a living, just by the way she dressed.*

"You're welcome...*secretary* lady."

The woman shot me a dagger-in-the-eye look, and flipped her business card my way. It read: GINA CARREY, VICE-PRESIDENT, NEW YORK BANK & TRUST.

"Have a good day...*doorman*," Gina whispered.

As I reached for the hand of the last woman, I couldn't help but notice how cold it was. I decided not to overthink my guess — this time I went on gut instinct. "Okay, you're a corporate lawyer, and you're here for the signing of a very hush-hush merger."

The cold lawyer lost all remaining color in her face. "How did you know?"

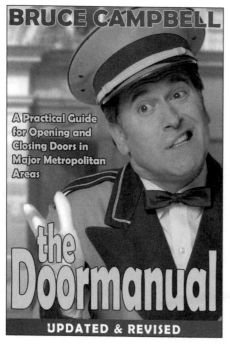

"Oh, lucky guess, I suppose."

"I have nothing more to say," she said curtly, and bolted toward the hotel.

One for four was a sucky average, but the exercise in human nature made me focus an otherwise wandering mind to laser-beam intensity. Through Foyl's eyes, I began to notice details of everyday life that would have eluded me otherwise, like fresh pigeon crap on a gargoyle's face, the color of the gum stuck to the bottom of my shoe, or the number of horn honks during a rush-hour minute. I knew that this new way of looking at the world would not only help me grow as an actor, but as a human being.

During my union break, I grabbed a ham-and-egg sandwich from the employee commissary and took my place among the army of Waldorf employees.

*One out of four,* I recounted. *Not bad for the first try.* I was also starting to get an attitude, and I liked it. In *Let's Make Love!,* my character, Foyl, was very assertive. I could do assertive.

As I hunched over to eat my sandwich, Eldridge passed by and put his hand on my back.

"How you doin', rookie? How's that actor's nose doing?"

"I'm okay, sir, it's just a little tender."

"That's good. You know, I like you Bruce, but if you worked here full time, I'd have to fire your ass."

"Really? Why?"

"I've already gotten three complaints about you, not including the guy who said your pushy behavior forced him to whoop your ass."

"I understand. I'm sorry, Eldridge, I let my character get the best of me."

"Just keep a lid on it. You only got two damn hours to go. Try not to make a scene."

"Aye, skipper," I saluted, wiping the excess mayonnaise from the corner of my mouth.

As I pushed through the opulent doors to the outside, I saw a brigade of dark sedans glide to a stop near the main entrance. On the sidewalks, men in plain suits scanned the area and escorted pedestrians away from the area beneath the distinctive gray-and-gold awning. Before I could figure out what was going on, I was approached by a clean-cut man with a receiver in his ear.

"May I see your I.D., please?" he asked, hand out.

"You first," I replied. "I work here, you don't."

Somewhat impatiently, the man showed me a U.S. Government–issue I.D., so I pulled out my laminated employee I.D. He studied it only slightly more closely than an ADD-afflicted airport screener. His furrowed brow should have tipped me off. "This is issued for only one day."

"Today, right, but it's still valid."

"That doesn't make any sense. Why would you have an I.D. badge that's good for just one day?"

"I have a reason, but it's none of your business, really," I replied.

The agent slammed me against the brick wall. "Do you know who I am?"

"Agent No Name?"

"Correction. I'm Agent Samuel Grunow with the U.S. Secret Service, so what you do is *all* about my business. Try again."

"I'm an actor, for God's sake," I croaked out of a partially crushed windpipe. "We hang around weird places to get the feel for a role. How do I know you're not an actor, studying for some new Fox reality show called *Asshole Federal Agents*?"

Grunow didn't respond — not to me anyway. "Uh, we've got a possible zero, three, niner, here, repeat, zero-three-niner, over?"

*Is that good or bad?* I wondered.

"Copy that," Grunow said, not looking at me. Then, "I'm going to have to ask you to remain in my immediate custody."

"But, if you're *asking* me, I have choice."

"You must remain in my immediate custody."

"I *must*. That sounds like you're telling me. And I'm a little fuzzy on the 'immediate' thing. Does that constitute a proximity?"

"Approximately."

"An approximate proximity. And, now this 'custody' thing — is that sole custody, or joint custody?"

"My immediate custody."

"Can I get a restraining order to cancel your immediate, approximate, proximity custody?"

"You have the right to remain silent."

"Whoa, cowboy, are you arresting me?"

"You are a Person of Interest," he said, showing a remarkable lack of emotion.

"A person of — hey, I'm a doorman, and I'm just here doing my job — on *private* property."

Just then, Colin Powell, who at the time was still Secretary of State, emerged from a black town car and headed toward the grand Waldorf entrance.

"Holy moly, that's the Secretary of State," I gawked. "You may have a job to do, buster, but so do I...."

If only our first encounter had been this civil....

I made my way quickly toward the front doors, appalled that nobody was there to open them. Colin was walking at a fast clip, and to beat him I had to break into a slow jog. Agent Grunow whipped around and began to transmit a heightened "alert code," and all of a sudden the plaza got real busy.

In case you've ever wondered, a "person of interest" shouldn't make fast moves toward the same person that a massive security detail is trained to protect. No less than seven agents descended upon me, barking hushed orders into hidden headsets, and I was tackled left, right, and center before I could reach the front doors. Within three seconds — the time it took to whisk Colin Powell to safety and dislocate my shoulder — I had blacked out.

Two hours later, I awoke in an "undisclosed location." Seconds after stirring, a door opened, revealing the same young, clean-cut agent.

"Mr. Campbell, I'm Agent Grunow."

"We met, yeah."

"Can I ask you a few questions?"

"Knock yourself out."

"What business did you have at the Waldorf hotel earlier today?"

"I was preparing for a role in an upcoming Mike Nichols film — you may have heard of him?"

"And why were you approaching the front door of the Waldorf?"

"Well, as a doorman, one tends to have a natural gravitation toward them."

"But with all due respect, Mr. Campbell, you're not a real doorman, you're an actor. So, according to the United States government, what you were doing at the Waldorf was technically unnecessary."

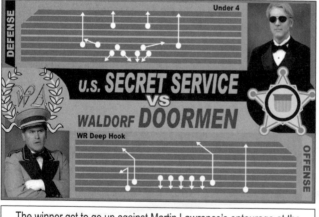

The winner got to go up against Martin Lawrence's entourage at the Hotel Niko in Atlanta.

"That's a little presumptuous, Mr. Grunow," I said, with my nose just a little in the air. "Art is subjective, and what I was doing was very necessary. I was rehearsing."

"Isn't acting just make-believe?" Agent Grunow countered. "Why do you have to go somewhere and pretend, before you go somewhere and pretend?"

I knew that the common man had no appreciation for what actors do to prepare, and James Lipton wasn't there to explain it, so I let it go. "Look, what exactly did I do wrong?"

"You refused to remain in my custody — an agent of the United States Secret Service."

"Sorry, but you don't sign my checks. And FYI, you were feeding me a lot of fuzzy law. What is a Person of Interest, anyway? Are they considered more like a suspect, or an Unlawful Combatant?"

Agent Grunow didn't respond. Behind him, the door opened, and another clean-cut agent handed him a dossier. After studying the enclosed material, with an occasional glance toward me, he closed the folder and pursed his lips. "You're free to go."

"That was a fast turn of events," I said, rising to my feet. "Am I now a person of 'dis-interest'?"

"With the exception of numerous calls to 900 numbers, your background check was clean."

"That's good to know, in case I run for Attorney General," I said, heading toward the door.

"But I should inform you, Mr. Campbell," Agent Grunow warned. "We are adding you to an ISL."

"Let me guess: International Shit List."

"Internal Security List," he explained. "It's a database, shared globally with cooperating law enforcement agencies. Our friends around the world will ask a few more questions next time you travel, check your luggage a little more closely — that sort of thing."

"Thank you, Agent Grunow," I said, shaking his hand firmly.

"Thank you for making America more secure."

At my hotel, I did the only logical thing a marked man could do: soak my aching feet in Epsom salts and surf the Internet. My Web guy, Kiffer, had recently posted a notice about getting the role, and I knew I would get a response, but I hadn't anticipated the tenor.

The first e-mail posted on the message board, from "XDethX," summed up the general sentiment rather well, with a subject line that read: "NOOOOOOOOOOOOOO! Say it ain't soooooooooooooooooo!"

Needless to say, this was from a hardcore *Evil Dead* fan. Admittedly, it was probably a mistake to announce that I wouldn't make the Cherry Hill, New Jersey, Spook-a-boo Horrorthon because I was working on a Mike Nichols film, but what was I going to do, lie?

Unfortunately, 99 percent of the e-mails were negative. To the average genre fan, working on an A-list Hollywood film meant that I had turned my back on the very people who shouldered me through years of struggle, only to walk away when the going got good.

I could feel their pain, but as an actor, as a purist, my first responsibility was to the character. In addition, I couldn't walk away from a story that would likely touch more hearts than a midnight showing of *Evil Dead II* in Gary, Indiana. When done right, movies are the best kind of goodwill ambassador — they uplift, inform, enlighten. I had a prime opportunity to enrich the lives of people all across the globe, not to mention myself through some serious residuals, and I wasn't about to let that slip away.

As I tucked my pruned, puffy feet under the covers, I ruminated about the e-mails, taking them to heart. Even though I was in an A movie, it didn't mean I had to let go of my B-movie sensibilities. Actors of my ilk had plenty of tricks in our low-budget bags, and I shouldn't be shy about using them.

**3**

# Sometimes a Great Notion

I walked into the first read thru of Mike Nichols's *Let's Make Love!* an emboldened, professional actor. I was early, had already learned my lines, and was bubbling with notes, ideas, and questions.

The routine is pretty much the same at all Hollywood table readings, particularly the high-end ones. Nobody gets up that early, so readings rarely begin before eleven o'clock. Coffee, tea, and a Best Western–style assortment of danishes are the standard layout. Most first reads are in hotel conference rooms or a production office, and the cast sits around a large table, usually in assigned seats, where they introduce themselves one by one, and read the script, page by page. This is followed by a question-and-answer session, then everyone glad-hands for a while, and splits.

Mike Nichols was different. He hosted the read thru at his brownstone/office, and there was a spread like you'd see in a magazine: omelets by Mike's personal chef (Rolfe), cappuccinos, pastries, chocolate-covered strawberries – enough sugar and caffeine to freak out a long-haul truck driver.

The reading itself took place in Mike's massive library, where the cast relaxed in overstuffed chairs around an imposing stone hearth. *A guy could get used to this,* I thought, dunking my second bear claw into a steaming cup of chai. *I hope I don't fall asleep.*

Renée Zellweger was seated next to me. I didn't recognize her out of makeup. She was very tiny, with curly lips and a calm disposition. Fortunately, I had the perfect icebreaker:

"Hello, Renée?" I asked casually, like a fellow actor would, even though I was oddly nervous about meeting this now-famous actress. "I'm Bruce Campbell. I play Foyl, the doorman."

"Oh, right," she said, smiling. "Nice to meet you."

"A good buddy of mine worked with you a few years back."

"Really? Who was that?"

"John Cameron. He was an assistant director on, what's that film? You were just an extra in it? It wasn't *Mall Rats*...."

"*Dazed and Confused*?" Renée prompted, not wowed with my recollection.

"That's the one. My buddy said he kept picking you out of the crowd and bringing you up front. He thought you were really gonna be something. Now look at you, with your award and everything."

Renée wasn't sure whether to be embarrassed or flattered. "Well, thanks...uh, this should be a lot of fun," she said, turning back to her script.

"This should be fun" is another phrase actors use, meaning: "I don't have any scenes with you, I don't really know you, and I don't have anything else to say to you."

I was about to hide behind my script when I noticed legendary producer Robert Evans across the room. He didn't seem overly occupied at the moment, and I knew him enough to break the ice.

"Mr. Evans," I said, extending my hand to this dapper man wearing a black suit and a cream-colored turtleneck.

Robert Evans looked at me through gradu-ated, owl-eyed shades. "Hello?"

"Let me reintro-duce myself. I'm Bruce Campbell. I'm playing Foyl, the doorman."

Before she was famous, Renée was dazed, confused, and squirting ketchup.

Robert's look remained blank until recognition dawned. "Of course. How nice for you."

"You know we almost worked together."

"Did we?"

"Yeah, back around ninety-five, you were doing *The Phantom* and I almost got the part that Billy Zane got."

As soon as the words had spilled out, I realized the zero inter-est a producer would have in discussing his bomb movie with an actor who didn't even get the lead role.

Robert didn't respond and was suddenly a thousand yards away. I pretty much froze in position as he walked away, not knowing what else to say that would make any difference. But before I could lament my lameness, a familiar catch phrase caught my attention.

"Groovy."

I turned to see what looked like a kid in his early twenties, wiping his hands together. He sported a beard, but it was a young beard, almost pubic.

**Rob Stern**
Meathead

Paramound Studios
Suite 1540
Los Angeles, California

(323) 555.9565, ext. 42
FAX: (323) 555-9566
e-mail: whipping_boy@paramound.con

"Hey, Ash," He said.

"I'm *Bruce*," I corrected, offering a hand. "Who are you?"

"Rob Stern — Paramount."

"Oh, one of the suits. What do you do there?"

"This is my project," Rob said, nodding. "I mean, I'm overseeing it."

"So, this one's on your watch, as they say. Big responsibility."

Rob laughed uncomfortably, pausing only to smell his fingers. "I guess you could say that."

"Do you like the script?" I asked, making conversation.

"Do you? What do *you* think of it?" Rob wondered, suddenly insecure.

"Well, it's very middle-of-the-road, but that was the idea, right? I'm assuming it's PG-13, and you'll release it next spring before the blockbusters kick in, blah, blah, blah — I get it."

Rob looked around as if what he was about to tell me was secret. "Well, we're in the middle of a *major* rewrite."

"I hope you're not going to cut me out before we even shoot, heh-heh."

"I wouldn't say that too loudly. Mike and I don't exactly agree about Foyl's role in the film."

"Meaning what?" I asked, mildly horrified that I wasn't entirely wrong.

"I'll give it to you straight, because I have a rep for that — Paramount never even wanted you in the first place. Do you have any idea how many A-list actors wanted that role? At one point, I had Costner, Cruise, and Crowe all on hold — all waiting for a yes.

Luckily for you, Mike made it happen because he's, well, Mike Nichols."

"So, what, you're waiting for me to fall on my face so you can replace me with Danny Bonaduce?"

"I wouldn't put it like that exactly, but he did do a hell of a read," Rob said, spotting someone more important across the room. "Well, gotta go."

Eventually, the socializing ended, and the read thru began. Actors took turns introducing themselves and when it got to me, I was as excited as I was nervous.

"I hope you don't mind, Mr. Nichols."

The director — *my* director — broke in. "Please, call me Mike." Then, to the cast, "Everybody, it's just Mike."

"Okay, sure," I said. "I hope you don't mind, I gave Foyl a last name."

"Oh, that's fine, we could use it on a name tag or something. June will make a note of it."

"It's Whipple."

"That sounds very...southern," Mike said, nodding. "A little obscure, but salt-of-the-earth." Mike looked to screenwriter, Kevin Jarre, his collaborator on the romantic comedy hit *Working Girl*.

"I think it's good," Kevin said, smiling.

"I also wrote his back story," I said, eagerly.

"Did you now?" Mike asked, with less enthusiasm. "Well, that's, uh, that's..."

"I made a copy for everyone. I hope there are enough to go around."

The room became silent as I walked around, handing them out. "It's three-hole punched so you can keep it in your script. The paper is reinforced, so it won't rip out. Those New York autumns can be wind-eee."

I handed one to Mike, who immediately handed it to June, his secretary.

"Wow, even a few left," I said, finishing my loop around the room.

I was about to sit down, when I realized I hadn't made the most important point. "Oh, uh, I'd also like everyone to refer to me from this point forward by my character name, Foyl."

"Thanks for that, uh, *Foyl*," Mike said, pointing to the back story in front of June, who was looking at it with feigned interest. "All right, let's keep moving along here, we've got a lot of ground to cover."

To facilitate the actual reading of a rather clunky writing format, Mike and his team used a customized screenplay which removed the minutiae, and deftly summarized the action that took place between the dialogue. We moved at a rapid clip, and arrived at page seven, scene nine — my debut — in no time.

"Mike, if I may?" I asked, raising my hand.

"Yes, Foyl."

"I'd like to try a little something with this. Just to fool around, you know?"

"Give it a whirl, Foyl. No time like the present."

Based on my character research, Foyl would have had a very pronounced Southern accent, so my line "Good evenin', Mr. Grayson, how are you tonight?" sounded a lot like, "Guuud eeeyvnin', mistuh Graiiison, haaaaur uuu t'naight?"

Richard Gere paused for a moment, adjusting to my approach, then recited: "Not so good, Foyl, not so good."

"Why not, Mr. Grayson?" Foyl asked, sounding like "Whaaa naught, mistuh Graiiison?"

Our director tried to hide his heavy sigh, but he couldn't. "Excuse me, Foyl?"

I didn't like being interrupted, but what can you do, that's the rehearsal process. "Yes, Mike?"

"Where are you thinking Foyl is from?"

"Outside of Savannah, Georgia — like it says in the back story."

Richard started laughing. "I'm sorry, but for a minute there, I thought I was acting across from Gomer Pyle."

The other cast members couldn't suppress their laughter. I could feel my face flush red from the negative vibes. *I may have to file a grievance with the Screen Actors Guild,* I noted to myself.

"But this is a romantic comedy, Mike," I objected. "Can't it be a little broad?"

"Foyl, as you can see, the Southern accent is funny," Mike explained, "but for the wrong reasons. Personally, I'd vote for an elegant Southerner, a gentleman, not a shit kicker. It's too on-the-nose."

Certain directors, particularly those of the caliber of Mike Nichols, have a way of making statements that are both explanations and decisions at the same time. Whatever the case, without a peep, I toned it down for the rest of the read thru, and avoided any further reprimands.

Afterward, the cast members mingled as expected, exchanging e-mail addresses, or discussing a particular scene. I worked my way past Renée, who gave

SCREEN ACTORS GUILD
5757 Wilshire Blvd.
Los Angeles, CA 90036

**GRIEVANCE FORM**

Name BRUCE LORNE CAMPBELL          Fake Phone Number (818) 555-6980

Website Address WWW.BRUCECAMPBELL dot COM

Last Speaking Role in a Film to Gross More than $100,000,000 Domestic Box Office SNOOTY USHER

Date of Occurrence 04-12-04

What is the nature of the grievance? HUMILIATION, SHAME, AND IGNOMINY

What effect, specifically, did said action have on you? I WAS SCARED AND WANTED TO HIDE

How exactly has your finely-honed craft suffered? SEE REVERSE SIDE

Additional Information (Give particulars and try not to adlib):

RICHARD GERE, RENEE ZELWEGGER, AND SOME OTHER JERKS LAUGHED

AT MY SOUTHERN ACCENT. ONE OF THE OTHERS (LINDA LAVIN) SAID

KEANU REEVES DID BETTER ACCENTS THAN ME.

Settlement requested ALL FOREIGN DVD SALES FOR SPIDER-MAN 3,

I hereby state that the information is correct and I am in accordance with California Laws in respect to the restrictions and/or privileges of vehicle licensing and transportation. I have read the SAG Handbook in regards to driving regulations administered on this particular campus and agree to abide by them.

Member's Autograph

Date 04-11-04

Bureaucrat's Signature (Associate Producer credit pending)

Date

FOR OFFICIAL USE ONLY     Date

Setup _____ Confrontation _____ Resolution _____

me that same semi-forced smile of recognition, to Richard, who was just saying good-bye to Christopher Plummer, the great actor who plays his father, the evil businessman.

Richard nodded when he saw me and walked over. "Hey, Foyl, I had an idea. What do you say, before we get into rehearsals with Mike, that you and I get together at my place here in town and we'll run the lines — massage the scenes. This is a relationship film; apart from the relationship that Renée and I have, my relationship with you has to be unique as well."

"I totally agree, Dick."

"Richard," he said, politely correcting.

"Right, Richard."

"You don't smoke, do you?"

"Not officially, no," I assured him.

"Okay, uh, well, it was great to hear a first pass at this. I'll have my assistant track you down."

With that, Richard bolted before I could respond.

The crowd around Mike thinned, so I thought I'd take a shot at talking to him. I got within his peripheral vision, and he looked over right away.

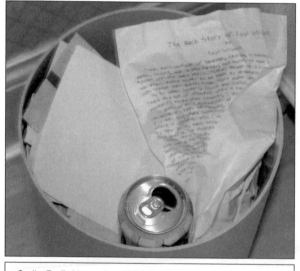

Sadly, Foyl's biography received a similar response to my own.

"There he is," Mike said, as genially as he could for being a little pissed off.

"Hey, Mike, I don't want to take up any of your time, but as you can see, I've been re-searching this role."

"Yes, yes, that was

very obvious," he said, nodding. "Just don't give yourself a hernia in the process. Today was a little rough, Bruce, I'm not going to lie to you."

"I'm sorry, Mike, I was pretty nervous."

"That's understandable, but don't get too lost trying to do a performance. Foyl never forces anything, he lets it happen naturally."

"Yeah, that's been a problem for me," I confided.

Mike shifted his weight uneasily. "If I might make a suggestion, Bruce, as an actor, you need to listen more. Half of communication is listening to what the other person has to say. I sensed that while the other character was talking, you were more or less just waiting to say your lines. Acting when you're *not* talking is even more important than when you are. Anyway, that's my take on it."

I found myself nodding with everything Mike said, but the word *communication* stuck. As an actor in search of a character, this single, simple word, understood and applied, could make the difference between a lousy performance and a memorable one. With renewed vigor, I marched past unread, crumpled bios, randomly abandoned in every direction, and out to the world at large.

*I hear you, Mike — I hear you loud and clear.*

# 4

# Mind the Gap

Communication is the glue that binds civilization together. For instance, my wife, Ida, and I don't share information all at once over a quiet supper; rather, we tend to spout things as we think of them during the course of a day. It doesn't matter whether we're on different floors or behind locked doors — we insist on doing it, knowing full well that it always causes two things: a breakdown in communication, and irritation.

Here's a typical conversation:

"Hey, Bruce, I'm going to the store," Ida would yell from upstairs. "Can I get you something?"

"Bye," I would call back, reaching for the remote control to mute the TV. "Hey, are you going to the store?" I would then ask.

"I just said that," she would say, growing increasingly annoyed.

"Great — can you get me something?"

You can see how even the smallest bit of missed or repeated

information can quickly turn what would ordinarily be a civil conversation into one that's twice as long, and half as civil.

I asked myself, what if relationship problems all boiled down to gaps in information? Finding the answer to this one would require wisdom, persistence, and the keen ears of Lester Shankwater.

With four days before Richard Gere and I planned to rehearse, I had plenty of time to meet Lester outside Sign of the Beefcarver in Sandusky, Ohio. When I was a kid in Detroit, it used to be called Sign of the Beefeater, but the makers of Beefeater's Gin threw a hairy fit and forced them to change the name.

On this balmy summer evening, Lester and I weren't there to sample the prime rib, which isn't bad, aside from slightly watery au jus. No, tonight we were sitting in his sky blue Astro minivan preparing to eavesdrop on a couple experiencing relationship problems. Lester's business card proclaims him to be a RELATIONSHIP CONSULTANT.

"At the behest of various clients, I record couples and analyze their communication skills. I also provide what I call the Cyrano Technique, that's what I'm doing tonight. I guide clients through rough spots in communication, in real time."

"Like 'love' coaching?"

"I like to refer to it as Unity Reinforcement."

"How does someone end up doing this for a living?"

"Well, it just sort of fell into place," Lester explained. "I used to sit in the Food Court at the Sandusky Plaza Mall — I worked at the Radio Shack there for ten years — and I would hear the most infuriating conversations between couples, and I thought to myself, I can help these people."

"What gives you special skills in this field? Do you have a degree? A Ph.D.?"

"Those are just words on a piece of paper. I have a great ear. I can fill in the blanks in most conversations, and I'm very intuitive.

The service I provide is goal-oriented. I don't want repeat clients, you know what I mean? I can only listen to idiots for so long."

"How does it work?"

"The deal is this: I discuss the desired effect he or she wants for a date, a party, a phone conversation, etc. Do they want to be funny? Do they want to sound more intelligent? More professional? I don't like to toot my own horn, but who do you think feeds Anthony Robbins all of his ideas — live, in real time?"

"That's damned impressive, Lester."

"Anyway, once you and the client agree on a strategy, I wire him with a very high-tech, low-profile, two-way communication rig. I can hear him talk, he can hear me. In special cases, like tonight, I've got a bug on her too. My client planted it on her purse. That's in case we need 'inside information,' know what I mean?

"This seems slightly insidious."

"*Discreet* is the word we like to use. Depending on the situation, I can also use my parabolic microphone. It can isolate specific sounds far away. They use them at football games. Let me show you."

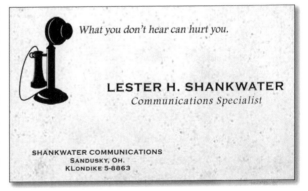

What you don't hear can hurt you.

**LESTER H. SHANKWATER**
*Communications Specialist*

SHANKWATER COMMUNICATIONS
SANDUSKY, OH.
KLONDIKE 5-8863

Lester stooped over and made his way to the back of the van.

"So if you don't mind my asking, what's with the sky blue Astro minivan?"

"For starters, blue is not a threatening or evil color," he said, moving a large case. "It's a heroic color, a good-guy color."

"And the minivan?"

"Answer your own question, fella," Lester urged, assembling a long, thin Senheiser microphone with a miniature satellite dish around it. "Say the word: *minivan*. Not very threatening, is it? Nobody's going to hassle a minivan. Besides, it's got plenty of cargo room, and the mileage is better than you might think."

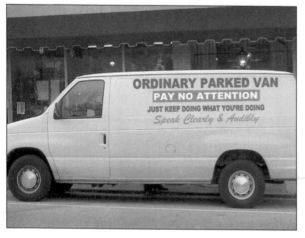

ORDINARY PARKED VAN
PAY NO ATTENTION
JUST KEEP DOING WHAT YOU'RE DOING
*Speak Clearly & Audibly*

Lester crawled back into the driver's seat with his parabolic microphone and rolled down the window. "Who shall we capture?"

I spotted a couple walking, or *trying* to walk, from the bar to their car. "How about those two?"

"Easy as a turkey shoot," Lester said, pointing the unusual microphone toward them. He fiddled with a few knobs and hit a speaker button. A man's voice came in startlingly clear, sounding very close:

"For your information, I can drive just fine, okay?" he slurred.

"That's amazing," I marveled, not really caring about the conversation. "It's creepy how you can hear them breathing, and the rustle of their clothes."

"It's fun stuff," Lester said with a smile. "Shit, I can tell what kind of slacks a man has on, just by the sound."

"How long have you been doing this?"

"Three weeks — full time, that is."

"But, you know, the average person doesn't have audio-visual aids when they're communicating," I protested. "People have to learn how to do that by themselves, don't they?

"Not if I can help it," Lester said, unapologetically. "I provide something better than probability — I provide *possibility.* Take this fellow tonight: his name is Darryl, he's got a hot babe, Mandy, but he lacks the confidence and sense of humor to make advances."

"So you're going to, what, feed him some one-liners?"

Lester looked at me like I was a fool. "This is serious stuff, Bruce. Darryl has problems communicating his thoughts and feelings. There is so much he wants to say to Mandy, but she'd never know it. I'm going to help Darryl break his cycle of self-defeat with positive, assertive, and sometimes daring prompts."

Lester pointed across the Beefcarver parking lot. Darryl was just arriving with Mandy in his Ford Focus. Lester jumped into action, flipping switches and adjusting dials. "This should be fun. Darryl's a very willing subject. It's always better during these live events when you don't have to argue with the client you're trying to help."

Darryl was a tall, thin thirty-something, with sandy blond hair that hadn't seen a style change in fifteen years. Or maybe I was just a little out of step with Sandusky, Ohio. He was sporting what I believed to be a leisure suit, and the plaid design was threatening to scar my retinas. Mandy, on the other hand, was petite and cute, though in a too-put-together sort of way. She had so much makeup on it was impossible to tell what she really looked like.

"Man, what a babe," Lester said, scoping her out with binoculars.

I looked slightly askance, but Lester shrugged. "Hey, it's Sandusky. Okay, Darryl, we're recording. Give me a nod if you can hear me."

Across the lot, Darryl nodded in compliance.

"Okay, tonight you're going to be a good listener, you're going to be more assertive, and you're going to try some humor. Here we go. Tell Mandy that she looks really pretty tonight."

Darryl tensed up as he escorted Mandy toward the restaurant. "Boy, Mandy, you look pretty...*tonight*."

"Don't improvise," Lester scolded. "And don't change the inflections either. This is about specific communication. She looks *very* pretty."

"You mean tonight I'm pretty, as opposed to every other night we've been together?" Mandy asked, teasing him.

Darryl got a confused look on his face. He wasn't sure whom to respond to first. "Very pretty," he said finally.

"So tonight I'm very pretty, but every other night, I'm just pretty?" Mandy asked, baiting him.

Darryl got the same confused look again, and Lester stepped in to bail him out.

"Absolutely not," he said, prompting. "You're always pretty, usually beautiful, but tonight you're stunning."

"Absolutely," Darryl said, repeating incorrectly. "You're always pretty usual, but tonight you're sunning."

Lester's jaw hardened audibly while his eyes narrowed. "Maybe he's impaired in some way...."

"Uh...thank you, I think?" Mandy said, not knowing whether it was a compliment or a psychotic break.

"You may have to dumb it down," I suggested, watching Darryl fumble for the front door of the restaurant. "What's he going to do when he doesn't have you around to feed him everything he says?"

"This is just a crash course," Lester said, defensively. "He'll eventually start using his own vocabulary."

"That could be scary."

"Be sure to help Mandy with her chair," Lester cautioned. "You're assertive, but you're also a gentleman."

Suddenly, a loud impact almost blew the speaker in Lester's van. It was followed by a few grunts, and a flurry of generally violent noises.

"Ow!" Mandy shouted.

"Whoa, sorry, Mandy, what happened?"

"What do you mean what happened? You kicked the goddamn chair right out from under me, and I fell on my ass."

"I didn't kick the chair on purpose, Mandy, but I think I may have tripped on it. Sorry."

Lester and I could hear Darryl helping Mandy up and into a new chair.

"That was smooth," I said.

Lester raised his eyebrows. "Okay now, Darryl, once you order drinks, it's time to make some magic."

We heard a new voice chime in. "Good evening, folks. My name is Carol, I'll be your server. Can I get you anything to drink right off the bat?"

"Let her order first, Darryl," Lester coached.

"Uh, she can go," Darryl said.

"Okay, well, to recover from my wounds, I'd like a vodka tonic."

Communications "specialist" Lester Shankwater.

"Complement her choice," Lester insisted.

"Hey, I love vodka too. Excellent."

Lester looked at me with increasing frustration. "Do we have a bad connection?"

I shrugged. "I'd be more worried about *Darryl's* connection."

"Okay, Darryl, order something different. Wing it."

"I'd like a...Long Island ice tea," he said, grinning. "With a flaming Jell-o shot chaser."

"Allll-right," Carol said, sensing what she was getting into. "I'll put those orders right in."

Lester referred to a few notes he jotted down. "Okay, Darryl, it's time to shine. Take her hand."

"Wooh!" we heard Mandy exclaim. "You scared me."

"I hear it's great!"
- Harry Caul, WKIF

Lester Shankwater is an eavesdropper. He drops eaves better than anyone. He can record an ant's fart from a mile away. Seriously.

But this time, he's heard too much. Or maybe not.

Another Parody of a Legitimate Movie Presents

**GENE CAMPBELL**
in
**"THE CONVERSATIONALISTENER"**

"Sorry," Darryl said. "Just wanted to hold your hand."

Lester winked at me. "We've got to kick it up." Then, to his guinea pig: "Okay, Darryl, I want you to look in her eyes — right in them."

"Why are you staring at me?" Mandy asked, sounding disturbed.

"Because I can't take my eyes off you," Lester suggested.

"Because I can't stop keeping my eyes off you," Darryl tried to repeat.

"Okay, that's nice," Mandy said. "Thanks. But don't grip my hand that tight."

"Mandy. I have to ask you something," Lester said.

"Mandy. I have you something to ask," Darryl repeated.

"He's either Russian or dyslexic," I said.

"What is it, Darryl?" Mandy asked.

"Do you know how much I think of you?" Lester offered.

Lester and I both winced, because we knew that Darryl was bound to disappoint.

"Do you know how often I think of you?" Darryl asked.

Lester looked at me, deadpan. "Close enough."

"No, how often?" Mandy inquired.

"Day and night," Lester said.

"Twenty-four seven," Darryl translated. "Non-stop."

"I hate when they embellish my simple and elegant statements," Lester lamented.

"So, like are you obsessed or what?" Mandy asked, not even close to being won over.

Lester let out a sigh, and continued. "No, Mandy, but I have a hard time expressing myself, and I just wanted you to know it."

"That was a pretty long sentence," I cautioned.

Lester shrugged. "What can you do? My course is one size fits all."

Darryl answered with, "No way, Mandy. I just have a time with hard expressions. And I just wanted you...to know it."

Lester and I weren't privy to Mandy's perplexed expression, but I'm sure it was worthy of *I Love Lucy.* "Hard expressions? What does that mean?" Mandy asked, really wanting to know.

"I can't get hard expressions across," Lester suggested, trying to salvage his failing operation.

"I can't get hard things across," Darryl tried.

"Okay, I'm trying to follow you," Mandy said. "You can't express hard expressions?"

"No!" Darryl said, uncharacteristically forceful. "I can't hardly express how much I...I like you."

There was a long silence. Lester looked at me with a glimmer of hope in his eyes. "See? Darryl is learning to swim on his own."

"I need to use the bathroom," Mandy said, not responding to Darryl's awkward declaration.

"Okay, I'm gonna have a smoke," Darryl said, quickly jumping from the table.

Seconds later, he emerged outside the restaurant and pulled a pack of Lucky Strikes from his jacket.

"Darryl, can you hear me?" Lester asked.

"Yo," Darryl said, nodding his head toward the van. "Going pretty well, don't you think?"

"Like gangbusters," Lester said, trying to stay positive. "Hey, hang on for a sec, we're doing some random monitoring."

Lester turned to me. "I'll bet you twenty bucks that Mandy's gonna make a cell call while she's in the little girl's room. And if she does, we'll get the inside story on how well he's doing."

Lester gestured behind him at a bank of high-tech gear. "Radio Shack don't lie. If Mandy dials out or gets a call, the sensor Darryl put on her phone will activate. From here, I punch in, match the frequency, and we hit pay dirt."

In about three seconds, a loud beeping filled the minivan. Lester smiled and activated the speakerphone.

"We get rid of everything we don't need," he said, as garbled signals and overlapping transmissions dropped away one by one. Eventually, we could hear the slightly nasal voice of Mandy, clear as a bell.

"Oh, not so good, Jackie," she said.

I glanced at Lester. "Is that Mandy?"

"Yep," he said. "The sensor on her phone syncs up with my unit out here. I'd explain, but it's pretty complicated."

The secret conversation continued:

"What's wrong?" Mandy's girlfriend asked.

"Well, this guy Darryl has been creeping me out all night. He's talking in weird sentences, his eyes bug out, and, oh my God, he almost crushed my hand."

"Is he at least rich?"

"Are you kidding me?" Mandy said, through derisive laughter.

"He's wearing a *leisure suit*."

As the girls gossiped, I couldn't help but watch Darryl. The poor sap didn't have a care in the world. He confidently hiked up his polyester pants and swiped a finger across his thin moustache, straightening any stray hairs.

"Oh my God! You gotta bail, girl," Jackie insisted.

"Please, Lord, let some man one day just take me away," Mandy pleaded.

Lester raised an eyebrow.

"Screw this guy," Jackie proclaimed. "Come on over. I got some cheap red wine. We'll get drunk and laugh at how useless men are!"

"Great! Sounds like a plan," Mandy said. "Well, I gotta go. I gotta pee real bad."

"Okay, love you, girl."

"You too. Bye."

"Trouble in paradise," I said to Lester, who was running his fingers through his hair and flipping switches off. "You don't seem terribly upset."

"Hey, I can't stop fate. If the guy is an idiot, he's an idiot. I'm gonna drain the lizard, and do a little, uh, sound check with Darryl. Do you need anything?"

"No, I'm good," I said, jotting a few notes in my actor's log.

From inside the now-silent van, I watched

In addition to all this equipment, the van also comes with passenger side airbags and six beverage holders.

Lester approach Darryl and give him a big pat on the shoulder. They had a brief, "educational" conversation, and Lester made his way inside the Beefcarver for a "drain."

What the hell is wrong with people? I wondered. *What's so hard about telling it like it is? Are we such freaks that we can't just deal with this shit ourselves? And why do we have to hire "experts" to explain and counsel us on every single detail of our waking lives? Most of the time, I'm pretty happy being a slob who doesn't know shit about anything.*

My wandering eyes fell on a bank of newspaper dispensers across the parking lot, lined up beneath the restaurant's large picture window. I checked my supply of quarters and hustled across the lot to see what local flavor I could find.

*Clink-clink.* I dropped in thirty-five cents and got myself a

The horribly misdirected Darryl.

*Sandusky Bugle,* "The Word of Truth for a Hundred and Fifty Years." But before I could glance at the headline, I spotted Lester inside the restaurant — and he wasn't going to the bathroom, he was headed directly toward a corner table. I shuffled closer to the restaurant for a better look, pretending to read the newspaper. From the closer vantage point, I saw Lester drop a folded piece of paper on a table without even slowing down. He deftly swung back around and slipped into the men's room.

*Tricky boy*, I thought. *What are you up to?*

Lester's timing was marvelous, because as soon as he slipped out of sight, Mandy exited the women's room and made her way back to the table. She couldn't help notice the paper, and she unfolded it for a look. Mandy looked around the room, but nobody responded. She glanced at her cell phone.

The door to the men's room opened, so I hustled back to the van, obscured by the local paper. Lester bounced out the front door and joined Darryl, who was just crushing out his cigarette.

Inside the van, I fished out Lester's parabolic microphone and aimed it toward the two guys. A few minor adjustments later, I was getting a fabric-rustling audio close-up of their conversation.

"Darryl, I'm proud of you," Lester said, grinning. "You've done really well."

"You think so?"

"So well, in fact, that I'm going to allow you to fly solo for the rest of the evening."

Darryl squinted at Lester. "Meaning?"

"You've graduated, you idiot — you're free!"

Darryl gasped. "Wow, really?"

"You can now pursue relationships on your own two feet," Lester assured him. "Repeat after me — I am a communicator!"

"Gosh, okay, uh, I am a —"

*Riiiiing* — the sound of Lester's cell phone interrupted Darryl's climax.

"Excuse me for a second," he said, turning away the slightest bit to answer. "Hello? Oh, *helloooo*." Lester turned to Darryl with a wink. "I have to take this, sport. Good luck and Godspeed."

"Okay, thanks for everything," Darryl said, and he marched inside the restaurant with new bravura.

I nodded, knowingly. *That little stinker.*

*Beeeep!* A red light flashed on the control panel. It sounded just like the one I heard when Lester tapped Mandy's phone. Looking at the dials, I located the two-button combination — the power to the receiver and the channel designator. Within thirty seconds, I had Mandy dialed in. She was giggling like a school-girl. A familiar, if faint, voice joined in:

"I'm a communications specialist," Lester Shankwater cooed.

I swung the parabolic mic toward Lester across the lot, and got perfectly clear reception. I couldn't help but notice a Panasonic CD recorder and a stack of seemingly empty CDs. I popped a CD in the sleek machine and hit Record. For a brief second, I felt like I was starring in a poorly reviewed, dumped-to-Saturday-night, syndicated action show, *Brick Brackman: Audio Detective.*

"I'd love to teach you some new ways to share information," Lester flirted.

"Yeah, I'd love that," Mandy agreed. "The guy I just ditched couldn't put a sentence together if his life depended on it."

"Well, I'd love to hear your story. I'm out in the lot."

"Okay, I ditched out the back. Want to meet at the Dumpsters?"

"Sure," Lester said. "Give me five minutes to do some ditching of my own, and I'll meet you there."

"Okay, I'll see you."

"Ciao."

Unless they're fifth-generation Italian, guys who say "ciao" are losers. This guy was a first-class chump. I recorded a few more seconds of Lester's happy whistling and self-affirmations, then hit Eject and stuffed the CD in my pocket. I placed the parabolic back where it was, returned the knobs to their original settings (more or less), and switched off the power.

Lester smiled as he approached the van, but I was already getting out the other side. "Hey, Bruce, listen, something's come up."

"Yeah, I know what's come up, and her name is Mandy."

Lester knew that for me to have such information I must either be possessed — or I must have used his stuff! "Yeah, well, you better keep my card, actor boy. You may not like what I do, but one day you may *need* what I do."

Larry's van squealed away, toward the Dumpsters in the back, where a lot more than love hung in the air.

As I walked toward the Beefcarver, Darryl came back outside and lit another smoke. His stooped shoulders told the whole story. Even though we had never met, I felt I knew him well enough to approach.

"Excuse me — Darryl?"

"Yeah?" he said, warily.

"You and I have the same acquaintance — Lester Shankwater."

SURVEILLANCE SUBJECT DATA SHEET

Name: Samantha "Mandy" Cooper
Bust: 33
Waist: 25
Hips: 29, "
Height: 5'4
Weight: 101
Birth Date: 11/23/81
Birthplace: Sandusky, Ohio
Ambitions: To be an actress, or even a television journalist
Turn-ons: Hopefully, communicat monster trucks, cats, man
Turnoffs: Lesiure suits, lack of ambition, men who don't like cats, body hair, bad teeth
Notes: She's a woman, so she won't care what kind of attention she gets as long as she gets attention.

She wears too much make-up, so Darryl should compliment her on her looks

Her friend Jackie sounds like a bitch

SHANKWATER COMMUNICATIONS
SANDUSKY, OH.
KLONDIKE-8863

"Yeah, well, I hope he isn't a close friend of yours, because I'd punch his damn lights out right now. He gave me bad advice."

"He did more than that, I'm afraid," I said, producing the telltale CD. "You and the Better Business Bureau might find this pretty interesting."

Darryl hesitated, as was his nature, but then he took the CD. "Thanks, mister."

"So. You hungry?" I asked.

"Well, I was, but I'm not sure anymore," Darryl replied.

"I'll buy dinner if you give me a ride to the Best Western afterward."

Darryl managed a weak smile. "I think I can handle that."

I put a hand on Darryl's slouching shoulder and we turned to head inside. "You know, Darryl, this could be the beginning of a beautiful friendship."

Small airports are sometimes more security conscious than large ones, simply because they don't have the big-ass machines to see inside all the luggage they transport, and it results in a lot more hand searches. I know this for a fact, traveling in and out of my small Oregon airport, and the Sandusky County Regional Airport was no exception.

"Darryl, this could be the beginning of a weird, heterosexual, male relationship."

As I stepped up to the head of the security line, impatient to leave this dreary part of the Midwest, Transportation Security Administration agent Bill Beasley put a palm up toward my face. "Boarding pass and I.D., please...."

I handed over the documents, and Agent Beasley gave them the once-over. He looked from my driver's license up to me and squinted.

"Why do you look so familiar?"

"I have that kind of face, I guess," I said, responding the same way I do to people who partially recognize me.

Bill looked me up and down to see if I was ready to walk through the metal detector. "Please make sure your belt and shoes are off."

"But my belt never beeps — even in L.A."

"Take it off, please."

"Same with the shoes. They don't go off in any airport."

"That's nice," Bill said, unimpressed. "Take them off, please."

"Oh, for crying out loud," I grumbled, tossing my shoes into a gray bin and shoving it on the conveyor belt. "In all the years of traveling, I have never *once* set off one of these —"

*Beep!* The metal detector sounded sharply as I passed through it.

"Oh, what now?" I said, tossing my hands in the air with a sigh.

TSA agent Ellen Heche was ready with a black, hand-held wand. "Please step over here and stand on the peanuts for additional screening."

"Why?" I asked belligerently, "Because I have a gum wrapper in my pants?"

"It could be as simple as that," Ellen said with a muted smile, waving the wand down and around my body. "Arms out. Let's hope it's —"

Ellen's wand started to make strange noises as it passed over a lower, cargo pocket on the front of my pants.

I reached down and pulled out a promotional pen from Lester Shankwater. "Typical. Heh-heh. Sorry about that."

"We're gonna have to put that through the machine," Ellen instructed. "Please put it in one of the bins."

I was set to launch into a lengthy tirade about pens and aircraft safety, but given the current security climate, I thought better, and dropped it into a small, blue tray.

Waiting for the stupid pen to roll out the other side, I put my shoes and belt back on. But as I approached the machine again, I saw no pen, just three agents huddled around the X-ray monitor, looking at the fifty-cent object with great interest and concern. Their attention turned to me, and the grim look on their faces said it all. A deputy from the sheriff's department stepped forward and gestured to a room with bluish, reflective windows.

"Mr. Campbell, would you please come with us?"

You never want to hear those eight words from a sheriff's deputy, but what choice did I have?

In the small, bare room, TSA agents Ellen and Bill sat nearby, while Deputy Willard Fitz paced menacingly in front of me. This was surely the most exciting thing to happen during Fitz's two-and-a-half-year career with the Oshgosh County Sheriff's Department, and he was going to make something of it.

"Are you aware that recording of any kind within one hundred yards of a TSA facility is against the law?" he asked.

"Not really, but okay, I'll go with you...."

"Particularly for a person on the ISL."

*The ISL?* I wondered. Then the connection hit me — the International Security List. I grabbed Lester's pen from the small desk in front of me and had a closer look. Sure enough, it wasn't just a pen with an advertisement on it; it was also a tiny recording device, capable of storing four hours of crystal-clear digital audio.

In a security environment where connecting the dots is a new priority, I could see how a rural airport, a recording device, and a previous brush with the Secret Service might set off a few alarms.

Officer Fitz got a stern look on his face and produced a small, laminated card from his back pocket. "Mr. Bruce Campbell, are you now associated with, or have you ever been associated with, the terrorist organization Al-Qaeda, or any of its affiliates in the known world?"

"Officer, for God's sake, I'm not a terrorist, I'm an actor. I mean,

I almost *played* a terrorist once — in *Collateral Damage* — but I lost out to Cliff Curtis."

Without responding, the deputy proceeded to the next of his appointed questions: "Do you harbor any ill will toward the United States of America?"

I slapped a hand on my forehead — it was going to be a long day. "Look, let's be reasonable. Why don't you just play what's on the device, which will be nothing, and I can go about missing my next seven connections. How does that sound?"

Federal law enforcement types are always suspicious of suggestions made by potential felons, but the three in this room exchanged shrugs and Deputy Fitz pressed Play for all to hear.

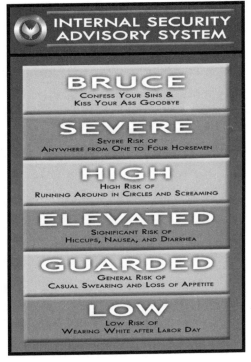

The initial sounds weren't very distinct, and had a muffled quality. Mostly, we heard the sound of fabric scraping across the microphone, like the device had been inadvertently turned on in my pocket. Then, the audio quality grew more hollow, as if the recorder were now in a large, bare room.

*Sounds like a bathroom*, I thought to myself. Oh, dear God, not that!

Before my brain could reconstruct an unfortunate bathroom incident, a barrage of visceral sounds too horrible to repeat in print boomed out of the pen. Earlier in the day, in a rush to get out of Sandusky, I grabbed fast food from a chain I hadn't seen since I was a kid, and it went down all wrong. Fortunately for the security of our country, Lester's mighty pen had captured the sounds of my gastrointestinal concert in excruciating detail.

Deputy Fitz managed to halt the noise coming from the damning pen, and we sat in silence, avoiding eye contact. The key word for the next few minutes was embarrassment, but the "evidence" convinced the agents that I was not the man they were looking for.

"Uh, I'd say you're pretty much free to go, Mr. Campbell," Deputy Fitz said, gathering up the papers in front of him. "Sorry for the hassle."

Civil liberty intrusions aside, and apart from the fact that my own government no longer trusted me, what disturbed me most about the incident was the fact that I wasted precious time away from my craft, particularly at a time when I was already apprehensive about my next appointment.

# 5

# An Idiot and a Gentleman

Richard Gere's pad was not hard to find. In fact, it was right where he said it would be, off Central Park West and across from Strawberry Fields, sitting on some of the most expensive real estate in the world. The exterior looked like it was rubbed down with fistfuls of money every morning. Decorations in the lobby were low-key and sleek. I checked out the doorman, who was, of course, nicely put together. As I passed him, we nodded in working-class solidarity.

The elevator ride up to the fortieth floor was fast and quiet. I found Richard's apartment and knocked on the door. It wasn't like we were dating, but I figured I should bring something as a courtesy for our work session. I knew he was a Buddhist, so I skipped the bottle of Chivas Regal and got him something better.

Richard opened the door, looking relaxed and happy in a comfortable, monklike outfit. I had no idea how old Richard Gere was, but he looked great. He had skin that actors die for, smooth and blemish free. His salt-and-pepper gray hair was very distinguished. "Hello, Foyl," he said, smiling. "Come on in."

Richard's penthouse was very different from others I had seen. With most of them you get the sense that the owner no longer has the slightest clue who they are or what their taste happens to be, and their living quarters invariably devolve into quasi–hotel suite extravagance — the hallmark of professional decorations. Richard's, on the other hand, far from being overdecorated, was subdued, almost serene.

"Hey, uh, we can skip the Foyl thing for tonight if you want," I suggested. "I don't want to get too crazy about that."

"Okay, Bruce, whatever you'd like. What have you got there?" Richard asked, referring to my gift.

"Oh, that. It's a little 'great to work with you' thing."

"Wow, that's really cool," he said. "Come in and make yourself comfortable."

I handed him the wrapped package, and he led us toward a sunken living room. "Would you like some white tea?"

"I don't even know what that is."

"It's the purest tea. You've heard of black tea, green tea, and so forth?"

"Yeah, I get it. So, Lipton would be considered a brown tea then, wouldn't it?"

"No," he said politely, "but I think you'll like the white."

"I'll take milk and sugar."

Richard looked back as he headed into the kitchen. "You don't put anything in white tea. It just is what it is."

"Okay," I said. "Sounds...*great.*"

Richard came out with a tray and joined me, cross-legged, on the floor. He poured us each a tiny cup of the herbal tea. "To this film," he said, raising his cup.

"To this film," I echoed, as we clinked. "May this film live long and prosper."

Richard and I sipped the brew and settled back. "How do you like it?"

I tried to think of something nice to say about his tasteless tea, which smelled like day-old hiking socks. "It's very different. Very savory."

"You don't like it, do you?"

If you think this is bad, you should see what he put in the soup.

"It's not a matter of *like*, really...."

"So let's see what you brought me," Richard said excitedly, as he grabbed at my hastily wrapped gift.

He tore at the newsprint and tape and eventually revealed a twenty-inch-high Buddha, happy, bald, and pot-bellied.

"If you rub his belly, he'll talk to you," I suggested.

Richard threw me a sideways glance, but rubbed Buddha's little belly nonetheless. A small, tinny voice emanated from a cheap speaker, deep inside: "If one speaks or acts with an impure thought, suffering follows one, like the wheel of the cart follows the foot of the ox."

"Wow, Bruce," Richard said, shaking his head. "It's... it's..."

At a loss for words, Richard carried the Buddha into another room like a stinky diaper, then sat back down, gathered himself, and got down to business. "So, Bruce, I thought we would start by talking about our relationship."

"Well, so far it's not *bad*. I mean, I just met you, but —"

"The *characters*," he corrected. "The way Foyl and Harry interact."

The surest way to never achieve Enlightenment is to use a photograph of Buddha in a cheap gag.

"Right, gotcha," I said, taking a sip of the fetid, lukewarm tea.

"I think our characters should be night and day, hot and cold, high and low. Know what I mean?"

"Sure," I said, playing along. "I'm the salt to your pepper, the Yin to your Yang, the cream in your coffee."

"Well...something like that," Richard acknowledged. "But you're the calm and cool one, I'm the hothead. We have to be very different is what I'm trying to say."

"I agree, Rich."

"*Richard.*"

"Uh, right. Can I pitch something to you along those lines?"

"Sure, Bruce," Richard said, calmly. "It's part of scene study. You and I will fool around with the material until it feels right, then we'll present it to Mike."

"Great," I said, feeling relieved, "because I'd say that our relationship isn't anywhere near what it needs to be."

"How do you mean?" Richard asked, intrigued.

"Well, it's pretty staid, isn't it? We're supposed to be these great friends by the end and all, but after what? The stuff that we go through should all be amped up to have more meaning."

Richard got a little worried. "Look, Bruce, I'm not a writer. If you're suggesting some rewrites..."

"No, no, not at all, just the way some of it's staged, and how we might react. Like, for example," I said, jumping to my feet, "the scene where you get mugged outside The Arms. Right now, there's just a tussle, and I come in to help."

"Right. I thought it works pretty well," Richard said. "Do you have a problem with that?"

"No, not if you want the audience to fall asleep."

"Well, I wouldn't add more violence if that's what you mean. I'm not a violence guy."

"I understand that, but it doesn't mean we couldn't dispatch this mugger with a little flair. Could we give something a try?"

Richard got to his feet, if hesitantly. "Sure."

"Okay, the script says that the guy comes at you from behind. You be you and I'll be the guy. He gets you in a bear hug, so what do you do?"

"I'd go limp and not resist."

"That might be what *Richard Gere* would do, but what about your character? He'd do what?"

Richard stepped in front of me, and I grabbed him from behind.

"I play Harry Grayson," he said, eyes squinting a little bit, "a tightly wound ad executive."

"That's right," I agreed, tightening my grip around his surprisingly good physique. "He wouldn't roll over for anybody."

Having uttered that, Richard heaved his arms up and arched his back. The strong, unexpected force sent me backpedaling across his shiny floor and directly into a Ming vase — CRASH! I dropped to the floor amid a hail of expensive pottery shards. All I could do was look up in horror.

Richard stood across the room with a wide grin. "That was fantastic!"

"Holy schmoly," I said, getting up from the shattered ring of crockery. "I am *so* sorry, man."

"Forget it, forget it, stay in character," Richard urged. "What next?"

"Well, as the guy was about to get up, Foyl would run in and give him the old one, two."

Richard, getting excited, ran over. "I'll be the guy now. Show me what you would do." He assumed the dazed position on the floor, and I ran in as Foyl, hoisting him to his feet.

"That's when I'd rear back and give him a haymaker."

"What's that?"

"It's a punch that has a real big wind-back, and a big follow-through. Okay, ready? I'm gonna go. You react how you think the guy would."

I reeled back and pretended to hit Richard. His timing was excellent, and it spun him sharply around — face first into his trophy case. Golden Globes, Oscars, and *People* magazine's Hottest Man of the Year awards tumbled to the floor, breaking and twisting.

Richard spun out of the debris and instinctively braced himself to receive another attack. "Damn, that was cool. You know I always turned down these kinds of films, but this is really a gas. I feel like this guy would charge you back, but then Harry could come back in and stop him somehow."

"Exactly," I said, snapping my finger. "You take him out with a roundhouse kick."

"A roadhouse kick?" Richard asked, as if struggling with the very concept.

"*Round*house kick. I'll show you. I had to do this once in a Sci-Fi Channel film called *Terminal Invasion*. First you start the turn, kicking the leg out."

Richard turned and kicked out. It was awkward at first, but he became more comfortable the more he tried it.

"FYI, it's the force of the extension that actually brings you back around," I suggested. "You know you've done it correctly when you land right back where you started."

"Right," Richard said, getting the hang of it. "Cool, let's try it. You play the mugger again."

"Okay, now since you're hitting my chest, go ahead and make a little contact. Sometimes, I can't react correctly if I don't feel it."

"Are you sure?" Richard asked, looking flushed.

"You bet," I said, wondering if I was pushing him too hard. "I'll pick it up from where I'm standing back up in the corner."

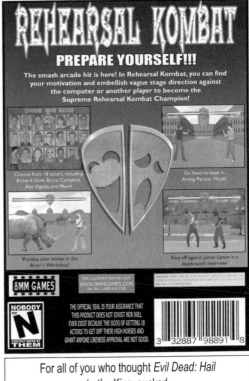

For all of you who thought *Evil Dead: Hail to the King* sucked.

I assumed the position of the mugger and slowly rose to my feet, preparing to charge forward. As I picked up speed, Richard let out a fierce yell, the kind that comes from someplace primal. He spun around quickly, and his right leg fully extended itself into my chest.

Stuntmen hate it when actors do their own fight scenes, and this is why: as if I had been pulled by a wire, the impact from Richard's kick sent me back in the opposite direction. The only obstacle between me and the floor was a thick glass table, which my bony back smashed into a thousand pieces.

I wasn't sure which to react to first, my impacted vertebrae, or the second-degree burns over 50 percent of my body from the overturned white tea kettle. Richard raced up to survey the damage, but the look in his eyes wasn't fear, shock, or anger — it was elation. "Hot damn," he said, trembling from the exertion. "Now *that* would be a scene."

I responded by coughing. A simple rehearsal had turned into a donnybrook. As I looked around the room, I realized that I hadn't seen such carnage since *Evil Dead II* — during what we called the "Zoom-Boom" sequence, where an entire cabin gets destroyed by possessed trees — and Richard Gere's New York penthouse was the last place on earth I ever expected to witness it again.

I began to worry that my background in rough-and-tumble films made me ill-suited for the subtleties of a romantic comedy geared toward adults, but Richard felt otherwise.

"I want to show this to Mike," he said, with fire in his dark eyes. "Foyl and Harry now have a new relationship, and I *like* it! Let me get you some arnica for your bruises, and we'll work the next scene."

# 6

# Dr. Schtup, I Presume?

Richard and I went at it until 2:30 in the morning, hashing over every detail of character in the movie, and our relationship. The last time I had so much fun acting was back in high school drama class doing "trust exercises."

Unlike the movies, where actors have the luxury of almost limitless takes of a scene or shot in which to nail their performance (or, in the B world, for "limitless" insert "two"), in theater, there are no "seconds," no opportunities to go back and get it just right — it's a one-shot deal.

In order to pull off a live performance with any kind of panache, the actors involved have to be completely in sync — and the glue that binds their emotional union is trust.

That's why high school drama teachers have their student-actors do silly things like stand blindfolded on a table and then fall backward into the waiting arms of their comrades. I find it ironic that trust exercises are taught in such an "every man for himself" profession. If they really want to prepare acting students for the real world, they might consider having them fall backward into a pool of irritable piranha — but I enjoyed them nonetheless. For me, it was a way to exercise demons that haunted me since Deke Swanson let me fall on my face during a similar, third-grade-playground exercise.

I always carry one of those dorky, pocket-sized notepads. It's something I've done since Junior High to capture fleeting, random thoughts before they evaporate. It came in handy that night, but to find an open page I had to go way in the back, past

— FOYL WOULD EAT SANDWICHES WITH MAYO ON WHITE BREAD

past

— ASK RICHARD ABOUT STARCH AND UNIFORMS

to where

— GET HEMORRHOID CREAM

already filled half the page (When Brando did it, they called it "method acting").

As Richard paced through the wreckage of his apartment, spouting like a summer stock player auditioning for *Richard III*, I scribbled notes, half-thoughts and ruminations until a familiar "writing dent" formed near the tip of my middle finger — something that hadn't happened since second grade penmanship class.

Richard and I decided to call it a night. We were both spent. The exhilarating high of the creative process is often followed by a tremendous crash, and I suddenly wanted nothing more than to be back in my hotel room. Richard promised to make an appointment to show off what we had come up with to Mike sometime in the next few days, and we bid each other a happy adieu.

Back at my hotel, a red light was blinking on the phone. It was too late — or early — to do anything about it, so I collapsed on the bed and hopped on board the Dreamland Express.

What seemed like five minutes later, the particularly shrill hotel phone rang me half out of bed. Phone calls early in the morning are always unsettling. In my life, it usually means that a friend is divorcing, an automobile is ruined, or the driver is downstairs waiting to pick me up and I'm late. This was something else entirely.

"Hello?"

"Bruce Campbell?"

"Who is this?"

"Dr. Albert Schtup."

Assuming the caller was David Goodman, an old friend with a longstanding practical joke vendetta, I hung up.

Thirty seconds later, the phone rang again.

"Hello?"

"Is it too early to call?"

"Look, I don't know any Dr. Schtup. What do you want?"

"I left a message for you last night."

"I didn't check it. Hey, let's cut to the chase — it's hard to talk when your face is stuck to the pillow with dried drool."

"Okay, sure," Dr. Schtup assured me. "I'll make it quick. I understand you're doing a sex picture."

"Well, it's not just about —"

"So you're gonna need a sex consultant."

"Hey, pal, I'm just an actor doing research. I can hold my own just fine otherwise."

"Brad Pitt said the same thing right before I coached him on *Thelma & Louise*."

I sat up in bed and turned on the nearest light I could find. "What exactly do you do?"

"Kid, you're talking to the Orson Welles of sex education — according to Roger Ebert in 1977. I teach, I'm an activist, but mostly, I'm a filmmaker."

"Anything I would have heard of?"

"Does *Rocket in Your Pocket* ring a bell?" Dr. Schtup asked smugly.

"*Rocket in Your Pocket*? Are you kidding? I saw that in eighth grade. Holy shit, you're that sex ed guy — you made those great movies that taught me almost everything about sex!"

"One and the same."

"Well that changes everything," I exclaimed, jumping out of bed and throwing the shades back to reveal a glorious spring day in New York. "I definitely want to talk to you. Where do you live?"

"L.A."

"I'm on my way."

I've been on the short end of the sex information stick. As a young, curious man, I never got that "sit down, son, let's talk" talk. My folks seemed satisfied to let me learn about the birds and the bees through osmosis, the costume designers on *Lost in Space* and *Batman* (Julie Newmar, not Adam West), and the sex ed films offered up in Junior High School.

I remember being herded, boys only, into a classroom and shown a sixteen millimeter film that dealt with "social diseases." I think it was a 1970s way to show reproductive organs without promoting "promiscuity" — or "comprehension."

The lack of passion in most of these films, combined with the excessive use of obtuse language, often caused me to confuse sex ed with drivers ed. After enough dreary seminars to bore Bill Clinton, my Playskool brain couldn't remember the difference between "Always use protection" and "Drive defensively." Between mild dyslexia and brainwashing phrases like "Always hold your hands at ten o'clock and two o'clock," it's no wonder Janet DeMarco slapped my face in the West Maple Junior High School parking lot — I honked her horn without signaling.

And while many of these films were boring, devoid of emotion and loaded with stale graphics, there were the occasional classics, the movies that stick with you and forever change the way you look at prophylactics. I'm grateful to Dr. Schtup for the entertainment value he always packed into his films. If I had to learn about venereal warts, at least the good doctor had the sense to convey such information with the help of a buxom woman in a low-cut nurse's outfit.

The good doctor never let a monotone announcer drone endlessly — he added rock music and sound effects to warn us about syphilis, herpes, and gonorrhea. In the capable hands of Dr. Schtup, sex ed was not only more enjoyable, it was far and away one of the few subjects with a future application. Despite my math teacher's insistence to the contrary, I have yet to find any practical use for algebra.

I navigated a rented Pontiac down Sunset Strip, a happening part of the L.A. scene since they started making movies there and it boasts blocks of star-studded clubs, bars, and trendy restaurants which snuggle up to the Hollywood Hills for miles on end. But as you head west toward the Pacific Ocean, the Strip — technically Sunset Boulevard — becomes more residential, more old-school. Or maybe just older.

Finally, after rifling through twenty pages of MapQuest print-outs (*Right turn in one half mile. Turn steering wheel twelve centimeters to the left through mild curve. Begin to get lost in a quarter mile*) and dodging an endless stream of contractors around hairpin switchbacks, I pulled to a halt in front of a sprawling, Roaring Twenties, Pickfair sort of mansion. The address matched my print-out, but the behemoth looked condemned.

As I waited in front of an impressive, albeit weathered, oak door, I thought about what the artistic visionary of sex education would look like. Would he go against type, a nebbishy guy, or would he be an aging Hugh Hefner, dashing and dissolute?

The man who opened the door was a cross between Danny DeVito and my high school gym teacher. He seemed to be in his early seventies, though it was difficult to tell due to his beef-jerky complexion and big round glasses. His wardrobe was straight from the *Love Boat* collection: sans-a-belt pants, loafers, and a pullover shirt that desperately needed the attention of a stain stick.

"Dr. Schtup, I presume?" I asked.

"Call me Al," he said, shaking my hand. "Albert Schtup is just a marketing gimmick. My real name is Al Glick. You must be Bruce."

"In the flesh."

"Are you a pool player?"

"I suck, but I enjoy it."

"Never trust a guy who can't handle his stick," Al said, turning away with a wink. "Waddya think of the digs?"

Al led me through a foyer that appeared to be doubling as the Greater Los Angeles Recycling Center. Pillars of *Variety, Hollywood Reporter, Adult Video News,* and *Educational Filmmaking Daily* towered over us. The date "1954" jumped out at me from one of the stacks as I squeezed past.

"I'm sure it was quite the palace in its day," I said delicately.

"I got this joint from Harold Lloyd, the silent picture actor," Al boasted. "Harold was having money problems then, and needed to downsize. It was a steal in seventy-one — pennies on the dollar. Me? I did fourteen sex ed pictures that year. Been here ever since."

Al escorted me down a long hallway with creaky floors covered by dank throw rugs. The walls were decorated with posters of his films, celebrity photos, and a myriad of sex ed memorabilia.

"You're the Forrest J. Ackerman of sex education," I exclaimed.

"There's a shot of me and Jimmy," he said, tapping a poorly framed picture of Al and James Colburn as he passed by. "This here was the actual thermometer used in *Mind the Behind*. I was proud of that picture, but I took a beating on it."

"Is there such a thing as an 'unsuccessful' sex ed film?"

"Sure. Like any other picture, sex ed had to grab the attention of sixteen-year-olds — you how hard that is, Bruce? Bruce?"

I wasn't listening. I had been distracted by the poster from his Korean War classic, *Erections are for Heroes*.

"Ain't she something?" Al asked, referring to his curvaceous leading lady who was featured, bursting out in every direction.

"I'll say. The scene where she ran around in that giant condom will be etched in my brain forever."

"Bunny Bellini."

"How many of your films did she star in?"

"Twenty-six."

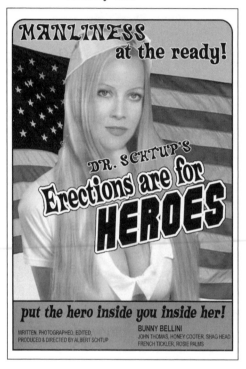

MANLINESS
at the ready!

DR. SCHTUP'S
Erections are for
HEROES

put the hero inside you inside her!

WRITTEN, PHOTOGRAPHED, EDITED,
PRODUCED & DIRECTED BY ALBERT SCHTUP

BUNNY BELLINI
JOHN THOMAS, HONEY COOTER, SHAG HEAD
FRENCH TICKLER, ROSIE PALMS

"Wow. Well, she was definitely my favorite. She taught me everything I know about premature ejaculation."

By now, Al and I were beyond the hall of shame, and headed down a flight of wide, marble steps to the basement, which was tricked out like a western saloon.

"Looks really authentic," I marveled.

"That's because it is. Harold Lloyd had it shipped in from Jerome, Arizona. Even the floorboards are original. You can still see the tobacco stains."

The ancient room was decorated with a modern pool table, jukebox, and foosball game.

"Okay, let's see those balls!" Al shouted, tossing me a cue.

"Pardon?"

Al pointed at the triangular pool rack and lit his half-cigar. "So, this picture you're working on. It's called *Let's Make Love!*?"

"Yeah, but mostly we *talk* about sex," I explained. "My character gives a lot of advice."

"Talk? People aren't paying good money to listen to a bunch of Hollywood types *talk* about sex. You gotta give 'em three things: shake, rattle, and roll. The *shake* is obvious. All my actresses are bustin' at the seams. The *rattle* means action. All my pictures have somethin' going on — drag racing, bar fights, chasin' broads — you name it. The *roll* is all about music. I had Bobby Vinton do an original piece for *How Wide is My Valley*. I'm the only guy in my business who went the distance. I wanted all my movies to be classy, to be the kind of thing you could see at any drive-in in America. The other guys cut corners; they didn't care about the craft. The Foster series sucked because it was all about charts and graphs, and the McCormack collection blew because it was too puritanical — totally in denial that people are screwing all over the planet every moment of every day. Trust me, Campbell, I know what I'm talking about. I've made a few sex pictures in my day — sixty-nine to be exact."

"How does a guy get involved in your line of work?"

"How does anyone? How did Frank Capra get started? Or William Wyler? That's the thing you gotta understand, Bruce: I'm a filmmaker first and foremost."

What could I say? I nodded and hit the cue ball with as much precision as I could muster. The break was mediocre.

"Little rusty?" Al quipped, as he took his cue and surveyed the table. "So, to answer your question, I got started making pictures for the Signal Corps. Ever heard of *Fight for Might*?"

"No."

Whack! Al put some heat on a stripe in the corner and it slammed down. "I'm stripes. That picture was pretty popular in its day. Anyhow, back in civilian life after the war, I was hoping to get into the industrial training film business — that's where all the action was."

Smack! Al banked his cue ball across another stripe and it fell.

"But all the good jobs were going to insiders," he continued, "so I offered to do a sex ed film just to get my foot in the door. It was a sleeper hit and the rest, as they say, is history. Next thing you know, it became a goddamn industry."

Al took another shot, but his ball jammed into a corner and spun out.

"What was it that clicked?" I asked, trying to find a shot.

"It was the fifties," Al said with a wave of the hand. "Parents were spared the agony of telling little Billy where to stick it. And the kids loved it because I made sex look like a blast!"

Crack! I sliced the cue ball into a solid and it looped around a corner pocket and dropped in.

*Halle-frickin'-lujah.*

"What was the subject?" I asked, attempting a fancy bank shot and sinking one of Al's balls instead. "How did you know where to start?"

"You start the beginning," Al explained, approaching the table.

Thwack! The cue ball buried one of his stripes in the corner. "My first picture was called *The Sperm Whisperer*. It was very simple: how women become pregnant. Beer?"

My brain attempted to process "sperm," "pregnant," and "beer." Various scenarios played out, depending on which order I put the words in, but the word "beer" kept coming back.

"Sure," I said.

Al shuffled off toward the kitchen. I did a quick inventory of balls. At four to one, the god of educational porn was kicking my ass.

Al returned with a couple of icy beers. "I knew there had to be a way to tell that story without any goddamn diagrams. That's where the actors-dressed-as-organs thing came from. I was the first to do it."

With this, Al slammed another stripe into the pocket. He only had two balls left, but his next shot fizzled.

"Shit on a stick," he muttered, taking a pull of his beer. "Of course, we could never show the wiener or the hoo-ha. And a man's willy was his 'manliness.' He couldn't have a stiffy, but it could be 'at the ready.' The vagina was a woman's 'willing valley' — and there were no orgasms, just a 'feeling of inevitability.' I caught some flack once for using 'ready to blast off,' but I didn't back down. My pictures always walked the line."

"How was the school board to deal with?" I asked, chalking my cue.

"They were my de facto studio. They controlled the purse strings, and had final cut, but I own all the negs because I was an independent contractor. Best deal in the sex ed biz. That's what allows me to live like I do," Al said, gesturing grandly at his crumbling estate.

I snapped the cue ball into a solid that was loitering in a corner and it went down.

**THE HUSTLED**

"I had to be very creative in those days. Try explaining woman's orgasm," Al challenged, "in Puritanical, post-WWII America, when you can't even say the word and you can't show her having one."

"How *did* you explain it?"

"A woman's orgasm? You don't!" Al roared.

I drilled another solid into the opposite corner.

*Now we got us a game, gramps.*

20th Century Kif presents
BRUCE CAMPBELL in IMAGINARY DIRECTOR's parodic side-splitting comedy **"THE HUSTLED"** co-starring Bunny Bellini · David Goodman and **ALBERT GLICK** as "Dr.Albert Schtup" with Janet DeMarco · Produced and Directed by Imaginary Director · Screenplay by Nonexistent Writer · Made in CINEMACOLORVISION

"People love to make fun of sex ed pictures," Al said, defensively, "but there was a lot of skill involved."

Thunk — my next shot was a dud.

Al chalked up. Crack! His cue ball rebounded several times and slammed into a stripe, knocking it down.

"The films caused quite a stir. I became an overnight expert, you know."

Thwack! His cue ball missed its target, but ended up in a perfect position for my next shot — a wonderfully clean, clear line to glory.

"Everyone wanted to talk to me, interview me, take my picture," Al added, sitting down for a sip of beer. "I was very popular — like this Stern fellow, on the Satellite."

I lined up my easy shot and managed to avoid a classic choke by dropping it in the pocket.

"So you're a doctor," I posed. "How did you get your doctorate? What was your thesis?"

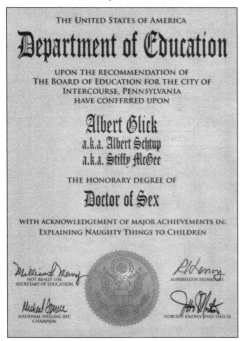

THE UNITED STATES OF AMERICA

# Department of Education

UPON THE RECOMMENDATION OF
THE BOARD OF EDUCATION FOR THE CITY OF
INTERCOURSE, PENNSYLVANIA
HAVE CONFFRRED UPON

## Albert Glick

a.k.a. Albert Schtup
a.k.a. Stiffy McGee

THE HONORARY DEGREE OF

## Doctor of Sex

WITH ACKNOWLEDGEMENT OF MAJOR ACHIEVEMENTS IN:
EXPLAINING NAUGHTY THINGS TO CHILDREN

NOT REALLY THE
SECRETARY OF EDUCATION

SUPERFLUOS SIGNATURE

Michael Spence
NATIONAL SPELLING BEE
CHAMPION

NOBODY KNOWS WHO THIS IS

"Are you kidding me?" Al chuckled. "I only graduated from high school, but my pictures were so influential, the Department of Education gave me an honorary degree. They don't give those out like bar napkins, you know."

My next shot impressed us both. Bak! The cue ricocheted off several banks, then tapped a solid in with just enough back-spin to avoid following it into the pocket.

"Lucky shot," Al said, swigging from his frosty mug.

"I know."

The next shot was pretty straightforward. I just had to roll a solid along the edge and into the corner pocket.

Whack! Mission accomplished.

Al wiped beer from his mouth. From his expression, I could tell he was trying to figure out whether I had intended to hustle him.

My last regulation shot was gonna be a pain, because it meant the cue ball had to make contact in close quarters, yet the pocket was clear across the table — a huge opportunity for error.

*It's only pool, fool.*

I took the shot. The solid ball rolled right across the table and dropped quietly out of sight in the pocket.

"I'll tell you," Al reminisced, "it all went to hell in a handcart in the eighties, when we had to include STDs. Because we had to appeal to a much broader audience, the scripts lost their edge."

My shot was simple — two feet away at the most. But images of professional golfers — and I'm talking good ones — missing amazingly easy putts flashed through my mind. Now, all I could think of was failure.

"Eight ball, corner pocket."

Tap — the eight ball rolled close to the lip of the pocket, but *close* didn't matter a damn in pool. I was dead meat.

Al eyed his last stripe.

Crack! He spanked the cue ball and it pushed his ball into a side pocket.

Then, from upstairs, a high-pitched squeal reverberated off the marble floor. "Al? Are you ready?"

Al looked up, a little perturbed. "Hang on!"

His final shot was even easier than mine, since I was kind enough to position the eight ball one inch from the pocket.

"Eight ball, corner pocket," Al announced, closing one eye for aim.

Tap — the eight ball dropped in the pocket and my crushing

loss was confirmed.

"And herein lies your education on sex," Al said, gesturing to the clean table.

Then, again from above: "Aaaaaaallll! Are you ready for me, baby?"

"Okay, okay, we're ready," Al shouted. "Come on down."

"Ready?" I asked. "Ready for what?"

"We're ready to make another picture. That's where you come in."

"No, that's where I leave, see —" I said, looking for the coat I didn't bring with me.

"You can't leave, kid. We got a deal."

"Deal?" I asked, my Campbell-senses tingling.

Al produced a single piece of paper and slapped it face-up on the pool table.

"You don't remember, but I got your autograph in ninety-six at the San Diego Comic-Con."

"What does that have to do with anything?"

"Let me put it to you this way: what you signed that day wasn't a still from *Crimewave*."

I sign so few photos from that movie that my mind actually recalled the obscure, lightning-quick incident. The autograph line was long and moving fast that day in San Diego, with convention handlers urging patrons not to dally once they reached the table.

At the time, Al looked like a lot of other guys there — sweaty, unshaven, assorted other hygiene issues. I signed his *Crimewave* photo and remarked how rarely I did that — something I do every time I sign one.

"You had a contract under that photo," I remarked, stringing the missing pieces together in my head.

"Why do you think I had you use a ballpoint pen instead of

a Sharpie?" Al asked, proud of his underhanded achievement. "Most worthwhile autograph I ever got — in *triplicate*."

I snatched up the contract and skimmed the page, looking for key bits of legalese, like *in perpetuity, artist agrees to, throughout the known universe,* and other thorny clauses. Al and his lawyers deserve a lot of credit — legally, they had had me sewn up tighter than lips on a shrunken head. I swore I wouldn't allow myself to be duped this way again after the *Assault on Dome Four* debacle, but I guess that's why those who refuse to learn from history are doomed to repeat it.

"Okay, you cheating weasel, what's the movie?"

Al blew the dust off an old manuscript and thrust it in my hand. The title page read: *Condom Nation*. "It was my best script, but the board of Education wouldn't touch it."

"Because of the condom issue?" I asked.

Al nodded, still stung by the memory. "Anyway, I tried to get it made for years. I sold the DVD rights, but I couldn't presell foreign to save granny's ass — my cast had no foreign 'cache.' Someone recommended getting either you or Wings Hauser. Wings doesn't do any conventions, but you're always out there with your hat in hand, so I figured you were an easy mark. Boy was I right. Once I got your signature, foreign fell into place and here we are. You play the lead guy, Jock."

"Who plays Nell?" I asked, fanning through the overly-long screenplay.

The click-clack of high heels drew our look to an aging, blonde bimbette arriving from upstairs. Her Rubenesque figure and pouty lips immediately triggered primal, childhood memories — it was Bunny Bellini, star of sex ed celluloid.

"I guess you would recognize Bunny." Al said, introducing her with perverted, fatherly pride.

Bunny was dressed as a cowgirl, with a buckskin vest that was unable to contain her twin protruderances, a cowhide choker, and red, white, and blue chaps. Her white tassels swished in the air as she waddled over, dimly evoking the hip-rolling sashay of Mae West in her prime.

Suddenly, I got very nervous around this sixty-something ex-vixen. It was almost as if she knew what I did in the bathroom after watching Al's films.

BRUCE CAMPBELL   BUNNY BELLINI-GLICK
DR. SCHTUP PRESENTS
CONDOM NATION

"Pleasure, Bruce," she said, holding out a bony, veiny hand. "Loved the *Evil Death* films. You were so cute as that guy with the girly name."

"The pleasure is mine," I said, kissing that same bony, veiny hand. "I feel like I've known you for years."

"I brought her out of retirement for this project," Al boasted.

Bunny let her hand linger for what seemed like a deliberate act of flirtation.

I suddenly felt a wave of dread. "Something tells me we're not doing a sex ed film.

"There ain't no Department of Education this time," Al said gleefully. "This picture is gonna take the 'ed' out of the sex ed. Okay, let's crank it up!"

Al's bellow prompted a flurry of activity as previously-hidden crew members poured into the room, setting up lights, cameras, and western props. Two wardrobe women descended on me as Al laid out the scene.

"Okay you two, we're gonna do the welcome home Jock scene — number thirty-two. There's no dialogue because *The Star Spangled Banner* will be playing the whole time, so don't worry about it. Jock just got back from working on the range. He just wants dinner and a beer, but his gal has other ideas. She wants dessert first. She wants him on the pool table."

*Eww — I just played a game on that.*

By the time Al was done explaining, I was dressed as a "cowhand," but felt more like a member of Village People.

"All right, get ready to shoot," Al called out.

His crew fanned across the bar, manning positions and readying equipment.

"What? No rehearsal?" I asked, a little indignant. "You may not know this, but I'm working on a Mike Nichols film, and this is definitely not how he would approach it."

"Sonny boy, when Bunny gets her paws on you, you'll wish your father never met your mother — it's not something you rehearse."

I knew I was in for a world of shit whether I stayed or fled, but my keen sense of professionalism took over.

*How would an A-list actor prepare for such a scene?*

"Al, I need two minutes," I said, holding up a hand, walking toward a corner of the bar.

"Okay, but only two," he shot back. "We got a fight scene to shoot before lunch."

Whenever an actor is faced with a serious challenge — and mine was being forced to make love to a woman twenty years older than me (on camera) — he or she must use every tool in their creative box to face, meet, and overcome that obstacle.

In this case, I called up a bizarre acting exercise that had lain dormant in my mind since high school: astral projection. Sometimes acquired knowledge doesn't pay off right away. In this case, for instance, it was a three-decade wait, but its ultimate value was immeasurable.

Through this technique, I was able to "project" myself back to Junior High School, when Bunny was the subject of countless adolescent fantasies. *Modern day Bruce* might not be able to service an aging sex starlet, but a *sixteen-year-old Bruce* would have the time of his life.

Also known as Retrograde Sensory Association, this is a radical, but highly effective technique used by actors only in the most dire circumstances. Side effects are typically mild, but may include headache, dizziness, and blackouts.

My ensuing journey was so intense, so *convincing,* I actually have no recollection of what took place here on earth. I was in a parallel universe.

What eventually brought me out of this life-altering, "far away place" was Al, shouting "Cut!" over and over.

When I opened my eyes, time had skipped easily an hour and a half into the future. I was lying on the pool table, next to Bunny, naked as an eight ball and drenched in sweat. Bunny, also without her cowgirl duds, took a deep drag off her cigarette. The look on her face was the most beguiling combination of awe and satisfaction I've ever seen.

*Something weird just happened.*

"An actor doing research my ass," Al scoffed, tearing our "contract" into a thousand pieces. "You wanted to get into Bunny's pants all along. Well, let me tell you something, buster — nobody gets to please my lady like that except me. Now BEAT IT!!!"

It was the first time I was ever thrown off a set, but the net result of growing as an actor and sharpening my professional tools made it all worthwhile. In case you're interested, Al and I later renegotiated, and the scene is available as a DVD extra on Al's newly-released collection, *Schtup-tacular: Sex Education Films of the '50s, '60s, and '70s.* The Tarantino commentary alone is worth it.

# 7

# Mike Mounts His Movie

At exactly ten o'clock the following morning, Richard Gere and I presented the new "mugging" scene for Mike Nichols and the screenwriter, Kevin Jarre, during rehearsal at Mike's brownstone.

Mike and Kevin had collaborated before on *Working Girl*, and were at a comfortable place in their professional relationship. I had been fortunate enough to work with Kevin on a TV pilot called *Missing Links,* and although it failed to mature into a full-blown series, we had enjoyed the experience.

The sound of Richard and me getting our breath back masked the quiet consultation Mike was having with Kevin. My sternum hurt like hell, but I managed to get through it. After a minute, Mike spoke.

"Hey, fellas, wow," he said, not necessarily happy. "Let me just say that I'm glad that nothing is broken and I hope you're both okay. But I have to ask you, what led you to take it in this direction?"

Internet - Showbase
http://www.showbase.con

SHOWBASE — The Internet Source for the Entertainment Industry

**Let's Make Love!**
(2004 - In Production)

Directed by
Mike Nichols

Written by
Kevin Jarre

Produced by
Robert Evans

**Slugline:** The perils of urban love unfold as two people try to fall in love in the heart of New York City.

**Cast**

| | |
|---|---|
| Harry Palmer | Richard Gere |
| Debbie | Renée Zellweger |
| Elder Palmer | Christopher Plummer |
| Foyl Whipple | Bruce Campbell |
| Mr. Jenkins | Ed Begley, Jr. |

Of course, nothing is official until it's on the internet.

I looked to Richard.

"Well, Mike, we just wanted to get the most out of the scene," he said.

"It was just a mugging, Richard." Then, looking at me, "you guys made it into a scene from *Walking Tall*."

"But, now Mike," Richard interjected, "let's not forget that Harry Grayson has a military background — Desert Storm, Desert Shield."

Mike walked over to the coffee machine, thinking. "Yeah, okay, I guess I could see that, but Jesus, I dunno."

"And he's a New Yorker, through and through, Mike," Richard pressed. "He's got coffee in his veins."

Mike put Cremora in his cup of coffee, swirling it around with a plastic stirrer, then stopped and looked at me. "And what was in Foyl's past that might make us believe that he can do what you just did? I didn't read 'has the ability to perform numerous karate moves' in your back story."

I couldn't expect Richard to bail me out on this one. "Well, Mike, Foyl had a brief stint in the National Guard, and he had a very domineering father, which led to numerous violent altercations."

Mike stared at me, unblinking. It's like that during rehearsals sometimes, where lots of long silences hang in the air simply because things have to be sorted out.

"Think of it, Mike," I urged. "This is a romantic comedy, but there's nothing that says you can't have some zingers, some mush-mush to give the flick a little kick in the ass."

"Mush-mush?" Mike asked.

"Yeah, that's my pal Sam Raimi's term. It's when he uses every available means to jazz up a scene, to goose it. You add *mush-mush*."

"Is this a story about mush-mush, Bruce?" Mike asked, with a lack of expression that was intimidating.

"Well, no, but it's like the seasoning of a meal, like the —"

"Mike," Richard offered, "could Bruce and I show you another scene that we worked on? It might give you a clearer idea of where we're coming from."

"All right, gentlemen, have at it," Mike said, walking slowly back to the worktable he shared with his secretary, June.

Richard and I had a quick confab.

"Look, let's tone this next one down a little," he said. "Mike doesn't seem to be a fan of the broad stuff."

"Okay, yeah," I said, agreeing. "He was about to eat me."

"But let's keep the intensity," Richard reminded. "In this scene, it's your job not to let me through that door, no matter what."

Richard was referring to a sequence near the end of the movie where Foyl must stop Harry from entering the building to see Renée's character, Debbie. It's a contest of wills, and Richard's character wins. We took our positions in the open floor, facing each other and began.

```
                    FOYL
            (trying out a
            more genteel
            Southern
            accent)
        Sorry, Harry, I cannot let you
        do this.
```

"Better, Bruce," Mike said, "I like that much better."

"I do too," Richard said, looking at me apologetically.

"Okay, fine," I said, mildly annoyed.

"Let's continue," Mike instructed.

```
                    HARRY
                (determined)
        I have to get in there, Foyl. I
        have to see Debbie.


                    FOYL
        Well unfortunately, sir, she
        doesn't want to see you.
```

That was Richard's cue to advance. Mike scooted his chair forward in anticipation. Kevin was paying close attention, not only to the words, but to our actions.

As Richard advanced, I retreated.

```
                    HARRY
                 (warning)
        We'll just see about that.


                    FOYL
        Don't push me, sir.
```

Richard forced me up against a side door, which we were playing as the entrance to the apartment building, and he put his hands on my collar.

Mike stood up. "Knock his hands off, Bruce."

I did, and it felt right. Richard is a very intuitive actor, and he reacted by putting his hands right back up, only this time more firmly in place.

```
                    HARRY
You know what she means to me,
Foyl.

                    FOYL
          (through gritted
          teeth)
Yes, I do. And that's the
problem, sir — she means nothing
to you.
```

"That's an action line, Bruce, move during it," Mike instructed. "Move away from the door. Richard, are you okay with Bruce forcing you back?"

"Sure, yeah, let's try it," he said, fully in the moment.

With a nod, I pushed Richard back from the wall. He resisted with his toned body, but I made some headway. "That yoga shit really works for you, doesn't it?" I said under my breath.

Mike took a step away from the table. June followed to take notes, because she knew he was prone to throw directions over his shoulder in the heat of a scene. "Now, Richard, you've got to get in that building," he reminded in a fatherly tone.

Richard and I looked at each other, getting set.

"You want to do the next bit?" I asked.

"Sure, why not?" he said, smiling.

With that, Richard swung an arm over my head and got me in a headlock. I quickly elbowed him, and his grip released enough to get free, but he was already working his way to the door. I tackled him from behind and we rolled around on the floor slamming into one of Mike's custom cabinets.

"*That's* the intensity," Mike said, becoming more animated. "Kevin, you onboard?"

Kevin shrugged, but he was chuckling just the same.

"June, you got those moves?" Mike asked.

"Pace, collar, push back, headlock, elbow, tackle, roll — got it," she said, writing furiously with a No. 2 pencil.

Richard had since rolled on top of me, and I worked my leg under to push him off. Mike saw what I was about to do.

"Make sure it's away from the building, Foyl. You want to keep him away. Let me see it!"

I let Mike see it, all right — and Richard too, because I pushed him back harder than I had intended. Richard backpedaled right past June and into the coffee station. Spoons, napkins, Nutri-Sweet packets, and freshly roasted, shade-grown Hawaiian blend coffee went everywhere.

"Oh, man, I'm sorry, Richard," I said, worried that I had broken the star's back.

"Don't you apologize to him, Foyl," Mike scolded. "Stay in character! You just did what you needed to do, and now Harry Grayson will do what he needs to do."

Richard took that as his cue and ran toward me. I got ready to perform the next bit of rehearsed action, but Richard was coming too fast. What happened next wasn't anyone's fault — in fact, it's a problem that often occurs when two actors are allowed to "fight" together in a scene. Actors and fighting is a little bit like wildfire — if it isn't watched closely, it can get away from you.

The move we rehearsed was this: Richard would charge, but I would step aside and whack him in the back, sending him to the ground — simple.

But Richard was going too fast for that, and his lunging shoulder impacted my thigh, sending me out of control.

Richard was also knocked off course, but inertia kept him going until he belly-flopped into a table of pastries, sweeping it clean — tablecloth and all. I was too busy spinning like a top to notice. In fact, the only thing I knew for sure was that the stairwell of the brownstone was getting closer.

When I hit the raised lip of the concrete stairway backward, I knew that what lay ahead was not going to be good. Any stunt-man will tell you, falling backward down the stairs is "a broken neck waiting to happen."

As I tumbled backward, the expansion of time caused by im-pending trauma allowed my mind to free-associate. I thought about the time I was acting in a Super-8 movie in Michigan, around 1976. Sam Raimi, boy wonder at that time, was direct-ing a film called *The Great Bogus Monkey Pig Nut Swindle*. My role, a bad guy, required me to take a punch over a concrete wall and fall into a "river" below. The camera rolled, action was called, and as I hurled myself over the wall, the same bubble of expanded time enveloped me. Below, images flashed in slow-motion detail: ripples moving across the dingy water, the twist of a leaf in the wind, the *concrete slab*, hidden two feet beneath the surface.

I hit the first set of stairs, and a loud snap from a damaged bone rang out as a harbinger of things to come. The sound of the fall was as spectacular as the visuals: *Whack – bam – "Ooof!" – clump – scrape – "Ow!" – duff – snap – wham!*

I finally got to the bottom of the steps, but momentum carried my cartwheeling body through a locked, metal fire door that will forever retain a torso-

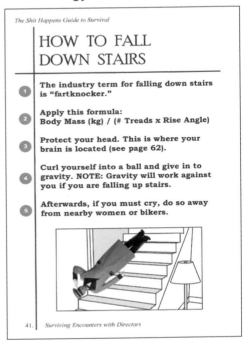

*The Shit Happens Guide to Survival*

## HOW TO FALL DOWN STAIRS

1. The industry term for falling down stairs is "fartknocker."

2. Apply this formula:
Body Mass (kg) / (# Treads x Rise Angle)

3. Protect your head. This is where your brain is located (see page 62).

4. Curl yourself into a ball and give in to gravity. NOTE: Gravity will work against you if you are falling up stairs.

5. Afterwards, if you must cry, do so away from nearby women or bikers.

41. *Surviving Encounters with Directors*

shaped dent. I tumbled into the adjacent alley, finally stopped by a row of metal garbage cans.

Mike ran to the top of the stairs. He could see all the way down to where I was sprawled among the wreckage in the alley. "Oh, my God," he yelled, sounding horrified. Then: "That was beautiful! June, did you get it all?"

"Let me see," she said, checking her notes. "Leg push, coffee crash, charge, hit, spin, table clear, stairs, including whack – bam – "Ooof!" – clump – scrape – "Ow!" – duff – snap – wham! Then, door and alley — got it."

"Excellent," Mike said, working his way down to me. "Now *that's* the way to mount a scene!"

I tried to roll over, but my back wouldn't allow it. Oblivious to my trauma, Mike knelt next to me.

"Bruce, I have to admit, I was pretty resistant to this new direction," he said. "I'm a character guy, you know? I don't really do the flashy stuff. But I think I'm starting to get it now, and to be honest, I love it."

Mike grabbed my wrenched arm and hoisted me up. "Let's not forget, in this scene Foyl loses the fight, but he's still a gentleman. That's the core of his being, it's what motivates him."

Mike gave me a healthy pat on the back and jogged back up the stairs, whistling a happy show tune.

Ready for a hot bath, a massage, and a nap, I stumbled through the lobby of my SoHo hotel looking like the loser of a bar fight — at 11:00 A.M. I approached the slightly disturbed desk clerk and smiled cordially.

"Good morning — any packages for Bruce Campbell?"

The clerk, an intern type, looked behind the desk. "All I have is a FedEx for *Let's Make Love!*"

"That's me."

"Could I see some I.D.?"

"They don't ask for that in Oregon, you know," I grumbled, rummaging through my bloody jeans.

"Well, you're not in Oregon anymore, are you?" she said, with obvious disdain.

I found my license and waved it in the clerk's face. Reluctantly, she handed over the package.

Every delivery from the outside world is like Christmas to the gypsy actor, so I can get excited by a gas bill. Back in my room, I ripped the box open immediately. Expecting the usual stuff from the home front, I instead found a strange amalgamation of used B-movie DVDs, VHS audition tapes (one marked Danny Bonaduce), news clippings, and a rambling note from Rob Stern, the Paramount punk I recently met.

The package was clearly not meant for me, but you know what they say about possession and the law. The attached note was addressed to Mike Nichols, and outlined Rob's agenda:

ROB STERN

Mike-o,

Stern here. As we strive to transform Let's Make Love! from something you'd sleep through on an airplane to something parents will hand down from generation to generation, the road may be a little bumpy.

To help pave the way, I've enclosed some additional doorman auditions that rock (hey, until we actually shoot, the "door" should stay open), and some great B movies of the past - check out the groovy shooting styles. Let me know if any of this helps.

Fighting for you from the coast,

Rob

I was surprised how quickly I could tear a piece of paper into a thousand pieces, flush it down the toilet, and cram an entire FedEx box into my undersized hotel kitchenette garbage can. For the record, it took exactly nine seconds.

"Doorman auditions my ass," I hissed, stomping on the parcel one last time. "Track that, motherscratcher...."

The little pissant really *was* looking for other actors, and had the audacity to flaunt it, knowing full well that Mike had already made his decision. My first reaction was to shove the audition tapes up Rob's generous ass, but the calm, resonant voice of Mike Nichols echoed in my head: "*Being a gentleman is what motivates Foyl...the core of his being....*"

If Mike wanted a gentleman, then by God he was going to get one. I was going to become the most gentle gentleman ever to roam the earth. It was time to go to the source, to the land of Dixie.

# 8

# The Gentlemen's Club

*Gentle man:* an oxymoron if ever there was one. Granted, modern men do come in all flavors — some are cute and cuddly, but most of them are rough and tough, and some are just plain pirates. I encountered a good example of this while directing an episode of *Hercules: The Legendary Journeys* in New Zealand. The Kiwis are a very hearty bunch. The Down Under men are manly, fearing nothing except their wives, girlfriends, and elderly aunts.

Through idle conversation between shots, I became friendly with a grip on the crew. He was a very nice fellow, but you wouldn't know it by his rough look. He was tall and wiry, and sported a plethora of scary-looking tattoos. He even had a gold patch over his right eye, and it fascinated me. Eventually, I became familiar enough to ask the fateful question:

"Hey, Rod, how'd you get that patch over your eye?"

"Oh, no big deal," he said with a wry smile. "I used to inject cocaine into it. Goes straight to the brain that way. 'Course, after

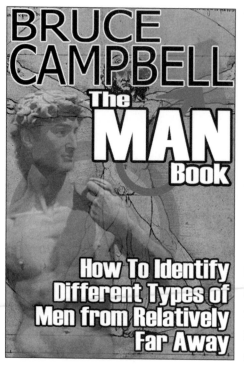

BRUCE CAMPBELL
The MAN Book

How To Identify Different Types of Men from Relatively Far Away

a while, the cornea wears out, doesn't she?"

I stared at Rod in horror. It was one of the most hideous stories I had ever heard. "Sorry I asked."

"No worries, mate."

But trying to focus on a genteel portrayal of Foyl Whipple meant putting away such macho memories. I had to erase the images of an overly aggressive modern man, a species bursting at the seams with testosterone, and replace it with the more restrained sensibilities of a Southern gentleman.

The Richmond Gentlemen's Society was housed in an antebellum mansion on Cotton Gin Lane. This grand estate wasn't just a place to stay, it was a living museum — a pristine link to a more mannerly time.

A dapper man of about thirty opened the door with a flourish. His Southern drawl was soft and long and syrupy. "Good afternoon, Mr. Hightower. We've been expecting you."

"Good afternoon to you, sir," I replied, my "sir" sounding more like a "suh."

I had decided to visit this mucky-muck establishment posing as a prospective member.

"Allow me to introduce myself. My name is Charles Butler, Associate Director. On behalf of the Richmond Gentlemen's Society, I'd like to welcome you. Please come in. Mr. Lee is expecting you."

I looked around. The foyer alone had more square footage than most homes.

"May I take your hat and coat?" Charles offered.

Fortunately, my wife, Ida, used to be a costume designer. Before I headed south, she outfitted me like a southern dandy from the old movies, right down to the spats. I handed over my top hat and coat.

Charles led me toward a substantial oak door at the end of a long, tongue-and-groove hallway. We walked past portraits of other famous southern gentlemen — Winfield Scott, Jefferson Davis, and Dale Earnhardt — all proud and firm in their resolve.

Charles opened the door and announced me. "Mr. Lee, may I present Mr. Hubert Hightower, from Savannah."

The paneled oak room was dark and plush and smelled like leather. Stuffed animal heads, plaques, and diplomas dominated the walls. But the real character of the room came from the two southern gentlemen who waited for me behind a large antique desk. One of them was Robert E. Lee. The other was his great-great-grandson, who was seated directly beneath the huge portrait of his famous ancestor, smiling approvingly.

"Mr. Hightower, I am honored to make your acquaintance," said Phineas T. Lee, coming around from behind his enormous desk, hand extended.

"The honor is mine, Mr. Lee," I said, trying to keep pace with his enthusiastic handshake.

"I understand you're interested in becoming a member of the Society."

"Yes, sir, most definitely. I feel as though my skills as a gentleman have diminished in this crude world of ours, and that your institution may very well be my salvation."

"Where is your family from, Hubert?"

"Virginia, originally, sir. My father is Major General Zachariah

'Zeke' Hightower, now retired."

"A military family," Phineas nodded approvingly. "Did any of your kin serve in the War for Southern Independence?"

"Of course, sir — we served with pride in the Seventh Virginia Regiment. Many of my family were lost at Antietam, Shiloh, Gettysburg, uh, Massa —"

In mid-word, I had forgotten the name of any more Civil War battles, so my mind flashed to the first Native American name I could think of: "Massapaquappa." It wasn't even a real Indian name, but that's what came out.

"Massa — ? I'm sorry, Hubert, I can't quite get that out."

"It was a...a little-known skirmish. Several of my kin were attached to a group called the Wart Hogs — special ops. Even to this day, I'm not allowed to discuss it, sir. Being a military man, I'm sure you understand."

"I see. Well, most honorable, son," he said, accepting my line of bull. "You come from good stock."

"From what I understand, sir, you yourself enjoy a heavy dose of pedigree in your lineage."

"Oh, I don't like to broadcast such things, but I suppose one could come to that conclusion."

"It's fitting that you should be the president emeritus of such an institution," I said, referencing the great Civil War general, "since Mr. Lee himself, ol' 'Ace in the Hole,' ol' 'Uncle Bobby,' was the mother of all Southern Gentlemen, if I may."

"And at the risk of sounding expansive, the distinction of our family goes back a wee bit further. Robert E. was the seventeenth direct descendant of Robert the Bruce."

"Of Scotland?" I asked, trying to hide my shock. I had been named after Robert the Bruce, and my relatives go back to those same misty Highlands.

"That makes me the twenty-first direct descendant," Phineas

added with notable pride.

*Holy shit — am I related to this windbag?* I wondered.

"Do you have a family yourself, Hubert?"

"I do, sir. I'm married to, uh..."

And then it happened again — I blanked on the name of Hubert's wife and kids.

"Uh...Mary Todd Hightower. And I have three wonderful sons — Jeb, George, and Jethro — two of whom do the Hightower name proud."

"And what occupies your time, Mr. Hightower?"

"Cotton, mainly."

Hubert's Confederate ancestor, Slim Hightower.

"A textile man. How wonderfully traditional."

"You will find, sir, that the Hightowers are steeped in tradition. My ancestors had a hand in something called the cotton gin. You may have heard of it."

"My goodness gracious, I should say I have," Phineas said, laughing. "I should say I have! Mr. Hightower, it will be my pleasure to introduce you to the ways of the gentleman. But first, a few formalities," he said, rummaging through a lower desk drawer.

He produced a small box and opened it. "Since you're not a member — yet — I must ask you to wear this medallion around your neck. It will let the members know that you're a guest, and to afford you such treatment. It also grants you, as a true son of the South, full access to our activities today."

"I'll wear it proudly, sir."

Phineas draped the thick medallion, supported by a fine silk ribbon, around my neck. "And if I may, Mr. Hightower, the fundamental rule for behavior in a club of this sort is the same as in the drawing-room of a private residence. In other words, heels have no place on furniture, ashes belong in proper receptacles, and there is to be no spitting or cursing."

"My good Mr. Lee," I said with a click of my patent-leather heels, "I shall comport myself in a manner that will uphold the dignity of this establishment and its esteemed membership."

"Very well, sir," Phineas said, digging a pocket watch out of his vest. "I'm due to regale the members on manners pertaining to manhood and courtship this very minute. Shall we?"

Southern gentleman, Phineas Lee.

Phineas took me by the arm and led me to the parlor of his grand if slightly crumbling estate. The light was dim, and the air was thick with cigar smoke. Liquor flowed freely, and there was a lot of back-slapping and friendly ribbing and a general air of masculine energy. Most of the members appeared to be well over sixty and carried themselves with the self-assurance of those already well established in life.

Charles Butler, upon noticing Phineas's arrival, addressed the gathering. "My distinguished associates, if you'll find a comfortable seat, we may enjoy the musings of our founder emeritus, Mr. Phineas T. Lee."

The men applauded respectfully and settled into overstuffed chairs as this leader of gentlemen walked to the front of the parlor. He orated like in the old days — by simply speaking loudly, though he was, in fact, an excellent speaker.

"Good afternoon to you, fine gentlemen."

"Good afternoon to you, Dr. Lee," came a perfect chorus.

"I wish to share a few precepts my grandfather passed along to me many decades ago. One morning, as I sat on his knee under a magnolia tree, he said, 'My boy, the honor of a gentle-man demands the purity of his word, and the incorruptibility of his principles. He is the defender of the defenseless, the cham-pion of justice — or he is not a gentleman.'"

A polite applause scattered across the room, with a few shouts of "here, here" thrown in for good measure. Dr. Lee hooked a thumb in his vest and began to stroll across the room.

"As a gentleman, you are a direct descendant of the knight. Your code of honor, particularly as it pertains to the matter of courting, must guide your motives. A gentleman, in the company of a female, will never be ostentatious or overbearing. These attributes are never to animate a well-bred person. Courting demands the utmost application of etiquette, which includes ethics as well as manners. This great association of ours, an association of gentlefolk, provides the necessary tools for us to apply good form in speech, charm of manner, and instinctive consideration for the well-being of others."

The men applauded vigorously. I threw in my own little "here, here" just for fun, and nobody seemed to notice. I was starting to feel good about my performance. If only Mike could see me now, he'd forget all about Danny Bonaduce!

"My good men, before we apply good courtship skills, I

would like to make you aware of a distinguished visitor. Mister Hightower, make yourself known," Phineas announced, unable to find me in the hazy room.

I raised my hand and the men turned their attention to me.

"Please welcome Hubert Hightower to our society. He is a man of impeccable character and background. I know that you will treat him as one of our own."

I nodded at the friendly, welcoming applause, embarrassed that the old fart had to make such a fuss.

Phineas worked his way to a nondescript black door and gestured grandly. "And with that, I bid you an afternoon of gentlemanly delight!"

He opened the heavy door and two dozen women worked their way into the room. There was a general hubbub of agreeability upon their entrance, and let me clarify why — these were strippers, dressed (albeit temporarily) in what looked like prom gowns. My suspicions were reinforced by a subsequent change of mood in the room — the genteel classical music turned into a pounding disco beat, and the light went from a lazy straw color to a pulsing white and blue.

Holy Plantation! This gentlemen's club really was a *gentlemen's club*!

Charles managed to find me amid all the activity and took me by the arm. "Before too many of our gentlemen become 'otherwise engaged,' Mr. Lee would like for you to join him in pontification."

"Pontificate away," I said.

We found Phineas, ever the teacher, address-ing a small group of men. "As you can see over here," he said, gesturing to two pop-eyed club members ogling a curvy stripper, "these gentlemen are exhibiting perfect etiquette through proper introductions."

One of the gentlemen bowed slightly from the waist. "Good

evening to you, ma'am. Allow me to introduce myself. I'm Sheriff Jimmy Jones."

"Notice how he didn't presume to offer his hand?" Phineas observed. "Strictly speaking, it is always the woman's place to offer or not, as she so chooses."

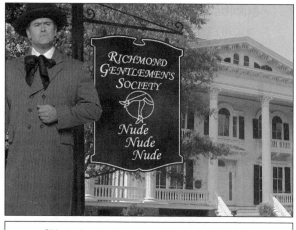

Chivalry is indeed dead, and it's buried in Virginia.

"Good evening," the brazen woman said. "My name is Scarlet." She then offered her hand to the next gentleman, who smiled and took it willingly.

"Evening, Miss Scarlet. Mayor Lloyd Dickweed. It's a real pleasure to make your acquaintance."

Scarlet took the Mayor's hand and winked at him. "It's going to be a pleasure making yours...." And she led him away through the crowd.

"Now there, we have a fine example of what happens when you apply what I call the three *P*'s," Phineas said with a nod. "Patience, poise, and persistence. Mayor Dickweed exhibited these three qualities in a fine manner, and his gentlemanly ways are being rewarded this very minute."

There was polite applause from the group of rapt men. Phineas made his way over to me as his entourage sauntered about the room, taking in the raunchy proceedings. "You see, Hubert, the value of these exercises to a gentleman is priceless. Here, he can hone his etiquette skills so that he may present the best of himself back home later."

"To his *wife*, I presume?"

If this acting/writing/directing/producing thing doesn't work out, I've always got my camera

"A gentleman never presumes, Mr. Hightower. And his presumptions are best kept to himself."

With that, Phineas walked into a dark lounge. This was where the old-time booze still flowed. None of that frozen daiquiri crap — these guys were sucking down top-end bourbon and whiskey. Every man in the place made sure to smile, nod, or wave as Phineas passed — he was the head honcho and everyone knew it.

"I'm quite pleased with the level of etiquette I've seen displayed so far. There is a hairbreadth between rudeness and reserve, you know," Phineas said, waving a finger in the air.

Then, from across the room, a Rebel yell caught everyone's attention. We looked up in time to see a burly man wind up and spank the rear of a full-figured stripper. "I'm gonna enjoy ridin' you tonight, darlin'!"

The woman turned to smack the lug, but she stopped short, because she could see what her aggressor couldn't — Phineas approaching from behind.

"Kind sir!" he bellowed.

The sweaty guy jumped out of his skin and turned to Phineas.

"Drummond, isn't it?" Phineas demanded.

"Yes, sir, Hank Drummond, but what did I do? I was just having some fun with the little lady."

"Hold your tongue. If you're a Drummond, then you know right well that it's not proper to slap a woman on her bottom side unless duly warranted."

"Yes, sir, I unnerstand," the man said, contritely. "Thank you, sir."

Phineas approached the woman Hank had slapped. "What's your name, my dear?"

"Ginger, sir."

"Now, we all know that a dusting on a woman's posterior is a sign of affection, even playfulness," and Phineas demonstrated with a light fanny tap on Ginger. "Now, ma'am, did I harm you in any way?"

"No," Ginger said, rolling her eyes.

"With regard to force, temperance must be the rule. A woman is a delicate flower." Phineas turned back to Hank with a little more fire in his eyes. "Let's have that apology, son. Say you're sorry to Ginger for your ungentlemanly behavior."

Hank rubbed his sweaty palms together and cleared his throat. "Miss Ginger, I'm sorry for what I done — powerful sorry."

"I accept your apology," Ginger said, and kissed Hank on the cheek.

Phineas clapped his hands together. "And there you go. Hank thereby redeems himself as a gentleman, and all is forgiven."

There was a joyous response, and Hank was rushed by his fellow gentlemen, welcoming him back into the charmed circle.

Phineas turned his attention to me. "I'm sorry you had to see that, Mr. Hightower."

"It's quite all right, Mr. Lee. The price you pay to be a gentleman, I reckon."

"A price that all must be willing to pay, without exception."

"Now, don't get me wrong, here, Mr. Lee. This is a fine institution to be sure, but I suspect that a man who spends too much time here will create troubles of his own at home."

"Son, I'll simply say this: men do what they do at this establishment, so as to avoid the need for such rambunctious behavior at home. We have, on many occasions, gotten letters from wives of thirty-five years, praising our name to the heavens for what we have done to tame their husbands and fiancÉs and sons. We are to be commended, Mr. Hightower — not questioned — for our service to society."

Phineas pivoted away from me as a means of politely changing the subject. "Another of the gentlemanly arts we encourage among our members is the art of conversation. Witness what we have over here."

I looked in the direction of Phineas's gesture and jumped at the sight: an octogenarian with a bad toupee being lap-danced by a red-headed bombshell. The man's face was breast height as he addressed her.

"I declare, Miss Tiffany, wasn't today the most ideal scenario for a walk in the park?"

Miss Tiffany giggled. "Why, Judge Green, the sun came through the clouds like a ray of hope upon the land."

"Your amplitude leaves me in arrears," the old geezer cooed to Miss Tiffany, who faked another giggle. "If I were to become one with your amplitude," he continued, "I fear that I may become hopelessly lost."

"You see?" said Phineas. "It is possible, even in this crude world of ours, to comport oneself with grace and aplomb."

Then, from across the bustling room, at a volume reserved for sporting events, we all heard, "Oh, my God, it's Ash!"

This incongruous shout caught everyone's attention, and we turned with great curiosity to the culprit: a busboy, bright red from embarrassment. "I am so sorry, but that's the guy from the *Evil Dead* films!"

"Hold your tongue, boy!" Phineas shouted, and the room fell silent. "Evil...Death?"

"*Evil Dead*, sir," he nervously corrected.

"What could those words have in common with this institution?"

"Uh, well, B-B-Bruce Campbell, sir," the pimply kid stammered, pointing directly at me.

Phineas didn't follow the kid's line of reasoning. "Why, we all know that he's Hubert Hightower, from Richmond," he said confidently, then — eyeballing me: "*Aren't* you, son?"

**CHARTER**

OF THE

**Richmond Gentlemen's Society**

The abridged version.

I was busted either way, so I decided to throw in the towel. How bad could it get? "Well, sir, not exactly," I said, minus the hokey Southern accent. "I'm an actor researching a role for a film."

A hushed murmur began among the men, and those that so easily brushed shoulders with me seconds ago stepped back.

"You're from Detroit, aren't you?" the busboy asked.

"Detroit!?" Phineas blurted indignantly, as if the city was from another planet.

"Yeah, that's right," I confirmed. "Outside the city."

"You went to Groves High School. I went to Seaholm."

"Really? You were a 'Sea-Foamer'?"

The kid chuckled and relaxed a little bit.

"What's your name?" I asked.

"Skip."

"Where you from?"

Phineas took in our exchange with building indignation. Skip held up his right hand, fingers together, creating the shape of Michigan — a sure sign of a native Michigander. He pointed to a spot just "east" of the tip of his pinky.

Fanboy Skip Lee.

"Northport Point."

"Holy crap, I went to camp there!" I said.

"Enough!" Phineas demanded, approaching menacingly. Two dapper men, sporting bouncer physiques, suddenly appeared on either side of me. "Sir, is it true that you are not the selfsame Hubert Hightower and that you are, in fact, an actor named Bruce Campbell?"

There was a courtroom feel to his questioning and I couldn't help myself. I took the bait. "Right-a-reeno, Mr. Lee."

"What? Ho! Say no!" the men cried out in agonized shouts.

"And is it also true, *Bruce Campbell*, that you are not from the great city of Richmond, the siege city, and that you are, in fact, from...Detroit?" he asked, having trouble even saying the word.

I puffed up my chest as I delivered the answer. "Yes, sir, it is true. Every bit of it. I'm from Detroit, and Detroit can kick Richmond's ass any day of the week!"

"Damn straight!" Skip shouted in support. Several men nearby began to reprimand him for his impertinence, but he knew his job was already toast, so he peeled off his waistcoat and flung it high in the air. "And you know what, you old farts? You can kiss my pimply, red-rashed ass, 'cause I quit this shit!"

Without warning, Skip dropped his pants and shot that roomful of stately men what was indeed a pimply, red-rashed ass of a moon. The ensuing dynamics were very strange. Members shouted and scolded and wagged their canes at Skip as he walked slowly out the door, tossing his fake bowtie into a trash bin.

"Order! Order!" Phineas bellowed above the din. The room settled somewhat, their attention returning to the inquisition. Phineas was red in the face, but the bluster was gone, and he was all about resolution.

"In light of the fact that, in front of many witnesses, men of impeccable character, you willfully and purposefully presented falsehoods, thereby disgracing not just my honor, but the honor of this establishment, and the honor of Southern gentlemen ev-erywhere, I hereby challenge you to a duel on the front lawn!"

The men cheered with great force. Their tone was changing too, from outrage to calls for action.

"A duel?" I asked in disbelief. "Get real, Phinney. I'm out of here."

"Mr. Butler, may I have my pistols, please?"

Without realizing it, I had become enmeshed in the workings of an ancient and deadly protocol. As Charles Butler walked toward Phineas's office, the men parted like the Red Sea — doors opened, feet shuffled, keys jangled.

I started to get creeped out. "Hey, you know, this has been fun, Mr. Lee, but your little joke is over. Where's the hidden camera?"

Phineas responded by nodding to his aides, who each placed a "you're not going anywhere" hand on my shoulder. Charles made his way toward a glass and mahogany cabinet. Inside, half submerged in a crushed velvet lining, two eighteenth-century flintlock dueling pistols glistened in the amber light.

"Mayor Dickweed, may I have the key to the dueling cabinet, please?" Charles asked, now more formal than ever.

The mayor, somewhat ruffled from his dalliance with Scarlet, fumbled with the keys, but eventually got the job done, and the cabinet doors swung open.

I was hustled outside by an increasingly unruly mob of old men and marched into place under the shade of a centuries-old magnolia tree. My senses sharpened by adrenaline, I found myself momentarily distracted by the manicured lawn. Their diagonal mowing process would be the envy of any golf course.

Standing twenty feet from me, Phineas removed his overcoat. He was sweating profusely, but kept his composure. One thing about these old freaks — when they commit, they *commit*. Phineas's two goons pulled my overcoat off, leaving us both in vests. As I looked around at the haranguing crowd, now formed into two rows on either side of us, I couldn't help but appreciate the authenticity of it all. This would have been a great plot for *Jack of All Trades*, I thought.

But the flintlocks brought me back to reality. Charles escorted them on a velvet pillow to a position directly between Phineas and me.

"We, as gentlemen, hereby agree to the guidelines set forth in the Dueling Code," Charles stated, as if he'd said those actual words before.

"In case you're interested, I didn't agree to anything," I shouted, so all could hear.

"Quiet!" "You've had your chance!" "Bah!" were the various gentlemanly responses.

"As the presiding officer, I, Charles Stonewall Butler, shall lead the proceedings. Will the challenger and the challenged please step forward?"

Phineas and I stepped forward. He wiped a sweaty hand through his hair. I responded by adjusting my visitor medallion.

"Bruce Campbell, you are hereby accused by the honorable Phineas T. Lee to have perpetrated a grave fraud on this society, and shall therefore be subject to the measures of justice this society sees fit and fair to administer. At the behest of Mr. Lee, this society therefore sanctions the use of pistols as an accepted method of resolving disputes, and shall commence imminently."

ZEKE HIGHTOWER'S HOW TO FIGHT A DUEL

Try to remember that violence never solves anything. Flintlock pistols, on the other hand, can solve almost anything.

Avoid potentially offensive phrases such as *redneck, cracker, hick, hayseed, hillbilly, democrat,* or *Detroit.*

If you happen to have a gift certificate for a local restaurant, offer it to your opponent.

A surprise punch to your opponent's nuts can work wonders.

Aim for the head. That way, if your opponent turns out to be a zombie, you still win.

### If None of the Above Works...

Accept death. Only after you face the fact that you are going to die can you really begin to live. Unfortunately, given your current predicament, you probably only have a few minutes to live life to the fullest.

If time allows, moon your opponent.

"Can I interject?"

"Not at this time, sir," Charles said, like an official at Wimbledon. "Not according to the rules."

"This is barbaric."

"On the contrary, my good man, this is tradition. Choose your weapon."

"I choose a grenade."

"Choose a pistol please," Charles repeated.

"Eeenie, meenie, miney —"

"Get on with it, man!" Phineas blustered.

Charles grabbed the nearest pistol and pressed it into my palm. He was obviously way more hip to these dueling rules than I.

"Point the pistol toward the sky, please, Mr. Campbell," Charles instructed with such assurance that I started to wonder how many duels he'd presided over.

Phineas took the other gun and we stood facing each other, barrels pointed in the air.

All I could think about was the state of my underwear.

"Turn away from each other."

Phineas and I adopted the desired position while Charles ran down the rules: "On my command, you will walk twenty paces in the direction in which you are presently facing. On my next command, you shall turn upon your adversary and fire. Your pistols each have one ball with which to inflict a mortal wound. Doctor Strom Tollison, are you present, willing, and able to administer to the dead and dying?"

A rickety man, easily a hundred years old, hobbled into view with his faded medicine bag. "Present, willing, and...what was that last one?"

"Able, sir."

"I am," said the doctor, hoisting his cane, and the surrounding men gave him a rousing cheer.

"When both adversaries have fired their shot," Charles continued, "the aforementioned disagreement shall be constituted null and void, and both parties, dead or alive, shall no longer carry the grievance forward. Are there any questions?"

"Yes, what's the difference between null and void?" I asked, stalling like a son of a gun.

"That is not a valid question, sir!" Charles snapped.

"I am prepared to settle this matter," Phineas stated with old-time resolve.

"Prepare to pace."

I tried to ready myself, but who was I kidding? If I could go out without soiling myself, that would be heroic enough.

"Forward — pace!"

*You've done a lot of dumb-ass things before*, I scolded myself, *but at least they were on film. My family won't even get the pleasure of watching me die, in slow motion, on national TV over and over and over. Okay, Mr. Actor Boy, You'd better run through all those cheeseball action films you were in, and think of some way to win this gunfight.*

As I paced off the twenty steps, I cursed the fact that I had never actually owned a gun. I didn't know how to aim that clumsy thing to save my life, despite the fact that that was exactly what was at stake. Pretty much every fight I'd ever been in had been resolved through stuntmen, sound effects, and judicious editing.

Being in films like *McHale's Navy* didn't help either, because I had used a fifty-caliber machine gun as a weapon, not a flintlock. The same reasoning applied for films like *Moontrap, Assault on Dome Four*, and *In the Line of Duty: Blaze of Glory* — in each case, I used a semi- or fully automatic weapon. Even in *The Adventures of Brisco County Jr.,* a western, I fired a single-action six-shooter, and you at least had six tries to kill the guy.

*What I wouldn't give for that sucker, right now*, I lamented. *I knew I should have purchased it on eBay last year.*

"And halt!" Charles yelled to us, now farther away.

*Okay, okay, think — what would my stunt pal Johnny Casino do right now? He'd drop to the ground and gut-shoot him, or he'd throw up some dust, just enough to cloud the opponent and give him that extra second to aim, or he'd scream and charge straight forward, freaking the guy out, forcing him to take a poorly aimed shot. It's a gamble, but if he missed, you'd have a huge edge — he'd be out of bullets, and by the time you shot back, you'd already be ten paces closer to the mark.*

"Prepare to fire!" Charles shouted with a terrifying seriousness.

Though I still hadn't figured out what I was going to do, my thoughts grew unusually lucid, particularly for an actor. Why must we always resort to violence when resolving disputes? Even though anger is a strong emotion and crimes of passion are many, we all know that violence only breeds more violence in an endless cycle of misery. That's it! I just won't take part in it. I'll do what Martin Luther King, or Jesus, or Gandhi would do — I'll resist violence, no matter what the cost.

Charles sucked in his breath and shouted, "Fire!"

As I turned, I made no attempt to raise my flintlock. Instead, I chose to greet my adversary with a smile. Even as Phineas T. Lee raised his flintlock in anger against me, with the full intention of inflicting great harm, I just looked at him, eye to eye, man to man, and hurled thoughts of peace, not a lead ball made in some death factory. I knew that even if my mortal body was taken away and forgotten in days to come, my gesture of peace was spiritual, and would remain undimmed forever.

The bastard fired his flintlock anyway. The ball hit me square in the chest, blowing me off my feet.

"Wooooh!" a unified cheer rang out. The men were very pleased with the outcome. Phineas threw his arms into the air, and a mob of joyous members rushed toward him in congratulation.

"Good gentlemen, in accordance with the rules and regulations of this society I, Charles Butler, hereby terminate this dispute. Phineas T. Lee shall go on record as the moral victor, and the name of the imposter, Mr. Bruce Campbell, who willfully misrepresented himself to be one Hubert Hightower, shall be stricken from the records so as not to sully the storied history of our esteemed organization!"

"Hurrah!" the men shouted in unison, many launching their top hats into the air. Phineas was hoisted up like a victorious football coach and paraded about.

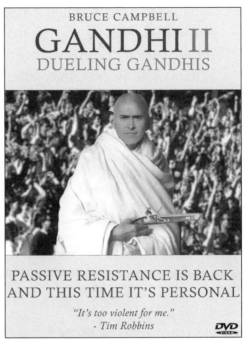

BRUCE CAMPBELL

GANDHI II

DUELING GANDHIS

PASSIVE RESISTANCE IS BACK
AND THIS TIME IT'S PERSONAL

"It's too violent for me."
- Tim Robbins

DVD

My senses began to shut down, as if someone had wiped Vaseline over my eyes and shoved cotton in my ears. As I struggled to stay conscious, I saw a blurred image of the old doctor, kneeling down to attend to me. As he squatted, he couldn't help but release a healthy fart.

"Pardon me, young man," he said, rummaging through his bag for a stethoscope. "Of course, you've got more to worry about than an old man's flatulence, I'll tell you that."

I could make out the shine off the doctor's naked head, as he listened for my heartbeat. After a moment, suspended in time, he slowly shook it in resignation. "Not much I can do for him."

Losing strength, my head fallen to the side, I got a wonderful whiff of the freshly cut grass, always one of my favorite smells. *My lawn in Oregon never looked this good,* I thought.

Then, everything went black.

*Beep-beep-beep* — the EKG machine marked out time with my

heartbeat. It was weak, slowed by pharmaceuticals and trauma. My mouth was so dry, my tongue had fused to the side of my mouth. I opened my eyes to see a dark, bland hospital room. I assumed that this was better than being in an operating room with five worried doctors racing about, pounding away on peoples' chests, yelling things like, "We can't just give up!"

In movies, the hospital room is also the place where you get the "you've got seven minutes to live" news, or the "I did everything I could, but..." news. That day it was the "you're a very lucky man, Mr. Campbell" news.

Now, acting isn't the only thing I have in common with Ronald Reagan.

"How do you figure?" I asked. "I've been mortally wounded. I'm dying in a hospital."

"Well, you *are* in a hospital," said the attending doctor, "but your wound isn't exactly mortal, and you're nowhere near death."

I looked around the room again, this time with a clearer head. There were no sobbing relatives, no Billy Graham, and thankfully, no lawyers. "How come I'm not dead? Last time I checked, I was inhaling grass clippings and the big light was coming."

"You've suffered a major trauma, no doubt, but what I mean by lucky is that the ball from Mr. Lee's pistol glanced off your metal medallion. It didn't even break the skin."

*Saved by the fact that I wasn't a member,* I thought, smiling. "Then why do I feel like I've been hit with a baseball bat?"

"That's essentially what happened. The force of the bullet pushed the medallion into your chest and fractured your sternum."

"My sternum? How long is that going to take to heal?"

"It's not really broken, but you're not going to want do a whole lot for a couple of weeks."

"Is it always going to be this painful?"

"Only when you breathe."

"Excuse, me, doctor?" a nurse said from the doorway. "Mr. Campbell has a visitor — a very distraught young man. He says he only needs a minute."

The doctor looked back to me for approval and I shrugged. "What the hell, as long as I'm not dying."

The "young man" happened to be Skip, the hapless busboy whose sharp eye and big mouth had precipitated my current condition. He entered the room, trembling. "M-m-m-mister Campbell," he said, eyes red from crying, "I am *soooo* sorry about all this. If I would have known that I, of all people, was responsible for you getting killed —"

"It's all right, Skip, I'm not dead yet."

"If there's anything you need here, any kind of treatment at all, you just let me know, and I'll make sure you get it."

"What, do you own the place?" I asked, not even trying to hide my smirk.

"No, but my dad does," Skip said, casually pointing to a sign which read PHINEAS T. LEE CENTER FOR ADVANCED MEDICINE. "And if it's any consolation, he feels pretty bad that he actually shot you."

"Wait a second," I said, with enough agitation to cause the *beep-beep-beep*s on my heart monitor to speed up. "You mean to tell me that Phineas Lee not only owns this hospital, but you're his son?"

"Right on both counts."

"I thought you said you were from Michigan?"

Skip hesitated for a moment. "Well, see, I'm his *other* son," he whispered, "the one he doesn't talk about. But he takes pretty good care of me, so you just say the word if you need anything."

"I sure will, Skip. Thanks."

"So, no hard feelings?"

"No," I said, reassuring him.

Skip's mood improved dramatically and he actually smiled. "Cool, then if it isn't too much trouble, could you sign my *Army of Darkness* poster?"

My first inclination was to tell this fan boy where to shove his poster, but I recalled the advice of Skip's old man, Phineas T. Lee himself, about what a true gentleman would do in this situation.

"Sure thing, Skip," I said, flexing my signing hand. "It's the gentlemanly thing to do."

# 9

# Dillinger's Dick

I've had exactly four relationships with women, and that's including two marriages. The expert sign does not hang above my
head in this category, but I do know this: there is no such thing
as a smooth relationship. A life shared by men and women is
always going to have an element of uncertainty. How could it
not? Living long-term with a member of the opposite sex is like
cohabitating with an alien — everything about them is different.

And just when you think you've got your own little E.T. figured
out, she turns out to be the Predator in disguise and rips your
head off. Personally, I'm a fan of the Gort-like alien spouse: mysterious, but ultimately peace loving and benign.

In the hopes of getting some much needed historical perspective on relationships, I headed north to our nation's capitol. The
first time I visited Washington, D.C., was in 1968, and I came
away with two impressions: The first? That soldiers are serious
people. On a miserable, Mid-Atlantic July day, where tempera-
tures easily topped a hundred, my folks dragged me to the Tomb

of the Unknown Soldier. For the forty-five minutes I was there, the man assigned to guard the monument never moved, never wavered, never flinched, even though salty sweat was pickling his eyeballs.

My second impression was that Washington, D.C., had all the information in the world. Even a rushed tour of the Smithsonian convinced my developing brain that all the treasures in the world could be stored in one place, and I'm sure this youthful impression played a role in my eventual return.

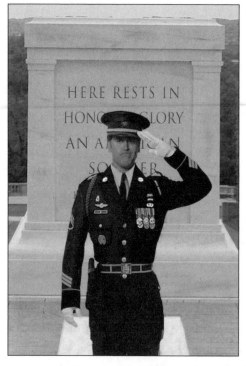

When I came back to D.C. thirty years later to write a TV pilot, I learned that it was much more than a place with big buildings and sweaty soldiers. My story, hauntingly similar to the Nicholas Cage film *National Treasure* — where the U.S. constitution is stolen from the National Archives — didn't light the TV world on fire, but I got a lot out of the trip, including a rare guided tour beneath Independence Hall. Please don't tell the authorities, but I still have a tiny piece of brick from the original 1732 foundation.

I also got a chance to visit "the stacks," a fairly sacred area within the National Archives where obscure artifacts are kept. In this case, I ogled original gear issued to Civil War soldiers, including maps, orders, and provisions. D.C. was that kind of crazy place.

Looking for a copy of the Magna Carta, George Washington's

teeth, or Richard Nixon's letter of resignation? Look no further than our capitol. Between the Library of Congress, the National Archives, and the Smithsonian Institute, there was more tangible history in our nation's capital than any other place on earth — other than the Franklin Mint.

The museum of all museums brought me back to D.C. this time — the Smithsonian Institute. Aside from exhibiting world-renowned artifacts like the vertebrae of John Wilkes Booth, Lincoln's assassin, the Smithsonian is also a prominent research facility.

In the Department of Records, I could review the great, troubled couples of our nation's history and glean insight into maintaining caring, mutually-supportive relationships under the duress of, say, having to go to the bathroom in a tin pot.

Washington, D.C., seems uptight and staid on the surface, but it's actually a hotbed of sexual energy: from phallic monu-ments to omnipresent scandals, sex is in the air as much as any fragrant cherry blossom, and I had much to learn. Besides that, I've always wanted to try the freeze-dried space ice cream at the Air and Space Museum gift shop.

The Smithsonian isn't one building — it's a complex of Victorian, turn-of-the-century and twentieth-century structures, some dating back to 1847. The granddaddy of them all is the Smithsonian Institution building. Straight out of *Harry Potter* as interpreted by Tim Burton, this palace of burgundy-colored brick was part Gothic church, part Willy Wonka's chocolate factory, but mostly Victorian. I expected to see Mary Poppins or Oliver Twist jump out at any moment and break into song.

Standing before that magnificent building, my cockney-colored daydreams were interrupted by a very un-Victorian combination of onion juice, grease, and melted American cheese that dripped off the tip of my chin before I could catch it with a hopelessly overwhelmed napkin.

A few feet away, my new best friend, Sasha, offered manly encouragement from behind his mobile Nuclear Sub stand. He had just sold me a hot, foot-long Philly cheesesteak sandwich with extra cheese and onions.

"Next big franchise opportunity. Watch out, Subway — Nuclear Sub is coming for *you*," he said, pointing a finger to emphasize his point. "My bags all have the new logo."

Sasha's sandwich was incredible, but the sheer weight of highly-processed animal flesh made it impossible to finish in one sitting. I stopped about a third of the way in, washing the last few inches of this cardiovascular nightmare down with a Diet Coke. I let out a belch that would startle a German, fired off a vaguely maritime salute in Sasha's direction, and stuffed the remaining food items in my satchel. It was time to shake hands with history.

Working my way through a labyrinth of American artifacts in the venerable Institution, I cut through the American Media section, where a very familiar piece of furniture caught my eye — the Archie Bunker chair. The Smithsonian had reassembled the original *All in the Family* set, and Archie's chair was the cornerstone of the famous TV room. As I approached it, I noticed that very few people were nearby.

*What could it hurt?*

I stepped over the red velvet ropes and plopped myself down in the overstuffed chair. It wasn't as big as I thought (the camera adds a few pounds), but it was as comfortable as it looked on TV. Growing suddenly paranoid, I moved to get up and a sharp *crack* sent the famous chair tumbling backwards. I fell to the fake floor and the ominous sound reverberated off a dozen perpendicular marble surfaces (would it kill them to put in carpet?) before finally dying away.

I heard distant shouting, and then footsteps clattering down the interminable halls. I crawled to the hopelessly damaged chair and tried to right it the best I could. Hearing a small noise, I looked up to discover the first eyewitness to the scene — a wiry ten-year-old with a summer haircut.

"Hey, what are you doing in there, mister?" he asked.

"I tripped. You can see that, can't you, kid?"

"No you didn't. I saw you. You were sitting in the chair and then it broke."

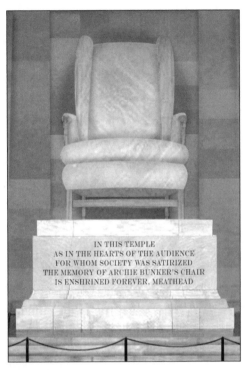

IN THIS TEMPLE
AS IN THE HEARTS OF THE AUDIENCE
FOR WHOM SOCIETY WAS SATIRIZED
THE MEMORY OF ARCHIE BUNKER'S CHAIR
IS ENSHRINED FOREVER, MEATHEAD

The kid had me cold, so I decided to try the "big lie" theory. I've found that kids are pretty good at spotting the small lie, but if your lie is outrageous enough — Santa Claus, the Tooth Fairy, compassionate conservatism — they'll fall for it.

I grabbed the young man by his shoulders and looked him dead in the eyes. "What's your name, son?"

"Zip," he said, unafraid.

"Listen to me, Zip. I have a nervous disorder and it makes me forget where I am. I thought I was in my grandfather's home. You can see how I might make that mistake, right?"

"I suppose — if you had a nervous condition."

"Right. Well, if anyone finds out, I could lose my job."

The squawk of two-way radios split the air.

"What do you do?" Zip asked.

I looked at his T-shirt. He had obviously been in town for the recent Earth Day celebration. "I help save the world."

"You do?" he asked, sounding like he was starting to believe me.

I decided to broaden the scope of my lie. "I own the largest recycling plant in the world."

"Really?"

"Cross my heart. And if I get thrown in jail because of this, I'll lose my job, and then the earth will become littered with sour-smelling, number-two plastic milk jugs. Do you want that on your conscience, Zip?"

At that moment, about ten security agents from all cabinet-level branches of government converged on the scene. I grabbed Zip by the arm and raised my hand in defense. "It's all right, gents, this young man didn't mean any harm. He was just playing around."

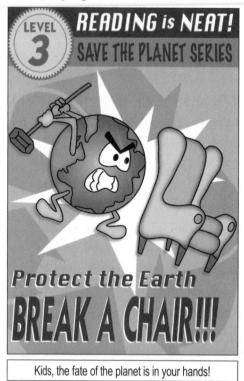

Kids, the fate of the planet is in your hands!

The good little soldier didn't miss a beat. "That's right. I went beyond the ropes and I played on the chair. This man begged me to stop — he warned me that I might damage an American icon, but I didn't listen," he explained, his eyes growing remorseful. "I broke the chair, but fortunately he stopped me before I could do any further damage."

*Good job, Zip. Right out of* Lassie.

I turned my attention to the anxious security force. "But rest assured, gentlemen, I'll pay for all damages or repairs. I wouldn't want the U.S. government, or this troubled young man, to be burdened by this tragic misjudgment."

A Department of Education cop put a hand on Zip's shoulder. "Come along, son. We're going to have to find your parents."

"Before you take him away, officer, may I have a word with the young man?" I asked.

"Sure."

I knelt down to Zip. He was handling this like a member of Earth First! at a logging site: scared, but resigned to carry out his duty for a greater good.

"Zip, you just saved a hundred billion soda bottles. Next time you snuggle up in a warm fleece jacket, thank yourself. Next time you sit on a recycled park bench, pat yourself on the back. You're a good kid."

"Thanks, man."

Zip was led away by the officer, but his spirit wasn't dimmed. In solidarity, he raised his fist high in the air. "Keep on rockin' in the free world!"

I was detained long enough to answer preliminary questions and give contact information, but otherwise I was free to go. As I made my way toward the research department, I thought about Zip and what would become of him. I decided that a year in juvenile detention was a small price to pay to save the planet.

I had only communicated with Daphne Terwilliger by email, and was surprised to find that the Smithsonian's associate director was almost six feet tall, with impossibly blonde hair falling to her waist and a high-wattage smile. She was the most stunning "Associate Director for Curatorial Affairs" I had ever met — light years from the shuffling, bowtie-wearing stereotype.

"Hi, Mr. Campbell, nice to meet you," Daphne said.

"Hi, Daphne. Nice place you have here."

"Thanks. You know, I watched you last night."

"Be careful when you say that," I warned. "All kinds of thoughts are racing through my mind, and most of them would prohibit me from running for public office."

"On *T.V.,* Mr. Campbell," Daphne corrected. "I saw part of *McHale's Navy* on Comedy Central."

As an actor, you know when someone says they saw "part" of something you were in, it's really code for: "It sucked so bad I had to turn the channel."

"Yeah, *McHale's Navy* is like a bad case of eczema," I joked. "It never seems to go away."

Daphne smiled. "You guys looked like you had a lot of fun doing that." Again, code for: "I'm glad you had fun making the film, because I sure as hell didn't have fun watching it."

"Mexico, hundred degree heat, no script," I mused, half out loud. "You bet we did."

"I have the list of couples you e-mailed me about. There are some, of course, that I can't help you with, like Torvill and Dean."

"No?"

"Sorry, ice dancing has never captured the imagination of the Smithsonian."

"That's a shame," I said. "Hey, can you confirm a rumor for me?"

"I'll try."

"A couple of years ago, I overheard some guys talking in a bar in Las Vegas. One guy was convinced that the Smithsonian had Sammy Davis Jr.'s glass eye? Is that true?"

Daphne looked at her watch. She was starting to think that she had been bamboozled by a moron. "I'd have to check, but I don't think so. Our knowledge might not be as extensive as 'some guy in a Vegas bar,' but you never know."

"Well, I can tell you this: Sammy's eye is as famous as

George's teeth."

"Aside from Mr. Washington's wooden teeth, we don't keep much in the way of 'parts' here. Incidentally, I see that George and Martha are on your list. I can help you there. And with, let's see, Mary Todd and Abe Lincoln, yes, and also with Mamie and Ike Eisenhower."

"I opted for the 'war-torn relationship' theme," I explained. "Love during a worst-case scenario. You know, two hearts, burning with the fire of an unquenched —"

"Uh-huh, sure," Daphne said absently, pulling out her two-way phone. BLEEP — "Armando?"

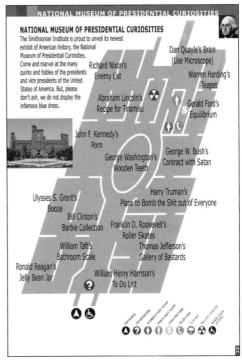

NATIONAL MUSEUM OF PRESIDENTIAL CURIOSITIES

The Smithsonian Institute is proud to unveil its newest exhibit of American history, the National Museum of Presidential Curiosities. Come and marvel at the many quirks and foibles of the presidents and vice presidents of the United States of America. But, please don't ask, we do not display the infamous blue dress.

Dan Quayle's Brain (Use Microscope)

Warren Harding's Teapot

Richard Nixon's Enemy List

Abraham Lincoln's Recipe for Tiramisu

Gerald Ford's Equilibrium

John F. Kennedy's Porn

George Washington's Wooden Teeth

George W. Bush's Contract with Satan

Harry Truman's Plans to Bomb the Shit out of Everyone

Ulysses S. Grant's Booze

Bill Clinton's Barbie Collection

Franklin D. Roosevelt's Roller Skates

William Taft's Bathroom Scale

Thomas Jefferson's Gallery of Bastards

Ronald Reagan's Jelly Bean Jar

William Henry Harrison's To Do List

BLEEP — "Yes, ma'am?" came the response, small and tinny.

BLEEP — "I need you to pull a few things. I need Ike, Abe, and George W. — the original — their personal correspondence — the juicy stuff. Could you meet us in the library?"

BLEEP — "Will do."

BLEEP — "Thanks," Daphne said, turning back to me. "Armando can find absolutely anything."

She scanned the other names on my list. "And I'm sorry, but I can't help you with Ma and Pa Kettle. They're fictional characters — certainly part of Americana — but not really a priority here."

"But Archie Bunker's chair is part of the permanent collection."

"You knew that, did you?" Daphne asked, almost impressed.

"Yeah, I just sat — uh, I just *saw* it. That was fictional, too," I reasoned.

"Yes, we know that," Daphne said, slowly, the way one might speak to Homer Simpson, "but the chair is here because of its impact from a social and pop-cultural point-of-view."

"Ah, well, there you go," I said, crossing Ma and Pa off the list.

"And as far as the blue dress goes, we can't help you there, either."

"Really? That's a little surprising, considering what my sources have told me."

"Are these sources based in Las Vegas as well?" Daphne asked, pointedly.

"Not this time — and they're very reliable."

"You wouldn't believe how many people call, or write, or e-mail about that goddamn blue dress."

"It's an important piece of 'Americana,' as you say — certainly from a pop-cultural perspective. That dress would make for a great traveling exhibition. Like King Tut. You'd see attendance spike, I can tell you that."

"Please, Mr. Campbell, don't go there."

"They toured the chair Lincoln was killed in, didn't they?"

"Yes, but it was very tastefully done."

"You're right — leaving the

blood on it was really classy."

"Keeping something intact is the most important part of the preservation process, even if some may find it unsavory."

"My case in point," I nodded.

"Are you still talking about the blue dress?"

"Yes. I think you should ring up the boys in Justice — tell them that the American public deserves to see the truth."

"How can you dare to compare the chair Lincoln was shot in, to the dress that Clinton, well, you know," she said, taking a deep breath. "Lincoln's assassination was a national tragedy."

"What do you think the blue dress affair was? I voted for the guy. All I'm saying is a little blue dress might go a long way toward paying for the upkeep of some of the more obscure items you have here."

Daphne didn't answer right away because she had finally gotten hip to the fact that I was baiting her. But eventually, her curator's curiosity got the best of her. "Like?"

"Like John Dillinger's penis."

"Where did you hear that one, a strip club in Phoenix?"

"No, that one is common knowledge — at least on Urbanlegend. com."

"It's simply not true," Daphne insisted. "It's just a very old, very *tired* urban legend perpetuated by immature men."

"Are you prepared to say unequivocally — on the record — that his penis is not stored in a pickle jar here at the Smithsonian?"

"Mr. Campbell, I am not going to waste taxpayer's money finding out whether or not the Smithsonian is housing a criminal's penis," she said, lowering her voice.

"Ah, go ahead, waste my tax dollars," I offered. "This one's on me."

Daphne wasn't about to get caught in an argument about penises or taxes. This was D.C. after all. "May I suggest, for the balance of your allotted time, you confine your research to artifacts whose existence is corroborated by more than a mix of hearsay and the *Weekly World News*?"

"Sure, fine."

"You'll need to wear this around your neck," she said, handing me a laminated 'Researcher' tag. "Shall we?"

Daphne led me down an incredibly wide hallway — within which I could have pulled a U-turn in an SUV — and through an archway. Just inside was a three-story library filled with rows of books, charts, treaties, and maps. Clusters of wooden research tables and chairs were scattered across the polished floor.

"I think you're going to enjoy this place," Daphne said, still sounding in awe herself. "We have roughly a hundred and forty-two million objects."

"Do you even know where they all are?" I asked.

Daphne hesitated. "I *think* so. We're getting better at that."

I looked at her in surprise. She was serious.

A man who I assumed was Armando, whom Daphne talked to on the phone, waited dutifully at one of the tables. On top of it were three file boxes.

"Thanks, Armando," Daphne said in a hushed, library tone. "I owe you."

"Yes, you do," he said, a little annoyed. "These were wedged between the Arc of the Covenant and Jimmy Durante's piano."

Before Armando could leave, I walked him a few feet away and made an additional research request — one that was accompanied by a fifty dollar bill. Armando nodded his understanding, scribbled something on a slip of paper, and shoved it into my palm. After this transaction, I rejoined Daphne at the table, who gave me a "What was that?" look, but didn't push it.

"Each president has his own box," she explained. "They're all personal letters from husband to wife, or vice versa, during the course of their marriage, catalogued chronologically and in some cases based on the topic. If you're a history buff, you'll be thrilled to know that Washington's letters to Martha, thought to be burned by her, were recently discovered in a storage trunk that came through as part of the Washington collection. Very few people have ever touched these letters, so please don't write on them, don't trace them, and don't make any new folds. I must also ask you to refrain from taking pictures."

"Yes, ma'am," I said, saluting in compliance. "Let's start with George."

As I slipped on a thin pair of latex gloves I got a chill, knowing that I was about to unlock the marital secrets of the father of our country. I cleared my head and nodded. "Okay, let's go for the tough times — the most extreme situation for George — aside from getting fitted for wooden teeth."

"That would have to be when he was camped out for the winter of seventeen-seventy-seven during the Valley Forge campaign. He had plenty of time to write, so there's an entire folder. Care to choose a letter?" Daphne asked, opening the portfolio.

I closed my eyes and picked a letter directly out of the middle and removed the plastic cover. Written in ink on an old parchment, the letter from George to Martha was dated December 13, 1777. I read aloud for the sake of Daphne:

My dearest Martha

This campaign has been long, but we must continue to rebuff these invaders, for this tender union of ours will not be extinguished in its infancy. Though our bodies may be weak, our minds are strong, and our hearts shall carry us through. The winter chill may stem the flow of my ink, yet the forthcoming spring shall cause it to flow as no other.

Yours in fortitude,
George

Frankly, for the Father of our country, I was a little disappointed. I thought I'd read syrupy passages about how good Martha's powdered wig smells, or holding hands on the plantation — but no such luck. "Geez, there he is, miles from home, and all he can talk about is the campaign."

"He's not talking about the campaign at all, dummy," Daphne said.

"What do you mean?"

"Washington isn't telling Martha his military problems. He was gone all the time, and he was an incredibly paranoid guy, which is a bad combination. The 'invaders' he's referring to are not the British — they were Martha's suitors, skulking around Mount Vernon, hoping George would be shot in battle."

"You're reading into it," I challenged.

"I don't think so. The only way Washington could keep order in his marriage, at least in his own mind, was to run everything like a military campaign."

Daphne took the letter from me and reread parts of it. "The 'union' he's talking about isn't the country, it's his marriage. And as for 'stem the flow of my ink,' I'm not going anywhere near that."

"Wow, so he was just a military guy, through and through."

"And by all accounts, Martha loved him for it."

"Let's compare George with Ike."

"Dwight D. was a different case altogether," Daphne said, reaching for the next box. "Figuring him out will make you a relationship expert, not to mention a first-class decoder."

Ike's box was different from the others. His was a standard-issue G.I. storage box — green, with blocky black stencil lettering stamped on the side: D. D. EISENHOWER

"Did Mamie and Ike get along?" I wondered out loud.

"Supposedly, yes, but those letters are a bore. To get the goods on Ike, you have to read the memos to his 'driver,' Kay Summersby."

I took the SUMMERSBY, K. folder and chose a page. Immediately, I could see that these letters were not dashed off in a trench while commanding the Allied forces — they were official military memos, on military stationery, hammered out in triplicate. Ike might as well have been writing to General Patton. I read out loud again:

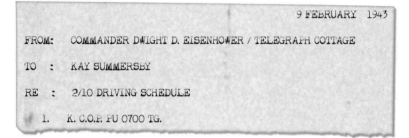

```
                                          9 FEBRUARY  1943

FROM:    COMMANDER DWIGHT D. EISENHOWER / TELEGRAPH COTTAGE

TO   :   KAY SUMMERSBY

RE   :   2/10 DRIVING SCHEDULE

   1.    K. C.O.P FU 0700 TG.
```

"C.O.P?" I asked.

"Change of plan — and 0700 is a.m.," Daphne explained, assuming that I didn't know military time, which was kind of insulting since she knew I was in *McHale's Navy*. "And TG is the Telegraph Cottage, where he was based during World War II."

I went to the next line.

```
   2.    STOP 1 - ACC BRF 0745 - 0830.
```

I looked at Daphne. "Translation, please."

"ACC — Allied Command Center."

"This is really steamy stuff, Daphne. I'm not sure I can handle it."

"Keep reading — and pick up the pace."

```
   3.    T.O. 0845-0915. AYS.
```

"T.O.?" I asked preemptively.

"Time off — this is where it gets good."

"What's AYS? At your service, or some shit?"

"As you suggest," Daphne translated. "It's military jargon, but with a new slant."

"Meaning, 'Hey, we have a half hour to do whatever you want'?"

"You're getting the idea. We have a wonderful internship program here, you know."

"No thanks," I said. "Interns are always getting in trouble. But, how do you know all this?"

"A few years ago, a researcher tracked down Eisenhower's typist in a rest home in Homosassa Springs, Florida. He interpreted the abbreviations shortly before he died."

```
4.   H.O.S. MTG 0945-1045. AVL 1100-1230.


              SIGNED EISENHOWER
```

"Okay, let me guess this one," I offered. "H.O.S. — "Have Oral Sex, 9:45."

"No."

"*Hot* Oral Sex?"

"No, 'H.O.S.' means there was a meeting at 9:45 with a 'Head of State,'" Daphne said with a sigh.

"Okay, I was close. AVL. AVL," I repeated. "All Vigorous Loving at 11:00."

"No!" Daphne said, hitting me on the shoulder.

I hadn't known her an hour, and I was already getting the older brother treatment.

"You said these memos were scandalous," I protested. "They could have played pinochle for all we know."

"Keep telling yourself that. AVL is an abbreviation for 'available'. Why else would this outrageously busy soldier tell his lowly female driver that he was available — so they could lollygag in the countryside? This schedule kept going for another *twelve* hours," Daphne exclaimed, waving the memo at me. "Ike the spike, that's what I call him."

"So, that was how Ike dealt with adversity in his relationship — a little action on the side."

Daphne nodded in agreement, then snuck a look at her watch. "But let's move on. My money's on Lincoln. There's a man who just plain loved his wife," she said, sliding the last box close. "Mary Todd was loonier than a fruit bat, but he stood by her until the end. He wasn't a soldier, so he wasn't gone on long campaigns. During the Civil War, he stayed in Washington."

I shrugged. "The country was falling apart, but at least she knew where her husband was for four years."

"Take a look at this," Daphne said, excited. "From a state dinner in eighteen sixty-three." She slid a coaster out of its plastic sleeve. Written in fading black ink was simply: VIXEN.

"Lincoln didn't have a series of letters to his wife or mistress because he was never away long enough to be in any trouble. Instead, he made things like this," Daphne explained, unveiling a tiny paper bird, folded Origami-style.

Handwritten on the side was a presidential haiku:

"In Lincoln's collection, we have a pile of these for two reasons: one — he loved his wife, and two — state dinners bored him more than anything else he did as a president."

All this talk of love, lust, and letters piqued my curiosity. "How about you, Daphne? Getting any memos from a distant warrior?"

"Not that I have to tell you, Mr. Campbell, but I'm a very busy woman with, as you can see, a monumental and never-ending task. That doesn't leave me much time for other 'pursuits.' "

"I can certainly understand, and I didn't mean to intrude." Suddenly uncomfortable, I stood up and began to gather my things. "Well, I guess that will do it."

Daphne left the presidential love letters with an associate and escorted me to the lower lobby, where a venerable iron staircase wound its way to the floors above.

"I can find my may out from here, Daphne. Thanks for all your help — you're a credit to your profession."

"I can't say that I enjoyed our little encounter, Mr. Campbell," she said, "but I certainly learned why actors can't hold a steady job."

Happy to part, Daphne left with a wave and a smile.

I had other plans, however. Referring to Armando's note, I made my way to the third floor and down a long, dim hallway where every other ceiling fixture was dark — probably to conserve energy — until I found storage room 315-A. Armando said that he would keep the door propped open, and that our clandestine exchange would take place there.

The door was indeed open a crack, but as I peered inside, I discovered Armando face down on the floor, his keys and walkietalkie next to him. Finding Armando out cold was surprising, but I was even more taken aback by the man dangling, spider-like above a small display case in the center of the room.

Making eye contact, the black-spandex-clad criminal and I froze. He was clearly in the processing of stealing an undetermined object and I wasn't part of his plan.

"Who the hell are you?" I asked, not knowing what else to say to a man who appeared to be very good at doing bad things.

"Leave now if you know what's good for you," he whispered menacingly through a wool mask which obscured his face.

I had to admit, it seemed like sound advice. After all, I could barely handle Richard Gere — what chance did I have against an honest-to-goodness international man of mystery? But as I turned to leave, I caught a glimpse of Armando, helpless and slack on the floor. What if he was really hurt? And what about Daphne, and Zip, and Mike Nichols — and all the other people out there who were counting on me?

As I rationalized a course of action that would involve little-to-no personal risk and still result in a story to which I could sell the movie rights, my eyes fell upon the display case over which the masked man was poised. Glare from the hallway lights behind me obscured the contents of the case, but I could make out the dim contours of what looked like an olive loaf. In the upper right hand corner, a hard-to-read P-Touch label read: ANATOMY — JD 1934.

*JD? John Dillinger? 1934? Dillinger was shot to death in 1934. Son of a bitch — the hoodlum was after the famous dick, too!*

I knew I had to act. Without warning, I leapt at the cabinet, shouldered the plastic display case to the floor, and wrapped my hands around what was truly a prodigious penis.

The thief, no slouch in the cat-like reflex department, slapped his gloves on my hands. "Not so fast!" he exclaimed, with what seemed like a hint of an English accent.

SHE ALREADY DID DALLAS.
NOW SHE'S GOING OUT FOR A LONG ONE.

**DEBBIE DOES DILLINGER**

starring
**BUNNY BELLINI** with
JOEY DILLINGER - RIP PANTS - DEE CUPS - RANDY MULLIGAN
OTTO EROTIC - DARYL HANNAH - BRONCO PELVIS - GLORY HOLE
Produced & Directed by CLARK JAMES Director of Photography BUDD WILLIAMS
Written by MARK VERHEIDEN Production Supervisor SLAPPY APPETITE

xXx

*Who is this English twerp?*

Turning, I tucked the penis away like a running back securing a handoff, and was about to reach the safety of the hallway when the thief's hand grabbed a fistful of my hair — my lovely, lush, movie-star hair.

"Ow! Let go, ya pasty, bangers-and-mash loving bastard!" I howled, reaching up to free myself.

The thief released my silken locks only to fasten his gloved hands on Mrs. Dillinger's pride and joy and ratchet himself toward the ceiling.

I felt my Scottish blood boil. Something deep inside, some DNA directive wouldn't let an Englishman get the best of me. I was not going to relinquish the prized penis to him or anyone else, so the airborne felon and I became engaged in an old-fashioned tug-of-war, with the pickled, stoutly inelastic organ pulled taut in our opposing grasp. I'm sure that somewhere, Dillinger was wincing. "What do you want?" he asked, straining from above.

"Same as you," I said through gritted teeth. "The dick."

"Why do you want it?"

"I've got a lovely spot for it on my new coffee table. You?"

"I was commissioned by a client — for his private collection."

This was too much. Knowing that such a vital national oddity might be lost forever in some rich jerk's private collection, I reacted without thinking. Heaving all my weight to the right in an attempt to either dislodge his grip or make him unpleasantly dizzy,

I instead threw us into a hopeless whirlwind, spinning across the storage room like a small tornado, vigorously destroying countless precious artifacts along the way.

I registered a blurry impression of a door, marked STAFF ONLY, just as it opened, and on my next orbit caught a glimpse of a stunned Daphne, gaping at our freakish fight.

"Oh my God!!!" she shrieked.

My adversary's head snapped up, trying to zero in on the source of the yelp, and I took immediate advantage of the distraction to yank Dillinger's member free. It was heavier than I expected — perhaps a result of the preservation process — and I nearly dropped it on the linoleum floor.

"Mr. Campbell, what is going on here?" Daphne demanded, as if this was somehow my fault.

"Well, I can't speak for Spider-Man here," I said, holding my prize well out of reach of the crotch bandit, "but I was preventing the theft of a priceless American artifact."

Daphne glared at both of us, and was about to expound on the inappropriate nature of the whole scene when her eyes fell on a prone Armando. "Oh, Armando!"

As she moved to comfort her fallen comrade, my (latest) nemesis unexpectedly released himself from his harness and dropped behind Daphne, swinging her around like a human shield. Then, in a one-handed bit reserved for cool guys like James Bond and stripper-cops, he ripped off his black spandex to reveal an arrestingly handsome middle-aged man clad in an Armani suit.

"Give me that artifact!" he demanded, sounding almost polite with the English accent.

"Artifact?" I asked, dubiously.

"What artifact?" asked Daphne.

Both of us ignored her for our own reasons.

"You know what I mean," the crook said, impatiently.

"And if I don't?"

The man tightened his grip around Daphne's neck. "The only way to guarantee her safety is to give me the artifact."

*Hmm. What would I do in this situation if I was playing a schlock action hero?*

Then I remembered that my characters usually get blown up or possessed.

*Okay, so what would Frank Stallone do? Or Rutger Hauer?*

But before I could think of any more B-action movie stars, Daphne's tears of panic began to streak her mascara.

"Okay," I said. "You got yourself a deal."

"But not here," he cautioned. "If I give her up, one of you could call security. We will do the exchange in the park across the street."

I glanced at Daphne to see if she was down with this plan. She nodded gravely.

"All right. What's your name?" I asked.

"Call me Roland."

"Roland." Daphne and I made our way toward security. Roland wanted to keep an eye on me and the world's most valuable schlong, but he also had to keep Daphne under control at the same time. Meanwhile, I had to keep an eye on Roland, maintain Daphne's safety, and protect my cargo. Daphne was probably kicking herself for having answered my e-mail in the first place.

Practically speaking, this meant that we moved together, through the halls and in and out of elevators, in a kind of shuffling, crab-like dance, not unlike a spastic polka.

Finally, the main hall — and the security check — came into view. Roland leaned in to Daphne. "Okay, Ms. Daphne, you're going to tell these nice security people that we're taking an artifact out for an exhibition."

"I'll have to tell them what it is," she said quietly. "For the paperwork."

Roland chose his words carefully. "It's an appendage."

"Belonging to whom, and why would we be checking it out?" Daphne pressed.

Roland was growing more irritable, perhaps because Daphne was thinking this caper through more thoroughly. "It belongs to John Dillinger, and it is being studied by the Harvard School of Criminology."

Daphne shot me an incredulous look that spoke volumes: underneath the abject terror associated with the threat of violence, there was a hint of wonder and apology.

Three burly security guards waited to check outgoing bags. Acting is bluffing, so I held my emotional cards close to my vest as I plunked my satchel down on a folding table.

Daphne was brilliantly cool, filling out paperwork and making small talk with officers Kimmer, Dominguez, and Smiddle. Roland was relaxed, but his eyes were constantly in motion.

Sergeant Smiddle, a beefy fellow in his mid-twenties, inspected the Dillinger relic briefly before continuing to rummage through my bag.

"Nuclear Subs, eh? Best in town. What kind ya got?"

"Philly cheese steak with extra cheese and onions."

"Man, that sounds good," the sergeant exclaimed, sliding the cleared bag back to me.

"Yeah, I can't wait to dig in before it gets cold," I said, organizing the items in my bag *extra carefully* before zipping it tight. "Well, you have a good one."

I slung the satchel over my shoulder and walked with Roland and Daphne into a humid D.C. at dusk. The park across the street was full of strolling tourists and kids — the perfect place to swap either state secrets or priceless museum pieces. Roland led us to a grouping of pine trees and turned his attention to my bag.

"All right, let's have it," he said icily.

"Sure thing," I said, removing the object, carefully wrapped in a "Nuclear Subs" emblazoned paper, from my bag.

Roland nodded approvingly. "Very clever."

"Now let her go," I demanded. "Like in the deal."

"Place it on the ground and back away," Roland said.

I complied and stepped back. Roland released his grip and Daphne ran — no, *sprinted* — to the safety of my arms.

"Oh, my God, Bruce — thank you. Thank you!" she said, tears streaming down her face.

"Thank me on the run," I urged, briskly leading Daphne away from the park and back toward the safety of the Institution, "because Roland's not gonna like all those onions."

"You mean you —?"

"That's right, Daphne," I said, gingerly handing her a plainly wrapped package that was also about the size of a foot-long submarine sandwich. "History is preserved after all — quite literally in this case."

Daphne was relieved, grateful, and embarrassed all at the same time. "I honestly didn't know we had *this* in our collection. I guess I owe you an apology."

"No need," I assured her. "It's enough for me to know that this national treasure is in your capable hands."

This time, Daphne and I parted as compatriots, fellow pre-servers of all things curious, and, dare I say — friends. It always feels good to end up on the positive side of human relations, and I turned down Pennsylvania Avenue feeling pretty good about my trip.

Most tourists come to D.C. to see monuments and walk away with nothing more than blurry, poorly framed pictures — hardly an accurate capsulation of a city. I came here on an altruistic quest for truth, fueled by a latent desire to help my fellow man. Instead, I was stymied by a massive bureaucracy and quickly derailed by bribery, greed, and betrayal. I may not have a photo album to show the relatives at Thanksgiving, but at least I could say my Washington experience was *real*.

**10**

# A Dash of Dash

I was having one of those phone dreams, the kind where the phone keeps ringing, but you know it's just a dream so you don't answer it — until you realize that it's not a dream.

*RRRRRIIIIIIIINNNNNNNGGG!*

I swatted at my cell phone, trying desperately to launch it off the nightstand, but the room was pitch black, and I didn't even know what state I was in. After about a minute of flailing with the covers, searching for a light switch, and swearing loudly, I managed to locate my cell phone.

"Okay, who died?"

"I'm sorry, did I wake you?"

I glanced at the clock. "At four o'clock in the morning? Hell no, I'm usually on my second breakfast by now. By the way, who is this?"

"Richard."

"Gere?"

"Yes. I'm sorry to call this early, but I had to talk to you about something."

"Okay...."

"I'm worried about scene forty-one A."

"Oh, I've got it right here," I said, snidely. "Hang on, lemme find it."

I lumbered groggily through my disaster of a hotel room. Weeks on location can be devastating, creating logjams of personal stuff in a room that always feels like it's shrinking. Rounding the foot of the bed, I bashed my knee on a protruding piece of luggage, then limped to my "executive desk," where the *Let's Make Love!* screenplay lay under a stack of unpaid bills.

"Okay...I'm back," I announced, returning to bed, but there was no response. "Hello?"

"I'm here," Richard said. "I was just meditating. Do you meditate, Bruce?"

"Not really. Whenever I try, I fall asleep."

"Then you're not concentrating hard enough."

"My mother said the same thing. Hey, so, scene forty-one A...."

"It's where I pick up Debbie for the first time."

"Yeah, it's kinda cute. What about it? I'm not even in it."

"I'm just not sure if I can pull it off."

I clicked the light up another notch and glanced at the scene. "What's to pull off? You're calm and cool, you've got some good lines and you sweep her off her feet. You'll be out of there by lunch."

**Spent PCS**

Charges for: BRUCE CAMPBELL
555-555-5555
bcact@aol.com

| | Date | Time | Phone Number | Call Destination | Caller ID Alias | Duration |
|---|---|---|---|---|---|---|
| 36 | 4/15 | 10:12 PM | 310-555-4373 | Incoming | Gere, R | 10 |
| 37 | 4/15 | 11:48 AM | 310-555-4373 | Incoming | Gere, R | 32 |
| 38 | 4/16 | 12:39 AM | 310-555-4373 | Incoming | Gere, R | 1 |
| 39 | 4/16 | 12:46 AM | 310-555-4373 | Incoming | Gere, R | 8 |
| 40 | 4/16 | 1:28 AM | 310-555-4373 | Incoming | Gere, R | 5 |
| 41 | 4/16 | 1:37 AM | 310-555-4373 | Incoming | Gere, R | 10 |
| 42 | 4/16 | 1:47 AM | 310-555-4373 | Incoming | Gere, R | 2 |
| 43 | 4/16 | 1:49 AM | 310-555-4373 | Incoming | Gere, R | 4 |
| 44 | 4/16 | 2:14 AM | 310-555-4373 | Incoming | Gere, R | 5 |
| 45 | 4/16 | 2:25 AM | 310-555-4373 | Incoming | Gere, R | 3 |
| 46 | 4/16 | 2:33 AM | 310-555-4373 | Incoming | Gere, R | 1 |
| 47 | 4/16 | 3:11 AM | 310-555-4373 | Incoming | Gere, R | 9 |
| 48 | 4/16 | 3:23 AM | 310-555-4373 | Incoming | Gere, R | 9 |
| 49 | 4/16 | 3:44 AM | 310-555-4373 | Incoming | Gere, R | 4 |
| 50 | 4/16 | 4:10 AM | 310-555-4373 | Incoming | Gere, R | 7 |
| 51 | 4/16 | 4:27 AM | 310-555-4373 | Incoming | Gere, R | 3 |
| 52 | 4/16 | 4:55 AM | 310-555-4373 | Incoming | Gere, R | 1 |
| 53 | 4/16 | 4:56 AM | 310-555-4373 | Incoming | Gere, R | 10 |
| 54 | 4/16 | 5:07 AM | 310-555-4373 | Incoming | Gere, R | 6 |
| 55 | 4/16 | 5:29 AM | 310-555-4373 | Incoming | Gere, R | 123 |
| 56 | 4/16 | 8:03 AM | 310-555-4373 | Incoming | Gere, R | 5 |
| 57 | 4/16 | 8:36 AM | 310-555-4373 | Incoming | Gere, R | 43 |
| 58 | 4/16 | 10:01 AM | 310-555-4373 | Incoming | Gere, R | 4 |
| 59 | 4/16 | 10:05 AM | 310-555-4373 | Incoming | Gere, R | 201 |

"It's not that simple. I've never picked up a woman before."

I held the phone away from my face. Sometimes you have to do that to get enough perspective during weird conversations. "Are you saying what I think you are, Richard?"

"I'm saying that I've never had to *try*."

"Oh, meaning that you never had to pick up a woman, because they were always picking you up."

"Exactly."

"Never?"

"No."

"You're breakin' my heart."

"Bruce, this really is an issue," he explained sincerely. "I never planned for my life to turn out this way, but there's nothing I can do about it."

"But, you know, Richard, the words are on the page for you, it's not like you have to make it up or anything. That's the beauty of being an actor — somebody else does most of the work for us."

"Then you don't know Mike Nichols," Richard said firmly. "A script to him is a rough guide. I know what's going to happen — after the first take, he's going to see right through my charade, and he'll throw out the words and force us to ad-lib, and I'm gonna be dead."

I didn't respond to Richard right away because I was too busy being amazed that even big actors have the same, silly fears that little actors do. It was both reassuring and terrifying at the same time, because Mike had essentially threatened me the same way.

"Now, your character would help me, Bruce," Richard continued. "And if you take this film seriously, you'll help me too."

"Okay, sure, but help you do what? Ad-lib?"

"No, help me pick up a woman."

I let that one hang in the air for a beat or two. "You're serious, aren't you?"

"I called you at four in the morning, didn't I?"

"Good point. But, you know, if you're looking for advice on how to snag a babe, you're better off talking to your real doorman, because I don't know shit about that world — just ask my wife."

"It's okay, you can still help," Richard said. "I need to find an expert, and I hear you've been running rings around us all in the research department."

"Oh, well, uh, what's your budget?"

"It doesn't matter, I'm dyin' here...."

"Okay, I'll get back to you."

I gave Richard a lot of credit. The majority of men are cowards — they're afraid to admit that they don't know their way around women. Mostly, they love to brag about their conquests, and while these boasts are almost always highly inflated — if not completely imaginary — not long ago, I had met a guy from Las Vegas who appeared to have some legitimate claim to the title of "King of all Ladies' Men."

I'd been to Las Vegas a bunch of times, hawking everything from horror DVDs to a western TV show, mainly because it's a popular place to hold conventions and stage huge promotional events. People love to mix business with massive quantities of gambling, booze, and sex, and Vegas is popular because it makes all three very convenient.

As a city, it's all about contrast — streets that are inconceivably hot, and casinos that are unfathomably cold. My emotional response to Vegas always takes the same form: horror, exhilaration, disorientation, amusement, then finally circling back around to horror. All in all, I can take or leave the place, but it's perfect for a guy like Dash Darwin.

I met Dash when I was in town to premiere an Elvis/mummy film called *Bubba Ho-Tep* at the Las Vegas International Film Festival. At a post-screening "afterglow," Dash had cornered me in order to pitch a movie based on his lifetime of sexual exploits. I thought he was perhaps the biggest B.S. artist I had ever met, but by the end of the night, almost every woman in the room — and there were some outstanding exhibits — had stopped to pay their respects.

The man had been *around*. I had to give him that.

Dash was the perfect teacher for Richard, but Richard wasn't the perfect student for Dash — mainly because he was too perfect. The chiseled jaw, the rugged chin, the molten eyes — if I was going to help him experience what it was really like to try and pick up a woman, he'd have to undergo an "extreme make-over" — *in reverse*.

Fortunately for Richard, I could, in fact, help him out. Having undergone special effects makeup of all sorts over the years, I had a few strings to pull.

"Melanie Tooker, Richard Gere — Richard, Melanie."

"Mel" extended her hand toward Richard Gere. As a special-effects makeup artist, she had worked with many "name" actors, but I could tell she was nervous around this particular one.

"Charmed," Richard said, kissing the back

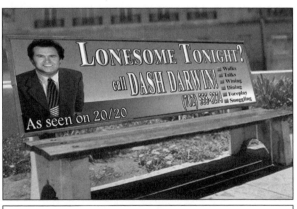

Just one of the ways Dash Darwin gets some ass.

of Mel's hand.

We had gathered in Mel's converted warehouse in Chatsworth, California, home of her "Ten Thousand Faces" workshop, to assess the situation.

Mel smiled unabashedly as she studied Richard's face. "Gee, in all the years I've done this, I never had to make a gorgeous man average."

Richard blushed, which is perhaps one of his many attractive qualities to women. It caused Mel to blush, and I must admit, even brought a little color to my face.

"Okay, Melanie, so the idea here is to make me look, not ugly, per se, but just not at all like myself," Richard explained. "Like I could sell insurance or something."

Mel walked us to a nearby computer, with a scan of Richard's face on the screen. "When I heard you wanted to do this, I did some renderings, and morphed your image with a picture I had on file. So we would go from this, to..."

Mel double-clicked on an icon, and a wonderfully bland version of Richard popped up on the screen. His features were similar, but dulled down enough to make him completely forgettable.

"...this."

Thanks to Mel's new gear, we ended up with a new Gere.

"That's amazing, Melanie," Richard remarked, impressed. "Who did you combine me with?"

"An old boyfriend. And just so you know, he couldn't get laid to save his life."

"Perfect," Richard nodded. "Let's do it —

make me unlayable!"

The amazing Dash Darwin swung open the door of his penthouse.

"Dash Darwin, you old dog," I said, offering my hand. "Great to see you again."

"Lemme see," Dash calculated, "that was about three hundred and fifty-two women ago...."

"Hey, that's between you and your STDs."

Dash laughed, then looked at Richard, who until now had been invisible.

"Is this our guinea pig?"

I pushed Richard forward. "Sure is — Little Dickie Simpson is his name."

Richard shot me a look like he was going to murder me in my sleep, but we hadn't thought of a name for him and I had to act fast.

"People call me... *Richie*," Richard added.

"Hey, Richie, Dick, it's all the same to me," Dash chuckled, slapping Richard on the back. "C'mon in, let me fix you boys a martini and show you the pad."

As Dash led us to his wet bar, which was outfitted like Appleby's, I cased out his biggie-size bachelor pad. The place fit right in with Las Vegas because everything about it was exaggerated.

"If you don't mind my asking," Richard asked meekly, "how did the label 'Mother of all Ladies' Men' come to be?"

"*Macho Magazine* labeled me that," Dash said, maneuvering behind the bar like a pro. "They took a poll of women in fifty-five cities who they thought was the best date they ever had — and I had the most votes. Two hundred and forty-four different women recommended me. That was a record," he said with pride, pouring tall martinis. "Hey, how about we take the nickel tour? For starters, we're in what I call the Entertainment Room. I designed it so the sound system can be different levels in different parts of the room."

Dash walked to a massive electronic control panel. "Atmosphere is the key," he said. "To woo a woman I need three nights. That requires three progressive programs, because each mood needs visual, audio, and sensory support. Check out program number one."

Dash hit a button and recessed lights came up full. The room really sparkled. Richard had a little notebook and was writing furiously.

"If you are meeting a woman for the first time, the room has to be light and bright. Safe. I use no filtration at all. She looks around and sees that the place is clean and that I have nothing to hide — except the *Playboys*. And those go here...."

Dash walked to the garbage can under the wet bar and pulled up the plastic bag.

"Under the trash bag in the garbage can. No first date will ever look there."

Dash closed his eyes. "Notice the music? It's upbeat, progressive, harmless. She's going to feel good about herself, pumped by the music. I also cool the place down, to maybe sixty-eight degrees. It makes my lady feel like it's okay to keep her clothes on. Anything less can restrict blood flow, and I'll say no more about that."

"Dash, what's your theory on first-date libations?" Richard inquired.

"I'll offer her an iced tea, or maybe a nice buttery chardonnay. You have to match the mood. As much as I like vodka and tonic, I'm not gonna be pushing that right out of the gate. Men are notoriously impatient. I have found that if you show even a little restraint, she'll be all over you. For the second date, program number two."

Dash hit a button, and the lights dimmed selectively. The mood was decidedly subdued.

"To achieve this 'warm' look, the lights are filtered with an amber gel. This tells the woman that the place is not only safe, but it's comfortable. She can kick off her shoes and spend an evening chatting in front of the fire. We talk about more personal things, about hopes and dreams. We get past the basics."

"And the music would be different too," Richard assumed.

"The music is still going to be progressive, but slower. It's not going to pressure her to feel sexy, but it's going to relax her. I'll turn the temperature up to seventy-two. As a libation, I would move into the red wines, maybe a nice port after dinner. She gets a little tipsy, but she's still in control."

Richard, an apt pupil, was like a sponge. "And phase three?"

"For the third date, otherwise known as the move-in-for-the-kill date, I pull out all the stops."

Dash hit several new buttons and the lights lowered half as much again. The room was transformed before our eyes.

"It'll take about thirty seconds for your retina to adjust," Dash said, walking around his love nest, gesturing. "For Date Number Three, I use darker colors. Reds and blues now take over the amber hues. The music is full-on Barry

The real reason your father never let you touch the thermostat.

White–style seduction. She sees that I'm not in a hurry, but she'll know that I'm also a man with needs like every other man. The temperature will rise to seventy-four, clinically proven to feel comfortable in lingerie. To calm her nerves, I'll go for the full-strength drink. It'll be something dark, like the room — maybe an aged whisky."

Richard nodded. I couldn't tell if he was impressed, or simply bewildered by the human condition. "Looks like you have it all figured out, Dash."

"Maybe not all, Richie, but I have created a 'romance pattern' that works for me."

"Do you take the same amount of pains with your clothes? I noticed that your robe is quite elaborate. Is that silk?"

Richard was referring to his fire-engine-red satin bathrobe with Larry King–style padded shoulders, black piping, and deep pockets on each side.

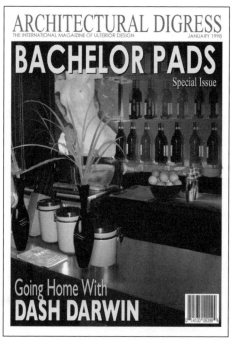

"Satin, actually," Dash corrected. "Silk gives me a rash. I had it tailored special. Ladies like it when a man puts himself together."

I couldn't help but ask, "But what's the distinction between 'put together' and 'overdone'?"

"I'll put it to you this way: most men can't match colors, fabrics, or layers, so they just don't do it. Women have had to lower their standards over the years as a result. If a man puts himself together — his socks match, he has a belt, there are no stains on his shirt — he will distinguish himself from the others."

Richard raised a finger. "Excuse me, is blow-dried hair necessary?"

"You bet. That's why I installed a 'preparation zone.'"

Richard began to write on the back of his spiral notebook pages as we moved from Dash's three-program entertainment room to his elaborate bathroom. The lights revealed an oversize personal hygiene bunker with all the trimmings.

"This is where the magic happens," Dash said, gesturing to the dual-head, multispray contraption. "A night out all begins with a good shower. I take three a day. Cleanliness is rule number one with chicks. If a guy stinks, he's history. That's why I use a hypoallergenic, antibacterial, antifungal soap."

Ever since moving into the bathroom, with its surgical lighting, I couldn't take my eyes off Dash's hair. That mane belonged to another species. The color wasn't just black, it was a raven blue-black, the color Richard Burton used in *Exorcist II* to look young and vibrant again. It's also impossible for humans to have that color naturally.

"How do you get your hair into that shape?" I realized it was something like the style used by the Big Boy restaurant mascot — equal parts Superman and Jethro.

"This? I've been practicing good hair technique since I was a teenager. I've got this down to about forty-five minutes."

Dash looked at Richard and cocked his head in thought. "Can I be frank with you?"

"Sure."

"Let's fix the hair," Dash said, gesturing to the mirror in front of Richard. "What kind of a style is that? Snoresville, that's what. For starters, you have nothing in it. You can't manage hair without product of some sort," he said, opening one of his many cabinets to reveal every hair product ever manufactured.

"Richie, your hair isn't going to be the same every day, and your hair needs aren't going to be the same either. But you can fight it with science. If your hair is feeling listless, you can perk it right up with KUP2 firming gel. If your hair is getting thin, you can fatten it up with Largess. If you're going outside, and it's going to be bad weather, you can set it in place with Perm-HLD fastening treatment."

Dash pulled out a tube of Natra-Gel, squeezed some of the clear goo into his hand, and massaged it into Richard's limp hair.

"Tonight, let's go with a look that says I just played half court with my pals — and now, I want to hang out and meet some ladies."

"A hair goo can say all that?" Richard marveled.

"The right one at the right time can," Dash said with a wink of assurance. "Something for every mood. But enough about hair...."

Dash flung open a new cabinet. Inside were a number of colognes. "A man's scent is as important as anything."

"Whoa," Richard said, reeling from the waft of aromas.

I stifled a sneeze.

"Cologne is the front line of communication between the sexes. What essence do you want to present to the woman you are dating?"

"That I'm...relatively clean?" Richard guessed.

"No," Dash insisted. "Tonight, you want to exude confidence, humor, and a wild spirit, yet with responsible undertones."

"One single scent can do that?"

"I shit you not," Dash said, producing a vintage bottle of Brut cologne. He held it up like a successful lab experiment. "The scent of kings."

Dash unscrewed the lid and held it toward Richard's nose.

"Don't tell me you never wore Brut?"

"I did wear it — once," Richard admitted. "But Brut made me feel like a loser."

"You mean a loser like Elvis?" Dash asked, challenging.

"He wore Brut?"

"And Hai Karate for a while, during his Hawaii comeback phase."

"But, Dash," Richard interjected, "I guess that what I still don't understand is, do you wear things, in this case, cologne, because you like it, or do you wear it because you think a woman will like it?"

"It depends on the type of woman I want to snare."

"You sound like you're going hunting."

"In a manner of speaking, I am. I use Brut primarily because it worked for the King, and I happen to enjoy the smell. If I just want to have sex, I'll wear yak scent."

Dash pulled a small, blue-tinted bottle out of his scent repository and took a whiff. "In very small doses, the scent a male yak emits when he's looking for a mate drives the chicks wild. Take my word, it works. I just don't care for the smell."

"I'll pass on the yak."

"I would too," Dash agreed. "Saturday night in Vegas. You don't need the big guns — dames are gonna be falling out of the trees. Oh, I almost forgot — the medicine cabinet."

Dash opened a hospital-style dispensary near the sink. Inside was every form of male "booster" in liquid, powder, and pill form.

"Time for my fun pack. I start with adrenal gland — it gets the testes going. Yohimbe is next. It's a bark from Africa. Shwing, shwing, ba-da-bing!"

Dash emphasized his point with a stiff forearm in the air, fist clenched. Richard turned to me with a look of horror. Dash popped the pill and turned his attention back to the cabinet.

"Siberian ginseng — the root for *your* root, as they say. Tons of garlic. It gets the blood pumping, know what I mean? And zinc to keep the reproductive chemicals in balance. Plus a buttload of vitamin E, because a guy has to have something to show for his manly efforts, doesn't he?"

"Are you referring to your 'essence'?" Richard asked, mildly appalled.

Dash winked and saluted. "On standby to replenish, sir," and he popped the pill. He then pulled a small vial from the top shelf of the cabinet and shook a substantial blue pill into his palm. "And finally," Dash said, checking his watch, "timing is everything with this little puppy."

Dash's lion's den.

"Oh, my, you have the Big Blue," I said, gawking at what was surely Viagra in Dash's hand.

"Harder by the yard." Dash downed the blue wonder pill and smiled. "I'm a slam dunk to have a little filly back here in two hours."

"And if not, you'd

better crack open the *Playboy*s," I said, "because you've had enough male stimulant to raise the dead."

Dash didn't want to talk about it anymore. "Come on, boys, we're trying to get Richie here a lady, and we haven't even gotten to clothes yet."

We followed Dash to his adjoining bedroom. I walked behind Richard, which proved difficult, because the Brut had removed all oxygen in its wake.

"This is my lair."

Dash wasn't kidding — his four-poster bed had lion heads on each corner.

"Lions are a symbol of masculinity."

"Where's the deer head?" Richard asked, half joking.

"Behind you."

Sure enough, we turned to see an enormous elk head with a twelve-point rack hanging above the bathroom.

Dash stepped into his walk-in closet. Outside, I heard a very muffled "Come on in."

He had an entire room devoted to the maintenance and storage of clothes. It was almost a closed-loop clothing operation with items you could only find in professional dry cleaning operations: a deluxe washer/dryer, a large folding table, a professional-grade pressing machine, ironing board, steamer and even a shoeshine machine.

"Level with me, Bruce," Richard whispered to me, half impressed, half horrified. "Are we on one of those reality shows? Am I being...what's the word? 'Punked'?"

Dash slid back a mirrored door to reveal a collection of undergarments that would rival an Asian sweatshop. "If you feel good underneath, you feel good on the outside."

"You aren't one of those purple minibrief guys, are you?" I asked.

"I wear an assortment of underwear. Am I fond of briefs? Yes. Why, you're a boxer man?"

"Not really, I like a good hybrid. I don't like the cheek squeeze of briefs, but I also don't like the wrap-around-your-leg effect that boxers have."

Dash pulled out a small pair of black briefs. "I hear you, but I need something to keep my package in line."

"Didn't I hear something about briefs and lowered sperm count?" Richard challenged.

Dash shook his head. "That was just propaganda from Fruit of the Loom." He plucked out a black tank-top T-shirt and tossed it at Richard. "Put that on under your shirt. It'll give you a multi-layered look. You'll appear more fascinating — one part of you is loose and light, the other is tight and dark."

Richard rolled his eyes, but he took off his dress shirt and put on the black T.

Dash walked over to a huge Lazy Susan and spun it around until he found a pair of black socks. "Socks have to be as slim as possible," Dash explained. "I want to be able to slip out of my shoes fast, because the last thing you need when some hot momma is ready to party is clingy loafers!"

Dash walked to the next and revealed a row of slacks, a row of sport coats, and a row of shirts, half of them dress, half of them Hawaiian.

"Tonight, we're going to the Pink Flamingo. It's not a formal place. I did some recon ahead of time. It's mainly bright colors, with an international flair. No sweat."

Dash pushed a button, and the row of pants started to move. He snagged a black pair off the rack and tossed it to Richard over his shoulder. "Those will look sharp." The Hawaiian shirts swung around, and Dash picked out a solid pink one, with black piping down the front. He held it up against Richard and the combination was suitably cheesy.

Having taken care of Richard, Dash assembled his own duds. Fully dressed, he looked like he was on his way to a Hamptons garden party — every article of clothing white, from head to toe, including the belt. The only exception (a glaring one) was a black T-shirt.

"The Flamingo is international, so in case you do some dancing, let's get you a shoe with a boxier toe — it's the rage." On the opposite wall, Dash revealed five rows of shoes.

"Are you related to Imelda Marcos?" Richard asked.

Dash, ignoring the jibe, slid back yet another mirrored door, exposing shelf after shelf of hats. "A man is put together from head to toe, my friend," and he picked out a matching pink Frank Sinatra fedora and tried it on Richard.

"Richie" looked put together, in that his pants were a little too tight and a little too short; his shirt was a little too open at the top and a little too wide at the collar and his shoes looked boxy and uncomfortable.

Dash grinned and put his arm around Richard. "Ladies of Las Vegas, watch out!"

The Pink Flamingo Bar was one of those ridiculous Vegas joints where the combination of money and grand ideas don't always go together. Personally, I think the decision to put a forty-foot-tall pink flamingo in front of this place was premature, but as a navigational aid, you can't beat it. I bet one hears, "Turn left at the big flamingo" a lot around here.

Inside, The Flamingo was a meat-market extraordinaire of mostly twenty-somethings but, because it was Las Vegas, plenty of forty-somethings as well, looking for a fling.

The ratio of women to men was really high, maybe sixty-five to thirty-five. Most of the women wore very little clothing, but compensated with lots of makeup. The men sported clothes from the casino gift shops and fresh burns from an afternoon at the martini-shaped pool.

We walked toward the expansive bar. Dash was in his element. "Right off the bat, Richie, you gotta become the bartender's best friend, and the best way to do that is grease their palm." Dash slapped a twenty on the bar. A cute bartender spotted it and hustled over. Dash winked at me.

---

## Horribly Ineffective Pick-Up Lines

**WARNING: These DO NOT work!**

- How'd you like gain 165 pounds for about six minutes?
- Is your father an astronaut because I sure am horny.
- Drunk yet?
- I may not be the best looking guy in here, but I'm the only one talking to you.
- They just called last call, and I'm out of options.
- My apartment is being fumigated. We should screw.
- Quick while my wife's back is turned!
- Your name must be Daisy because I sure am horny.
- So, are you the fat friend or what?
- Anybody else here live with their parents?
- Personally, I found *The Fountainhead* to be a bit pedestrian.
- I designed Bruce Campbell's website.

---

"Evening, gents, what can I get for you?" she asked.

"A cold drink and a hot bartender. What's your name?" Dash asked smoothly.

"Misty."

"You can play me all night, sweetie," Dash said with surprising charm. Like any good salesman, Dash believed every word he said.

"What can I get for you?" Misty repeated, not changing her tone.

"A Pink Flamingo, baby," Dash said, winking.

I looked at my watch. Thirty minutes had passed already since he dropped that Blue Bomb on his system. He was going to be doing a lot more than winking pretty soon.

"What's in a Pink Flamingo?" Richard asked.

"It's the house specialty," Dash said, smiling. "Rum, vodka, gin, scotch, bourbon, triple sec, and a dash of bitters."

"Sounds like a heap of hurt to me," I said. "I'll take an Amstel Light."

Dash immediately went into scope mode. "I like this place because the bar is a semicircle. Do you know what's good about that?"

"You can see every lonely guy across the way?" Richard guessed.

"If your glass is half empty you will," Dash scolded. "No, you can see all the available chicks."

Dash was right on this occasion. Circling around us was an impressive array of women, mainly grouped in twos and threes, though scattered among them were also plenty of singles.

Richard turned to Dash, all business. "Okay, so Dash, let's have it. What's the secret of the pickup?"

"I'm not gonna tell you, Richie, I'm gonna *show* you. Okay, see that blonde over there?"

Dash pointed to a woman who was very tan, very blonde. Her clothing and makeup were both sparkly. She seemed a likely target.

"I'm gonna do the ol' bait and switch."

Richard furrowed his brow. "Is that a card trick?"

"No, it's where I'm *not* gonna try and pick her up. Here, watch. I'm gonna talk about anything other than her or me. I'll sit on her left. You go around the other way and sit on her right — and get your little notepad out."

Dash looked at his watch and took a shot of breath spray. Richard circled around and sat to the right of the blonde, trying not to make eye contact. I parked myself nearby on a stool, strategically positioned to observe the play-by-play and help myself to a bowl of Chex party mix.

Dash took a seat on the blonde's left. She knew she was surrounded, but remained remarkably cool. Dash did his best to mind his own business, so the threesome sat, ignoring each other.

Eventually, the blonde spoke first and, surprisingly, to Richard.

"Well, hello," she said, in a very friendly tone.

The way she added "well" in front of "hello" gave it a slightly different meaning. Richard made contact with her piercing blue eyes.

"Good evening," Richard said, trying to be Mr. Regular Guy in a Bar.

"Where's your ring?" the woman asked.

"That's a mighty big assumption," Richard said, truly surprised. "I'm Richie, by the way."

"Richie what?"

"Richie Gere-er-ing," he stumbled, trying to ad-lib a last name.

"That's nice. What brings you to Vegas?"

Dash shot Richard a "why are you talking to her?" look.

"Oh, I'm just here visiting friends," Richard explained casually. "What is your name?"

"Tonight, my name is...Anastasia, Richie," she said, placing a delicate finger on his lips. "I love the way my lips move when I say your name. Riccchhhiee," she whispered, puckering up lasciviously.

Over the blonde's shoulder, Dash was giving the hunched, palms in the air, "what the fuck?" look.

Richard stared for a moment at his stunning blonde friend, glanced at Dash, and said something that (for him) was an utterly foreign phrase. "Will you...come home with me?"

"I'll get my purse," "Anastasia" said, halfway out of her chair.

Richard smiled infectiously and mouthed "thank you" as he passed me.

Dash watched in shock and awe. "That son of a bitch shattered my land speed record of 2 minutes and 38 seconds."

I watched "Richie" and his date leave the Flamingo, and marveled. "Well, Dash, don't be too hard on yourself. After all, you lost out to Richard Gere."

"What are you talking about?" Dash asked, still miffed.

"My buddy Richie — he was Gere in disguise."

"Get out of here."

I nodded yes.

"Well no wonder he got the chick," Dash rationalized. "He's a goddamn Hollywood movie star — I can't compete with that."

Dash glanced at his watch nervously. More precious time had elapsed. "Shit, I'm about to turn into a pumpkin."

Dash scanned the bar like Robo Cop looking for a mutant sex offender. He zeroed in on a brunette, seated alone. "See that saucy little thing over there with the fabulous bags?"

"The one with the low-cut dress?"

RACE: CAUCASOID
HEIGHT: 5' 5"
WEIGHT: III
EYES: BLUE
HAIR: LONG
BREASTS: 34B

LIKES:
TENNIS, READING,
NON-DAIRY CREAMER
DISLIKES:
MARMOTS, ALGEBRA,
CEREAL WITH MARSHMALLOWS

SCANNING...

Dash's POV.

"Yeah. I'm goin' for the full-court press. Get ready to be impressed."

Dash went for his target, and I circled wide to view from afar. Dash parked it next to the statuesque woman and pulled out his

Zippo lighter to fire up a cigarillo, the classy kind with the plastic tip.

"Do you always case out women?" the brunette asked, not particularly upset.

"Can you blame me? If I was you, I'd stalk myself," Dash explained, smirking. "But hey, I'll just sit here and mind my own business."

Dash's master plan, of course, was to let his prey make the next move — and she did.

"Where do guys get shirts like that?"

"Oh, this? At the cool-guy clothing store."

And finally, Dash Darwin himself.

"I'd have thought the Salvation Army, because it's so butt-ugly."

By now, any mortal man would have been thrown for a loop, but Dash was not exactly a neophyte at this game. "It's not the shirt that matters, sugar, it's what's *under* it."

"All I see under it is a T-shirt. What's that for, to soak up your sweat?"

Dash was taken aback. This woman obviously had his number.

"And what's that stinky thing? A Tiparillo?"

"A Cigarillo."

"Whatever. It's not a cigar or a cigarette — it can't make up its mind. Christ, my *father* smokes those. He chews on the plastic tip for days."

"Your father is a great man," Dash said defensively.

"My father is a louse. And something smells like a medicine cabinet."

"It happens to be Brut."

"It happens to suck," she said without remorse.

"It was good enough for Elvis."

"Oh, I should have known by your hair — or is that a fright wig? When does the lounge act start, Wayne?"

"Are you referring to Wayne Newton?" Dash said, his hackles rising.

"I am."

"In a negative way?"

"Is there a positive way, Pompadour Pete?" the brunette said, her delivery devastating.

In the middle of this shooting war, I slid the Chex mix a little closer and ordered another Amstel Light.

"Hey, if you haven't got anything nice to say about the King, or the Prince of Vegas, maybe you shouldn't say anything at all."

"Maybe you're right, you hairsprayed, freeze-dried, limp dick."

The brunette grabbed her clutch and left without a further word.

Dash glanced at me, looking beaten and sheepish. "Heh-heh. What can I say? Sometimes it's a good news/bad news scenario: the good news is, she's talking to you — the *bad* news is, she's talking to you. You never know how it's gonna go down...."

Just then, a drop-dead sexy woman sashayed past, nearly giving us whiplash. Dash's reaction was more audible than mine, mostly because two hours had elapsed since he popped Mr. Blue Pill, and something biological was long overdue.

Dash got a look in his eyes that only guys can appreciate. It was the "I'm out of time" look. He pointed at his watch, and mouthed the word *trouble.* A waiter passed with an empty tray, and Dash yanked it from his hand to cover up his *bonis maximus*. As he ran away, a pretty full room got a good idea of why Viagra is regulated.

I decided to walk back to my hotel from the Flamingo. Las Vegas is best after dark, mainly because it's the only time you can walk around outside without feeling like an egg on a giant skillet. Lots of people were on the street, mostly en route to a bar or casino, and I wondered about the games they'd play tonight, trying to pick each other up.

Personally, I think guys like Dash — and we're all Dash to varying degrees — are idiots. His life would be so simple if he stripped off the fake hair, gave up the scents, the color coordinating, and the methodical planning, and never went to places that made him feel desperate. He'd never have to use pickup lines, per se, because he would never try to someone else. He'd save all kinds of money that he could put toward a hobby, which would enrich his life, not just his nightlife, and he'd probably meet someone within a year and settle down forever. Okay, that's not going to happen, but you know what I mean.

Back at the Best Western, I rounded the last corner on the fifth floor and came face-to-face with a polka-dot handkerchief wrapped around the doorknob of our shared room (in a mutual effort to keep the actor's "eye of the tiger," Richard and I decided to bunk together). The prearranged signal was clear: handkerchief on knob = "do not enter" or, in this case, "Richard got laid."

I was happy for him. From an actor's perspective, he really punched through a brick wall, and it was exciting to watch him grow firsthand. But I was so tired I couldn't see straight, so I did what any forlorn roommate would do — I sat my ass on the floor and began to root through the leftovers on his room-service tray.

Fortunately, Richard is a classy guy, so there was really good stuff to scavenge — a third of a bottle of Dom Perignon, a half-eaten turkey croissant sandwich (the mayo was easy to scrape off), with white-chocolate-dipped strawberries for dessert. It wasn't easy, but somehow I managed to make it through the night.

# 11

# Dial "M" for Marriage

The crick in my neck from sleeping in the hallway didn't keep me from meeting with Mike in New York the next day. The message on my voice mail was simply that Mike wanted to "talk." Being naturally paranoid, I assumed that I had done something wrong, and booked the earliest flight available.

"Thanks for coming, Bruce. Have a seat."

Mike had this infuriating way of being both cordial and demanding at the same time, but he never had to tell me twice. I sat in a plush chair to one side of his desk.

"Two things. First, thanks for Vegas," Mike said, choosing to remain standing. "Whatever the hell you and Richard did there worked wonders. Richard called me in the middle of the night, exploding with ideas. He's like a kid again. Second, and the main reason why I wanted to talk to you: have you had your 'woohoo' moment yet?"

"My...'woohoo' moment?" I asked, missing his point.

"Yeah. The big breakthrough — the moment when you've

skinned the character alive and you finally see what's inside."

"Well, uh, I could lie to you, Mike, but no, I haven't exactly had that moment yet. I didn't know I was supposed to."

Mike took a few commanding steps toward me. He's not a big guy, but he carries himself well. "I don't want a woohoo-less actor in my cast, Bruce. We're getting damn close to shooting, and I want my actors to know where their characters came from, where they're going, and how they got there. Once that portrayal is committed to film, we're all going to have to live with it."

"Yes, sir," I said, sheepishly.

"Now get out there and find your woohoo moment!"

Mike made his point: I had fallen short, again. Foyl was supposed to be a relationship expert. He was happily married and a font of wisdom on that particular topic. I'm on marriage number two, and though I have been joined in matrimony for 18.5 years collectively, it doesn't mean I know the first thing about it.

I knew a horse wrangler one time who had the perfect plan for avoiding the institution of marriage altogether: "You treat 'em [women] real good until you hear 'em talkin' about getting married. When this happens, you gotta do something shitty — I mean *really* shitty — out of nowhere. It'll take 'em awhile to get back to marriage talk after that, and if they do, you just do it all over again. It's kept me out of marriage for years."

I couldn't envision Foyl Whipple dispensing that same advice to Richard Gere. For the sake of *Let's Make Love!* — and perhaps my career — I decided to crawl back into the womb of marriage and experience it with new eyes. I hadn't said a vow in fourteen years, so I figured it wouldn't hurt to get some insight from the pros.

"Let me get this straight, Mr. Campbell, you want to work with us as a wedding planner, but just for one wedding? Isn't that a little unusual?"

"I'm an actor," I said. "I'm just doing research for a part."

Neither Dick Patterson nor Reed White, co-owners of Patterson & White: Your Wedding Planners, seemed reassured. "You're not one of those damn actors who's only in straight-to-video sequels and Sci-Fi Channel movies, are you?"

What could I say? "I won't charge you for my services."

"Uh-huh. Well, that's a little more attractive, but there is the issue of training and capability and liability."

"I'll assume all liability, and as far as capability, you guys don't have a worry in the world."

*Patterson & White*

BRUCE CARLSON *Wedding Planners*

~~Dick Patterson~~
Wedding Planner

3689 Paved Road Drive
Columbus, Ohio 43220
(614) 555-3429 tel
(614) 555-3499 fax
plans@patterson-white-weddings.con
www.patterson-white-weddings.con

Dick Patterson turned to his business partner. "Reed, can you believe this fellow wants to walk in here and plan one of our top-end weddings for no particularly good reason?"

"Sounds like a secret camera show to me," Reed said. "How do we know that this isn't some kind of *Caught on Tape* horse-shit?"

"Lots of actors have reality shows these days," Dick added.

"Especially ones that haven't had anything new on the air in a few years," Reed said, looking directly at me.

"Hey, guys, this isn't a hidden anything," I explained. "I'm just honing my craft."

The men huddled and whispered to themselves while I continued the hard sell.

"In fact, you can even video the whole process," I assured

them. "Use it as promotion for your company — but we'd have to talk if you ever went national."

As the men talked, they gestured and nodded, sometimes with emphasis. The overall length of their deliberation wasn't a positive sign, so I assumed a no was coming. Suddenly, the intensity of the two men dissipated. Their huddle relaxed, and Dick came toward me smiling.

"All right, Bruce, you're on board," Dick relayed with a smile. "But if you fuck us over, we'll kneecap you in the parking lot."

I looked at the two businessmen who had owned and operated, for the past thirty-two years, Patterson and White Weddings in downtown Columbus, Ohio. There was something very "Detroit" about their warning, in that it also seemed very real.

"Sounds like a good deal to me, fellows," I accepted with a smile. "Thanks."

Without delay, Dick pulled out a thick folder. "Okay, you've got the Boils — Lance and Jackie. They're getting married Friday the twentieth."

A fan sent me this picture... a weird fan.

"Holy cow," I blurted, looking at my watch. "That's only two weeks from today."

"That's pretty typical, kid," Reed said. "These bastards come in at the last minute and want everything for nothing — fast, good, and cheap."

"'Pick any two,' is what I tell clients," Dick chuckled. "Here's the lowdown: the bride — Jackie Troutman — her old man, Ed, made a ditchload of money by paving half of Columbus. The kid,

Lance, doesn't know shit from shine-ola, but he works for her daddy and is next in line to be the paving king."

"Your job as a wedding planner is part sales, part planning," Reed added, playing the second half of the tag team. "This is a big day for these people, right, Dick?"

"Biggest day of their life," Dick shot back, with the timing found only in well-rehearsed routines. "If Daddy is going to spend money on any day in his life, it's going to be on his little girl's wedding day."

"It's actually why we're giving you this gig," explained Dick. "This one's a no-brainer."

"I can see what the kid wants from her," I reasoned, "but what does she get out of him?"

Reed became visibly agitated by my question. "Never do that, kid," he said, with a hint of reprimand in his voice. "Never bring it up. You're part defense lawyer, too. Your client is always innocent and perfect — unless the check bounces, in which case you sue the shit out of them."

"Cash-flow problems aside," Dick added, "the couple-to-be is always a great match. Your personal opinions don't count, and your job is never to question the pairing or the in-laws, just keep the wedding on track."

"It's like working air traffic control," Reed offered. "You don't care what airline they are, as long as they all land safely."

Dick and I looked at each other. Neither of us could make sense out of that scenario.

"It doesn't matter," Reed said, rummaging through his desk. "It's like Mickey Rooney once said: 'As long as the wedding takes place without loss of life, you've succeeded.'" He tossed a hefty wedding catalogue in my lap. "If you're ever having trouble sleeping, this'll do the trick. It's the ultimate marriage bible. You think marriage is about love and happiness? Think again. Marriage is about cakes and catering and stationery and limousines and gifts. Marriage is about moola."

"Marriage isn't a question of 'am I going to spend money?', it's a question of 'how much money am I going to spend?'" Dick said, unconsciously jingling the coins in his pocket.

"It's ugly," Reed agreed, "but it's all part of getting hitched in the modern world."

"For many, marriage is a dream come true," Dick said, walking across the room to me. "At this company, we help make dreams a reality. If our client wants rose petals falling from the sky as they walk down the aisle, even though later that night they're going to beat the crap out of each other, then by God, rose petals it is."

I never saw the dog-eat-dog sales play, *Glengarry Glen Ross*, but I imagined it was kind of like this.

"Sell!" Reed shouted, escalating the energy in the room.

"I will!" I said, pumping a fist in the air.

"Wedding!" Reed yelled.

"Best day of their lives!" I answered.

"Money!" Dick bellowed and the three of us danced around their stuffy office, pumping our fists in the air like the beginning of an Anthony Robbins infomercial.

Dick caught his breath and shoved a piece of paper in my hand. "That's the address to the Troutmans'. They're expecting you at six o'clock sharp for drinks, dinner, and a planning meeting."

"Uh, okay," I said, trying not to appear addled. "Who's going to be there?"

"Everyone."

I wasn't sure if they heard me gasp, but Reed put a reassuring hand on my shoulder. "We'll follow up tomorrow and see how you did. Now get out that door, son," he said, like Knute Rockne, "and plan us a wedding we can all be proud of!"

The Troutman estate had the longest black asphalt driveway I had ever seen — almost half a mile through the rolling hills of northern Columbus. Given Ed's vocation it made sense, but I could have done without the antique Caterpillar bulldozer at the entrance, elevated six feet on huge footings as a monument to the paving industry.

Ed Troutman's house was a sprawling, L-shaped ranch, mid-sixties in its sleek styling. As I swung up in my bug-splattered Ford Explorer, the proprietor himself was the first one out the front door.

"Hey, friend, I didn't hear anything about a Ford coming on my property."

"I'm sorry, are you Ed Troutman?" I asked.

"I am," he said, "but we're not talking about me, we're talking about the Ford, son."

Before Ed could get up to speed, his daughter Jackie, a cute, bubbly young woman of twenty-four, hugged her father from behind. "Oh, Daddy, how would he know we're a Chevy family?"

"He could have called ahead and asked," Ed said, indignant.

"I'm Jackie, and this is my daddy, Ed Troutman," she said to me with a smile. "You are most welcome here."

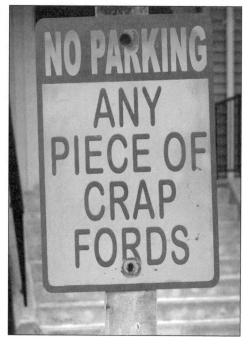

"And hello to you," I said, getting out of the Explorer and offering my hand. "I'm Bruce Ca —" And then it happened again, I realized I hadn't bothered to come up with a fake last name. "I'm Bruce... *Carlson*, I'm the wedding planner."

"We know who you are," Ed said. "Now, pull that car around to the side. I don't want anyone to see a Ford in front of my house."

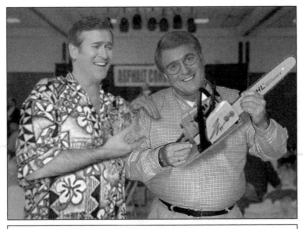

Ed Troutman with the occasional mid-grade celebrity.

"Are you from Detroit, sir?"

"Why do you ask?"

"Well, that's where I'm from, and we used to talk like that. Some folks were Ford families, others were Chevy or Chrysler. I know where you're coming from. I came from a Chevy family, too."

"Then why are you driving a goddamn Ford?"

"I bought it off my neighbor in Oregon when the weather was really bad. I lost my head, I wasn't paying attention. I'm sorry, sir."

"You can't do that to your brand, son. It just ain't right. Besides, I'm on the Columbus city council, and Chevy is the largest employer in the metropolitan area, if you catch my meaning. So, pull it around to the side, then come on in and I'll pour you a tall one."

As I walked back to my "goddamn Ford," Jackie gave me a withering smile as if to say, "I know my daddy's an asshole, but he's the only daddy I've got."

Ed Troutman had money, and he knew how to spend it. After

meeting his diminutive wife of few words, Pearl, I got a ten-dollar tour of the house from Jackie while Ed supervised the makings of a Tom Collins.

The Troutmans enjoyed a state-of-the-art entertainment room, a big-game trophy room, a wine cellar, sauna, walk-in closets, bathrooms around every corner, and pictures of Ed with politicians, athletes, and the occasional low-to-mid-grade celebrity.

I admired the one with Sonny and Cher. "This one's my favorite. Your dad looks like Clark Gable."

"That's Ed Troutman, he's just larger than life," Jackie sighed.

"How is Lance adjusting?"

"That's an interesting word. I guess I'd say it's a process," Jackie said politely.

This was not the type of family to come out and say, "Lance is a dweeb, Dad is an asshole, and Mom won't say anything about anything."

"Are the Boils due to arrive soon?"

"Yes, we're waiting on the Boils," Jackie said. "We're *always* waiting on the Boils."

=Ding-dong=

Jackie raised her eyebrows. "Not anymore."

The Boils, father Vic and second wife/stepmother Tina, pulled up in a Chevy Nova. I'm sure Ed was very happy about that. Son Lance was right behind in his Pontiac Trans Am. His car wasn't a Chevy, per se, but at least it fell under the General Motors umbrella.

Vic Boil, sporting a thin moustache and a serious comb-over, was a tool-and-die shop manager. Tina, an overweight secretary, worked for the mayor's office, which apparently was a source of friction between her and Ed.

Lance Boil, twenty-seven, and going in every direction at once, was a doofus. He worked as "vice president of sales" under Ed. It wasn't a job he excelled at, but then, he didn't really have to.

As the Boils and the Troutmans converged in Ed's family room, I could sense the clash of styles, tastes, and social standing. The Vic Boils of the world tended to hate the Ed Troutmans. Whenever Vic could get in a cheap shot at corporations he would, while Ed was more than happy to lob back insults about the "lazy-ass" working class.

Tina and Pearl never really gelled either. Tina was, in Pearl's eyes, a "step" parent, and always would be. In fact, of the two families, the only positive dynamics were between the bride and groom, who seemed to genuinely enjoy each other's company.

"A Collins, Vic?" Ed boomed across his wet bar, which was decorated like a NASCAR pit stop.

"A Bud'll be fine, Ed, like always," Vic said, taking a seat on a bar stool. "How's business?"

"We're paving the way to the future, Vic!"

"I walked right into that one."

"How about you, Bruce? A Collins to get your engine running?"

"No thanks, Ed, I'm working tonight," I said. "Do you have Dr. Pepper?"

"Mr. Pibb all right?"

"Sure."

"Hey, dumb ass!" Ed bellowed.

I wasn't sure whom he was insulting, but then I saw Lance, hugging family members in the foyer.

"Yo!" he yelled back.

"Want a Tom?"

"You know it, boss man."

"How about you, Tina girl?" Ed urged.

"Diet Pepsi, thanks," she said, joining the group at the bar.

Ed grabbed a soda from his fully stocked fridge and popped the top. "How's life with numb nuts?"

"If you mean 'how is working for his honor the mayor,' it's just fine," sniffed Tina, "and a lot more friendly than the snake pit down there at the city council."

"It's where the rubber meets the road, darlin'."

"And we'll provide the road," Lance blurted out, joining them.

Ed jammed a drink into his hand.

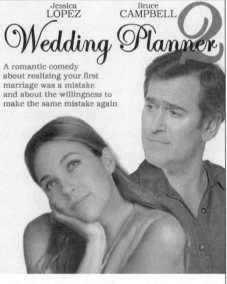

Jessica LOPEZ    Bruce CAMPBELL

*Wedding Planner 2*

A romantic comedy about realizing your first marriage was a mistake and about the willingness to make the same mistake again

"Better than My Second Marriage!"
-Albert Ross, WKIF

*"Keep the wedding on track,"* I heard Reed say. "I propose a toast!" I said, raising my Mr. Pibb high. "To Lance and Jackie: a terrific couple. I'm look forward to this wedding, I'll tell you!"

"I'll bet you are," Ed mumbled to himself.

In a delivery that would make my employers proud, I announced: "It's a once-in-a-lifetime day, isn't it?"

Lance kissed Jackie and there was sporadic clapping.

Ed forced a smile. "So when do we get to hear them big ideas, Bruce?" he asked.

"I'll be making my presentation after dinner."

"Why wait?" Ed insisted. "What else are we here for? We can eat dinner any ol' time. Someone get Pearl in here."

"I've been here the whole time, jackass," Pearl barked, startling everyone from a dark love seat in the corner.

"Sorry, honey, you're so damn quiet sometimes...."

I knew my time was at hand. "Folks, I'd love to share some life-changing ideas with you."

The family migrated across to the Ethan Allen Mt. Vernon family-room set and formed a semicircle, with Jackie and Lance in the middle. Ed, too nervous to sit, paced behind them. I took a sip of my Mr. Pibb and recalled what Dick and Reed told me: *"Always have three wedding pitches ready, because the first two are going to get rejected."*

"Lance, Jackie, you're a young, dynamic couple," I said, subtly flapping my hands behind me, trying to make the sweat dry. "But getting married is a big step. It's more than that — it's a leap, actually. And what better way to demonstrate that than by skydiving your way down to the wedding?"

Lance began to smile like an idiot, and Jackie was definitely intrigued, but the look between Pearl and Ed spoke volumes.

"That sounds like a great idea. I'm for it," Lance said, looking around for support.

"Uh-uh," Pearl uttered, shaking her head from side to side. "No way on God's green earth."

"I paced it out," I interjected. "Ed, you've got twenty acres here, am I right?"

"Give or take."

"That's plenty of land, even on a day with light to moderate winds."

"Shit, boy — jumpin' out of a damn airplane?" Ed exclaimed. "That's my *daughter* you're talking about."

"It might be fun, Daddy," Jackie responded.

"Fun? You seen them power lines on the south end of this

property? I can't let my daughter, let alone my vice president of sales, get strung up and fried on their wedding day," Ed said as he walked back behind the wet bar.

"I don't like the idea," Tina said, "but I must say, you could only consider something like that with the current zoning laws Mayor Coleman supported."

Ed blew a raspberry at Tina as he loaded up the stainless-steel blender. "It's just a bad idea all the way around."

In my two hours of formal training, one thing Reed said really stuck with me: *"If you bomb, kid, just make a joke out of it. Keep tap dancing."*

"Hey, I'm not *married* to it," I chuckled. "This has to work for everyone."

"I was...all right with it," Lance said, defeated.

"Why don't you tell us what you really had in mind," Ed called out.

"I'm glad you asked, Ed," I said, turning to the newlyweds-to-be. "Lance and Jackie, I've done some research on you two. You both went to Ohio State, one graduated, and Lance, you once played side by side with the great football coach Woody Hayes."

I conveniently left out the fact that Lance had been a third-string defensive end on the kickoff return team. "Ed, you and Pearl have Buckeye fever, am I right?"

"Class of sixty-six," Ed acknowledged, raising his Tom.

"So what better way to share your love than to get married in the stadium?" I proposed.

The men in the room perked up, particularly Ed and Lance.

"Right on the field," I continued. "The same field as the 2002 National Champions. But that's not all. The colors of the wedding will be scarlet and gray, the school colors. If it's been good enough for Ohio State since 1878, then it's good enough for Lance and Jackie."

Jackie wrinkled her nose at this idea, but I kept the sales pitch moving. *"Never let a lack of enthusiasm slow you down,"* Dick Patterson's voice echoed in my mind.

"The bride and groom enter the stadium through a victory arch formed by the members of the wedding party."

"That would be beautiful," Pearl imagined.

"Almost as beautiful as the day you met Ed in the stands in 1963," I said, closing in on Pearl. "He was the most handsome field maintenance man you'd ever seen."

Pearl blushed. "It's true, you know."

"Shit," Ed said, waving her away with a smile.

I started to get a good feeling about this pitch. The right people were responding. Vic and Tina were noncommittal, but Vic never had much to say anyway. Jackie, for her part, seemed to have become strangely unengaged in the process.

"And who is on the field to greet them, in formation, but the Ohio State marching band! And I don't need to tell you what T-B-D-B-I-T-L means...."

"The Best...," Ed started.

"Damn Band...," Lance continued.

"In the...," Pearl added.

"Land!" The three of them pounced on the final word together.

"That's right," I said. "And after the ceremony, instead of the traditional scripting of Ohio, the marching band will spell out 'Lance and Jackie' in cursive, and play the 'Buckeye Battle Cry,' rewritten by a former *Simpsons* writer."

Reaction in the room had been building, and my pitch was met with enthusiastic hoots, clapping, and laughter.

"Shadddap!" A voice boomed.

Ed and the other merrymakers stopped to look at Vic, who had shouted. "I'm sorry, folks, but I'm gonna have to put a kibosh on that one."

I stifled a cough. Lance sat back in his chair with a "whoa." Ed came from around the bar.

"You been sitting there pretty quiet until now, Vic," he said. "What's the matter?"

"I'm just the father of the groom," Vic responded. "So, what I think doesn't really matter a damn in the whole marriage deal, but I marched in the University of Michigan marching band — class of '68 — and I don't think my son should participate in a ceremony that is so obviously slanted."

"Slanted? I went to college there," Lance said.

"So did I," Jackie added.

"I understand that," Vic said, trying to remain calm, "but you were never on the other side like I was. Even before the game, dressed in our maize and blue, little old ladies would spit and swear at us as we walked down the street."

"I never realized that," Pearl said, slightly alarmed.

"Believe it," Vic said, still agitated by the memories. "I been around, okay? I been in 'Nam. I didn't come home to no picnic then either, but I never come up against bigger assholes — you'll excuse me, ladies — than the goddamned Buckeyes and Woody 'chew your hat' Hayes."

Vic, I would later discover, was from Taylor, Michigan. There are only three things you do there: work, drink Budweiser, and watch University of Michigan football, arch rival of Ohio State.

"Watch how you talk about Woody in this

house," Ed cautioned.

"Hey, I was tryin' not to say anything, 'cause I know how much you love that fat idiot, but enough is enough, Ed. There are two sides to this family."

An awkward silence followed, during which, little eye contact was made. Finally, Ed broke the impasse. "Okay, hey, I got no problem *not* paying to rent Ohio Stadium and the entire band," he said, clearly disappointed and pissed.

"All right, good," Vic said, with a nod. "Got any more Bud?"

"In the fridge," Ed gestured, not making any effort to get one.

Since I was now 0 for 2 in sales pitches, I assumed that this would be a good time for my third and final attempt.

"Lance and Jackie," I said, pointing my finger at them as if I planned this all along. "You both went to Ohio State, but ironically, you never met there — you met where?"

I not-so-subtly hinted at a huge banner for the Columbus Speedway above Ed's wet bar.

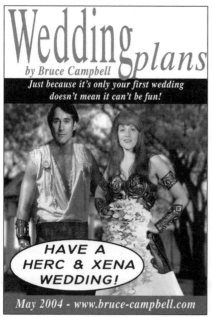

"The Speedway," Pearl said, her eyes lighting up. "I like that place. Those boys drive fast."

"That's right, Pearl," I said, playing the room. "And what were the circumstances?"

"Lance was a mechanic for a car Ed's company was sponsoring," Pearl said, fond of the memory.

"Jackie came down for a pit stop, and she never left — did you, baby?" Lance said through a Tom Collins smile.

"Nope," Jackie said, smiling back. "And it went from there."

"I'll say it did," I continued. "From humble beginnings to a full-blown love affair for the ages, the race track has been your bond, the asphalt that has kept you two together."

"FYI," Ed blurted, "we resurfaced it in ninety-five. Helluva good contract."

"And what better way to cement your love," I asked, "than by standing in the middle of the oval track of Columbus Speedway?"

"Now you're talking my language, Jack," Vic added with renewed interest.

"Each member of the wedding gets to race a lap against — and he's only a phone call away — none other than Jeff Gordon."

The idea of a NASCAR theme turned Ed around quickly. "Hey now, that would be a kick."

"The hell you say," Lance said, grabbing hold of Jackie. "My woman isn't goin' anywhere near Jeff Gordon!"

"The hell *you* say," Pearl said, getting everyone's attention. "He can keep me in the pole position any day!"

The men all burst into rowdy laughter. Nothing bonds drunken idiots like sexual innuendo.

"Betcha I could take Gordon," Vic said, nodding. "Betcha I could."

"Betcha I could too," Tina said, winking at Vic.

"Can we get Garth Brooks to sing?" Pearl asked.

Lance and Jackie exchanged unexcited looks.

"Anything is doable," I said, snapping a finger. "We just have to make it worth his while."

"He hasn't had a hit in a few years," Ed chimed in. "He couldn't be all *that* much."

"Never know until you try," I said, smiling like Robert Preston in *The Music Man.*

"He can sing, 'Ain't goin' down 'til the sun comes up,'" Vic suggested.

*"The best ideas sell themselves,"* Reed had said to me at the end of our "seminar." For all the crap he fed me in two hours, that notion made the most sense. As I looked around, the family members — the parents anyway — were excited enough to spitball their own take on what would make for the perfect NASCAR-themed wedding.

"You present the ring on the awards podium," Vic threw out, getting suddenly very verbal. "I've always wanted to stand up there."

"And for the big finale, I'd go for a mock accident," Ed added. "Hell, I could come zoomin' around, smash into Jeff Gordon, and he could bounce off the wall. You could even have some dummies and shit that go flyin', I mean, really blow the lid off that place."

"Did you know that the Speedway is wired to do closed-circuit TV broadcasts?" I asked.

"Could our friends in Iowa tune in?" Pearl wondered.

"If they have a TV set, you bet," I said, sounding like game show host Wink Martindale. "They're also set up to record and edit the wedding in real time. Everyone will get a finished DVD on their way out."

"I'll be damned," Ed nodded, really transfixed.

The third time was the charm. I could name my price. "Well, you folks can talk it over. Ed, I'll call you in the morning."

"Sure, but I can tell you now, this is a slam dunk," he said, pumping my hand.

"I'll have Reed give you a call to discuss the details," I said, excusing myself.

Vic sat back down at the bar. "Isn't that something? Hey, Ed, got any more Bud?"

"Sure thing, buddy. Let me get that for you, now that we're in-laws! Ha-ha-ha!"

Vic joined in the laughter, and the two men were instant friends again. Meanwhile, Tina and Pearl converged on a full-size, cardboard standee of Jeff Gordon in the corner. A high-spirited conviviality was spreading through the room like petro-chemical fumes, and the parents, having inhaled deeply of their high-octane fantasy, didn't seem to notice that Jackie and Lance had disappeared.

Going around the side of the house to where my offending Ford was parked, I saw the glow of a cigarette. The husband-and-wife-to-be were by them-selves, having what looked like a serious discussion, so I decided to say a quick hello and good night and then get out of their way.

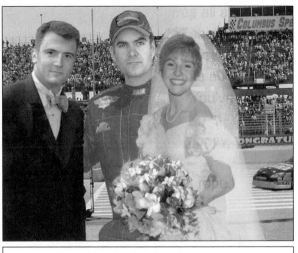

Instead of throwing rice, they'd throw beer cans.

"Well, the big day is coming up," I offered.

"Yep," Jackie said, nodding, not really wanting to start a conversation.

"Well, we'll try and make it memorable for you."

"Maybe too memorable," Lance said, dissenting for the first time.

"You think so?" I asked.

"I mean, whose wedding is this, anyway?" Jackie questioned, with uncharacteristic intensity.

"Yours, of course," I said.

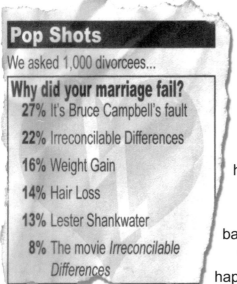

**Pop Shots**

We asked 1,000 divorcees...

**Why did your marriage fail?**

**27%** It's Bruce Campbell's fault

**22%** Irreconcilable Differences

**16%** Weight Gain

**14%** Hair Loss

**13%** Lester Shankwater

**8%** The movie *Irreconcilable Differences*

"Did anyone once ask *us* what we wanted to do?"

"No," Lance said.

"Where *we* wanted to go?"

"No."

"Who *we* wanted to invite?"

"No."

"You two don't seem very happy," I said.

"We're not," Jackie sniffed.

"But don't tell them that," Lance backpedaled.

"We were afraid this would happen — that our parents would totally forget what the day is all about and force us into something we hate."

"Well, what do you really want to do?" I asked.

"What *can* we do? Nothing," Lance said.

"You have plenty of choices. You can go along with everything we talked about tonight, or you can bail on the whole thing."

"We don't want to bail," Jackie said. "We want to get married."

"Yeah, just not in this bullshit way."

"We'd rather just run away and tell everyone after we're married. I know that they want to share, but it's so personal. What do they know about us?"

"You could do that," I agreed, "but it would cause a big fuss."

"Well, what's more important?" Jackie wondered. "A wedding where everyone has fun, or a marriage that lasts?"

"The latter," I said, sliding two first-class tickets out of my pocket. "Vegas okay?"

"Are you serious?" Lance asked, as if his cell door had just been flung open.

"Any wedding planner worth his salt has to have a contingency plan. My job, ultimately, is to plan a nuptial, not please the parents," I said, half-expecting Dick and Reed to appear from the shadows and deliver the much-discussed crippling.

"Oh my God, thank you so much," Jackie said, with tears welling up. "What are you going to tell them?"

"I'm not going to tell them anything. Why spoil the fun? By the time they realize you're gone, Jeff Gordon will be dancing on a table with your mother and it won't matter. And personally, I recommend the Elvis Chapel of Love. The guy does a great 'Hunka Burnin' Love.'"

"Okay, thanks, man," Lance said, whipping off his tie and taking Jackie by the hand.

I watched as they ran to his car and peeled away down Daddy's fresh asphalt driveway. As I hopped in my Ford, I wondered what the odds were for Lance and Jackie in a world where half of all marriages fail. If the strength of a union is to be judged by early, key decisions, I'd give them better than fifty-fifty.

I called Ida from the airport on my way back to New York City and we discussed the events in Columbus. We agreed that while we may not know what marriage is, Ida and I certainly know what it is not. There is no "fairy dust" sprinkled on your head when you wed, and happiness isn't guaranteed by symbols like a ring, a license, and certainly not by a prenuptial agreement. A decent union comes from both parties trying like hell for as long as they have the strength, and that's just the beginning. Marriage isn't fixed, it's a work in progress from the first vow, and anyone who tells you different is full of beans. At least, I decided, that's the opinion of one very wise New York City doorman.

# 12

# A Fitting We Will Go

I stuffed the last of a grilled corn muffin in my mouth, washed it down with lukewarm tea, and buzzed number twenty-two. I had arrived at Sandra Demming's costume shop in New York City's Greenwich Village.

"Can I help you?" squawked a voice from the little box.

"Yeah, Bruce Campbell here for a *Let's Make Love!* fitting."

The door buzzed and I was in.

Sandra's loft/sweatshop was mostly a huge open area with wall-to-wall windows and uneven wood floors. Assistants were scurrying about, making phone calls, hemming pants, and doing whatever else you need to do to win two Academy Awards.

An unflappable, supremely confident, four-foot-tall field marshal, Sandra had the energy of three people. "We're late, and you're early," she declared, "so you can have a seat and read a year-old fashion magazine, or you can see some of the things we're doing with Renée."

"I'll go for the fashion show," I said, and promptly followed

Sandra through a maze of fabric, machinery, and testy gay men.

Turning a corner, we came upon a large fitting area with mirrors on three sides and flanked by comfortable chairs.

"Park it," Sandra said. "Renée will be out in a sec."

Before Sandra could finish her sentence, Renée emerged from a changing room, resplendent in a riding outfit that looked straight out of *Town & Country*, circa 1987.

"Hi, Brad," she said, seeing me.

"Bruce."

Renée made a face like she had stepped on a frog. "I'm so sorry. *Bruce.* I knew that — duh."

"It's fine. Brad Pitt and I get confused all the time."

"Well, now that you two have caught up," Sandra said, nodding, "I think the suit is marvelous."

"I do too," Renée said, turning around in front of a mirror. "It's fun, elegant, and very —"

"Baggy," I said, cutting her off.

Renée and Sandra looked at me in shock, but then back to her outfit.

"It's not baggy," Sandra said, defending the fit.

"Well, I'm not the Academy Award winner, but to a layman's eyes it is — particularly in the butt."

"Do I have a saggy butt?" Renée asked, turning her back to the mirror and looking over her shoulder.

"No, not you," I explained. "You have a very nice butt. You must work out a lot."

"I do," Renée said, frowning. "A *lot*."

"For my money, I'd like to see it a little more celebrated."

"Well, fortunately for us, this isn't your money, Mr. Campbell," Sandra scolded, "it's the money of Paramount Pictures, and we're going to —"

"Oh, but I beg to differ. It's the money of the guys who are coming to see Renée. They still have the image of her from *Chicago* swimming in their heads."

Sandra stepped toward me. "This movie is not for that type of person. This is a Mike Nichols film, and I know for a fact that his only concern is the story."

COMBO ITAN

This magazine is stupid and so are you

MAY 2004

**WHY YOU'RE SO DAMN FAT**
6 WAYS TO STOP EATING SO MUCH RAW BUTTER

HE'S PAYING, GET THE LOBSTER

EITHER HE'S GAY OR YOU'RE UGLY

**OOPS!**
STUDY SHOWS LOVE IS JUST ONE BIG STUPID LIE

**FAUX FACE?**
HOW TO TELL IF A FAKE HEAD APPEARS ON A MAGAZINE COVER

**PURGE WITH PANACHE**
THE LATEST TRENDS IN SELF-INDUCED VOMITING

**EVEN MORE MEN ARE PIGS THAN YOU THOUGHT**

**MAKE LOVE THE RENEE ZELLWEGER WAY!**

YOU'LL NEVER LOOK LIKE HER, BUT KEEP TRYING

OUR EDITOR HAS A LOT MORE MONEY THAN YOU DO

**SELF-TAUGHT GRAPHIC DESIGNERS ARE HOT!**
SUBSCRIBE NOW AND YOU MAY WIN SOMEONE ELSE'S HUSBAND

"Wrong, smarty-pants," I shot back. "I know for a fact, being a guy, that the only thing male audience members care about is the shape of Renée's booty. Sorry, Renée."

"Oh that's okay," she said, starting to doubt her outfit.

"This is a date flick, Bruce," Sandra argued. "Seventy-five percent of the viewers will be female."

"Well, whatever the percentage, if you want to get men in theater seats, you'd better dish up some serious eye candy."

Sandra shot me a "shut your mouth, or I'll shut it for you" look.

"What about the waist, Sandra?" Renée asked. "Do you think it needs to be tapered more?"

"It's fine, Renée — very flattering. You have to ride a horse, don't forget. It has to be practical. Don't listen to this blowhard."

"Okay, let me ask you both a fundamental question: When a woman gets dolled up for a night on the town, does she wear the sexy outfit for herself, or for the enjoyment of men?"

Renée bit her lip out of bewilderment. "Well, it depends on what the goal of the evening is, doesn't it?"

Sandra, eager to use almost any topic as a means of shutting me down, jumped right in. "For herself," she stated flatly. "If a woman feels sexy, the man will pick up on it."

"Okay, let's run with that scenario," I offered. "Renée, do you feel sexy in that outfit?"

"What kind of a question is that?" Sandra asked indignantly. "Of course she does."

"Why don't we let Renée answer for herself, Sandra?"

Renée looked at herself in the mirror and hesitated. "Well, it's certainly cute...."

"Cute? Yes. Sexy? No. Normally, I think you're sexy as hell, Renée, but I'm not picking up any vibes from you." I turned to Sandra. "You want my honest opinion?"

"No."

Ignoring her dismissal, I appealed to Renée. "Most of the guys I know who get the wood for you —"

Look, kids, it's the official Renée Zellweger magnetic dress up kit!

"Excuse me?" Renée said.

"Well, you can't expect paying customers not to treat you like a commodity. They cough up the dough, they want to see the goods. I'll bet fan mail from men spiked when you did *Bridget Jones's Diary*."

"Well, it did, actually,"

Renée acknowledged. "But I assumed it was because they liked my acting."

"You were great in the movie, Renée," I assured her. "But guys liked you because there was *more of you to like*."

"I am *not* gaining thirty pounds ever again," Renée said, shaking her index finger at me. "Not counting sequels, of course."

"I'm not suggesting that at all, but there are plenty of ways to get more of the hourglass thing going."

"This I'd love to hear from the B movie expert," Sandra said, probably wishing that I had been run over by a bus on the way to the fitting.

"Well, we did this film called *Army of Darkness*, and Dino De Laurentiis, the producer, was used to actresses from the fifties, with curves that went on for days. The only way we could get a starlet approved by him was to make her look like she had a twelve-point rack, if you know what I mean."

"Renée has a beautiful bust," Sandra insisted.

"Could have fooled me," I said, casually sitting in one of the overstuffed chairs.

"And what would you have us do? Foam-inject her like a molding process?" Sandra wondered sarcastically.

"Nah, you stuff a few gel sacs into a larger bra and walk away."

"Okay, it's official — you disgust me," Sandra said, turning away.

"No, I hear what he's saying," Renée said, trying to bring Sandra back to the table. "You want to try it and see? Isn't that what these fittings are for — to experiment?"

Sandra paused for a second, then looped her measuring tape around her neck. "All right, you want boobs? I'll give you boobs."

Within ten minutes, Renée was virtually bursting out of her

MAKE LOVE!... THE BRUCE CAMPBELL WAY

riding outfit in all the right ways. She walked back and forth in front of the mirror, taking in the new look.

"Tell me this isn't better, Sandra," I said, impressed at what they had pulled off in such a short time.

"Okay, it isn't —"

"I love it!" Renée said, cutting in. "It's provocative and pronounced."

"Well, honestly, neither of you count," Sandra said. "This is a case where an outside opinion is needed."

"But all the men who work here are gay," I protested.

"Sure, but they know a thing or two about sexy."

"Sorry, Sandra, not when it comes to women. I'll find a straight man for you."

I looked toward the entrance and saw a bicycle messenger getting a signature for a package.

"Excuse me, sir," I said, approaching him, "You're not gay, are you?"

"No," the messenger said, a little put off. "Why?"

"We could really use your help with something. Have you heard of Renée Zellweger, the actress?"

"Sure. She's a babe."

"Would you like to see what she's going to wear in her new film?"

"Shit yeah, dude, are you serious?"

I grabbed the messenger and walked him to the fitting area. As we rounded the corner, his jaw dropped. "Whoa" was all he could say.

Renée's face lit up.

"Tell us what you think," I prodded the messenger. "Be descriptive."

"Well, it's tight, and she's awesome. She looks like that chick from *Tomb Raider*."

"Very descriptive, thank you very much," I said.

The messenger started to fidget. He was wearing tight bicycle shorts and Renée's appearance was challenging his "comfort."

"Hey, well, if that's all you need me for, I'd better get going," he said, hurrying to the exit, messenger bag shielding his growing embarrassment.

"I rest my case," I said to Sandra, trying not to be smug.

"A" MOVIE STAR    "B" MOVIE STAR

"Hard to argue with that," Renée agreed, slightly uncomfortable. "I think we may have to take a second look at the other outfits."

Sandra looked at me with disdain. "Perhaps Mr. Campbell would like to stay and comment while we go through them all over again?"

"Oh, could you, Bruce?" Renée asked excitedly.

"Sure," I said, winking at Sandra. "How did these A-list productions ever get along without me?"

# 13

# Midlife Miasma

When I was a kid, I had recurring "failure" dreams. If I were playing baseball, for example, I could smack the ball deep into the outfield, but I wouldn't be able to round the bases. Or, I'd be chopping wood, but just as the axe met its target, the blade would turn sideways. Prepping for *Let's Make Love!*, my failure dreams revolved around the telephone. The calls were always important, but the phone would ring and ring because I could only hear it faintly, like it was off in the distance, and by the time I got to it, the caller hung up.

I heard the phone ring again that morning and, as always, it was a thousand miles away. But the sound grew, and soon the phone was only a hundred miles away, then a hundred feet, then it was up on my nightstand...where it had been all along.

The early morning caller was Mike, my fearless — and relentless — leader. "Good morning, Bruce. It's Mike. I assume you're already up."

"Uh, yeah...of course," I said, trying to lubricate my dry mouth enough to form a sentence.

"Listen, I'm in the middle of a production meeting so I can't talk long. We're adding a car chase at the end of scene seventy-two, and we were about to pick a car, but it just occurred to me that Foyl is the one who chooses the car for Harry."

"You want me to choose the car for the chase?"

"No, I want your *character* to choose the car. We're playing for keeps here, Bruce, work with us."

"Yeah, sure, sure, how do you want me to go about it?"

"Quickly. I'm sending you to Dallas. Ever been there?"

"Uh, yeah, once — and why there?"

"It's home of the single largest car dealership in the nation. If you can't find Harry's car there, you can't find it. June, my secretary — you remember her — she'll meet you at the dealership to take notes, arrange payment, etcetera."

"Okay...when?"

"Today. People will call you about all that. Have fun. Get busy."

*Click.* Mike was done.

There were several things I noticed while shooting a film in Dallas a few years ago. First, the place was flat. Architects love it, because there are no mountains, rivers, or oceans to "distract" from their designs. That's why, architecturally speaking, you see so many weird buildings spread willy-nilly across the city.

Second, the world's largest car dealership made sense in Dallas because you've got your oil-drilling fat cats (still living off money they made two decades ago) and your general assortment of fortune seekers in a regulation-be-damned town.

I met June in the football-field-size, fry-an-egg-hot parking lot of Mid-Life Motors. I can't use their real name for legal reasons, so let's just stick with that. It wasn't hard to spot the sales manager, Duff Jenkins, Jr. His hair was perfect, his moustache was perfect, and his "I ain't got a care in the world" smile was perfect.

On this bright day, Duff wore a white cowboy hat that was impossible to view directly without protective eyewear. His suit was a hybrid of sorts — shit kicker meets city slicker: a silver sharkskin jacket and pants; a sky blue shirt with a string tie; an oversize longhorn buckle attached to a belt that was cinched tight around his expanding "shot and a beer" belly.

Duff was the number-one car salesman in Dallas, five years running. His hand was extended easily a dozen feet before we actually shook.

"Mr. Campbell?"

"Bruce'll do just fine."

"Duff Jenkins, Jr. Nice to meet you, sir. I sure loved *Cisco Kid.*"

"*Brisco.* Uh, Duff, this is June — she works with the director."

Duff nodded politely. "Missy."

"June will be fine," she said curtly.

"Sure, okay. Now, you're doin' some re-search for a film, or whatnot?"

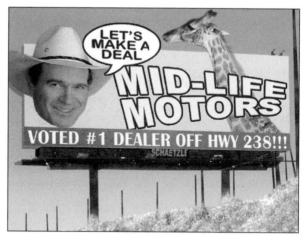

"Yes," I said. "I need to pick a car for an upper-middle-class, recently divorced man who wants to redefine himself."

Duff winked. "Got just the thing."

We walked to the "Import" section, where a canary yellow Subaru Baja sparkled in the sun. Duff went right into his thing:

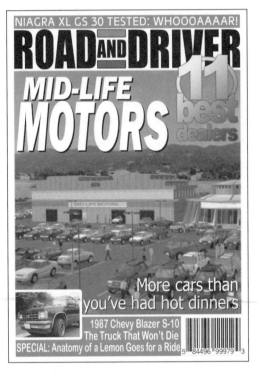

NIAGRA XL GS 30 TESTED: WHOOOAAAAR!

# ROAD AND DRIVER

## MID-LIFE MOTORS

11 best dealers

More cars than you've had hot dinners

1987 Chevy Blazer S-10
The Truck That Won't Die

SPECIAL: Anatomy of a Lemon Goes for a Ride

5 84496 99979 3

"Subaru Baja Sport — turbo-charged, sixteen valve, single overhead camshaft, all-wheel drive."

"Okay, so what does this car say about the guy who buys it?" I asked.

"It depends," Duff pondered. "How old is he?"

I wasn't sure, and I glanced at June.

"Fifty-ish," she said.

Duff sucked air through his teeth like he just saw a dog get hit by a car. "In that case, it says 'I'm fifty trying to be eighteen again.'"

I shook my head. "Nope. Not quite right. He's having a midlife crisis, but he's not that desperate."

"I'll tell you a secret," Duff confided. "Thank God for men like him because he keeps men like me in business. I was just at a sales conference in St. Louis, and the keynote address was about the economics of a midlife crisis."

Duff walked us over to a small, stylish BMW. "The 2004 BMW MX9. The Bond car. Pierce Brosnan himself drives one."

"Yeah, because the car company gave him one for free."

Duff gestured to the rear of the car. "Notice that there is virtually no room for luggage of any kind. The man who drives this car doesn't want any more *baggage*."

"Interesting." I looked at June, and she was already jotting notes. "But the character we're buying for isn't that irrelevant."

Duff had obviously heard every reason ever given *not* to like (and therefore buy) a car. "This car gives you precision crafts-manship, ergonomics, and an on-board nav system. These features are not 'irrelevant,' Bruce, they are timeless."

"Duff, I can't blame you for trying. This car was cool for a couple years, but it's very 'then.' Let's move on to something new and different."

Duff steered us toward the cars closest to the main show-room — the high-end section. "The Lexus XL 5. Top of the line," he said with his trademark right-handed, palm-up presentation. "This car says CEO of a Fortune 500 company."

I hopped into the Lexus and had a look around. The interior was plush as hell, with heavenly seats and an instrument panel befitting a small airplane.

"You're right, I feel like a CEO."

Duff continued his pitch from outside the car. "I've sold this car not only to CEOs, but to politicians, athletes, movie stars —"

"Yeah, but it's not right. My guy isn't a CEO, and he isn't an asshole."

"Beg pardon?" Duff asked, taken aback.

June looked up from her notes.

"When I see them on the road," I explained, "they're driven by well-dressed, stern-looking guys, usually accompanied by some face-lifted, bottle blonde who looks miserable. This is also the kind of car you're most likely to see parked illegally in a handicap spot, or sideways, taking up three spaces. Close, but no cigar."

"Damn, this friend of yours is a picky sumbitch, ain't he," Duff said, suppressing his anger, "'cause we sell these like hot-cakes."

Duff led me across the lot to the "muscle" section and ges-tured to a silver behemoth. "Here you go, Bruce. No man can resist the temptation of a Dodge Niagra 4X4 2500 XL GS 30 twin cab."

Huge is a word that is overused, but I'm going to use it — the truck was huge.

"This Dodge could fit that Baja in the back bed," Duff continued. "It's got three hundred and forty-five horsepower, with a Hemi Magnum V8 standard. By owning this car, you say to the world: Get out of my way."

"By owning this car, you say to the world: I have a needle dick," I countered.

June dug the tip of her No. 2 pencil into her legal pad.

Duff looked at me like he hadn't heard properly. "Come again?"

"The guys who drive these gigantic trucks are all little Napoleon bastards. They can't get it up, so they put a monster under their gonads. I'd be afraid that women would think my friend was impotent if he drove that truck. Christ, in a few years, he'd need a handicap ramp just to get up into it."

Duff invaded my personal eighteen-inch bubble to ask a question. "Bruce, does your friend suffer from erectile problems?"

"Actually, Duff, I have no damn idea. What kind of a question is that?"

"It's been clinically proven that the tire-to-frame vibrations from this truck stimulate blood flow to the extremities of the body, and I think you know what I'm talking about." Duff cracked a Texas-wide smile and rocked on the heels of his boots. "Not to mention what it does for the little lady. There's a reason why it's our number-one seller."

"I can think of cheaper ways to get a hard-on."

"C'mon, now," Duff said, holding up a puffy, ringed finger. "Don't make fun until you've tried it. Get up in there, take it for a spin around the parking lot, and then tell me I'm crazy."

I thought about de-clining, but my Motor City sensibilities made me weak. "Okay, Duff, sure — once around the parking lot."

Duff grinned and winked at June, who turned away, mildly horrified.

I climbed into the truck's elevated cab. Looking out, I could see the entire parking lot. Feeling like the king of my vehicular domain, I started the Dodge and revved the engine like a sixteen-year-old in a Wal-Mart parking lot.

Whoooaaaar!

*Wow, that was smooth.*

I did it again.

WHOOOOAAAAAA AHHHHHRRRR!!!

June stepped back a couple feet, cringing at the loud noise and Duff, ever the gentleman, grabbed her by the elbow.

Duff Jenkins Jr. modeling the megalithic Niagra 4x4.

"Do you know what I think when I see this car?" Duff shouted over the heavy idling. "I think strength, I think rugged reliability."

I've got to drive this monster, I convinced myself.

I shifted into "D" and let my foot off the brake. The powerful engine propelled the truck forward. I pressed the gas, but the truck didn't lurch like my ranch junker — it was smooth, like a sports car. The tachometer bounced as I revved, braked, and turned my way around the parking lot.

It didn't take long for a tingle to work its way across me. The entire truck was vibrating like a coin-operated mattress. I swung around in front of June and Duff, but I couldn't bring myself to stop. His B.S. about what the truck does for the male species wasn't B.S. at all — I had a hard-on that would impress my dad. I turned beet red from embarrassment, but I found myself laughing at the same time. Soon, I was laughing so hard, I had to roll up my windows. The more I drove around the parking lot, the harder I laughed, and the harder I got. It was an insane scenario that caused a near miss with a Lamborghini.

"Ha-ha-ha!!!" I laughed. *I'm driving a real truck!*

Duff was laughing too. "I'll start the paperwork," he called.

I put the truck in park and wiped the tears of joy from my eyes. Towering above a row of brand-new Hummers in front of me, I felt like some sort of fuel-injected deity. Even the small, red pickup truck speeding along next to them amused me.

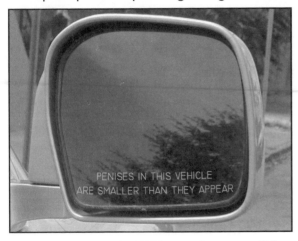

*There is room for all vehicles, big and small, in my SUV kingdom.*

Then I noticed that two masked men in the bed of the pickup were dumping liquid on the Hummers as they passed each one.

*Holy ecoterrorist, something bad is about to —*

*KA-WHUMP!* The entire row of Hummers became engulfed in ten-foot-high flames.

"Lord almighty!" Duff screamed, losing his hat from the concussion. He grabbed his cell phone and dabbed out 9-1-1.

June stumbled back and slammed into the side of a BMW. She dropped to the ground, notes scattering.

The little red truck screeched out of the parking lot and down a residential side street. From my high vantage point, I could see exactly where the ecoterrorists were heading. Intent on cutting them off, I put the Dodge in gear and hit the gas.

The red truck was quick. More important, it wasn't as wide as my all-terrain oil tanker and fit neatly down a narrow alley. There was no way to follow, but I could blaze my own trail across a nearby backyard. I slipped the Dodge into low gear and roared across the freshly sodded yard, narrowly avoiding a kiddie pool and an angry pit bull.

I emerged out about ten lengths behind the red truck on a short straightaway and opened the monster up. The ensuing rush of speed was better than any truck commercial could possibly convey. Within seconds, I was poised to ram the destructive little fuckers off the road, but glancing down, I realized that I was also poised to embarrass myself.

*Enough with the vibrations already!* I thought.

Ecowarriors must prepare for various scenarios, in case their destroy-in-order-to-save-the-world plan goes awry, and these guys were on their game. Bags of nails and glass bottles hailed down on the road behind their truck. Consequently, I was too busy avoiding punctured tires to notice the Molotov cocktail sailing through the air, but I did perk up when it shattered on my front hood and erupted into a wall of flames.

I couldn't see through the inferno, but I knew I was reasonably close to their truck, so I opted for one last hurrah and jammed the gas pedal to the floor. The V8 propelled the Dodge forward, engaging the passing gear, and I hit something, *hard.*

The impact blew out the gasoline fire, revealing the crippled mass of the red truck, spinning out of control. My truck had nailed it square in the back and sent it careening down a steep grass embankment, directly toward oncoming traffic.

I turned my attention toward my own vehicle, which was lurching irrevocably toward the same fate. The two front tires had blown from the collision, reducing navigation to a cruel joke. I jammed on the brakes as hard as I could, but from the lack of response, I knew right away that inertia was not to be overcome.

With no other choice, I kicked open the door and jumped out as the truck reached the lip of the hill. I tried to hit the ground running, but I misjudged the rate of travel and my legs were swept out from under me. I connected with Mother Earth at an awkward angle, and momentum kept me tumbling on the hard-scrabble for what seemed like a hundred yards. Ahead of me, the Dodge rolled out of sight, and the rest could only be heard — the terrified screams, the twisting metal, the report of a huge explosion. Things didn't sound good for the ecoterrorists.

By the time I limped back to Mid-Life Motors, the gigantic fire was almost out. Duff and June had collected themselves and were giving interviews to the local police. The recent turn of events convinced me that I had found the right car.

"June, pay the man," I said. "I'm going to drive the Dodge back to New York."

Word traveled fast about the Hummer incident, so by the time I rolled the truck up to the loading dock behind Mike's brownstone, the production office was ready with an impromptu celebration. I revved the beefy engine to the delight of the assembled cast and crew, which included Mike, June (taking notes, now with a bandaged elbow), Richard, and even Renée.

I jumped out of the truck, stood on the hood, and raised my arms in victory. Instead of applause, there was a slight gasp from the crowd. In all the activity, I had forgotten the side effects of a long road trip in that particular vehicle.

Renée blushed. "Well, at least you're happy to see us, Bruce," she said, staring unabashedly at my emboldened manliness. It was the first time she got my name right — and the last time she ever forgot it.

# 14

# Testing, Testing, One, Two, Three...

The next morning, safely back in the land of *Let's Make Love!*, the next thing on our preproduction agenda was a camera test. Unlike low-budget movies, which tend to eliminate any proce-dure that costs money, big movies test everything before filming begins — cameras, lighting, even how the actors look in makeup and wardrobe.

I've always enjoyed the testing process, because it's more of a social event than a work day. The studio Mike used was big enough to accommodate plenty of film equipment, but it was small enough not to be intimidating. I took a sip of Earl Grey tea and walked to a designated mark on the floor, decked out in full doorman splendor.

The camera crew was led by the great cameraman Vilmos Zsigmond. He is without a doubt one of the greatest living cin-ematographers. What I respect about Vilmos, apart from his distinctive, natural lighting style, is the fact that he got his start filming low-budget exploitation movies.

"You know, Vilmos, as much as I like your work on *The Deer Hunter* and *Close Encounters*, I also really liked what you did with *Echo of Terror*."

The title didn't immediately register with Vilmos.

"Also known as *Psycho a Go-Go*," I added.

"Oh, years ago, you mean," he said with a slight Hungarian accent. "Yes, yes, 1965."

"That's the one," I confirmed. "You had some wicked handheld sequences in that, and they were not the annoying kind — yours were focused and sharp."

"Yes, we did quite a bit of it," Vilmos said, lighting up at the fond memory. "That was hard on the shoulders, that one, carrying a goddamn Mitchell camera around all day. You know, we had seven days to shoot the whole thing."

"Get out of here. It looked way too good for that."

"Thank you. I developed something of a natural style because so many movies I worked on didn't have the time or money to light."

"Are you going to do any cool handheld shots in this production?" I asked.

Vilmos shook his head, somewhat resigned to his high-end movie fate. "No. Not this time around. This is a Hollywood movie. We're going for *pretty*."

"But scene seventy-seven, where Foyl chases Harry down the street dodging traffic, could play really well handheld, don't you think?"

"I know, believe me, I talked to Mike about this already."

"What's this?" Mike asked from across the room. He was known for caninelike hearing. "Is someone saying my name?"

Vilmos explained as Mike joined us. "Well, it's the sequence with the traffic. Bruce and I were just longing for some handheld in the middle of it."

"Really? You're not sold on the 'long-lens-keep-our-distance' approach?"

"Of course, that will still work," Vilmos reasoned, "but handheld might be a good way to put the audience in the middle of the chaos."

I almost brought up Vilmos's applicable work in *Wild and Willing* (also '65), but I decided not to be the expert; I was happy just to have introduced the topic.

"Well, on the day, we might do a pass at that," Mike said, waffling a bit. "But let's keep the telephoto stuff on hand."

Vilmos took this film off his résumé a long time ago.

"Of course, sure," Vilmos assured Mike.

A peculiar feeling came over me as I watched these two legends interact. There was a mutual respect there, a reciprocity of esteem that momentarily raised the grubby business of moviemaking to an art. This, I realized, was why I was here. I wanted to be acknowledged by these men as a fellow artisan, a laborer in the machinery of the sublime. Desperate to make an impression, I used the tools I had. "You know, you could go shaky cam," I blurted.

There was a brief silence as both men took in this suggestion. I was certain that a "mind your own fucking business" speech was on its way, but I was pleasantly surprised:

"What is a shaky cam?" Vilmos asked, curious.

"It's just a camera mounted in the middle of a two-by-four with a bolt. You get a guy on either end of the board, and it becomes pretty stable. You can screw bicycle grips to the ends if you want, but the cool effect is that you can be chasing someone, like Foyl and Harry, through traffic, and the camera can rise up and glide over things, like taxicabs, garbage cans, people — whatever. A Steadicam operator can't do that. It also works great for demon P.O.V. shots."

"Ever work with one of these shaky cams, Vilmos?" Mike asked gamely, ignoring my last comment.

"No, but it sounds like it might give a great perspective above the traffic, so you can see the chase."

"I agree," Mike said. "Let's check it out. You're just full of good ideas today, aren't you, Foyl?"

"Well, I just reread the script again last night, and I got curious about things. Like, uh, how were you going to do the scene where the concierge falls out the window?"

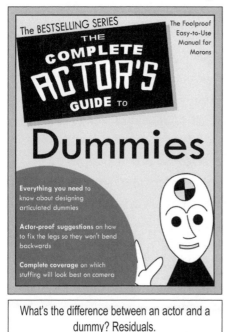

What's the difference between an actor and a dummy? Residuals.

Mike and Vilmos looked at each other. "Same as we planned," Mike explained. "A high fall stunt that the second unit crew will shoot."

There was another silence as I considered his approach. "I was kind of hoping you were going to use a dummy."

Vilmos couldn't help but snicker, and I turned to him. "If you can use a dummy in *Deliverance*, Vilmos, you can use one on this film," I scolded.

"There was a dummy in *Deliverance*?" Mike asked Vilmos.

"There was," Vilmos admitted. "Just a quick shot. It was too dangerous of a stunt. This kid has a good eye."

"There was also a dummy used in *Bridge on the River Kwai*," I explained.

"Really?" Mike asked. "In a David Lean film? I always associated dummies with cheap and cheesy."

"They're cheap all right, Mike. They're one of the cheapest, most effective special effects around. A dummy can do what a stuntman will never attempt," I argued, basking in the director's attentive gaze. "I was thinking a dummy, because in the script it described as 'a blur, happening out of the corner of Harry's eye.' It read funny to me, and nothing says comedy like a dummy, as long as the arms and legs don't bend backward."

Mike whirled to June, who always manages to stay nearby, yet never too close. "June, remind me to put in a call to Marty Sossin, the mechanical effects guy, about a dummy." Mike turned back, every bit the energized director. "Okay, Vilmos, Foyl, let's shoot this thing!"

As makeup, wardrobe, and hair did their final touches, Vilmos turned to Karen, his very butch camera assistant. "Take the camera off sticks. I want to shoot this test handheld."

When Mike heard that, he looked up from his monitor. "I like that, Vilmos. It's gritty. It's New York."

"I thought you might," Vilmos said, slipping a pad on his shoulder and hoisting the Arriflex camera up. "This is a lot lighter than a Mitchell, I can tell you."

Mike stood on his feet. He expected to see a bit of my character, Foyl, come out today. "Foyl? You ready for this?" he asked. "Are you feeling handheld?"

"Any time, sir," I said, slipping into a southern gentleman drawl.

"Okay, let's have it. Let's have the back story — action!"

And I was happy to oblige, riffing for long periods about my character, and the world according to him. Meanwhile, Vilmos was getting very creative in the handheld arena, dropping low at times, getting up close at others, all to Mike's great delight.

"And...cut!" he shouted. "Good, Bruce. You've been doing your homework!"

"Thanks Mike," I said, more relieved than I sounded.

Mike turned his attention to Vilmos, now sweaty from the camerawork. "You old dog, that was really effective. Let's talk about this shaky cam...."

Mike escorted Vilmos to the craft service table, chatting excitedly about camera techniques. I was filled with pride, knowing that in my own humble way, I had influenced their conversation.

People tend to make fun of low-budget movies, often because they lack the smooth sophistication of slick Hollywood fare. But what the average viewer fails to recognize is that low-budget movies, with almost nothing to lose, are far more likely to push the creative envelope. Granted, most of them fall flat on their face because of poor writing, choppy editing, and bad acting, but you have to love them for trying.

Before *Let's Make Love!*, I used to think that working on high-budget movies was boring, simply because they never tried anything new or daring. I also felt slightly out-of-touch working on blockbuster movies, mainly because the process of making them tends to be impersonal. But after a few weeks hacking around this interesting Mike Nichols movie, I hadn't had a boring day yet and, best of all, I was beginning to feel like I was part of something special.

# 15

# Seven Brides for Seven Husbands

Richard Gere's character, Harry, gets divorced in the first scene of the film, and Foyl, the trusty doorman, is there to counsel him. Having been through the big D once myself, I wasn't willing to do it again in the name of research, but I could sure talk to an expert on the subject.

America is full of multidivorced people, but few can hold a candle to the queen of Splitsville, Elizabeth Taylor. As fate would have it, Ms. Taylor was slated to appear in *Let's Make Love!* as Richard Gere's mother, and she was staying in New York City at my old stomping grounds, the Waldorf.

I knew the chances of actually scoring an interview were pretty slim, so I hinged my plea on the fact that I was a costar doing research, not a reporter digging up dirt.

"Hey, everyone's gotta eat," were the first words out of Elizabeth Taylor's mouth over the phone. "What are you doing tonight?"

"Having dinner with you, Ms. Taylor," I said, sounding cool, yet pumping my fist in the air silently.

Elizabeth Taylor is about as close to royalty as you can get in the States, so she feels comfortable in really nice places, like the newly restored Visaro restaurant in the Waldorf. We agreed to meet for dinner at seven o'clock. I wore the best suit I could find, but I still felt like a homeless person as I stepped out of my cab in front of the famed hotel.

Waiting dutifully was Vinnie, a fellow doorman during my single day of work. "Well, well, well," he said, with a wry smile. "If it isn't John Hinckley, Jr. What brings you back here?"

"I'll have you know, Vinnie, I'm here as a guest."

"Okay, well, try not to start another incident, 'cause a certain you-know-who is coming here again tonight."

"No shit, Colin Pow —?"

"Ix-nay, Owell-pay," Vinnie said, hushed.

I nodded silently, then looked at him expectantly. "Aren't you forgetting something?"

Vinnie looked around, then realized he hadn't opened the hotel door. "Oh, sorry, man," he said, swinging it open wide.

I tipped him a buck and stepped inside. The Visaro restaurant, which was across the lobby, looked like a movie set: well-

Acting for Dummies: boning up on Elizabeth Taylor.

dressed extras eating fine cuisine in low light. I approached a stuffy-looking fellow about locating my date.

"Good evening, my good man."

"Good evening, sir," he said in a thick English accent. "May I help you?"

I have a theory about why there are so many English chaps working as hosts and receptionists in New York and Los Angeles: It's because there are truckloads of unemployed British actors in both cities, many from the Royal Shakespeare Company, and what else are they going to do to pay the rent? Rich enclaves tend to max out on the pretension thing, and nothing fits that image better than a snooty English fellow who isn't particularly interested in helping.

"You sure can, slick," I said casually. "I'm here to sup with Ms. Elizabeth Taylor — you know, the movie star?"

"Of course I do. You must be Mr. Campbell. Right this way. Ms. Taylor is already here."

Yikes, I thought to myself. I thought only people from Michigan showed up early.

The maitre d' led me to a quiet, corner booth. Seated alone was Elizabeth Taylor. My knees buckled a bit when I saw her for the first time, just thinking about all the movies she's been in, from the epic bomb *Cleopatra* to one of my all time favorites, *Who's Afraid of Virginia Woolf?* Even in her golden years, Liz was still pretty and elegant. She held out her hand as I approached the table.

"Hello, dear, you must be Bruce."

"Yes, ma'am. It's a real pleasure to meet you."

"I'd get up, but my hips aren't what they used to be."

"Oh, that's quite all right, uh, how should I address you? Ms. Taylor? Dame Taylor?"

"Liz is fine," she said with a smile. "Dame makes me sound like an old battle-axe."

"Although you must have enjoyed being crowned."

"Oh, it was marvelous — so opulent, deeply opulent," Liz said.

"When I heard you were crowned, I thought to myself, well,

from one Queen Elizabeth to another."

"Oh, you dear man, sit down right next to me," Liz said, patting the chair nearby. "Jules, let's get some iced tea for this charmer."

Jules, the snooty English fellow, didn't quibble with Liz. He nodded and was gone in two seconds.

"I gather from your note that you're playing Foyl, the doorman," Liz said.

"Right, and since he's full of relationship advice, I thought I could round out my research by talking to you, a woman who's, uh —"

"Been around the block?" Liz offered.

"Well, you have had quite the life."

"With quite the men, yes." Liz nodded. "I'm sure I'm the perfect subject. Where do you want to start?"

"Well, let's see, you've been married seven times."

"Have I? I lost count," Liz said, obviously numb from the amount of times she's talked about this.

"I just want to know what it is about marriage you enjoy so much, seeing as how you went through the process so many times. Most people would have stopped riding that horse after the third or fourth time."

"Well, if you fall off a horse, you have to get right back on, don't you, or you might never want to ride again — I learned that from *National Velvet*. I like the company of men, I don't hide that. I find them to be fascinating creatures."

Liz finished her last words while looking directly at me. I'd like to flatter myself in thinking that her burning, violet-eyed stare, the one that went right through me, was the result of my wit and obvious charms. Sadly, Liz is just a dynamic woman — when she looks at you, you know it. I guess that's why she's a movie star. My trance was broken by Jules, returning Liz's iced tea.

"And Jules, could you fetch me some Sweet 'n Low?" Liz asked sweetly.

"Of course, ma'am. I'll *fetch* it right away," he said, turning on a heel, briskly.

Liz watched him go approvingly, then turned to me. "I don't even use Sweet 'n Low, I just love to watch him walk."

I cleared my throat and continued. "I applaud your attraction to men, being one of them myself, but that doesn't mean you have to get married in each case."

"No, but I was married for the first time in 1950. In those days, if you dated a man for any length of time, you were more than likely to end up married. I was eighteen, but that wasn't unusual then, except for the fact that I was a movie star. Movie stars were expected to make a little whoopee before they tied the knot. You're married, aren't you?"

"Yes ma'am, second time around."

Liz held her hand up to her mouth in shock. "Oh, you've been divorced?"

"Yeah, I'm afraid I have," I said, enjoying her antics.

"And how long did you know her before you got married?"

"Whose interview is this, Liz?" I asked.

"Shush, answer the question."

"A year — she was married when we met."

Liz held up her hand again in horror. "Oh, the scandal!"

"Wait, it wasn't like that," I explained. "For the first six months I just worked with her."

"I'd like another husband, please."

0046 1070+1@  KIF3 4539  3936+1@

6T00:08:36:12     R200:00:04:09

"Hold that goddamned cue card closer, moron!"

"Okay, so you broke up a marriage and got hitched six months later. I don't feel so bad now."

I opened my mouth to explain the situation, but Jules arrived with her Sweet 'n Low.

"Here you are, ma'am."

"Thank you, darling."

Jules walked away and Liz watched him go, a faint smile across her classic lips.

"Liz, I ran the numbers the other day. You've been married seven times, encompassing about thirty-three or so years. That's an average of almost five years per marriage."

"Yes, but my goodness, if I wasn't an actress, I wouldn't have been married nearly as many times. Every party I went to — and in those days you couldn't say no because it was all arranged by the studios — I'd meet rich men, and famous men, and powerful men. It was all too irresistible. Hollywood, in its day, was just one big playground."

"Yes, you have had your share of each of those types. First time around, it seems like you went for the money."

"You're referring to Nicky Hilton — Conrad, Jr."

"Son of the hotel magnate, yeah."

"Nicky was a combination of things," Liz said. "He was very cool, a classic playboy. He would do crazy things like get his father's jet and take us to Miami for the weekend. As an eighteen-year-old, what did I know? It was all marvelous. The studio fought it at first, but they relented and, of course, I got married in a studio wedding dress."

"Membership has its privileges."

Liz smiled, but it was slightly sad. "And then, of course, it all turned to custard."

"Out of eight months with Nicky, how many were good?"

"Was that all it was? You've done your research?"

"I have, and yeah, it was. If it's any consolation, my wife has a friend who stayed married only four months."

"Some marriages just burn hot, then burn out."

"Then you married an actor, for God's sake."

"Yes, Michael Wilding. I thought he was gorgeous."

"There must have been more than that — you had several children with him."

"Well, because we were in the same profession, we just had so much in common. And he was so charming with his British accent. Jules reminds me a bit of Michael."

"That marriage was about four and a half years," I elaborated. "Just about the average. I love the fact that Michael was, at one time, a stand-in for Douglas Fairbanks, Jr."

"Well, you have to start somewhere, Mr. *Evil Death*."

"*Evil Dead*. You've heard of those films?"

"I've heard about them but I haven't seen them. It's a chain-saw film, isn't it, lots of gore?"

"Yeah, that's the one," I said, sipping some tea to wet my dry throat. "But next time out of the gate, you went higher up the food chain. You went for a producer."

"Yes, and that was the beginning of what I call the scandal years. All the hoopla hid the fact that I was still marrying these people, it wasn't like I was just shacking up. Have you ever lived with a woman, Bruce?"

"Uh, well, yes, I have."

This time, when Liz put her hand up to her mouth in shock, I

Make Love!... The Bruce Campbell Way

joined in and we performed it in sync.

"Now, Mike Todd was a big thinker, a pioneer of sorts. His company, Todd-AO, developed the 65-millimeter film frame thingamajig. It was the best big-screen system in its day."

"You know, women are attracted to men for all kinds of reasons," Liz explained. "But I always liked men who had a plan. Besides, that marriage doesn't really count, because Mike was taken away from me," she said, dabbing her brilliant blue eyes with a tissue.

"You obviously loved the guy."

"I sure did. He was loud and bombastic, but he got things done. He was one guy who never crapped around."

"I guess things got sticky later with Eddie Fisher."

"Well, sure, because Eddie was Mike Todd's best man, and he was married to Debbie Reynolds, a national treasure. You couldn't have planned a more ludicrous scandal, but it all happened pretty organically."

"What was the appeal of Eddie Fisher at that time?"

"You can't be serious. Eddie was bigger than Elvis Presley in his day. He had one of the largest endorsement contracts ever. People always talk about me getting a million bucks for *Cleopatra*. Granted, that was a lot of money in the sixties, but it was a lot more when Eddie got that much from Coca-Cola in the *fifties*! I didn't know the world drank that much Coke. I went for Eddie because the rest of America was after him too."

"But he had a lot to lose at that point. You at least were coming from a sympathetic situation."

"Sure. Eddie had a lot to lose, and he lost it all. Love is a gamble. Eddie knew that to divorce his terrific wife in the fifties, he would face repercussions, and he sure did, bless him."

"Of course, he wasn't jumping ship for chopped liver exactly," I corrected. "There are a lot of men who would take a leap for you, Liz."

"Oh, you delightful man, you," she said, playfully pinching my cheek.

"But by your own calculations, that marriage actually *exceeded* the average. You were married to Eddie for five years."

"I guess I was," Liz said with a nod. "Not bad for a tabloid marriage. Eddie and I had been around the block even before this blew up. You learn to develop a stomach for the scrutiny, the pressure. I'd love to see what would happen to the average marriage if they were photographed and written about twenty-four hours a day."

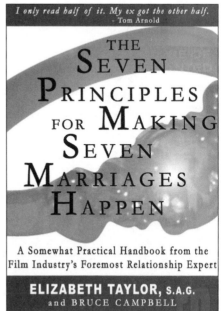

*I only read half of it. My ex got the other half.*
- Tom Arnold

THE
SEVEN
PRINCIPLES
FOR MAKING
SEVEN
MARRIAGES
HAPPEN

A Somewhat Practical Handbook from the Film Industry's Foremost Relationship Expert

**ELIZABETH TAYLOR, S.A.G.**
and BRUCE CAMPBELL

"They have a TV show like that now."

"Oh that's dreadful," Liz said, truly horrified. "You know, Richard and I put up with a lot of scrutiny, both professionally and as a couple."

"I'm assuming you're referring to Richard Burton."

"Of course, silly."

"He seemed like a pretty dynamic guy, enough so to marry him twice."

"Dynamic, that's a fun choice of words. Yes, Richard was bigger than life. Our marriage was bigger than life. Our work during that time was bigger than life. I guess we were looking for a bigger than life experience and we found it. We fought loudly, we loved loudly, we laughed loudly, we cried loudest of all."

"It sounds very theatrical."

"Yes, it was as if we were both 'on' the whole time. It was very memorable, though. I don't regret either marriage to Richard, because he was so extraordinary. And I didn't worry about the scandal because by then everything was a scandal. I was even rebuked by the Vatican, you know."

"You got me beat there," I said. "Of course, I'm guessing the Pope hasn't seen *Evil Dead* yet."

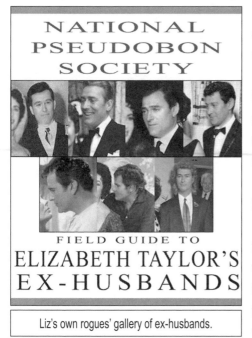

NATIONAL PSEUDOBON SOCIETY

FIELD GUIDE TO
ELIZABETH TAYLOR'S
EX-HUSBANDS

Liz's own rogues' gallery of ex-husbands.

"They published a statement denouncing my 'erotic vagrancy,'" she said proudly.

"Well, lewd behavior aside, I thought you and Richard worked really well together and that you did some great stuff during that time."

"In between the chaos, yes, I think so too," she agreed.

"Now, while I won't use the term 'love of your life,' Richard was certainly the most long-term marriage. Counting both times, you were together eleven years."

"Yes, that's the equivalent of sixty-seven years in Hollywood," Liz giggled. "It lasted that long because we were working a lot and we were working together — it kept us out of trouble. We kept the trouble between us."

"Okay, I have to ask: John Warner, husband number six. What was the deal with that?"

"What do you mean 'what's the deal?' When I was with him, he was a statesman, a powerful man, a true gentleman."

"But he doesn't seem very exciting."

"You're not up on current events," Liz countered. "John has done it all: Secretary of the Navy; work with the Defense Department; a five-term senator. You don't have to be snapping your fingers all the time to be a type-A go-getter. He had a strong will and genuine drive. I couldn't help but admire that."

"I understand he called you his 'little heifer.'"

Liz smiled. "John called me that because of how often I had a cow," and then she lifted her head, roaring with laughter. "It suited me well, I guess. I think Richard Burton would agree."

"So, there's only one husband left," I said, glancing at my crumpled list with six names crossed off.

"Now, be nice. I've heard a lot of jokes about Larry, who is a really sweet man."

"I have to say, with Larry, you really shook the pattern up. You'd been married to famous actors, singers, politicians, business moguls, but that was the first time you ever landed a teamster. You have to understand the public's fascination with that one."

"Of course — the newspapers jumped all over it," Liz said, still angry, framing the imaginary headlines with her delicate hand: QUEEN ELIZABETH MARRIES A PAUPER, LIZ FINALLY GETS HER DREAM HOME — BUILT BY LARRY! My God, it was absurd. And then there was the 'age' issue."

"I didn't want to bring it up."

"There's no way to avoid the topic. That was the second part of the scandal. It wasn't bad enough that he was 'just' a construction worker, he was also twenty years younger than me."

"Yeah, the year Larry was born, you married your second husband, Michael Wilding."

I raised my hand to my mouth, and Liz brought hers up as well — another shared, shocked moment.

"But I'll tell you what," Liz explained, "by the time Larry came along, I was ready for a man like that. The downside of a whirl-wind life is that it's a whirlwind life — you can't keep playing can-you-top-this forever. Very successful men can also be very unpleasant to be around, and Larry was just...Larry."

"Was it really that simple?"

"Yes, it was. When we met in group therapy, I wasn't there hoping to find a younger man, I was there to get sober."

"Well, something must have clicked, because you stayed married for five years."

"Aside from making his lunch every day, being married to Larry wasn't bad at all. It was the closest I've ever had to a 'normal' life."

"Okay, so the obvious question after all this is: what makes a marriage go bad?"

"I think people either oversimplify or overanalyze that concept. Divorce is different for each person. For me, marriages ended for a variety of reasons, usually a combination of growing apart, *being* apart too much, the occasional abusive situation, boredom — the same reasons anyone else gets divorced."

"What makes one work?"

"Oh, honey, I don't have any idea. I think the entire institution is something of a flawed notion."

"All right, so last question. You've had a lot of divorces. I only had one, and I barely walked away from it. How did you manage those dark days, after a divorce?"

Liz was about to answer when an incredibly fit blond man arrived at our table. Liz looked at me knowingly. "Oh, you get by," she said, gesturing to the beautiful man. "He's my head of security, aren't you, Lars?"

"Ya," he said simply.

Liz held out her hand for Lars and he helped her up. "You know, I've had a lot of heartache in my life: failed marriages, movies that bombed, health problems, I've been in and out of rehab," she said, snuggling up to Lars. "But the rest of the time, it's great to be Elizabeth Taylor. I mean, what do you expect me to do, sleep alone?"

This ageless beauty winked at me and escorted Lars back to her Waldorf penthouse. I glanced at the check ($147.40 for iced tea, a mint julep, and a fruit plate) and gasped. *Thank God for the Screen Actors Guild.* Being on location, I had a week's worth of per diem burning a hole in my pocket, so I paid the bill in cash and walked out.

FAMOUS GUY STARES AT CAMERA

HORRIBLE CREATURE TELLS ALL

ZODIAC DIET KILLS SEVENTEEN PEOPLE

**EXCLUSIVE**

St∘∘e LIZ'S NEW BOY TOY

"She Must Be Blind," Say Friends

4 53758 63086 1

They say there's no such thing as bad publicity.

On my way across the very familiar lobby, I noticed a lot of activity. Men in dark suits were prowling about the entrance, excusing their way though the usual Waldorf clientele, while keeping one finger on the communication device in their ear.

Secret Service agents are trained to notice body language. They look at hands and eyes, and take note of erratic ticks. I made eye contact with a familiar, clean-cut Agent Grunow, looked away too quickly, knew I'd made a mistake, and bolted for the exit.

"Halt!" Grunow shouted, and began running after me.

I just wanted to get the hell out of there so I decided to ignore him, and by the time we converged at the revolving doors, we were both in a full-out sprint. Grunow dove at me from behind, and our combined inertia took us through the doors and out the other side — directly into Colin Powell, who had just reached the entrance himself.

The three of us did a painful group hug down the broad steps of the Waldorf. Secret Service agents, doormen, taxi drivers, and guests all watched in horror as we rolled past the first landing and kept going down the second set of stairs.

At this point, Secret Service agents began doing what I would describe as a World Series pile on, hurling themselves at our tumbling group until we became a human mass, undulating down the steps and finally crashing to a halt by the horse-drawn carriages waiting out front.

At the bottom of the pile, I was pressed face-to-face with Colin Powell.

United States Secret Service

**MOST WANTED**

ATTEMPTED AGGRAVATED ASSAULT OF SECRETARY OF STATE; CONSPIRACY TO AGGRAVATE SECRETARY OF STATE; "JACK OF ALL TRADES"

## BRUCE L. CAMPBELL

**Aliases:** Ash, Brisco County Jr., Snooty Usher, Jack Stiles, Autolycus, Peter Perkinson, Wedding Guest, Ring Announcer, Final Shemp, Virgil, Ally McBeal, etc.

### DECRIPTION

| | | | |
|---|---|---|---|
| Date of Birth: | June 22, 1958 | Hair: | Dark Brown |
| Place of Birth: | Birmingham, MI, USA | Eyes: | Two |
| Height: | 6' 1" | Sex: | Male |
| Weight: | Variable | Complexion: | Spotty |
| Build: | Svelte | Citizenship: | USA |
| Languages: | Limited English | | |

Scars and Marks: "L"-shaped scar & mole on face

Remarks: Bruce Campbell is an actor by trade and therefore may be able to easily assume new identities (unless Chris McDonald assumes them first).

### CAUTION

Bruce Campbell has been trained to use firearms and edged weapons, and as he proved in "The Quick and the Dead" is able to disappear completely from sight.

### REWARD

The Rewards For Secret Service, United States Treasury Department, is offering a reward of up to $25 million for information leading directly to the apprehension or conviction of Bruce L. Campbell.

"Mr. Secretary, it's not what you think," I explained through lips that were pressed against the bottom of someone's dress shoe.

Before he could respond, I was hoisted to my feet by a baker's dozen Secret Service agents and shoved into a waiting town car. Colin Powell got the "human shield" treatment back inside the hotel, and aside from a few bumps and bruises, he was no worse off.

I couldn't talk my way out of this "incident," and it necessitated a call to Dale, my dutiful lawyer. Unfortunately, because of my new status on the ISL (Internal Security List), no amount of legal wrangling or corroboration (and Liz Taylor wasn't happy about being interrupted that night for questioning, let me tell you) could spring me before they ran a more detailed Security Threat Analysis, or STA. The fancy title meant that they were going to take a deeper look into the ways I had irritated the U.S. government in the past.

As I lay in the holding cell, numerous past infractions flashed before my eyes, any one of which could land me on an ESTL (Elevated Security Threat List): parking violations, late library books, failing to renew my Jefferson County Sheriff's Association membership.

It was a long, cold, sleepless night.

# 16

# Lights, Camera, Mayhem!

I must have checked out clean enough to avoid "Enemy Combatant" status, because I was discharged from my "undisclosed holding cell" at 6:15 A.M. — forty-five minutes shy of call time for my first shooting day on *Let's Make Love!*

My cab screeched to a halt outside New York's Astoria studios at 7:05, exactly five minutes late — a miracle, considering the fact that I had no idea where I was coming *from*. I paid the driver, but didn't get very far before a harried woman with a walkie-talkie and a name badge swooped down on me.

"Good morning, Bruce, I'm De-BOR-ah, the DGA trainee," she said, already grabbing my arm.

"You don't have to grab me, Deborah, we'll make it," I assured her. "And please refer to me as Foyl from now on."

Deborah sighed and let go of me. "Sorry...Foyl. And, my name looks like Deborah, but it's pronounced de-BOR-ah."

"Okay, sure."

"Base Camp is this way," she said, leading us through the

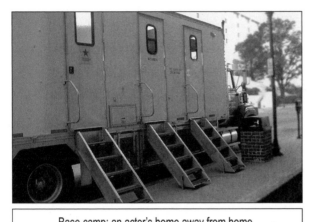

Base camp: an actor's home away from home.

Astoria complex.

"So, how's the shoot going?" I asked. "You've been at it for what, a week now?"

"God, it seems so much longer than that," Deborah exhaled.

"That didn't sound very optimistic — this is a Mike Nichols film!"

No sooner had the words come out of my mouth than we had to pause to let a half-dozen grips move a twenty-foot-square portable green screen — an indispensable special-effects tool, used for compositing layers of motion-picture images.

"Well, because of things like that," Deborah said, "this film is two weeks behind after only one week of shooting."

"Wow," I said, surprised. "Is that typical for Mike? I know he likes to improvise."

"Improvise? We should be so lucky. No, this is about rewriting, rethinking, reinventing."

Just as she said this, Deborah and I steered clear of a group of puppeteers, each dressed in ninjalike black clothing and wearing harnesses with rods attached to surreal human figures.

"Is Cirque du Soleil shooting on the lot?" I asked, looking back after we had extricated ourselves from the puppeteers.

"Script changes started coming so fast, the crew never had a chance to read them before a new batch would come in. Now, we're all just winging it one shot at a time."

We had to sidestep a stake bed truck that was backing up to unload what could best be called a shaky cam on steroids. Some ambitious young go-getters in the mechanical effects department had since gotten their hands on the same primitive camera rig I told Mike about. For a device usually comprising a two-by-four, bicycle grips, and a bolt, it was far more tricked out now, with leveling capability, safety devices, a gyroscope, and even a drink holder. Either way, I was intensely pleased to see it was now part of this massive operation.

Deborah and I got to the edge of Base Camp, a loose configuration of vehicles, generators, catering equipment, and trailers. My trailer was the type affectionately known as a "double banger." I'm not sure which snide teamster named it that, but a double banger is the duplex of actor housing, meaning that I shared a wall with some other unsuspecting thespian.

I unloaded my stuff and had a look around. Every so often, an actor gets lucky and the trailer is brand-new, with the latest perks. Mine was hot off the assembly line, and that meant the lights worked, the toilet flushed, and there was even hot water.

In the corner, I noticed a climbing harness draped over my padded swivel chair, with a note pinned to it:

The note was from my buddy, Johnny Casino, the stunt coordinator. *Harness? What the hell is the harness for?* I wondered. My wardrobe was laid out, and as I sifted through the clothes, I noticed a pair of pants that had been prepped for interfacing with stunt rigging.

*Knock-knock-knock*

I opened the door to a tall, thin man with a cigarette in his hand.

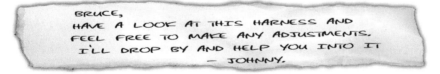

BRUCE,
HAVE A LOOK AT THIS HARNESS AND
FEEL FREE TO MAKE ANY ADJUSTMENTS.
I'LL DROP BY AND HELP YOU INTO IT
— JOHNNY.

"Hi, Randall Klein, wardrobe supervisor. Is it true we should only refer to you as Foyl?"

"That's right."

"Are you finding everything okay?"

"I think so," I said, "but I wonder if I'm in the right trailer. What's with the harness, and the rigged clothes?"

"We're doing the harness first up. I left a note pinned to your jacket."

"For what scene?" I asked, growing concerned.

"Well, it's not a scene, per se, it's...an *enhancement* — yes, that's the word we're using now — an enhancement to scene seventy-six, where you fight with Richard, or should I say Harry? Let me know if you and Johnny need any help putting that thing on."

"Sure."

Randall sucked on his cigarette and scampered off. I shut the door, locked it, and rifled through the script to scene seventy-six, where Foyl confronts Richard's character. We grappled and wrestled, but why did we need wire work?

*Knock-knock-knock*

I opened the door to a tall, muscular fellow.

"Bruce, how are you, buddy?" Johnny asked, flashing his trademark rodeo grin.

"Confused," I said, "but come on in and let's chat about this harness."

Johnny followed me in. I shut the door, and we exchanged a hearty handshake.

"Been a while," Johnny said, hooking a thumb into his belt. "Not since the *Death* movies, right?"

"Yeah, pretty much. Hey, so, what's with the harness? What part of the scene is it for?"

"It's during the fight. You get Richard in a bear hug and he throws you off. And Mike, well, he wants to add some 'mish-mash.'"

*"'Mush-mush?'"*

"Yeah, that's the term. I gotta tell you, it's a little weird. I've worked with him for twenty years and I've never seen him like this. I gaffed *Wolf*, and he left all the stunt stuff up to me because he hated it. Now, it's like he's John Woo or some shit, but, hey, we aim to please — and cash the check!" Johnny slapped his hands together. "So, we're almost ready out there. You just slip it on and cinch it up. We'll tighten it on the set."

"Okay, Johnny, thanks," I said, somewhat resigned to my fate.

I locked the door again and changed out of my street clothes. I wriggled into the harness, which is similar to the type of rig worn by rock climbers, and a terrible wave of dread swept over me. The last time I wore a similar harness was for the film *Army of*

*Evil Dead 2*: Some of my best harness work.

*Darkness*, and my memories of the experience were anything but fond — the toll on my extremities, the nausea, the strap rash on my inner thighs. To this day, I walk with a slight limp because a nylon strap did a number on my left hamstring.

*Knock-knock-knock*

De-BOR-ah was back with an update. "Makeup and hair are ready to see you, Foyl."

"Thanks."

I slipped into the flannel robe they provided, and found my way to the brightly lit makeup and hair trailer.

0094 1090+1@ KIF2 0049 3296+1@

GT00:07:21:03    R:00:00:45:13

"Hold that goddamned cue card closer, moron!"

"Good morning," I said, shielding my eyes from the white fluorescent light. "I'm Foyl, reporting for duty."

"Hi, Foyl — we got the memo about your name — please have a seat. I'm Anne Herono, and I'll be doing your makeup."

Anne put on a pair of small, round glasses and leaned toward my face, inspecting it.

"Just get rid of the bags under my eyes, and we're gonna get along great," I said, winking.

"I'm going to do a lot more than that, Foyl. Scene seventy-six is the middle of a fight scene. You're not allergic to anything, are you?"

"Just fake blood."

Anne was only mildly amused. "I'm going to apply two bruises, a cut on your forehead, and pavement rash on your nose."

"Don't you think that's excessive for just a scuffle?"

Anne shrugged. "This came directly from Mike. He's the director, right?"

The one nice thing about enduring long makeup applications is that I can get a forty-minute catnap out of an hour-long procedure. Drooling has been an issue in the past, and I'm told that I snore on occasion.

My last stop on the glamour train was Jeri Feldman, hair stylist. She was a little too full of good ideas so early in the morning.

"Foyl, as you know, we're in the middle of the fight. Mike wants the hair to be really active and adaptable."

"What does that mean?"

"I'm not sure exactly, but that's what he said. Mike's been saying a lot of things, lately. We're all tap dancing as fast as we can."

"Sure, well, take your best shot," I said, thumbing through a fashion magazine.

Between makeup and hair, two and a half hours had elapsed. I emerged from the trailer looking like a man who had been on the losing side of a soccer riot.

Deborah led me to stage eleven, where an entire facade of the Park Avenue Arms had been built. Under these conditions, Mike would have complete control over the atmosphere. It was an impressive scene, with extras and cabs bustling everywhere, their movement coordinated by a squad of assistant directors, and the Shaky Cam Deluxe, standing by for use.

"Where's Mike, De-BOR-ah?" I asked.

"He's by the camera," she said, pointing. "They're setting up."

I waddled to the set, since that's all you can do when a harness is wrapped around your gonads, and caught Mike's eye.

"Good morning, Foyl, you ready for a little fun today?" Mike asked jovially.

"Yeah, the harness gag is an interesting touch."

"I'm just driving the truck down the highway that you and Richard have been paving. I'm running with this and having a ball."

"Okay, I hear you," I said, smiling. "But where does this piece fit in the scheme of things?"

"I'll show you," Mike said, walking over to his multimonitor video setup. "June, have you got the boards for this scene?"

"Right here," she said, handing Mike an immense binder with easily three hundred pages of storyboards. "I've marked the page with this shot."

"Thanks, hon," Mike said, opening the binder to storyboard number 7...-A7.

"Since when did you start using storyboards?" I asked, surprised.

"Well, there are so many gags in this scene now, I had to lay it out shot for shot. Okay, in this one, you and Richard are here in the foreground. On action, he'll throw you back. I'll be shooting handheld —"

"You actually shoot too?"

"Well, I haven't before, but this film has cracked wide open for me. I'm going to Shaky Cam away from you, as you go away from us."

"Uh-huh...."

Mike grabbed me by the arm. "You're over here." He led me to a neon yellow, T-shaped mark on the sidewalk. "You'll be ratcheted back from here."

"To where?"

Mike turned to a group of fit, T-shirted guys and whistled. "Terry, let's get Johnny." He turned his attention back to me. "Up there, to the second story. Just get as far as you can. You don't actually have to reach the windowsill, because when you're halfway up, we'll paint you out and fill in the rest of your movements with a digital rendering. Okay, good luck!"

Mike patted me on the shoulder and headed back to the camera as Johnny arrived.

"Sorry, just setting a pick point for another gag," he said, slightly out of breath.

"It's fine, I'm in no hurry to lose my breakfast. Now, Johnny, give it to me straight — is this going to be ugly?" I asked.

Johnny looked at me with an expression that lacked his usual cock-sure smirk. "Yeah, coyote ugly. They're gonna jerk you into next week, so I better cinch you up like a son of a bitch."

"Do what you must," I said, wincing at the thought.

Johnny performed a series of painful strap checks, then turned to Steve "Overtime" Krasner, the first assistant director. "All set here, Steve!"

Richard Gere arrived on set, looking refreshed and happy. "Hey, Foyl!"

"Vegas high five," I said, smiling and offering up a hand.

Richard slapped me loud and proud. "Hey, I did my first stunt today, a high fall, about twenty feet, into boxes. It was awesome, like ballet. I wish I had gotten more into this physical stuff a long time ago. I have you to thank for that. And listen, that Dodge is absolutely crazy. I used to have a thing about gas-guzzlers, but in this day and age, I'm willing to be more open-minded. Thanks."

I had myself to thank for what I was about to endure as well, but I wasn't as giddy as Richard.

"First positions!" Steve called out.

I stood behind Richard and wrapped my arms around his shoulders, assuming the "bear hug" stance.

Mike tells me that Foyl will ultimately be replaced by a CGI character nicknamed "Door-Manimal."

"Be glad of two things, Richard: one, that you're wearing a hat, and two, that I had a light breakfast."

"Okay, here we go — roll sound!" Steve shouted, and the crew went through its usual pretake gyrations.

"Speed!" the sound man shouted from afar.

"All right — three, two, one, *action*!"

Before I could say Mary Poppins, I was yanked off of Richard's back and catapulted forty feet into the air. The sudden, violent movement knocked the wind out of me, and when I finally came to a stop, high above the soundstage, I found myself suspended, upside down.

The crew whooped in delight, the "cut" bell rang, but I remained in place.

"We're gonna release you in a second, Bruce," Johnny called from below. "How you doing?"

"Just...keep...doing your thing," I said, turning red in the face.

In my unbridled youth, I used to enjoy the freedom of being suspended and heights never bothered me. In my maturing years, however, the antigravity thing doesn't sit well at all. Then I got a nasty taste in my mouth.

*Is this triggering some kind of heinous acid reflux?* I feared. "How you doing, guys?" I asked, trying to sound unworried.

But the previous night's incarceration, plus the nervousness of the day, combined with the height, the motion, and that second goddamn Sausage McMuffin with Egg were all just too much.

"Hey, folks, sorry, better watch it down there, I think I'm gonna —"

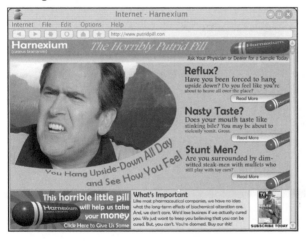

And I blew — the fast food, the hot tea, the "curiously strong" Altoids — I blew it all. Several lucky crew members were able to heed the warning and dive to safety, but a group of four stunt guys, responsible for keeping me aloft, were not able to abandon ship and took the brunt of my acidic offering.

Let me go on record by saying that the stunt guys took their sweet damn time lowering me to the ground. By the time I got down, I was more dizzy than ashamed, and the only crew remaining was a hazardous materials team, brought in to sanitize the set.

The barfed-on stunt guys were getting towels from wardrobe as I waddled past.

"Really sorry, guys."

"That's okay, Mel Gibson blew chocolate cake into my face during *Braveheart*," one stuntman offered.

"That's good to know."

I looked over to where Mike was stationed; he was getting ready for the next shot. I could only walk as fast as a person who needed a hip replacement, but I caught up with him eventually. "Hey, Mike, that shot go okay for you?"

"Yeah, pretty good," he said, already on the move. "I think between the four cameras we should have it. Got a hell of a barf shot on B camera — extreme closeup."

"Yeah, good, hey Mike, can I ask you a couple of questions about some upcoming scenes?"

"Sure, as long as they're quick. I have to look at a dummy the effects guys made, for when you land from that last gag. It's wild, we just did an expensive digital shot, and now we're just going to throw a dummy out a window. I love it — I love that grab-bag thing you were talking about."

"Oh, good, good — but beyond this scene, I had a quick question for you about tomorrow's monologue in scene seventeen."

"Seventeen — the one in the foyer?"

"Yeah, I was hoping you'll let me really work the room in that scene — you know, get some movement going."

"Room? There is no room. We're shooting the whole foyer on green screen."

The look on my face must have urged Mike to continue.

"We're playing a much more fanciful look, Foyl," he explained. "This is a romantic comedy. We're injecting helium into this whole thing, so the foyer is going to look huge, very big, like Grand Central Station, and it won't be real, it'll be computer generated, so I'm not sure what there will be to work, but you're welcome to have some fun with it on the day."

"I see," I said, not hiding my dismay.

"But that's been pushed on the schedule anyway, so we can kick some ideas around as we get closer."

Mike and I arrived at the rear end of the mechanical effects trailer, where Marty Sossin, a bear of a man, was inside, putting the finishing touches on his latest work of art.

"What do you think, boss?" Marty asked, displaying the dummy from the back of his effects trailer.

Mike shrugged. "Looks pretty spiffy, but what can it do?"

Marty lifted the dummy high over his head. "Well, it's a titanium frame for starters, so it's really light."

He tossed the dummy down a set of metal steps where it bounced and shuddered before slumping to the pavement below. The movements of this inanimate object were eerily accurate, and I felt suddenly overwhelmed by a strange fondness for it. What that thing could have done for us in the Super-8 filmmaking days. Without having to restuff it with newspapers, or reattaching the head after every take, we could have thrown this Robo-dummy off the highest parking lot in the land with nary a scratch.

"That's the most beautiful dummy I've ever seen," I said, enviously.

"Not a bad endorsement," Mike said to Marty, walloping me

on the back again. "Consider it approved. Another triumph, Mart-o."

Mike winked at me and turned to go. "Great first day, Foyl. Big one coming up with Renée in about a week."

I waddled back toward Base Camp, wondering what the hell Mike was talking about. The only big anything on my schedule was a simple bump and "excuse me" with Renée — just an eighth of a page of material. But I had more pressing issues, like returning the flow of blood to my loins.

Back in the comfort of my double banger, I wiggled out of the Harness of Death and threw it against the shared wall. I felt nauseous and sweaty, like I was coming down with a fever. I grabbed a bottle of jojoba oil, plopped into the recliner, and slathered the healing salve on my raw, rashy inner thighs.

Ruminating about the day, I wondered if Mike Nichols was just having a renaissance in his directing career, or if this classy production was being infected by my B-movie sensibility? The changing schedules, frantic rewrites, lack of communication, and unpredictable director made my first day on *Let's Make Love!* feel exactly like a B movie.

*Dear God, I've spent twenty-five years climbing up the food chain in this business, and it all culminates in this, another goddamn B movie? Maybe all that "evil" stuff is real after all and I'm diseased — cursed!*

I stood up to get a bottle of water and suddenly felt very light-headed. I steadied myself on the linoleum counter and tried to get centered, but it was impossible — images of the past weeks flashed forward and rewound backward in my head:

The nerve-wracking audition process; Rob Stern busting my chops; dummies falling through the air; Mike lecturing me; shaky cams floating by; handheld cameras moving up to my face; crew members laughing at me, always laughing....

I looked around the trailer and the walls began to move in, ever so slightly. The place was shrinking. I became short of breath, tearing at my collar to let more air in, like the Wolf Man under a full moon.

Wracked with guilt and horror, I ran outside to my appointed Lincoln town car and dove inside.

My driver, Julio, was startled awake. "Ready to go, Mr. Campbell?" he asked politely.

"I'm ready all right, Julio. This worthless, B-grade nobody is ready to go nowhere, so hurry up and take me there."

Julio shrugged and put the car in gear. "Whatever you say, man."

He interpreted my ramblings as a request to take me back to the hotel, but upon arrival, I knew I couldn't stay there either. I couldn't go from one box to another; I had to roam, like the free-range actor I was, and sort out my confusions.

My belligerent meanderings led me into nearby SoHo and past a familiar theater, the Angelika, which specializes in revivals, off-beat stuff, and lots of independents.

Bleary-eyed from sensory overload, I looked up at their marquee. Showing, through special arrangements, was a "Troubled Child" film series, featuring filmmakers who fought the studios. The films currently in exhibition were *Apocalypse Now*, *Brazil*, and *Bonfire of the Vanities*.

*Yeah, fought the studios*, I thought. *And lost.*

Each of the three films had great potential, but were hamstrung by a volatile mix of auteur excess and studio meddling. *Let's Make Love!* had all the warning signs of a troubled movie, but Mike Nichols was never prone to such excess in the past. Something stunk in La-La-Land. I began to suspect that Mike was being manipulated by that movie geek of an executive, Rob Stern, but the only way to know for sure was to puncture the corporate world of Paramount Studios and sniff around. I had a week off, and I had connections — they weren't A-list, but they were connections nonetheless.

# 17

# Last Supper

Lanny Sticks, my costar from *Death of the Dead,* was a fine actor. I met him in Detroit, years prior, on a training film for Chrysler where Lanny played a mechanic and I was a disgruntled customer. During the three-day shoot, we shared dreams of acting in films that would be seen outside of car dealership conference rooms, and became fast friends. In the late '80s, we both relocated to Los Angeles, and our professional association continued for the next decade.

But work slowed for Lanny and, like many actors, he took a job to make ends meet, as a security guard at Paramount Studios. "At least I'm still in the movie business," he used to joke, trying to keep a brave face on his economic situation. Over the next decade, big-city distances and faraway locations diminished our contact until we lost touch entirely. It was time to change all that — I needed Lanny to get me in.

"Hey, Lanny —"

"Who is this?"

"Bruce."

"Bruce who?"

I rolled my eyes. Surely, my costar of big and small screen hadn't forgotten so quickly. "Bruce Campbell, your only true friend."

"Oh...."

This was followed by a pause that made me think the line had gone dead, but Lanny broke the silence.

"It's been awhile."

"Yeah, when was the last time I saw you, two, three years ago?" I asked.

"Seven."

"No way."

"I haven't heard from you in seven years," Lanny confirmed. "Does my pal Bruce call me just to shoot the breeze? Nah. Does he call me when he's doing the special-edition DVD for *Death of the Dead*? No, too much trouble. Why are you calling me now? Did someone die?"

"No, no, everyone's all right. Hey, Lanny boy, easy. I know I was lame at keeping in touch, but it's a two-way street, my friend. I haven't heard boo from you either."

"You moved once a year, on average, for a decade," Lanny said, with building anger, "and never forwarded — well, not to me, anyway — your contact information. Great way to maintain friendships, amigo."

"Okay, Lanny, I'm guilty. It's all my fault. Can we move on now?"

"What do you want?" he asked tersely.

"I need your help."

"You're right, Mr. B-Movie Man. You do need help. I saw your film *Icebreaker* the other day on cable, and I got two words for you: 'acting lessons.'"

There was a distinct hang-up click on the other end of the line. I stared at the phone as my mind veered toward self-doubt.

Had I been cruel to him? Had I been insensitive? Had I really been that bad in Icebreaker?

Well, okay, he had me there, but Lanny's role of a backwater hick in *Death of the Dead* was a lot of fun for him. And while maybe I had been a disappointment in the friendship department, I didn't recall Lanny reaching out over the years. My thoughts shifted to anger: *That bastard! Here I am, calling to see how he was, and he bites the hand that has fed him in several films.* But then I thought, *Okay, let's give it one more shot. If he blows me off after this, at least I can say that I tried.*

I let Lanny's phone ring long enough to get his answering machine: "This is Lanny, and *this* is the beep —"

*Beep*

"Lanny, this is Bruce. Hey, I'm just looking for some help, for old times' sake. If you won't do it for me, I understand. All a guy can do is —"

*Click* — "What do you need?"

The shock of Lanny picking up the phone made me jump. "Well, I'm working on *Let's Make Love!*"

"The Nichols flick, sure. I hear it's in trouble."

"Yeah, same here. So here's the deal: I need to be a fly on the wall — get on to the lot, catch some dailies, and nose around the executive offices a little bit."

"Let me get this straight. After ignoring me for seven years, you

THERE IS ONLY ONE THING WORSE THAN THE DEATH OF THE LIVING...

THE PRODUCTION VALUE WAS
**HORRIFYING!**
-LES CRAVEN

LANNY STICKS MADE SOME
**FRIGHTFUL**
CHOICES
-JUAN CARPENTER

DEATH OF THE DEAD

DVD

want me to risk getting fired to sneak you into a place I'm paid to protect?"

"Yes."

"Okay, I'll do it."

"Really?"

"Yeah. Long story. Come on over tomorrow night for dinner and we'll talk."

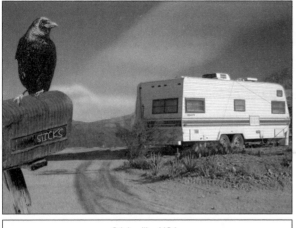

Sticksville, USA.

Lanny lived out in Canyon Country, California, where I bought my first house west of the Rockies. In the mid-80s, this area was just beginning to experience a building boom. Almost twenty years later, it was completely out of control.

I took the Soledad Canyon exit off the Antelope Valley Highway, made my way past brand-new, homogenous, "American Beauty"–style developments, and pushed into the Los Angeles backcountry.

Lanny had a modest trailer on a small piece of desert. He lived alone these days, mostly because he wanted to and, frankly, because he was so cantankerous. His four dogs surrounded my car as I drove up. Two rottweilers, one pit bull, and a German shepherd — not the friendliest dogs on earth.

Lanny stepped out, grinning that troublemaking grin of his. He was weathered and unshaven, and seemed comfortable with both.

"Aren't you gonna come and say hi?"

"Hell no. I have a wife and kids and these dogs look hungry."

Lanny shouted something guttural and unintelligible, and his dogs immediately sat on the ground, eyes still on me, tongues wagging in the hot air.

"They only understand German," he explained. "It's a strong language."

"And so romantic."

"You can get out now."

I stepped around the dogs gingerly and greeted Lanny on his porch. I offered a shake, he went for a hug, and it was all a little awkward, mainly because he had a double-barreled shotgun in his right hand. Lanny squeezed me hard, like he was pissed off.

"Hey, man, great to see you. Welcome to my humble abode."

"Thanks," I said, getting the air back in my lungs. "You've got yourself some place here."

"I make do. I bought this with *Death of the Dead* money, you know."

"Did you? That was smart. I pissed my money up a rope."

"It's a blessing and a curse."

"How do you mean?"

Lanny began to walk around his expansive rock-and-garbage-strewn lot.

"Well, some days I look out at this forty acres and I think, *my God, I own this*, and other days I look out, and I think about...the injury."

"The injury?"

"You say that like you don't remember," Lanny said, with hurt in his eyes. But before I could respond, he slapped me on the shoulder. "Great to see you, Bruce — let's get some grub!"

The moon was full over Canyon Country that night. In the desert, an exposed moon makes everything look like a 1950s western — fully illuminated and washed in a blue tint.

Inside the trailer, Lanny was acting as short-order cook, and he had a greasy mixture of fried eggs, onions, and hamburger spread out on his oft-used grill.

"Lanny's hash — served twenty-four hours a day."

I was at his dining table, looking at an overhead schematic of Paramount studios, map grid number 593-G6. Latitude: 34.08365; Longitude: -118.32219 — otherwise known as Hollywood, U.S.A.

"I borrowed that from the maintenance department," he said proudly.

"So, Lanny, any ideas how we pull this off so there's no paper trail, or 'drive-on pass' hassles?"

"Easy. Look north to the cemetery."

According to the map, the Hollywood Memorial Park Cemetery, resting place of Marilyn Monroe and other Hollywood heavyweights, was due north of the studio. The second I saw the configuration, a story told to me fifteen years ago suddenly made sense.

"Wait a minute. I know this place. My makeup man on *Maniac Cop* — another film where you beat me up — was a young makeup apprentice on *The Ten Commandments*."

"I think I know this story," Lanny said, squinting at the memory, "but I thought it was just Hollywood B.S."

"No. This guy was there. His job was to spray dark body makeup on the extras in a special ventilated shed on the Paramount lot. But, as the wind blew, so did the makeup residue —"

"Directly on the tombstones in the cemetery," Lanny said, finishing my thought.

"Cecil B. DeMille was so horrified when he heard the news that he dispatched a small army of U.S.C. students with brushes and buckets to scrub the tombstones."

Lanny laughed at the image. "That's how close together they

are. There's a hidden gate back there that connects them. I know the ground-skeeper. We used to hook up and raise hell — gave 'graveyard shift' a whole new meaning. Now, look, if you want to sneak into the Paramount lot, here's what I would do: I'd go to the cemetery, pretending I was visiting the grave of some big star. Who do you like?"

I COMMAND YOU TO WASH THOSE TOMBSTONES!

"The old-fashioned guys, like Tyrone Power — is he there?"

"Sure as shit — right next to Harry Cohn, the prick who ran Columbia."

"Hey, don't say that — Columbia is responsible for *The Three Stooges*."

"He was still a prick. The point is, you stop by to pay your respects to Ty or whoever, and then make your way back to Rosemary Avenue, the road behind the pond, until it dead-ends. The gate is back there. I'll meet you."

"Sounds like a plan," I said, smiling. "But Lanny, tell me your reason for doing this. On the phone, you said something about a long story."

Lanny was about to answer, but dinner was fried up and ready. "Grab your plate, cowboy — grub's on!"

I held out the mismatched plates to my bachelor friend, and he heaped on the food like it was our last meal together. Sitting down at his Formica-topped table, I couldn't help notice Lanny's pressed guard uniform hanging on the back of a chair.

"Pretty snappy duds, Lanny."

"I tailor mine," Lanny said, digging out two Coronas from his small refrigerator. "I picked that up from the film *The Border*, with Nicholson. He tailored his uniform. At first I thought it was just an ego thing, but then I realized that it makes a lot of sense. When you're put together, you look together, and when you *look* together, folks assume that you *are* together. It's all smoke and mirrors, but hey, we *are* in Hollywood, right?" Lanny said, dropping a beer in front of me. "If you were being squeezed out, you'd do the same thing."

Variety Reporter

## Trouble at Paramount
## Upstart Sticks makes
## waves, egg salad

By Mike Avalon

Hollywood and the entertainment industry can be stubborn sometimes, and a certain major film studio off of Melrose is no exception.

Yet, it seems this fact is not common knowledge to all of the studio's employees. Recently, a relatively young and new Security and Studio Wellness Associate Officer had the audacity to approach his [obviously] superiors with a list of ways the studio's security forces and valet parking could ...energized and neofitted ...paradigms.

"You're being forced out by the studio?" I asked, wiping my greasy lips.

"Yeah, it's been a long time coming. I made a name for myself right away there, see? I started as a pass checker at Gate Two. That's where they break you in, see how you do under pressure. My failure rate was 4 percent the first year of my guard career —4 percent. Most guys are 13, 14 percent."

"You were a climber."

"It wasn't that," Lanny continued, "I was just a natural. So they moved me up to the Gower shipping gate. I did check-ins there and turned a few heads. I caught five loads of stolen shit going *out* the door in the first month. In thirty days, I saved the studio my entire year's salary. That's when the squeeze began," he said through a clenched jaw.

"For doing a good job?"

"Yep," Lanny said, taking a slug of beer. His quiet, understated reserve fell away, and a hidden anguish played out like Marlon Brando in *On the Waterfront*.

"I was too good, Bruce — that was the problem. I started to shake up a good-ol'-boy guard system that had been in place since the Great Depression. Some of these guys used to drink with John Barrymore, for Chrissakes, you know what I'm saying? Suddenly, here comes a guy who ain't makin' mistakes, and he's payin' attention, and he starts to see that the security infrastructure in place here isn't any good. And what did they do to reward me?"

"It doesn't sound good, whatever it is."

"They gave me 'the watch.'"

"I hope it was a Rolex."

"No," Lanny said impatiently. "They put me back in what we call the DMZ, no-man's-land. They did it to break my will. Because of the isolation, most guys would crack within three months. I did it for *five years,* Bruce."

There was a clunky pause, as I tried to think of something to say that wasn't stupid, rude, or insensitive. How do you say, "Yeah, that must have sucked," without saying that exactly? The best I could do was, "Yeah, freaky shit. Why not just quit and work at Universal, or Sony?"

Lanny turned his hash over and over, defiantly. "That's just what they would want me to do."

After a second helping of everything, Lanny and I watched the sun set from the porch of his trailer. Across his small patch of desert, a cacophony of barking dogs serenaded us. We shared a beer and talked about the good old days, before *Death of the Dead* and "the accident," whatever that was.

# 18

# Dailies from Hell

Parking in Hollywood is a nightmare: No Parking without a Special Permit; No Parking between the Hours of Ten and Two on Tuesdays for Street Cleaning; No Overnight Parking. Why not just put up a concrete riot barrier around the entire city?

That's why I took a cab to 6000 Santa Monica Boulevard, the address of the Hollywood Memorial Park Cemetery.

"You know, Mary Mon-roe is buried here," my Pakistani driver informed me, counting out the change from my twenty.

"Do you mean Marilyn Monroe?"

The driver looked at me like I was a fool. "Tha's wha I say — Mary Mon-roe."

I stuffed the change in my pocket and stepped out of his gypsy cab. There it was before me, the cemetery that housed the tombs of Hollywood's greatest old-timers: Rudolph Valentino, Douglas Fairbanks, John Huston. It was a classic cemetery, built in 1899, with Gothic tombstones, and giant mausoleums for the long-forgotten elite. The only time I saw it before this was on an episode of *Charmed*.

I glanced at my watch. The time read 5:30 P.M. — half hour until closing. I was to meet Lanny at 5:45, so I paid ten bucks to get in, and consulted the free map they included. From the main entrance, I turned left and headed toward the pond. Lanny's secret gate was on the far side. As I walked along Lakeview Avenue, I began to pass the final resting places of well-known showbiz people. Cecil B. DeMille, the Steven Spielberg of his day, was housed in a giant tomb.

*And it probably went over budget*, I reasoned.

Around the corner was Jayne Mansfield, a blonde bombshell made prominent as a studio threat to Marilyn Monroe. Marion Davies, a forgettable actress from the 1920s and '30s, had a massive tomb as well — but then again, her sugar daddy was William Randolph Hearst, the newspaper magnate.

Raimi favorite Tyrone.

Just beyond Marion, my man Tyrone Power was laid out in a fine memorial. Ty was a man's man from the old school, with dark, penetrating eyes, and a cigarette-enhanced voice. This dashing leading man had a permanent place in my friend Sam Raimi's household. His mother, Lu-Lu, was so crazy about him, she hung framed portraits everywhere. Sam even faked his autograph on one picture, convincing Lu-Lu to this day that it was real.

Tyrone's hypnotic powers

were still in evidence. A woman in her sixties was standing silently by his grave, cradling an old black-and-white glossy of the handsome star, and dabbing her glistening eyes. As I got closer, the fan spotted me, but she didn't try and hide her sorrow — or rage, for that matter.

"Damn you. We could have had such a life together. Why did you have to leave me so young, so virile? You bastard!"

Assuming she was talking to Tyrone Power, I offered my condolences. "Rumor has it, ma'am, he died of a heart attack while in the act of bedding a much younger woman. At least he went with a smile on his face."

"That's not true," the fan shot back defiantly. "We made beautiful love in the afternoon. Ty told me he was tired, so I let him drift off to sleep. I tried to wake him several hours later, but he... he was gone...."

The grief etched on the woman's face seemed real, not some delusional story.

"You're the woman?" I asked incredulously.

"Not everyone in this town is a phony, mister," she said bitterly.

I decided against baiting her further, and headed north to Rosemary Avenue. Near the end of the poorly maintained street, I spotted an overgrown, rusted gate with a simple lock. There were no others like it in this part of the park, but Lanny was nowhere in sight.

Then, through the thick foliage, I heard the secret call: "Where do you think you're goin'?"

It was one of Lanny's favorite lines from *Death of the Dead*, when his redneck character takes control of a group of people in an isolated cabin and forces them outside to certain death. I walked over to the gate as Lanny was unleashing the padlock. With a quick look around, I ducked into an obscure, overgrown section of the Paramount back lot.

"This is it — the outback," Lanny said, gesturing around.

"It's creepy as hell."

"And this is during the *day*," he added, leading us along a footpath through this overgrown area. "Try being here at three o'clock in the morning, when the freaks have Marilyn Monroe parties in the cemetery. My job was to keep fans of dead actors from getting into the studio that once employed many of those same actors. How sick is that shit?"

Lanny and I arrived at the edge of the "New York City" portion of the back lot. One particular brownstone seemed oddly familiar.

"Was that Ally McBeal's apartment?"

"Sure was. Hell of a nice gal."

We walked past Ally's place in silence, mainly because Lanny was still stewing about his situation. "See, the payback is to stay, Bruce," he said, rubbing his hands slightly, "and to stick their noses in it by excelling."

We got to the end of the "block." To our right, administration buildings began.

"We cut through Eddie Murphy Plaza," Lanny said, indicating the route with his hand as he walked. "Turn left at the Gene Kelly Building, and the DeMille Building is all the way down on the right — that's where the screening room is."

The Eddie Murphy Plaza was very tidy, and the early evening light, refracted through the Los Angeles smog, bathed the area in a warm glow, which I'm sure is exactly how Eddie would have wanted it. As we approached the Gene Kelly Building, the plaza narrowed to a two-person pathway. Just ahead, a sunny courtyard revealed the immaculately maintained Cecil B. DeMille Building, a vintage complex from the '40s.

"This is it," Lanny said, gesturing to the building. "When

DeMille was working, he insisted on his own private screening room, so they put one in the basement. Now, it's an execs-only situation. We, of course, will go in the service door."

Lanny rifled through his ring of keys and opened the door. Inside, typical of all the old office buildings on the lot, the décor was faded plaster, rounded edges, and a myriad of hallways.

"Just keep heading down," Lanny said, pointing to a stairwell on our left.

A dark doorway at the bottom posted a cheery sign: AUTHORIZED PERSONNEL ONLY. Lanny selected a new key, and the door opened easily.

"Angelo's the projectionist. He's been on the lot since time began — a little crabby, but a great old geezer."

Lanny arrived at a nondescript metal door. He knocked lightly.

A gruff voice came from behind the door: "Just a fuckin' minute!"

Lanny smiled at me, as if to say, "See?"

The door swung open, and we were greeted by a bald, cigar-chomping, cardigan-wearing curmudgeon.

"Angelo, this is that fellow I wanted to bring by — Bruce Campbell, one of the actors in *Let's Make Love!*"

Angelo looked at me, rolled his eyes, and shooed us inside. "Okay, hurry up, the execs don't like the smell of my cigar, and we're ready to roll."

Inside, Angelo led us toward his projection booth. "*The smell of my cigar*," he repeated derisively. "Let me tell you something, the executives who used to sit in this screening room smoked nothing *but* cigars. I couldn't get two feet out the door before Zukor, or one of the top brass, would shove a Del Fuego in my hand the size of a ham sandwich. You could tell how much work a picture needed by the amount of cigar smoke in the room. Now, these little pricks are playing Nintendo during reel changes — sheesh."

We rounded the corner to Angelo's "lair." The large room was encrusted with fifty years of movie-projection-booth stuff — some of it work-related, like strips of film hanging above an editing bench, and some of it just items that piled up over time, like posters, clippings, and notes pinned to an overflowing bulletin board.

Anchoring the room were twin Peerless movie projectors. I had seen a few over the years, hanging out in projection booths during theater appearances, but never this pristine.

"Holy cow," I exclaimed, "Peerless."

The first dailies shown through the Peerless.

"The originals," Angelo said with pride. "Carbon arc. You gotta adjust 'em every fifteen minutes as they burn, and replace 'em every two hours. You got sixteen different lube spots to keep oiled, so you can't just walk away like they do in the multiplexes. These should be in a museum. A hundred and two thousand hours projecting dailies, rough cuts, final cuts, first trials, trailers, recuts — you name it — without a major problem, and that's only since '52, when I got here."

I was enjoying Angelo's crusty ranting, but I was more interested in saving my movie from the scheming of the man I had begun to think of as my nemesis.

"Dailies are when?"

"Right now," Angelo huffed. "Back off while I crank this sucker up."

The Peerless came to life and it purred smoothly as the film fed through its sprockets. I walked over to one of several viewing windows. A small speaker, held up by a coat hanger, broadcast the accompanying sound.

"Turn it up if you want," Angelo said, jamming his stub of a cigar out in an overflowing ashtray. "Don't know why you would bother. No offense, but this picture is a stinker."

I looked back to Angelo in horror. "Really? Why do you say that?"

Angelo cracked a wizened, jaded smile. "Kid, I can tell a stinker from the first take of the first reel of dailies. It's not about the star, or the writer, or the director, it's the whole ball of wax. You make a picture, and it's a collision of elements — sometimes it's magic, and sometimes it, well, it's this," he said, jerking a thumb at the dailies, now playing.

I turned up the volume and watched. Stylewise, Mike Nichols was indeed going ape shit. His footage, while gorgeous to look at, was frenetic, choppy, and full of gags. Something comic and ingenious might emerge once assembled, but currently, the dailies had the feel of a Roger Corman movie with a bloated budget.

"A 75-million-dollar movie, and they're throwin' fuckin' dummies around. That never would have happened when Zukor ran this place. The execs now, they're more worried about stock options, golden parachutes, and production deals than making pictures. The punk screening these dailies is a classic example," Angelo said, pointing to Rob Stern, lounging in one and a half seats, with his feet draped over the back of the leather chair in front of him. Looking at him was the visual equivalent of chewing on tin foil.

"He's on the cell phone half the time, or he's dictating some B.S. to his big-tittied secretary. Listen to this...."

Angelo turned up an ambient speaker. "We use this to check the sound in the room itself. We also use it to listen in on the schmucks. The things I've heard, kid."

Through the speaker, we could hear Rob spouting off: "You know what, Kari? Move my detailing to tomorrow morning. I'm sorry, Johnny, go ahead."

"He's watching dailies, dictating, and talking on his cell phone — all at the same time," Angelo said with disgust.

"When you're good you're good," Lanny interjected.

Angelo tended to the Peerless as the last of the dailies threaded through. "Thank God they're over."

Rob Stern could be heard swinging into postdailies, high-gear executive mode:

"Okay, memo to Mike: 'Mike — saw Tuesday's dailies. While I enjoyed the handheld stuff, I think it's too confining. Suggest more crane use and wide-angle lenses to give us more of a sense of scope. General note: more extras, the streets look too empty — maybe we could add digital people in post? In addition, please talk with Bruce Campbell re: his first day of shooting. Loved the barf — a great DVD extra, but suggest reshooting the shot — too stilted. He looked like he was waiting to get pulled back. Not organic. More notes later. Yours in making a classic, Rob.' Okay, memo to Kevin Jarre, re: dialogue...."

I turned the volume down and glanced into the screening room below. Rob was dictating, and punctuating his long sentences with frenetic hand gestures. His legs, as if working an invisible Thigh-Master in fast motion, never stopped wobbling open and closed.

"The worst part," Angelo complained, "is that the punk leaves the biggest mess you've ever seen — candy wrappers, memos, Doritos. What am I, his mother? And let me ask you: how the fuck can anyone drink sixty-four ounces of anything? In two reels of dailies, he can go through an entire Big Gulp. Go figure."

Down below, Rob gathered his things and headed toward the exit, still blabbing on the cell phone. "Hey, Kari, is the conference call still on with Mike and Terry?"

I glanced at Lanny. "I'm assuming 'Mike' is our Mike. Who's Terry?"

"Executive vice-president of production at Paramount," Lanny explained matter-of-factly.

"Could be interesting. Think we can tail him?" I asked.

Rob Stern multitasking.

"Who do you think you're dealing with, amigo?" Lanny asked in return, a little put off.

We said our good-byes to Angelo (I even got a free cigar, though Ida doesn't abide them) and slipped out the side door. The difference between Angelo's dungeon and the afterburner brilliance of the late-day California sun was something like a thousand percent, and I stumbled about blindly, trying to spot Rob Stern before my eyes adjusted.

Lanny, smart enough to slip his shades on before exiting the building, kept the fledgling executive in his sights. "He's on the move — let's take a short-cut."

**Terry Feingold**
*Head Meathead*

**Paramound Studios**
Suite 297
Los Angeles, California

(323) 555.9565, ext. 19
FAX: (323) 555-9560
e-mail: penny_pincher@paramound.con

"Where is Rob's office?" I asked.

"On the third floor of the Sturges building," Lanny said. "His boss, Terry Feingold, is on the fourth — dead ahead."

Lanny and I headed toward the southeastern corner of the lot, taking a shortcut through every building we encountered.

"See, the heavy, dark keys are part of the original lot. Those will get you into the older buildings on the older parts of the lot. The next generation, between '37 and '79, used these silver jobbies. Brand-new buildings have swipe cards that can be re-programmed. Either way, there isn't a door I can't get into."

"So, Lanny, Rob is about to have a conference call with this guy Terry. Any way to listen in?"

"As long as you're not claustrophobic there is," Lanny acknowledged, using his second-generation key to open a loading door of the Sturges building, then a smaller key to activate a service elevator inside.

We arrived on the fourth floor and Lanny led us hurriedly to an unmarked door almost vibrating from the hum of machinery behind it.

"The old air duct routine," Lanny said, smiling as he produced yet another odd-shaped key.

"Really, that's possible?"

"You bet," Lanny said, throwing open the door, revealing a metal stairway. "You can have a bird's-eye view of any office built after '43."

"How do you know all this?" I asked, sizing up the ladder and the network of metal ducts looming above.

"Sunday nights are usually pretty slow on the lot," Lanny said. "Me and a buddy used to play Dungeons and Dragons. This is the one place he could never find me. Now look, you'll see a vent at each office. Terry's is three vents down. Good luck."

"Wait, you're not going with me?"

"Hell no. Last time I was up there, I drank a can of Coke and my belly swelled up enough to trap me for an hour. That's why now I carry Tums wherever I go."

Lanny unclipped a small, rubber-coated flashlight, and flipped it on. "You'll need this."

"Okay, see you soon," I said, ascending the rusty ladder.

The duct system was very tight indeed. I cursed every bacon cheeseburger ever consumed as I dragged my carcass thirty horizontal feet to the first grate. I peered into what looked like a casting office. The walls were lined with actor headshots, and a heated negotiation was under way.

"Look, I could give a shit if Corey got a pinball machine in his trailer on *Trancers III*. After the third failed drug test, he'll be lucky to get per diem!"

I didn't need to hear the rest of that tragic conversation, and dragged myself to the next grating. Down below, a money guy of some kind was deep in the middle of a convoluted explanation:

"It's very simple, actually," the man continued. "The first eight hours are straight time. The next four are time and a half, and every remaining hour after that is double time. No, that doesn't include night premiums, meal penalties or forced calls...."

Before I fell asleep, I hauled myself forward, to what would hopefully be the office of Terry Feingold, who was one of about ten executive VPs at Paramount. When I arrived, Terry was on the phone:

"No way. Look, you blew a big deal for me because of it, and I'm not going to let it happen again...."

*This Feingold is a tough cookie*, I thought. But his conversation continued:

"No, next time, *you're* taking him to soccer practice. Yeah, well, whatever — talk to the lawyer."

Terry slammed the phone down and stared at it in silence. The downward tilt of his head revealed a substantial bald spot that was in the process of being "restored." Pressing my face against the metal slats in the vent, I could see that his office was typical of a midlevel executive, decorated in a Southwestern theme, with a faux stucco fireplace and generic tapestries.

*Bzzzzzz!* Terry's intercom came to life, and the slightly bored voice of his secretary came across the speaker phone. "Terry? Rob's here for the conference call. Should I send him in?"

"Do me a favor, wait five minutes, then let him in."

"Sure," his secretary responded.

With that, Terry leaned in his relax-the-back executive chair and put his feet up on the desk. Was he finishing an important call before Rob came in? Freshening up? No, he was simply making his subordinate wait because he could.

After wasting exactly five minutes, lying on the cold metal duct, I watched as Rob entered Terry's office. The dynamic between studio executives was usually cautious, to say the least, but even accounting for the usual Hollywood paranoia and ambient venom, "warm" is not a word I would use to characterize their relationship.

Unlike Terry, Rob was hired as a "creative" guy at the studio. He'd be *making* movies instead of "overseeing" them if he had a creative bone in his supersize body. Rob was all about "development." I was told by a writer I knew that the kid had many failings, but was nonetheless regarded as a sort of wunderkind who could "develop the hell out of a script." I wasn't sure if that was a compliment or not, since far too many decent scripts have been shanghaied in "development."

The subject of the day, of course, was *Let's Make Love!*, the film assigned to the two execs. Mike Nichols was about to call in for a status conversation, and they wanted to get their stories in sync.

"Well, financially, he's going 'Kurtz' on us," Terry said, rifling through a stack of paperwork on his desk. "He's projected to go over by 25 percent, and that's *after* burning through a 10 percent contingency already."

Even from my ridiculous vantage point, I could see Rob's eyes suddenly ignite. "Listen, Terry," Rob spat, "Mike is attempting to do something really special here, and I think we should all be cheering him on rather than... than...."

Where's Lester Shankwater when I need him?

For just a moment, Rob had appeared to be in danger of stating an actual opinion, but his deeply ingrained sense of self-preservation returned just in time, assisted by Terry's withering stare. *Interesting,* I thought to myself. *Stern seems to have an awful lot invested in Mike's new "vision."*

"This is a romantic comedy, asshole, not Arma-frickin'-geddon," Terry barked. "Can't you creative guys rein him in?"

"Hey, whoa, whoa, there," Rob said, putting his hands up, trying to erase any hint of his previous backbone. "You bean counters say the same thing every time a creative force — and this is Mike Nichols, mind you — changes his mind or enhances a script."

"Shooting entire sequences green screen isn't enhancing, Robbie, it's reinventing the wheel."

"I was brought here to breathe some life into these old Paramount walls, Terry. Personally, I have enjoyed watching *Let's Make Love!* blossom into a higher-concept, albeit slightly more expensive, story. It's gonna appeal to a much younger, and *broader* audience than Mike Nichols ever had before, and marketing will back me up."

"We already got our slate of high-tech action flicks, Rob, we don't need another one to kneecap us when we're down."

"Wow, that's a real hard line," Rob said, dabbing the sweat along his hairline.

"It's my ass, is what it is," Terry said, poking his own chest. "Glick gave me the max I can spend under the new cap — remember the one we all agreed on in writing? I can't let this, or any picture, go over it, and I'm putting the onus on *you*, to bring your genius director around."

"But the new stuff is really cool," Rob protested, weakly.

"No, the new stuff is really expensive. Can't we have cool stuff that isn't expensive? When I first read this script, it was three people in a room

"LET'S MAKE LOVE!"

Producer: Robert Evans    Shoot: 32 Days
Director: Mike Nichols

Budget Date: 02/11

| Acct# | Category Title | Page | Total |
|---|---|---|---|
| 11-00 | STORY, RIGHTS & SCREENPLAY | 1 | $1,192,040 |
| 12-00 | PRODUCERS | 2 | $1,820,750 |
| 13-00 | DIRECTION & SUPERVISION | 3 | $2,314,300 |
| 14-00 | CAST | 4 | $18,130,762 |
| 15-00 | ESPRESSOS | 5 | $514,204 |
| 16-00 | TRAVEL & LODGING | 7 | $2,828,703 |
| | TOTAL ABOVE THE LINE | | $26,800,759 |
| 21-00 | PRODUCTION STAFF | 9 | $644,739 |
| 22-00 | CAMERA | 11 | $537,438 |
| 23-00 | ART DEPT | 12 | $293,420 |
| 24-00 | SET CONSTRUCTION | 14 | $1,193,194 |
| 25-00 | SPECIAL FX | 14 | $1,226 |
| 26-00 | SET OPERAT | 15 | $453,237 |
| 27-00 | ELECTRIC | 16 | $338,041 |
| 28-00 | SET DRE | 17 | $331,991 |
| 29-00 | PROPS | 18 | $348,404 |
| 30-00 | FILM | 18 | $428,834 |
| 31-00 | EXTR | 19 | $220,386 |
| 32-00 | WAR | 19 | $431,691 |
| 33-00 | MAKE | 20 | $215,178 |
| 34-00 | MEAL | 20 | $160,701 |
| 35-00 | SOUN | 21 | $222,923 |
| 42-00 | LOCATI | 21 | $568,516 |
| 43-00 | TRANSP | 23 | $530,951 |
| | PRODUCTI | | $6,920,870 |
| 61-00 | EDITING | 25 | $422,150 |
| 62-00 | MUSIC | 26 | $734,126 |
| 63-00 | SOUND | 26 | $232,376 |
| 64-00 | FILM & STOCK SHOTS | 26 | $152,502 |
| 65-00 | TITLES | 27 | $77,126 |
| 66-00 | OPTICALS | | $51,126 |
| 67-00 | POST PRODUCTION ESPRESSOS | | $278,234 |
| | TOTAL POST PRODUCTION | | $1,947,640 |
| | TOTAL ABOVE THE LINE | | $26,800,759 |
| | PRODUCTION PERIOD TOTAL | | $6,920,870 |
| | TOTAL POST PRODUCTION | | $1,947,640 |
| | GRAND TOTAL | | $35,669,269 |

$1,947,64...

$35,669,269

Before...

talking, 95 percent of the time. Who's been taking growth hormones here? How did this one get away?"

A buzzing sound prevented Rob's answer. "Mike's on the line, Terry."

"Okay, tell him to hold just a sec," he said, turning his attention back to Rob. "I'm always bad cop. Can you be bad cop for once?"

"I'm no good at being bad cop," Rob said, shaking his head no. "And as the creative exec, it isn't really my job."

"But you always complain that when I'm bad cop, I'm too bad," Terry reasoned. "Maybe if I play good cop, and you're bad cop, we might get somewhere."

"Okay, I'll try it, but no guarantees," Rob warned.

The two wary allies nodded, and Terry stabbed at a blinking phone button.

"Hello, Mike," Terry said, warmly. "Rob Stern is also here on speaker."

"Hey, Mike," Rob feigned cheerfully, "how's everything going?"

"Not bad, but I'd like another week of shooting," Mike said flatly.

Terry and Rob exchanged a panicked look, then broke into laughter. "Hey, Mike, you're a funny guy!" Rob said, smiling, as a fresh drop of sweat rolled along his sideburn.

"Is that a no, then?" Mike asked, not joking.

As the reality of the request sank in, Terry signaled to Rob to be quiet, and a stony silence followed.

"You still there?" Mike asked over the speakerphone.

"Oh, we're here, Mike," Terry said, now pacing in front of his desk. "That's a pretty tall order, particularly after all the new expenses, like a storyboard artist, helicopter shots, forty new digital effects, and a special armature dummy. I could go on."

Rob shot Terry an "I thought you were going to be *good* cop" look. "But, Mike, make no mistake," he urged. "It's all terrific stuff, it's just starting to add up, heh-heh."

Rob tried to continue, but Mike interrupted him.

"You know, fellas, I haven't exactly been making this movie in a bubble," Mike said, as politely as he could under the circumstances. "I've got enough memos from Rob alone to fill a book — and not one of them was to tone it down, they've all been about making this movie bigger and bigger. Now, I haven't heard a bad word from corporate on any of this, so, until I do, I'm going to continue to make a great movie for this studio. I'm sure you bright young men have it in yourselves to help instead of hurt. Good day."

And with a faint click, the three-way conference suddenly dropped to two. Terry immediately turned his wrath on Rob.

"You call yourself 'bad cop'?!"

"Hey," Rob countered, having sweated through an undershirt, a dress shirt, a tie, and an outer jacket, "your 'good cop' shouldn't have been worse than my 'bad cop'!"

"I had to do that, numb nuts," Terry hissed, "because your 'bad cop' was such a pussy!"

The two fell into silence, Terry slumping into his chair behind the desk, and Rob blotting his shiny forehead with a hankie.

"Now what?" Rob asked forlornly.

Terry leaned back, plopped his feet on the desk, and shrugged. "It's up to you, Rob. As I recall, you brought this project to the studio, not me."

"What?" Rob protested. "We did it together, don't you remember, Terry?"

"As my e-mails and interoffice memorandums will prove, I fought against this project, yet you continued to champion it."

Rob flinched at the mention of a paper trail. "Are you saying you're not going to cover my back on this?" Rob asked, incredulous.

"Not this one, amigo," Terry confirmed. "If *Let's Make Love!* tanks, you're taking the fall. Life's too short. I'm going to fiddle while the whole thing burns."

Rob's eyes turned arid and reptilian. "Terry, I couldn't agree more with your assessment of this project. It's flatlining. But that's no more my fault than it is yours, or even Mike's. No, I think that once everyone has had a chance to

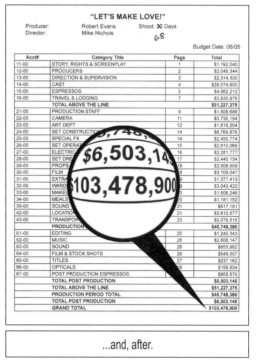

...and, after.

review the facts they'll see that this entire fiasco can be laid at the feet of one man: Bruce Campbell. Just check out the Internet Movie Database — everything he touches turns to straight-to-video crap. He's like a carrier for a B-movie Ebola virus. I heard he almost brought down *Spider-Man 2* and he was only in that for five minutes. He's in *Let's Make Love!* for, what, almost thirty? We gotta make him disappear," Stern said definitively.

"Well, do what you gotta do," Terry said in a dismissive tone. "This baby is yours now."

I began to shiver, not only because of the chilling scene I had just witnessed, but because the cold metal duct was lowering my body temperature to a dangerous level.

Shimmying backward to the access ladder, which was much harder than forward, my mind reeled.

*So, I wasn't going crazy — that little prick Stern was the evil puppetmaster after all! First he tries to keep me out of the movie, now he's trying to blame all of his dumbass decisions on me. I should have guessed he was a troublemaker from the first time I saw him smelling his puffy fingers.*

Lanny and I rode back across the lot in silence. He had upgraded our means of travel to a golf cart, mainly because he felt sorry for me. At the vine-riddled back gate we shook hands.

"Well, Lanny, I almost wish I hadn't seen that," I said, finally.

"Yeah, kids today," Lanny said, jingling his ring of keys. "He came over from New Line. He was their 'franchise' guy. He has a lot to prove, I guess."

"He's proven a lot to me already," I said.

"Well, watch your back," Lanny urged grimly, closing the gate between us. "Say hi to Ty for me."

With a wink, I vanished into the cemetery, en route to the Los Angeles Airport. I was due back in New York in two days.

# 19

# Bad Day at Black Rock — The Sequel

Stuntmen, as a rule, are funny. But the stuntmen working on *Let's Make Love!* were downright hilarious. Waiting in my trailer the next day was a gift basket of Egg McMuffins, Earl Grey tea, and a can of Altoid mints, nicely laid out like haute cuisine.

The attached note read:

Before I could say "har-dee-frickin'-har-har," there was a knock on the door.

HEY BRUCE —
THOUGHT YOU MIGHT WANT THIS BACK!
— JOHNNY AND THE GUYS.

"Hang on!" I said, in a tone reserved exclusively for annoying assistant directors.

"It's Mike," he said, through the door.

"Holy shit." I stumbled to unlock the door. "Hey, good morning — come on in."

Mike stepped into the trailer and smiled politely, looking around. "You actors have it pretty rough, don't you?"

"We make do."

"Hey, listen, Foyl, I have to talk to you about the dailies. May I sit down?"

"Sure," I said, gesturing to my "lounge" chair.

"It's like this," Mike began. "What we're making here is a film that wants to break out, do you know what I mean?"

"I'm not sure I do, Mike. No."

"Maybe that's the problem," he said in that irrefutable director tone. "I need to know that you're going to be on board."

"On board? I'm not sure what you mean. What do you need from me, specifically?"

"I need you to start rounding out your performance."

"Mike, I've only been in one shot," I protested.

"And it was flat."

"Flat? You could tell that from me being flung forty feet into the air?"

Mike nodded. "Foyl, a shot is a scene and a scene is a shot. I need you, for lack of a better expression, to camp it up a little."

I let out a bitter, ironic laugh. "Well, this is the first time I've been asked to do *that*!"

"Are you with me?" he asked, in his no-nonsense manner. "You're either in or out, bucko. I need to know."

And it appeared that Mike was happy to wait for my answer. Blushing at the embarrassment and confusion of the situation, I shook my head yes. "Sure, of course. Anything you want, Mike."

"Thanks, Foyl," he said, rising. "See you out there — big scene coming up."

And he closed the door behind him.

*Stern probably put this in his head,* I fumed, looking at the flimsy wall in front of me and wondering if I could put my fist through it like countless other actors had in the past. But before such wicked thoughts could get the best of me, someone began pounding on the door.

"Damn them to hell," I growled. "What?"

I whipped open the door to reveal Kevin Jarre, the screenwriter, smiling awkwardly. "Good morning, Foyl. Is this a bad time?"

"Oh, hello, Kevin. No, I got nothin' but time. Come on in."

We assumed the same seating arrangement, and Kevin looked around the trailer as all visitors do.

"These things are getting much better."

"Yeah, they sure are," I said, not wanting to get drawn into an inane trailer discussion. "What's on your mind?"

"Well, Mike and I were kicking around today's scene last night, and these are the new ideas. I just wanted to sit down with you, to see if you had any questions."

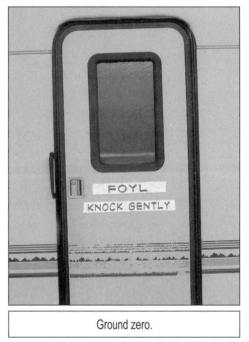

Ground zero.

"Okay," I said, glancing at the single page. "I thought this was just a bump-and-go with Renée."

"It was, Foyl, sure, but Mike is having quite an *evolution* as a filmmaker. I'm sure you can appreciate that."

"Sure," I said, scanning the new page, "I'm just trying to keep up." As I read on, the new action sequence seemed not only extensive, but exhaustive. "Wow, this is pretty, uh...."

"Fun?" Kevin offered.

LET'S MAKE
# LOVE!

Screenplay by
Kevin Jarre

Directed by
Mike Nichols

REVISION HISTORY
Revised Buff Re-Write - 06/21/04
Second Pink Polish - 06/20/04
Second Draft of Third Revision - 06/18/04
Revision with Half the Carbs - 06/15/04
See Also Other Revision - 06/11/04
Gratuitous Nudity Revision - 06/06/04
Writer Wants a Boat Revision - 05/31/04
Fishing Rod Revision - 05/24/04
Goldenrod Revision - 05/17/04
Plaid Revision - 05/09/04
Berber Revision - 04/30/04
Pink Revision - 04/20/04
Blue Revision - 04/09/04
Shooting Script - 03/28/04

"If you're a triathlete, yeah," I wheezed, getting tired just from reading. "And what's with my last line?"

Kevin smiled at his own handiwork. "We thought that would put a nice button on the scene."

"But that line is from the *Evil Dead* films."

"'Groovy'?" Kevin said. "That's not even a line, that's a single word."

"I know, but in context, it's too weird. I've already said it in movies twice, and I'm afraid of the cliché association."

"So, what, you can't say 'groovy'?"

"Did Stern make you write that?"

"Stern? Are you insane? No. Nobody tells me what to write."

"Well, either way, I'm not sure if I want to go there," I said, shrugging helplessly.

Kevin paused to gather his thoughts. Not all writers roll over and play dead when an actor has script issues — particularly playwrights. "Look, neither you nor I nor your pal Sam Raimi made up, or owns the rights to, the word *groovy*. I'm comfortable with it. The word is appropriate for your character and the situation, and if you'd like to change it, you'll have to take it up with Mike."

Without a further word, Kevin stood up and left my trailer. I watched him go in silence, then grabbed a cold Sausage McMuffin with Egg from my "gift basket" and wolfed it down angrily.

Out in front of the Park Avenue Arms set two hours later, the cast was assembled to block the new scene. Mike was laying it out for us all, helping us to see the big picture.

"Okay, gang, now we begin with Harry and Debbie exiting the building. Foyl, you tip your hat as she passes, but you didn't know that they were in the middle of a real knock-down-drag-out-fight. Debbie turns to clock Harry, but he ducks, and Foyl gets smacked in the face. Meanwhile, Harry gets around in front of Debbie and stops her from leaving. Foyl is shaking off the hit, and he steps forward to see what's going on. That's right when Debbie winds up with her purse to hit Harry, and she whacks Foyl on the back-swing, sending him backwards into the revolving doors — which are rigged to spin around — and they throw him back out, right into Debbie who clotheslines him with another backswing, and Foyl drops to the ground. Debbie and Harry then make up, and jump into the back of a waiting cab. End of scene."

"Sounds like a 'oner' to me," Johnny Casino joked from the sidelines, and the entire crew let out a raucous laugh.

"That's exactly right," Mike said matter-of-factly. "I want it as one continuous shot."

The residual laughter subsided almost immediately, because the crew knew that Mike never joked about what he wanted to do. Renée and Richard Gere exchanged a slightly worried, albeit excited look.

"You really want to do this in one, chief?" Johnny asked, shifting his weight uncomfortably from boot to boot.

"Yes," Mike nodded. "The scene requires a single, uncut piece that plays out in real time. The pacing has to be exact."

To accomplish this, we began a grueling trial-and-error period where the scene was paced out slowly, methodically, then performed with increasing speed, and for longer periods without stopping. Tragically, advancements were not without collateral damage. During a three-hour period, I managed to bash my knee on the side of the building, get an ankle caught in the revolving doors, and take a full-on punch in the face from Renée Zellweger.

"Oh, my God!" Renée exclaimed, as I tumbled to the pavement, clutching the bridge of my nose. "I am so sorry."

"I'm okay, I'm okay," I assured her, going the stalwart route. "I'm good to go."

"Good to go, my ass," Johnny said, not fooled by my false bravado. "You're bleeding like a pig. Let's get the medic over here!"

Steve, the first assistant director, looked at his watch and rolled his eyes. "Okay, that's lunch, one hour!"

As the crew stampeded away from us, Mike walked over to offer his condolences. "Hey, Foyl, for what it's worth, that last go-around was finally leaning in the right direction."

I weakly gave Mike the thumbs-up as the medic shoved cotton in each of my nostrils.

De-BOR-ah approached. There was a grim look about her. "Mike, you have some visitors who need to see you."

"I don't have any visitors today," Mike said, dismissing it as unimportant. "June handles all that business anyway."

Deborah took Mike aside. Her words were lost to me, but from Mike's reaction, I could tell that she was relaying serious news. Mike glanced at an idling black Cadillac Escalade, and took a deep breath.

My stomach bested any further curiosity, and I joined the lunch line. The prime rib was looking really good. Lunch is always a great time to people-watch, but as I looked around, I noticed that crew members were socializing in small groups, and the mood wasn't as happy-go-lucky as usual.

*Must be middle-of-the-shoot doldrums*, I assumed.

Digging into a cold beet salad, I tried to make peace with what Mike said in my trailer. Deep down, I knew that my job as an actor was to be a good soldier and to carry out the vision of the man in charge, regardless of whether I'd do things the same way. I finished a massive piece of cherry pie, washed it down with a cup of hot tea, and worked my way back to the trailer.

When acting, my post-lunch regimen is very specific: I brush the lunch out of my teeth, take a fistful of vitamins, and grab a catnap. But after the physicality of our run-throughs, I decided to skip parts one and two and proceed directly to the catnap.

Two hours later, I awoke in a panic, haunted by recurring dreams about forgetting lines — an actor's worst nightmare. I got up slowly and shuffled to the bathroom. The mirror revealed a serious case of Pillow Face, and a glance at my watch confirmed the elapsed time.

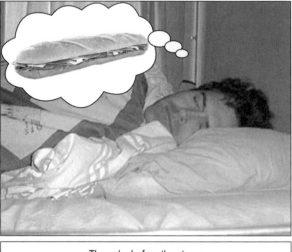

The calm before the storm.

I opened the trailer door and squinted into the late-afternoon sun. Across the base camp, Deborah spotted me and hurried over. "Hello, Bruce. Sorry you haven't heard from us."

"What the hell is going on?" I muttered, feeling the pull of dried drool on my face. "Why haven't I worked?"

Deborah looked around nervously. "Well, it looks like you've been...*released*. I can sign you out."

"Oh, wow," I said, confused. "What about the scene we were rehearsing?"

Deborah struggled to find the right words. "It's being retooled, they say, but I'm always the last to know. Sorry."

"That's fine. What's my call time for tomorrow?"

Deborah fixed her eyes on the pavement between us. "There isn't one right now. You're a 'will notify.'"

# 20

# Quest for Liar

"Will notify" in movie lingo means that the production doesn't have a firm idea of when an actor will be needed. I was in my executive suite watching the Home Shopping Network at eleven o'clock at night when I received official "notification." It came in the form of an emotional phone call from my agent, Barry.

"This is huge," he said, choking back tears. "This is fucking awful."

For an agent to cry, I knew it was bad. "Okay, Barry, let me have it."

"Paramount wants to...get out of the Bruce Campbell business," he said, sniffling.

"Wow. He did it. He really did it," I said, chewing on my lower lip.

"Who did what?"

"Who else? Rob 'Big Gulp' Stern. He had it in for me from the start."

"Look, they admit that it was their mistake," Barry said, trying to reassure me. "Mike Nichols himself told me that he loved working with you, and that he would keep you in mind in the future."

"That and a buck fifty will get me a cup of coffee."

"Hey, you're pay-or-play, so don't worry, you won't be out any money."

"Good thing, because I smell a drought of biblical proportions coming on."

"Please don't do anything stupid, Bruce. I have a call into Paramount."

"Don't do anything stupid, he says," I repeated with venom. "Let me tell you, Barry, I already did something stupid — I agreed to audition for this goddamn role!"

I expected Barry to come back with some sort of plastic bromide calculated to calm me down. But there was nothing but dead air.

"What?" I asked.

"There's more," said Barry, hesitantly. "Have you ever heard of something called a 'B movie virus'?"

My own little lost weekend.

I slammed the phone down so hard I cracked the base and split a fingernail. I quickly decided to vacate the premises before I could inflict any more damage to the hotel room or myself, and proceeded to tear up the "city that never sleeps" with an all-night bender.

The long flight back

to the West Coast gave me plenty of time to do three things: recover, rethink, and regroup. I have a very healthy ego, but I wasn't concerned about my own well-being — I was concerned about my bank account. Potential employers in this fickle industry could easily get the wrong impression and run for the hills. Abominable behavior has long been tolerated from big-name stars, but the average thespian gets no such slack.

An actor who has a blowout with a director might be labeled "difficult," regardless of the circumstances. If he or she shows up late for call enough times, or forgets their lines often enough, they'll become "unreliable," and the label will stick like residue from a Band-Aid. But no one, to my knowledge, had ever been stricken with a "disease carrier" tag. If word got out that I was not only fired from a supporting role in an important film, but that I had infected that film — and possibly the director, cinematographer, and other actors — with some sort of career-killing pathogen, the ripple effect could be staggering.

Back home in Oregon, I typed the name of a certain Big Gulp–sucking executive: R-o-b S-t-e-r-n, into a movie database website. The information that popped up both surprised and horrified me. *Army of Darkness* was listed as one of his credits — an acting credit.

Army of Darkness? *That was back in 1991. How old was he, fourteen?*

I rifled through storage boxes in my attic that contained research from my last book, *If Chins Could Kill: Confessions of a B Movie Actor*. In it, I included snippets from production reports showcasing what a perilous shoot *Army of Darkness* was.

Production reports, depending on your point of view, can be a beautiful or horrible thing. Each day, at the end of shooting, the Unit Production Manager, in conjunction with the First Assistant Director, fills out this form, detailing exactly what happened that day, down to who worked, how many lunches were served, how many feet of film were exposed, etc. A production report is often cited in legal and insurance matters, so the information included is usually corroborated and almost always exhaustive.

One particular part of the form, from which I got the best material, was the "comments" section, where the assistant director would include delays, accidents, and anything else of interest to the production. One such comment section indicated the hiring and subsequent firing of an underage extra. My jaw dropped as I read:

*Rob frickin' Stern*, I said to myself. *The bitter little liar.*

I decide to consult with my Paramount insider, Lanny Sticks, and gave him a call. He sounded groggy and unfocused at eight-thirty that night.

"Hey, Lanno — BC here. How are ya?"

"Uh...hi. Better than you, I guess. I still have a job."

"Yeah, funny. It's that little know-nothing, Stern. He may have gotten a few cheap shots in, but if I go down, I'm takin' him with me. Are you in, Lanny? Can you help me?"

There was an unusually long pause as Lanny considered this.

"Hey, look, man, I'm just a security guard. What can I do?"

"You can help me get back in there and kick some major executive ass, that's what," I urged. "All I need are your keys, Lanny."

"Sorry, buddy, but I gotta think about my future. I didn't make a zillion dollars like you on all your failed TV shows. They have a good retirement package here at the big P, and I want to take advantage of it."

"But you said yourself they were forcing you out," I countered.

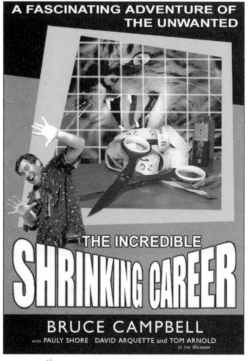

A FASCINATING ADVENTURE OF THE UNWANTED

THE INCREDIBLE SHRINKING CAREER

BRUCE CAMPBELL

with PAULY SHORE  DAVID ARQUETTE and TOM ARNOLD
AS THE MILKMAN

"Let's just say things have changed."

I knew there was no talking him into it. On top of it all, his subtle personality shift made me suspicious, so I didn't want to tip my hand any further.

"Okay, Lanny, I understand. Be well."

I hung up the phone and walked outside to enjoy a brilliant Oregon sunset. The image of refracted light beaming through the clouds was hauntingly surreal, and it reminded me of the esoteric ending of *The Incredible Shrinking Man*. The lead character was shrinking uncontrollably, and became so ineffectual that normal-size adults were no longer aware of his existence. I felt that way right now — so small and helpless that I was virtually invisible.

But I wasn't going to go out like that. I was going to crawl back from a planned obsolescence and clear my name in Hollywood. The information age leaves a vast, digital footprint and I knew a doofus like Rob Stern would leave a slimy trail everywhere he went. I could link his jiggly ass to this whole disaster, but to do it I needed those e-mails.

# 21

# Belly of the Beast

"Why would you want to be Robert Evans?" makeup queen Mel Tooker asked.

"He's the producer of *Let's Make Love!*, and I want to pull a gag on him. It has to work, Mel. I have to be able to pass as him for a couple hours."

Mel smiled and shrugged. "Don't ask, don't tell...."

Together, we sorted through a stack of miscellaneous Robert Evans photos she had assembled, taken over the years at numerous Hollywood functions. Robert got his start as an actor back in the studio era, so there was a plethora of reference material on his distinctive face.

"This should be no problem at all," Mel said, in her usual chipper voice. "Let's get busy."

The procedure was very similar to the transformation I underwent in order to play Elvis Presley at seventy. Guessing that Robert Evans was hovering around that age, we salvaged the jowl moulds from *Bubba,* and even adapted a hand-stitched

Elvis wig to suit the desired look.

Two and a half hours later, I emerged from Mel's warehouse and squinted into the L.A. haze. I was a new man: a powerful producer who could throw his weight around where he needed to. Robert Evans has been a fixture at Paramount since the 1970s, and I was going to milk every bit of deference and privilege he had coming.

Lincoln town cars in Los Angeles are a dime a dozen. With plates like Snoop, FilmCo, and Star21, they roam the hills and valleys of Los Angeles in search of dark-shaded famous types to ferry about. In my New Zealand TV days, Executive Class Limousine Service was the appointed carrier, and I got to know the drivers on my way to and from the LAX airport.

I still had a card from George, a wannabe actor who drove for them. We always got along well because he hated Los Angeles as much, if not more, than I did, and he was always up for shortcuts and funky routes. On top of that, he owned his own town car, and that would suit my nefarious scheme better.

"George, Bruce Campbell here, how are you doing?"

"Hey, dude, what's up?"

"I need you for another adventure."

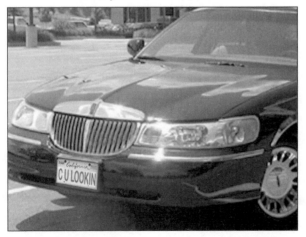

"Sure thing — I'll call dispatch and we'll schedule it."

"No, George, this one has to be under the radar. I want to hire you separately from the limo service."

"I see," George said, getting more interested. "What's the deal?"

"The deal is this: On Sunday, I play Robert Evans, and you play his driver. Together, we crash the Paramount gate. Think you can do that?"

"In my sleep, daddy-o. Can we do it after the Rams game — about three-thirty?"

"Sure."

"Cash?"

"Of course."

"You got yourself a deal, Mr. Robert Evans."

It turned out that George had also driven for the real Robert Evans, and according to him, he always entered Paramount at the Van Ness gate, a lesser-used shipping entrance on the east side of the lot.

The basic drill at studios is that the only way you can get on the lot is to possess a coveted "drive-on" pass, usually called in by some authorized person affiliated with a current production. I was sure that Robert Evans, once head of the entire studio, wouldn't put up with any of that, so George and I had nothing to display but sheer bravado as we neared Gate Four.

"Okay, George, I'm thinking we pull up, I'll do the 'I do this every day' wave to the guard — you do the same — and odds are we're in the door."

"Sounds good, boss," George said, nodding dutifully.

The town car swung in front of the guard shack, and my heart sank for two reasons: the attending guard was very young, and *Lanny Sticks was training him.*

"Fuck," I spat, under my breath. "Okay, George, stay sharp."

The twenty-two-year-old guard, Luis Rodriguez, stepped forward, clipboard in hand. "Can I help you?"

"Robert Evans," George said simply, with just the right amount of boredom in his voice to sound convincing.

"Do you have a pass?" Luis asked politely.

Lanny Sticks took note of the name, and stepped toward the town car. Instinctively I rolled my window down and nodded to him.

"New guy?" I asked, delivering my first line as Robert Evans.

"Yes, sir, Mr. Evans, thanks for your patience. How are you today?"

"Just fine, Lanny," I said, smug in knowing that I didn't even have to look at his tag. That reading *must* have sounded convincing.

Lanny held my look for a beat, then glanced at Luis. "This is Mr. Robert Evans, Luis. He's one of the most famous movie producers in the world. He comes here all the time. He's one of the few people who doesn't need a drive-on pass. You might want to put his name in that special column on the right — see it there?"

"Yes, sir, okay — I got it," Luis said, jotting the name down.

Lanny looked back at George, who was waiting in a wonderfully passive mode. "Mr. Evans, where's Keith?"

Before I could answer, George jumped in. "He's sick as a dog," he said. "He showed up this morning at the dispatch office, and barfed in his own car while he was cleaning it. Naturally, we swapped it out for Mr. Evans."

"Naturally," Lanny repeated, giving George the once-over.

We had complied with the basic needs of the gate guards, so I wanted to avoid further interaction. I thanked Lanny and rolled the window back up.

George let his foot off the brake, and the town car groaned forward in another subtle indication that we wanted to leave.

"How's that new office working for you, Mr. Evans?" Lanny asked.

*That bastard.* Could he kick back on a Sunday afternoon and wave a few cars through? No, my pal, Lanny Sticks, had to be a fastidious prick.

"Just fine," I said, rolling the window down two inches. "It smells like a new house in there."

As I was saying this, my hands rifled through the latest *Hollywood Creative Directory*, an exhaustive quarterly listing of where to find virtually anyone in Hollywood, and located the production office of Robert Evans.

Bruce the Robert.

"Of course, the Adolph Zukor Building is worth all that effort, wouldn't you say?"

Lanny rocked back on his heels. "Sure is, Mr. Evans."

He signaled to Luis, and the arm rose up. We were free to enter. Lanny and his new recruit watched in silence as we drove past.

Around the corner, in a reserved parking lot, George and I caught our breath.

"Well, that was a first good test," I said, slumping back in the plush seat.

"Can I change my shorts now?" George asked. "That was close."

"Too close. But George, I have to say, you were at the top of your game. That might go down as one of your finest unseen performances."

8100

Memo 42 of 1974                    LML

-Add the line "We've got company"
  prior to a car chase.
-15% more ninjas.
-Increase usage of "f" word.
-Shower scene(s).
-Add a wise-cracking stereotypical
  ethnic supporting character.
-Sex scene involving exercise bike.
-Hotel should be built over sacred
  burial ground; evil spirit is pissed.
-Buckets of blood pouring out all
  over the place.

( Done )  ( More )

Rob's latest brilliant ideas.

"Well, thanks," he said, modestly, pointing to his head. "I'll always have it up here."

Trying to reference the location of Rob Stern on the map Lanny Sticks pilfered was almost impossible. The Paramount back lot became what it is in 1926, and grew in fits and starts. An overhead schematic is like looking at the maze of a secret garden designed to confuse and disorient.

"I know the studio pretty well, if it means anything," George offered. "What are you looking for?"

"The Sturges Building."

"What's your plan?"

"For your own sake, I shouldn't tell you any more than I already have."

George rolled his eyes and took the map from my hands. He pulled out a yellow highlighter from his glove box and traced the route for me.

"There you go, mystery man. Enjoy."

"Thanks, pal. It's for your own good."

"Whatever."

"Now, do me a favor and just hang right here. I'm going to need between fifteen minutes and a half hour."

"You got it," George said, sliding his chauffeur cap over his eyes.

I walked with confidence down the colonnade in front of the administration building, glancing at George's markings occasionally.

*So far so good*, I thought. My getup was working, even though I felt like a Disney character at a theme park.

I cut behind the Lubitsch Building, across an open plaza, and slipped around the Dressing Room building, hoping to duck into the rear of the Preston Sturges Building. As I approached the door, a frumpy young man stepped out — Rob Stern! Holy hell, I was hoping to find his office, not the man himself.

*Why are you here on a Sunday?* I cursed secretly. *Shouldn't you be home, mowing your mother's lawn or playing Nintendo?*

"Hello, sir," Rob said, reverently. "What brings the great Robert Evans to my little building on a Sunday?"

I suddenly realized that the actor in me was relishing the encounter. I was Robert Evans, the producer of *Let's Make Love!* and Rob was just a little pissant junior executive from East Nowhere. It didn't make up for being fired, but it soothed my ego somewhat.

"I know you put in a lot of time on this project," I explained. "I mean, you're the one who brought it to the studio, kid. You're responsible for its development, responsible for its *current state*," I added, with an edge in my voice. "So, I knew you'd be here working today. I wanted to get your notes on the latest *Love* draft."

"It's funny you should ask that, Mr. Evans," Rob said, inflating himself. "I just e-mailed them out to everyone."

"Great, I look forward to reading them," I said, with genuine sincerity.

"Cool. Well, I'm off to the Buddha Bar to meet some friends about a new project."

"Hey, kid, before you go — quick question about the Campbell situation."

Rob bristled at the subject matter. "Uh-huh?"

"What really went down there? I don't see what the problem was. I never heard anything negative about him from Mike."

"It was an internal situation," Rob said, hesitantly.

"Who authorized it?"

"The decision was made on upper levels."

"Don't bullshit me, kid. I used to run this place. Give me a name."

Rob pursed his lips. "I say this with due respect, Mr. Evans — the Campbell case is a Red file. You've been there before, so you know I can't talk about it."

"Well that's fine, kiddo," I said, blowing him off as Robert Evans would have. "Red, blue, green — pick whatever color you want, but I'm going to get to the bottom of this Campbell thing. You studio chumps can't muscle me. I know where the bodies are buried around here — literally."

"Sure, I understand, Mr. Evans," Rob said, his face flushing from the threat. "I wonder how these things happen myself."

*You're going to wonder all right. You're going to wonder how my right shoe got so far up your ass.*

"Well, I'll let you get back to your nice, new office," Rob said, unable to hide his resentment.

"Yeah, got some big deals coming down — better get to it."

I stepped toward the Sturges Building, but Rob stopped me.

"I thought your office was *that* way," he said, jerking a thumb behind him.

I turned to see a low-profile building, with a facade like something from the set of *Chinatown*, the classic film produced by Robert Evans. Then I noticed a sign above the door: ROBERT EVANS INTERNATIONAL.

"Of course, kid. I've had so many offices here over the years,

I get turned around. Ciao."

"Have a good one," Rob said, pausing to see if "Robert Evans" actually entered "his" office.

I waved back and ducked into the plush lobby.

That brief encounter accomplished two things on my mission: 1. though risky, I was able to glean useful information and get under the weasel's skin, if only a little bit; 2. I now knew definitively that he was not going to be in his office for the rest of the day.

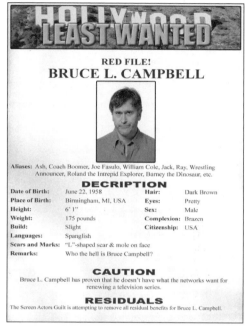

**HOLLYWOOD LEAST WANTED**

**RED FILE!**

**BRUCE L. CAMPBELL**

Aliases: Ash, Coach Boomer, Joe Fasulo, William Cole, Jack, Ray, Wrestling Announcer, Roland the Intrepid Explorer, Barney the Dinosaur, etc.

**DECRIPTION**

| | | | |
|---|---|---|---|
| Date of Birth: | June 22, 1958 | Hair: | Dark Brown |
| Place of Birth: | Birmingham, MI, USA | Eyes: | Pretty |
| Height: | 6' 1" | Sex: | Male |
| Weight: | 175 pounds | Complexion: | Brazen |
| Build: | Slight | Citizenship: | USA |
| Languages: | Spanglish | | |
| Scars and Marks: | "L"-shaped scar & mole on face | | |
| Remarks: | Who the hell is Bruce Campbell? | | |

**CAUTION**

Bruce L. Campbell has proven that he doesn't have what the networks want for renewing a television series.

**RESIDUALS**

The Screen Actors Guilt is attempting to remove all residual benefits for Bruce L. Campbell.

"Bob, there you are."

I turned to the bored, supermodel-type receptionist.

"Jack's waiting to see you," she said.

"Jack?" I asked, trying to hide my utter confusion.

"How many Jacks do you know, silly?"

"Ha — right!"

"I put the usual on your desk."

"Thanks...kiddo," I said, not knowing her name, and I walked out of the lobby.

At the end of a dimly lit hall was an enormous oak door, the kind you'd see in an old library. Some people in Hollywood earn a lot of money making movies. Some people in Hollywood earn so much money they spend more time decorating their offices than actually making movies.

I swung the heavy door open to see a man with his back to me, dressed in golf attire, putting at the far end of what was my enormous, seventies-era office. Large enough to host a full-scale party, but sprinkled with enough cozy nooks to accommodate intimate business dealings, this was a Hollywood mogul's wet dream.

I almost tripped over the shag carpeting as I entered, and my guest, *Jack Nicholson*, turned around with that characteristic Cheshire grin.

"Hey, Bobby," he said simply.

It was *that* Jack, after all. *Christ, I'm dead.* Jack Nicholson and Robert Evans went back thirty years, and surely knew each other's ticks and tastes.

"Jack you old dog," I said, initiating a hug, but Jack pulled back, surprised by my intimacy.

"All touchy-feely again, Bob?" he asked, a little confused.

"I'm just happy to see you again, Jack."

Jack and Bob.

"What, you missed me since playin' poker last night?"

My blank stare didn't help the awkward situation, so I shifted topics. "What can I get for you, Jack-a-roo?"

"The usual, thanks."

*Of course he would say that.*

I gestured to the expansive wet bar, trying to get more information. "Pick your poison."

Jack looked at me like I was off my nut. "Tomato juice, same as always." He went to the mini fridge and got it himself.

On top of a slightly agitated Jack Nicholson, I had yet another conundrum to deal with: I had no idea why we were meeting, or who initiated it.

Taking a deep breath and exhaling loudly, Jack pulled the tab on his can of low-sodium tomato juice and sat down on a plush sofa. "So...."

"So..." I echoed, nodding my head, as if we shared a secret.

"Wanna hear it?" Jack asked.

I was a nanosecond away from saying "hear what?" but I caught myself and sat down in an adjacent chair. "Sure do."

Jack took a swig of juice and stood right back up. "All right, here it is: the other day, I was makin' some salad dressing in the kitchen. I had a little water, I had a little oil, but I was out of vinegar. And then it hit me — we need to make another *Chinatown.* The first one was about water, the second was about oil, and the third should be about *vinegar*!"

"Vinegar," I said, looking confused, but still nodding yes.

"Work it backwards in your head, Bob — vinegar, wine, grapes — the land they're grown on. *The Two Jakes* was set in '48. You set this one a few years later in the Napa Valley, when Jake is retired, see, and it turns out the land he owns is tied up in this whole scheme to pave the way for a vineyard."

I kept nodding yes. Having already jeopardized the fate of one film, what else could I do?

"I'm calling it *Grapevine.*"

You didn't have to be an executive to know that *Grapevine* stunk as a title, but that never stopped movies like *Ishtar* and *Gigli* from getting made, and who was I to judge?

Jack interpreted my continued lack of response as a sign of disinterest. "Townsend is in, what more do you want, Bob?"

"Well, Jack, uh, you know how I feel about these movies —"

"Is it the deal? Is that's what's buggin' you?"

I had to stay neutral; I couldn't intimate that my deal was any better or worse than Nicholson's, since I didn't have a whisper of inside information. "No Jack, not specifically...."

"Look, I talked to Townsend. He'll give you five gross points and I'll give you five gross points."

He was referring to Robert Townsend, one of the luminaries of seventies screenwriting, and he was also referring to gross profit participation, money from dollar one at the box office.

"Will that do it, Bob?" Jack implored, getting impatient. "Can we make the deal?"

Considering the fact that I just got Robert Evans 10 percent of gross revenues for a *Chinatown* sequel starring Jack Nicholson, I felt pretty good. It was the most productive ten minutes I'd ever spent in Hollywood. "Jack, if you feel that strongly about it, sure — let's do it."

Jack's Cheshire smile came back in full force. "Good thing — my tee-time is in twenty minutes."

Jack initiated the hug this time, but I was the one who pulled away. Our verbal exchange was sweat-inducing, and I smelled like a rubber glove simmering on low heat. Jack got a good whiff.

"Whoa, Bob, you're sweatin' up a storm there, amigo. Everything okay? You don't look so good."

I realized that a dreaded "edge" of my makeup appliance began to show. On a film set, hiding makeup lines is a never-ending battle, requiring constant attention between shots. In a live context, it meant that my time as Robert Evans was limited, even under the best of conditions.

"I just had a little work done," I whispered to Jack in a knowing, sotto voce, "and the results were not exactly what I had hoped for."

Jack gave me a say-no-more wink and excused himself from the office. "I'll be in touch, Bob."

I decided to remove myself from Robert Evans International

before I could green-light another project.

"Hold all my calls," I said over my shoulder as I dashed outside.

Rob Stern's office was on the third floor of the Sturges Building. I knew for a fact that there was a generic bathroom on the second floor where I could take the makeup off, wash up, and continue my quest without incident.

Bathrooms on back lots aren't what you might think. Far from opulent, the average biffy-in-a-bungalow was closer to the Navy than Hollywood. Color schemes were either drab brown and creme, or dark gray with a light gray trim. But it didn't really matter how many coats of paint had been added since the days of Adolph Zukor, because all I was gonna do was rip my face off and get out of there.

I pushed the door open, expecting to see exactly nobody on a Sunday evening. I was wrong. Chris McDonald, a very busy actor, was washing his hands in front of the mirror. Chris kept busy as an actor, mainly by stealing roles from me. At last infuriating count, he was up to seventeen. He and I play the same "type" a lot — the smarmy, snotty, or obnoxious guy, only he lands most of the roles I'm trying to get.

WHY I HATE CHRIS McDONALD

ROLES HE STOLE FROM ME

1987: Jeb, Eight Is Enough: A Family Reunion
1991: Darryl, Thelma & Louise
1993: Frank Kelso, Fatal Instinct
1994: Jack Barry, Quiz Show
1996: Shooter McGavin, Happy Gilmore
1997: Ward Cleaver, Leave It to Beaver
1997: Jon Krakauer, Into Thin Air: Death on Everest
1997: Wilson Croft, Flubber
1998: Mr. Frank Connor, The Faculty
1999: Kent Mansley (voice), The Iron Giant
2000: Mitch Gibson, Takedown
2001: Macadam Salesman, The Man Who Wasn't There
2004: Bruce Campbell, Comic Book: The Movie

MY NAME IS CHRIS McDONALD. THPT!

ROLES I WON

1995: Raffle Winner, The Demolitionist
... um...

ME

I met Chris once at a function in Century City, and unfortunately he turned out to be a very nice guy — I say unfortunately, because it made it more difficult to hate him. I knew exactly why the bastard was here — for an *audition* — and he was killing time in the bathroom.

If I didn't take action, I knew what was going to happen: Chris was going to tell me, Robert Evans, about his latest gigs, and how nice it was to meet me, how he'd love to work with me some day, and blah, blah, blah, and then he'd notice that something was wrong. With makeup that was about to take itself off, it didn't take long to devise a plan.

"There's that actor I see everywhere," I said, going the gregarious route. "Bob Evans."

"I know who you are, Mr. Legendary Producer," he said, offering his hand. "Chris McDonald. Great to meet you."

I shook Chris's hand all right. I shook it long and hard, enough to get a worried look out of him.

"You here auditioning for something, kid?"

"Uh, yeah, the new Zemeckis film, *Double Down*."

"Oh, that picture. What role are you reading for?" I asked, curious.

"The lieutenant who gets killed at the end — Ryan."

"Ahhh, it's funny, Bob Zemeckis is a good friend of mine. He used to shine my shoes on Sundays. All I ever hear him talk about is this Campbell kid."

"Bill Campbell? That bastard always gets my stuff!" Chris said, shaking his head.

"No, no, the other one," I corrected.

"Glen? He's a singer."

"No, *Bruce* Campbell."

"The *Evil Death* guy? Why would Bob want him?" Chris asked, puzzled.

"Something about a certain quality," I said, shaking my head. "Look, I don't know, kid, I'm not directing the picture."

Chris became utterly befuddled, wringing his audition sides in his hands. "But if Campbell is already a lock — and you would know, Bob — then why should I even bother to read? You were an actor once, what would you do?"

"Well if it was me, I'd go home, check the mail for residual checks, and make a sour apple martini. But, it's Hollywood, kid, anything can happen."

"Yeah, I guess you're right, Bob, I —"

That's when I started to tear my face off. Sticking a thumb into the foam crevasse that had opened up earlier, I began to pull the prosthetics away from my face.

"Oh, my God, I'm melting!" I whimpered, in my best horror film reading.

Chris reeled back. The blue-green fluorescent light and the gray-on-lighter-gray bathroom lent itself perfectly to a ghoulish atmosphere.

My right hand was able to separate a huge chunk of my cheek, and I threw it into the sink. Chris almost vomited on the spot.

"Don't just stand there, Chris, get help!" I wailed, tearing my lips clean off.

Chris ran out of the bathroom, cupping a hand over his mouth, presumably to either barf or spread the word that something horrible had just happened to Robert Evans.

"Try and audition with *that* on your mind, Chris McDonald," I said, nodding ruefully.

Three hours of sweat had loosened the makeup substantially, so I finished tearing off what was left of Robert Evans and dumped him in the trash.

I emerged from the bathroom as a pasty-faced Bruce Campbell, and walked up to the third floor. I worked my way toward Suite 3350, passing a night cleaning crew that was going from office to office. *Had they passed Rob's office, or were they working their way toward it?* I wondered.

As I rounded the corner, I realized that Suite 3350 was being cleaning at that very moment. Acting is bluffing, so I took a deep breath and plunged into Rob Stern's office suite. A Latina woman was vacuuming, and another was spraying every surface with a horrid pink cleaning solution. As I entered Rob's world, I didn't hide the fact that I hated the smell.

"Whooh," I said, waving my hand in front of my nose. "Hey, it's okay. No more."

The spraying woman looked at me. "No?"

"No, thank you." I turned to the woman who was vacuuming. "Hello. It's okay. No need to do that."

The vacuuming woman finally noticed me. "No?"

"That's okay, really. Don't empty anything, no vacuum, no spray. Thank you. Good night. I have to work. *Mucho trabajo.*"

The women were happy to shave ten minutes off their work schedule. I ushered them out, threw the deadbolt behind them, and then turned to face Rob's world. Strewn around the office were posters of *Star Wars* and *American Pie*, *Evil Dead* action figures, signed photos from miscellaneous celebrities, and — I actually did a double take — the sword from *Army of Darkness*!

Rob had it mounted above his desk on a plaque, the way you display a beautiful elk rack.

"That little thief," I muttered, as I worked my way behind his desk through stacks of unread scripts. I yanked the sword off its display and twirled it in my hand. I knew immediately that it was authentic. The aluminum swords used on *Army of Darkness* were very sturdy and mercifully light — they felt like no other.

Hating him even more, I put the sword aside and scanned the surface of Rob's black, wood composite desk. It was littered with memos and candy wrappers, neither of which applied to my case. I turned my attention to his computer terminal. Rob had mentioned to "Robert Evans" that he had recently e-mailed his notes on the latest draft, so the challenge was to hack into his e-mail system.

His *Lord of the Rings* welcome screen displayed an access window, waiting for the correct password. If this were all a movie, I'd be a computer wiz and I'd hack in, get what I needed, and change the timing of the stoplights in Beverly Hills just for kicks.

But this was reality, and I had no such computer skills. I stared at the blinking cursor for a solid minute, until a shiny glint on the monitor led my eye over to the aluminum sword, which gleamed under Rob's bright halogen lamp.

I looked from the sword to the sign-in screen and typed "deadite." No response. I typed "Ash," and got nothing. Breaking into a cold sweat, knowing that many computer systems give you three attempts at the password, then shut you out, I bit my lip and typed the third and last try: "groovy."

The transition from soul-swallowing ghoul to film producer was an easy one for Stern.

Instantly, Rob's welcome screen changed, the *Army of Darkness* theme came up, and the character Ash said "Groovy." I was inside!

The inner workings of network computer systems have always been daunting, but I managed to navigate his e-mail system enough to call up a search mechanism. I typed in two words sure to get matches: *Campbell* and *Love.*

| Mailbox - Inbox | | | ⊕ ⊡ ⊗ |
|---|---|---|---|
| Mailbox   File   Edit   Options   Help | | | |
| ⊘ ◀ ▶ ⊘ ↑↓ | | | Campbell love |

**Inbox**

| From | Subject | Date Received | |
|---|---|---|---|
| e-auction | You won your bid on "Transformer... | Monday, June 12th, 6:04 AM | ▲ |
| R. Evans | RE: Does it have to be Bruce Cam... | Monday, June 12th, 6:59 AM | |
| Middle Earth Webguild | We missed you at the re-enactment | Monday, June 12th, 8:04 AM | |
| Mike Nichols | Campbell's in, deal with it | Monday, June 12th, 8:27 AM | |
| Anaheim Girls Gone Wild | Your subscription confirmation | Monday, June 12th, 9:24 AM | |
| R. Evans | RE: LML, Matrix meets Love Story | Monday, June 12th, 9:59 AM | |
| Jarre_K | I didn't like your idea. | Monday, June 12th, 11:22 AM | |
| Mike Nichols | I beg to differ. | Monday, June 12th, 11:59 AM | |
| Chicks with Chimps | Your subscription confirmation | Monday, June 12th, 1:04 PM | |
| R. Evans | What's up with all the CGI? | Monday, June 12th, 2:14 PM | ▼ |

**Sent Mail**

| To | Subject | Date Sent | |
|---|---|---|---|
| Kiffington | Can you get pix of BC's house? | Monday, June 12th, 7:51 AM | ▲ |
| Mike Nichols | But, I'm a producer!!! | Monday, June 12th, 10:59 AM | |
| Terry Feingold | The budget. | Monday, June 12th, 11:04 PM | |
| R. Evans | RE: What's up with all the CGI? | Monday, June 12th, 3:14 PM | |
| Jarre_K | Does he have to be a doorman? | Monday, June 12th, 3:16 PM | |
| Gere, Richard | Don't pull your punches. | Monday, June 12th, 4:15 PM | |
| Clarence | No! Sit! | Monday, June 12th, 4:20 PM | ▼ |

Probably a hundred e-mails, dating back almost a year, sprang up on a list. As a studio executive, I knew he wouldn't have deleted them — and what, erase his legacy? Randomly, I opened enough of them to learn that Stern had slowly, methodically masterminded the "*Army of Darkness*-ization" of the *Let's Make Love!* script, ignored budget implications, and when things began to go horribly wrong, blamed it all on an enthusiastic but undeserving actor (that would be me). I now had enough to take this kid down.

As fast as my mediocre computer skills would allow, I download-ed the damning e-mails to Rob's desktop and copied them to a blank CD-ROM.

"Ha! I'll show that punk —"

I headed for the door but before I could exit, a mixture of Paramount security guards and plain-suited men poured in, all led by Lanny Sticks.

"That's him," Lanny said, pointing at me. "That's Bruce Campbell. He's the perpetrator."

I froze.

"Robert Evans, my ass," Lanny said, approaching me with a mangled chunk of my Robert Evans appliance in his clenched fist.

"How did you find out?" I asked, my mind racing, churning through one B-movie-inspired escape after another. Suddenly I noticed that the aluminum sword that had helped me a decade before was within easy reach. I began inching toward it.

"In all the years I would say hello to Robert Evans," Lanny explained simply, "he never once called me Lanny."

"So it all boiled down to a name," I mused.

"The call about Robert Evans's face melting off helped too. That's when I —"

That's when I grabbed the sword. In a neat two-step move I learned on the failed TV show *Jack of All Trades*, I deftly stepped behind Lanny and placed the jagged aluminum blade tight across his neck.

The other security guys freaked and backed away, one falling over a chair.

"Get away from the door," I barked.

Using Lanny as a human shield, I made my way toward the exit.

"Let him do it," Lanny urged, feeling the discomfort from my blade. "I'm good, don't worry about me."

I backed out the door with Lanny in tow and we worked our way to the edge of the nearest stairway.

"You're gonna take a big fall, Bruce," Lanny warned. "If you let me go right now, I can clear this up. You keep going with this, it's gonna get serious. Studios have heavy-duty backup when they need it."

"I'm innocent, Lanny," I explained, grabbing the enormous ring of keys from his belt. I clipped his walkie-talkie to my pants and shoved him to the floor. "From one actor to another, I'm telling the truth."

"I don't care," Lanny scowled, massaging an elbow.

I ran down the stairs and past the "meltdown" bathroom, side-stepping the Haz Mat team that was hosing the place out.

Out on the relative expanse of the back lot, I picked up speed and made my way past the administrative offices, where George and the town car were parked. But as the Lincoln came into view, I discovered George spread-eagled across the hood. He was being rousted by four serious-looking men.

*Poor bastard. To serve the greater good, one must be pre-pared to sacrifice a few innocent chauffeurs.*

Caught on tape: "Bob Evans" lurking around the lot.

I took off in the opposite direction at a dead run, checking in on walkie-talkie broadcasts as I went. Between four channels, I did the best I could to monitor what Lanny and his men knew — or *didn't* know.

Channel 1:=SQUAWK=

"I'm heading south on Ave E...."

Channel 2: =SQUAWK= "I'm gonna be here awhile, Stu, the police want the melted face stuff as evidence...."

Channel 3: =SQUAWK= "on 5th Street, westbound...."

Channel 4: =SQUAWK= "no, no, it was liverwurst with mustard — in a bag under the desk. Can you check again?"

My only logical escape route was due north, through the cemetery. I knew Paramount well enough to know that avenues ran north and south, and streets were east and west. The guards were obviously covering the main drags. As long as I stayed on the streets, I wasn't safe, but a man with keys could head north, to freedom.

The Crosby Building was right in front of me. I tested the keys methodically, just as Lanny had explained, and within a minute I was inside.

I quickly realized that I was on a scoring stage — one that was actually scoring a film. Fortunately, I had come in through the rear and was facing the backs of some forty musicians. They, in turn, faced a large digital screen, which played a climactic chase scene from some unnamed Adam Sandler movie. I scoped a door on the opposite side of the paneled room and predicted an easy walk around.

All actors love props, so I used the walkie-talkie to engage in a very important, silent conversation as I eased past the woodwinds. But just beyond the percussion section I became distracted by some good sight gags in the film. I became the guy at baseball games who walks back to his section, a beer in each hand, looking up at the scoreboard rather than straight ahead. You don't want to be behind the idiot, because he walks about one mile an hour, and you don't want to be in front of him, or seated in his row, because half of his beer is emptying in all directions.

My version of that guy was walking into a drum set, sending the cymbals crashing to the ground at exactly the wrong time. The music stopped, lights came up, and all heads turned to me. I fumbled with the cymbals before resorting to the walkie-talkie gag.

"Yeah, ten-four, good buddy — just checking out some strange noises in the Crosby stage, but it's nothing unusual, over."

Before anyone could penetrate my cunning ruse, I slipped out the north door and found myself in a hallway lined with other doors, all leading to rooms seemingly related to postproduction sound.

I chose a door toward my end of the hall and promptly stumbled into an active Foley stage. These recording studios are almost always dark and are floored with a number of surfaces that simulate anything from a concrete walkway to a grassy knoll. Before my eyes could adjust, I stumbled noisily across every surface except the one the engineers were trying to match — Meg Ryan walking barefoot in the sand, for some soon-to-be-released romantic comedy.

*Don't these guys ever take a day off?*

I pushed through a side door and realized that I was now interrupting an ADR session, the process where dialogue is replaced in a controlled environment, after-the-fact. "Controlled" became more of an abstract concept as I plowed my way into George Clooney's session.

"Hey, hey, what the...?" George wondered as he spun away from the microphone to see who was behind him.

"Sorry, Mr. Clooney, just a routine security check," I said, hiding my face, never really stopping.

"That was good, George," the technician said over the studio speaker, "but the line is: 'Hey, hey, *where* the ...?' Let's try one more."

Before the big-shot star could explain, I snatched a seed-less grape from his complementary fruit basket and snuck out. George gave an incredulous look to nobody in particular, and put his headphones back on.

The exit led to an alley adjacent to Studio 15. No sooner had the door closed behind me than a familiar, angry voice echoed down the alley.

"Well, I guess it's just you and me."

I turned to see Lanny Sticks blocking my exit. He wasn't car-rying a gun, just a big riot stick.

"Mano a mano," he said, twirling the baton like he had paid attention during training.

I was bigger than Lanny, and had a sword, but I didn't feel like risking a rubber-coated bash to the kneecap if I could avoid it. The only way out was a door to Stage 15, immedi-ately to my right, but unlike the other ones, it was older, funkier, and harder to key. It would be a race between my door-opening skills (mediocre) and Lanny's police brutality training (unknown but possibly extensive).

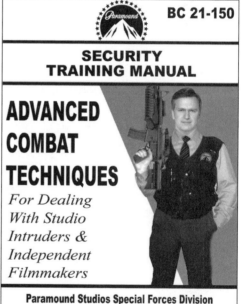

BC 21-150

**SECURITY TRAINING MANUAL**

**ADVANCED COMBAT TECHNIQUES**

*For Dealing With Studio Intruders & Independent Filmmakers*

**Paramound Studios Special Forces Division**

I decided to risk it. I took off toward the door and whipped out the key ring. Lanny charged, baton in attack position. I tried the first key, but it was no good. I spun around and — *whannnng!* — parried Lanny's approaching baton with my sword, then kicked him in the chest and tried a second key — still no good!

I spun back and head blocked the next swipe from Lanny, but

I knew aluminum was no match for steel, and that this type of contact wouldn't last long. Based on a move a stuntman taught me during *Mindwarp*, I dropped to the ground and swept my legs under Lanny, knocking him on his ass. He fell hard, losing both his breath and the baton.

I tried a third key, and it worked! I pulled open the insulated doors and walked right into a full-fledged barbarian fight scene, staged courtesy of American Express. There must have been a hundred leather-and-fur-clad warriors, hacking away at each other with crude weapons. I promised myself it would be the last time I infiltrated Paramount on a Sunday, and fought my way north, through the smelly Angelinos.

Lanny was soon on my heels, blocking blows from wooden swords, and shoving unsuspecting extras out of his way. As we neared the exit, he inadvertently walked into the middle of two stuntmen diving at each other and got sandwiched in the middle.

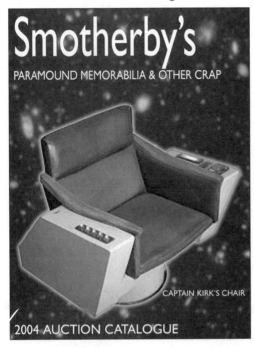

# Smotherby's

PARAMOUND MEMORABILIA & OTHER CRAP

CAPTAIN KIRK'S CHAIR

2004 AUCTION CATALOGUE

Across the stage, in "video village," a goatee-sporting, baseball-cap-wearing director leaped from his low director's chair.

"What the *fuck* was that? Cut, cut!"

I pushed open the doors to 12th Street, one of the most northerly on the lot. The outback was close. The last building standing in the way of victory was a storage facility. Inside the musty, damp place, unused sets from movies and

TV shows were stored. I hustled past saloon sets, bank facades, and...*Captain Kirk's chair?!*

The original *Star Trek* had been one of my favorite shows as a kid, and I would imitate William Shatner for days on end. I wiped some residual dust off the wide vinyl arms and sat down. The chair wasn't nearly as comfortable as I had assumed, and it didn't swivel or do anything cool, but it didn't matter. I leaned back and assumed command of the starship *Enterprise.*

"Gentlemen, I suggest you get my ship out-of-there," I bellowed to an empty warehouse, in perfect Shatner staccato.

"Aye-a-eye, sir," came the reply from across the large room (though not, I might add, in a particularly convincing Sulu).

It was Lanny, with a big lump on his head, back for more. I bolted out of Kirk's chair and kicked open the side door.

Blessed wilderness awaited at the fringe of the back lot — my way out. I ran through the dense underbrush. Shrubs and pickers tore at my clothes and skin, but nothing could affect the elation I felt now that freedom was within my grasp.

But at the overgrown gate to the cemetery, Lanny was there, waiting.

"I knew you'd go out this way," he said, tapping the baton in his palm. "A word of advice: never try to out-shortcut a security guard. They'll beat you every time."

Before a standoff could occur, I reached down and threw a fistful of dirt at Lanny's face and then rushed him. It was a surprise move, and it gave me a momentary edge, but Lanny hadn't slept through that 20-minute self-defense video. Using his baton as a barrier, he made sure the butt of it impacted with my chin when we landed on the ground.

A split second of white-hot pain exploded in my head and I released my grip. Lanny rolled over and readied his baton for a crippling blow, but not before I backhanded him across the face.

You see it in movies all the time, but in reality it hurts like hell, and is absolutely no good for your knuckles.

Either way, it was enough to get this little bulldog off me and we squared off again. The similarity of this scenario triggered a vivid flashback from *Army of Darkness*. I was rehearsing swordplay in the gravel parking lot of the Polsa Rosa Ranch with our sword master, Dan, and he taught me a slick, disarming maneuver where you attack and evade at the same time.

Before you could say "action," I ducked, swiped, rolled, and knocked his heavy baton high into the air. The cool move ended with me placing the tip of my sword against Lanny's jugular vein.

"Ow, shit, that hurt!" Lanny complained.

"Sorry, man, it never worked on the first take before."

Lanny and I faced each other, breathing heavily. I could hear the rustle of footsteps and shouting near the edge of the outback — trouble was closing in.

"If I didn't know better, Lanny, I'd say you were pissed about something. What the hell did I ever do to you?"

Lanny shot a hard look at me. "Think about it, Bruce. Do you ever see me with women? Did you ever notice that I don't have any children?"

"Wow, I never knew you were gay, Lanny."

"I'm not gay, dumbass!" he barked. "Did you ever wonder that maybe it's because ol' Lann-o is shootin' blanks?"

"You're...*sterile*?"

"Why don't you just come out and say it?" he said, looking around nervously. "You know the scene. *Death of the Dead* — I'm Snake, you're Nash. I'm takin' you outside the cabin at night and I knock you in the back of the head with the butt of my shotgun."

"And Nash flies off the porch to the ground below," I finished.

"Yeah I remember — it hurt like hell."

Lanny turned back to me, eyes glistening at the tragic memory. "You have no idea. When you fell off the porch, you kicked a back leg in the air, didn't you?"

"To balance myself, yeah," I said defensively. "I always do that with falls."

"You put the heel of your boot right into my dingleberries."

"I did?" I asked, puzzled. But then I remembered Lanny approaching me after the take that night, sweaty and pale, mentioning that he was in some kind of pain. "I did. I did kick you in the nuts, Lanny," I admitted. "That made you sterile?"

"It was a hell of a shot," he said, avoiding eye contact.

"But why didn't you say something before?"

Lanny wiped his eyes and smiled, but it was forced and tragic. "Hey, it's not something you talk about while shootin' pool with the guys on a Friday night, you know?"

The advancing footfalls grew louder. A flashlight swept the woods, and we began to hear the tinny, "blah, blah, blah" of walkie-talkie chatter.

"Then it won't matter if I do it again," I said, kicking Lanny dead center in the Planters. He buckled instantly, an indescribable look of pain carved onto his face.

I turned my attention to the lock on the gate and pulled out the prodigious collection of keys. *Too long,*

The exact moment the term "Brucectomy" was coined.

I reasoned, and swung the fake sword with all my might. The aluminum blade pinched the metal chain against the stone wall and severed it. The lock fell off and the gate swung wide open. I raced into the cemetery just as officers of all jurisdictions swarmed upon the scene. It was now an old-fashioned foot chase.

# 22

# Run, Bruce, Run!

I retraced my steps backward through the maze of the large cemetery, praying I wouldn't get lost. With a couple of Paramount security guards setting time trials behind me, my decision-making process became very spontaneous.

I rounded a corner near Tyrone Power's tombstone, and his devoted lover was there again, placing fresh flowers on his grave. I grabbed the middle-aged, frumpy woman and looked deep into her eyes.

"Kiss me once — for old Ty's sake?" I implored, as sincerely as I could for being completely out of breath.

"Anything for Ty!" the woman said, throwing her arms around me.

Our kiss was convincing enough for the security team to run right past without stopping. After an uncomfortable moment of trying to disengage from this surprisingly strong woman, I thanked her profusely and headed on my way.

Out by the main cemetery entrance, the security guys were

chatting with the groundskeeper and I slipped out undetected. But as I approached Santa Monica Boulevard in search of a cab, I was amazed to see that the entire street seemed to have been closed off. A few blocks away, an official-looking motorcade approached, while a group of men in suits milled around, fingers to their ears.

Behind me, an agitated voice rang out: "It's him — it's the guy!"

When you're on the lam, you don't always have time to examine a situation as carefully as you'd like. So it wasn't until after I had hurdled the concrete security barrier lining Santa Monica Boulevard and collided with a strangely familiar man wearing an unseasonably warm dark wool suit that I realized harassing a world figure for the third time wasn't the best way to make a clean getaway.

"You?!" Agent Grunow hissed accusingly as I struggled to extricate myself from our impromptu embrace.

"Are you following me?" I asked suspiciously, buying time while I unhooked my pant cuff from his gun belt.

"I'm here on official business," he explained. "Secretary Powell has been invited to a screening of *The SpongeBob Squarepants Movie*. Hey! Come back here!"

As with so many things in life, zigzagging between screeching black government SUVs was fun for the first thirty seconds, but got old fast. As I ducked and weaved my way across the boulevard, my new Sprint PCS phone kept thumping around in my breast pocket. I trapped it against my chest and fished it out. I'm not a gadget freak, but this sucker had it all — photo/video capability, wireless access, text messaging, even video games, which is why I had it in the first place, because the phone was given to me to approve an *Evil Dead* game (buy yours today!).

It occurred to me, between huffing and puffing, that although I didn't live in Los Angeles anymore, I still had plenty of close friends in pseudo high places. Any one of them would help me at a moment's notice; all I had to do was call.

The first person I dialed was good buddy Sam Raimi. Since the *Spider-Man* movies kicked major box-office ass, Sam's stature as a director had grown considerably. Now he was an A-list director, and I knew he could pull some strings.

As expected, I got Sam's assistant, J.R.

"J.R., Bruce here, how are ya, buddy?"

"Fine, thanks. What can I do for you?" he asked.

"Well, I'll tell it to you straight because I don't have much time — I'm in trouble, and I need Sam's help desperately."

"Okay, I'll give him the message."

"The hell you will, J.R.," I said, starting to wheeze, "I need to talk to him *now*."

"Sorry, man, Sam's writing *Spider-Man 3*. He's not returning anyone's calls until the end of the day."

"Even if I said I was being chased by dark forces of evil?"

"He was pretty adamant."

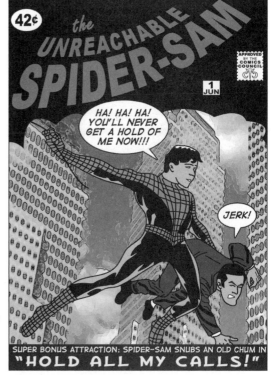

"Okay, no sweat. Tell Sam it was nice knowing him."

"Okay, will do," J.R. noted, as if he were taking a message to pick up a loaf of bread.

I hung up the phone and cursed *Spider-Man*. How dare those films do so well! I shouldn't have given such great performances!

*The hell with him*, I rationalized, *I'll call my pal Rob Tapert.*

Rob was a successful producer, and he would no doubt have major connections, legal or otherwise, that could help. I dialed Rob and, of course, got his assistant, Sue.

"Sue...Bruce here. How are you...doing?"

"You sound like you're running a marathon," she said.

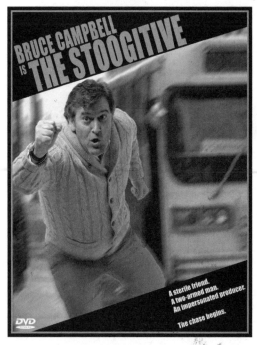

"Something like that. Listen, I need to get hold of Rob — it's really important."

"Rob's not here right now, but I can give him a message."

"Sue, you don't understand — I really need to talk to him."

"That might be a little difficult. He's on a flight to New Zealand right now to prep a film. He won't touch down for about five more hours."

"All right, forget it. I'll be making national headlines by then."

I flipped the phone closed and cursed New Zealand. Goddamn global economy — why the hell can't Americans make movies in *America*?

I ducked up an alley on the north side of Santa Monica Boulevard. and glanced back at my pursuers. Fortunately, they were making phone calls too, and it kept them at a corresponding distance.

*Okay, L.A. sucks for friends.* I needed someone who would support me unconditionally. Who would be there when the chips were down? Who would be there even when I wasn't at the top of my game? That's when I realized that the help I sought couldn't be found in my Rolodex — what I needed was a fan!

Even with a squad of angry, trained men after me, the notion of calling a fan to ask for help made me laugh. I laughed so hard I dialed up the Internet and connected to my website. Or rather, that's what I attempted to do. The buttons on my PCS phone were tiny, which made it impractical to surf the web while jumping fences and eluding rottweilers. Nonetheless, after slowing to a dead run, I was able to download a fan database.

The next challenge was finding the nearest fan. I cleared another fence and thumbed through the addresses that popped up on the nice color screen ("visible even in low-light conditions," the rep had assured me). The names Jan and Ryan Gritton were easy to find, because they were the only listing for Hollywood, U.S.A.

I maneuvered around a line of fresh laundry, blowing lazily in the breeze, and pasted Jan's address into MapQuest. While the operating system's tiny hourglass symbol taunted me, I sprinted across Huckleberry Lane and jumped over a cinderblock retaining wall.

The directions eventually popped up, and I made my way to 509 Beech Lane, a small bungalow, tucked off the street.

*Bam-bam-bam!* I pounded on Jan's door like a cop.

An exhausted-looking woman in her late thirties opened the door and looked me over. "Not interested," she said, slamming the door in my face.

*Bam-bam-bam!* I pounded on the door again, even harder.

The door was opened the second time by sixteen-year-old freak Ryan Gritton. With a classic *Evil Dead* fan look of dyed black hair, an ashen face framed by black horn-rimmed glasses, tattoos, and multiple piercings, he was clearly trying to intimidate me.

"Look, dude, what do you want?" he demanded.

I took a wild guess. "Ryan Gritton?"

"Yeah?"

"Don't you recognize your only true friend, Bruce Campbell?"

It took a moment for Ryan to alter his posture from defensive to unbelieving, but the transformation was fun to watch.

"I don't believe it!" Ryan exclaimed, half jumping in the air. "Mom, it's okay, it's Ash!"

"That's right," I said in my best game-show-host impersonation. "And you've just won the 'Make Dinner for Bruce Campbell' Sweepstakes!"

Jan stepped out from behind her son and became more animated. "Oh, my God, when do we get to make dinner?"

"Right *now*," I said, pushing my way into their cramped, cluttered bungalow.

The Gritton home was a loving one, but their interior had been decorated by a gang of howler monkeys on crack.

"Nice place you have here," I said, allowing my eyes to slide past the piles of as-yet-undone laundry heaped in the kitchen. "Say, uh, do you have a computer with a CD-ROM drive?"

"Sure do. In Ryan's room," Jan offered. "You're free to use it, while I whip up dinner. Grilled cheese okay with you?"

"You read my mind, Jan," I said, following Ryan to his room, which, in keeping with the general aesthetic, was a shithole.

"It's dial-up. I hope it's fast enough for you, Ash," Ryan said.

"Right now, I'd use an abacus if it would help," I said, turning on Ryan's Gateway 2000 computer, the same brand I had purchased years ago and threw in the trash because of piss-poor performance.

I logged on to my account and quickly deleted a wave of spam. The CD-ROM in my pocket had gathered a dew of sweat from my body during flight, but it loaded just fine. Now, all I had to do was send the damning information to parties that might clear my name — the execs at Paramount, the Screen Actors Guild, trade magazines, my mother, and aint-it-cool-news.com, a fan website that thrives on inside information.

But just as I slid the compact disc into the Gateway's lame drive, the walkie-talkie I stole from Lanny Sticks squawked: "Uh, yeah, 212, we've sighted the suspect in a bungalow in Hollywood — please advise."

This intercepted broadcast confirmed my fears that the big hammer of the law was about to fall. I quickly gathered Jan and Ryan and sat them down on their Ikea living room couch.

"Okay guys, look — I came here under false pretenses. You see, there are dark forces arrayed against me, forces that want to sully my otherwise good reputation. I need you to stall while I use your computer to clear my name."

"Are they punishing you because of *Jack of All Trades*?" Ryan asked. "Because that show sucked ass."

"It's not that," I explained, not wanting to debate the particulars of why a TV show succeeds or fails. "But if you don't help me get this information

Ryan Gritton and his "only true friend."

out, I'm going to prison. And if I go to prison, I won't judge any more costume contests at horror conventions, I won't be in any more failed TV shows, there won't be any more small roles in big movies, and there sure as hell won't be any more cult classics like *Maniac Cop*."

I had to stop myself because prison wasn't sounding so bad.

Ryan gave his mother a grim look. "Mom, break out the heavy metal," he instructed.

"Damn straight," she said with a nod. Then, to me: "You've got some e-mail to send, big guy."

Jan didn't have to tell me twice. I ran back to Ryan's room and began composing a heartfelt, clear-my-name/here's-my-proof letter. In the adjacent room, I could hear the muffled sounds of shotguns being breech-loaded, shell boxes being emptied and tossed on the floor, Tasers being charged.

My walkie-talkie squawked again: "Stand by, 39, waiting for enclosure signal...."

*Shit, the feds are closing in.* "Hey, guys, it's go time!"

Ryan ran down the hallway to the front room. He was packing a Desert Eagle in his belt and a Remington Wingmaster Magnum 12-gauge double-barreled shotgun in his arms. Jan was close behind with her Browning Citori Feather 12-gauge over/under shotgun, and a snub-nosed .38 pistol tucked into her jeans.

"Damn this dial-up!"

Above us, the *whop-whop-whop* sounds of a circling helicopter rattled the windows. My letter complete, I decided to send it in one mass e-mail to everyone I knew. I attached the incriminating files on the CD and hit Send. There were several megabytes of information, and I knew from living in the dial-up hell of rural Oregon that the transfer was going to take time, something we had precious little of.

Then, without warning, federal agents swooped in from several directions — some on foot, some in souped-up SUVs — and surrounded the bungalow.

Inside the main room, Ryan and Jan were locked and loaded. The bright glare of spotlights poured through the checked curtains.

"They got us surrounded," Ryan said through gritted teeth. "Bastards."

The files were:

`███ 15% _____`

Trying to buy some time, I keyed the walkie-talkie and used my best NASA radio voice. "He's on the move, he's on the move! The perpetrator just took off on foot, heading north in the alley behind the bungalow!"

The airwaves immediately filled with chatter, and the helicopter swung its light away from the house. I cracked a self-assured smile, but before I could make a snide comment about how dumb they were and how smart I was, the chopper came back, hovering even closer to the house.

I glanced at the computer monitor:

`██████ 30% _____`

"Damn this dial-up connection," I said, cursing telephone lines everywhere and slamming my fist on the keyboard.

"Hey, buster, I'm a single mom, okay?" Jan said defensively. "I can't afford that Ethernet shit, so screw you!"

"I'm sorry, Jan," I apologized. "I'm not mad at you, I'm mad at the world."

Then, my Sprint PCS rang.

"Hello?"

"Mr. Campbell, this is Agent Grunow, Secret Service. We

should talk."

I switched on the handy speakerphone feature, and gestured for Ryan and Jan to listen.

"I told you never to call me here," I said. "What do you want?"

"We need you to safely evacuate the occupants of the house," Grunow insisted.

"Over my dead body, pig!" Ryan shouted into the phone.

I shushed him, and checked the transfer.

`[=========================== 67% ===========================]`

I swore under my breath, but tried to keep cool and stall. "Have I done something wrong, Agent Grunow? Am I charged with something?"

"You are considered not only a fugitive, but you are, because of prior infractions, now a security threat to the United States of America."

*Guantánamo Bay, here I come.* "Yeah, well, you'll have to come and get us," I snarled, hanging up.

Ryan threw me a high five, and the three of us shared a moment of elated defiance, knowing we had taken on the Man. But my personal excitement was tempered by recollections of the F.B.I.'s well-known heavy-handed tactics. They had sharp-shooters, and they knew how to use them.

"Turn the lights off — quick!" I warned, and we all dashed for different lights.

I bent down to click off Ryan's Lava Lamp and a federal bullet shattered the globe, sending glass, water, and red paraffin everywhere.

"Take cover," I yelled, running back to the computer to check the upload.

`[=========================== 74% ===========================]`

"That was my favorite lamp, assholes!" Ryan shouted, busting the glass out of a side window with the butt of his shotgun.

*Boom! Boom! Boom!* The fireworks began. Ryan pumped hot buckshot toward several of the bright spotlights, darkening one of them as a piercing scream filled the air — most likely from a S.W.A.T. team member.

Tear gas came next. Hissing canisters, spitting noxious plumes of yellow smoke crashed through three windows. The small dwelling didn't take long to fill up with the debilitating gas, so I grabbed a T-shirt off Ryan's pile of dirty laundry and shoved it over my mouth and nose. This was followed by a brief, internal debate as to whether a teenager's T-shirt stench was preferable to tear gas. Reluctantly, I stuck with the shirt.

Jan and Ryan began to hack uncontrollably, but never abandoned their posts, each flanking a different side of the bungalow and slinging lead into the haze.

I tried to open my stinging eyes long enough to see the upload. A quick glance to see "82 percent" was too much to bear, and I had to close them again.

Then, behind me, a dark figure burst through the window. It was like the end of a creepy horror film where you think everything is going to be okay, and then all of a sudden — *Boo!* — someone reaches out and scares the living crap out of  you. In this case, it was Agent Grunow, my nemesis, and he was bent on bringing me into custody.

I was able to square off before he tackled me, but it didn't really matter — I couldn't see worth a damn. Grunow and I tumbled across dirty laundry, gum wrappers, and stray CDs until we hit the opposite wall. Neither of us could get the upper hand, but Grunow was able to get a clear look at the monitor. He assumed that my upload was something devious, and made stopping it his new number-one priority. He lunged for the mouse, but I grabbed his leg and twisted. Grunow crashed to the floor, and I put a knee in his back, hoping to stabilize him long enough to let the remaining 9 percent go through.

In the front room, all hell was breaking loose. The S.W.A.T. team had a highly armored battering ram, and proceeded to use it on a front door that was worth maybe three or four good hits.

But as far as Jan and Ryan were concerned, nobody was getting inside their home.

"Stay here, Ryan," Jan ordered, pulling back a portion of rug to reveal a crawl space. "I'll hit 'em from below."

CHAPTER 23

# EMBELLISHED THREAT RESPONSE TACTICS

## S.W.E.A.T.

### PRELIMINARY TACTICS

1. Exaggerate probable cause.
2. Ignore due process.
3. Shoot all pets.
4. Shoot all spouses.
5. Set lots of stuff on fire.
6. Shoot all fires.
7. Play lulling sounds of woodland creatures being slaughtered.
8. Shoot the guy next to him.
9. Set all dead pets on fire.
10. Have a quick game of tag football with the ATF.
11. Repeat.

*Ruby Ridge*

*Waco*

*Gritton Household*

"Okay," Ryan shouted above the din, reloading as fast as he could.

Grunow turned out to be one well-trained son of a bitch, because he had squirmed out from under me in less than four seconds and was now maneuvering to gain the advantage. As we wrestled, we had a perfect view of the power strip underneath the computer table. Grunow lunged for it. I tried to get there first, but the agent was exactly one second ahead of me. Before he could unplug the power strip, and my hopes of career salvation, I clamped a hand on top of Grunow's and froze his momentum.

Under the house, Jan crawled toward the front of her bungalow like a commando. From below, she soon had a clear shot at the rather broad side of a federal agent's butt — no Kevlar protection for that. She took aim, but decided against removing his cheek, and instead blew away several feet of dirt around his boots, sending him and the other battering ram operators scrambling for cover.

"Get gone if you know what's good for you!" Jan yelled after them with contempt.

For a layman, I was doing a damn good job holding my own against one of Uncle Sam's finest, but, hey, I wasn't trained in Quantico, so I didn't expect what came next, which was Agent Grunow's pointy elbow, lodging itself deep in my left temple. The impact stunned my brain long enough for him to finish his prime directive, and the power strip was effectively unplugged.

"No!" I screamed in horror, looking up at the monitor, expecting to find that the remaining 1 percent of the file had died somewhere in cyberspace, thereby ruining the transfer. But nothing was wrong, because the computer was actually plugged directly into a wall socket on the *opposite side of the table.*

Grunow looked at the monitor in amazement. He quickly shouted into his headset: "Cut the power, cut the —"

My fist prevented the agent from repeating the traitorous phrase. He was now a resident of dreamland.

The screen read: 99...100 percent — the file finished uploading, and AOL cheerfully announced:

File Sent

And with that, the power to the bungalow was, in fact, cut — but not before the truth had echoed far and wide.

Immediately following the outage, the Feebs administered

"Flash-Bangs," devices that deafen and disorient by emitting a huge booming noise accompanied by a blinding flash. Three or four of these got going at the same time, and none of us knew which direction was up.

A full-front assault began, and a mixture of F.B.I., local S.W.A.T., and Secret Service agents came through windows, doors, floors and attics. I was tackled by three guys at once. With my face shoved into the 1980s polyester carpet, I could hear the muffled cries of both Ryan and Jan as they were hauled away. The jig was up.

**23**

# Aftermath

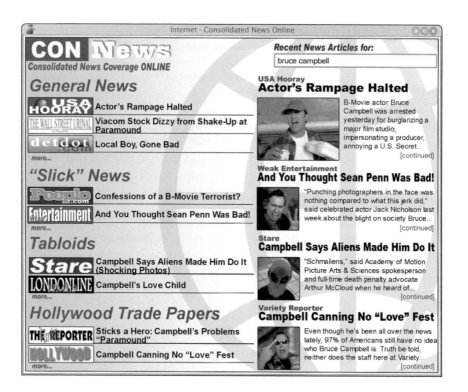

## FILM/TV

# Campbell in Shambles?

**Artie McCloud**
*Associate Press*
••••••••••••••••••••••••••••••

The bizarre legal saga surrounding Bruce Campbell came to an end today as the actor, best known for his role as an 18-inch-tall action figure, was turned over to the custody of the California penal system. Federal prosecutor Gummo Wolverton, who had promised to make an example of Campbell to other out-of-work B movie actors, proclaimed that "justice had been served."

Campbell, upon his arrest for domestic terrorism and other charges last fall, immediately employed the services of celebrity lawyer Johnny Cochrane, who argued effectively that corporate giants can't discriminate between an "A" actor and a "B" actor. Cochrane felt that the issue "should play out on a big canvas."

Campbell was eventually found innocent of all state and local charges, including sabotage, and therefore not liable for the entire negative cost of *Let's Make Love!* as Paramound had alleged. The film in question, helmed by veteran Mike Nichols, was shut down three weeks after Campbell's departure.

Paramound Studios, in response to the news surrounding Campbell's sen-

*See **Campbell**, Page G4*

# Campbell

*Continued from Page G1*

tencing, issued the following statement:

**Bruce Campbell**

"Paramound Studios and its affiliates are relieved to hear that the legal issues pertaining to Mr. Campbell have been resolved, but remain troubled that a once promising actor who had appeared in our company's *Congo* and *Escape from L.A.* could 'fall so far, so fast.'

"And, because of this remarkable incident, we're going to take a fresh look at actor Lanny Sticks. He's done some impressive work, both in front of and behind the camera, and this studio - which is proud of its long-term commitment to talent - owes him a big one. Thanks, Lanny."

Paramound also announced that it had decided not to renew its contract with up-and-coming executive Robert Stern because of "poor creative choices" and "reckless disregard for fiscal matters." As part of his severance package, Mr. Stern will retain a first look deal at Paramound, through his newly formed production company, Know-it-all Pictures.

The federal trial, which wrapped up today, left Campbell, a member of the dreaded "Terror Watch List," charged with three years for "threatening and endangering a federal official." Johnny Cochrane felt that the sentence, considered a slap on the wrist by some, to be "a fair and just verdict."

# 24

# Bruce Man of Alcatraz

I'd been incarcerated before, dozens of times, in fact. I know what it's like to sweat under the hot lights of a lineup, or cry myself to sleep in a ten-by-ten cell. And unlike other men, I had actually planned great escapes and executed them, picked locks, and gone over the wall, laughing all the while. I even ripped off a prison laundry system, just to see the look on the warden's face. Granted, it was all while acting in films or TV shows, but the experience prepared me for doing time in the Chino Men's Facility in southern California.

It wasn't as bad as you might think. I got three squares a day, my own bed, and plenty of Latino-themed television. In return, all I had to do was empty the garbage once a day for two hours. Sure, you get the shit jobs at first, that's how the joint works, but with a little ingenuity and two cartons of Kool Extras, I worked my way up to cleaning executive offices.

Mostly, though, I just exercised, or read books in my three-man cell. It took awhile, but I also earned a write-in degree in electrical engineering from the DeVry Institute.

One day, I had a visitor, which was unusual.

"Campbell — fresh shirt!" the jack called out.

I walked across the hardscrabble yard to the visitation room. There, waiting for me behind reinforced green glass, were Rob Stern, nemesis extraordinaire, and a lawyerly-type fellow.

"No offense, but of anyone on the entire planet I *wouldn't* want to see, it would be you," I said, taking my seat on a wobbly plastic chair.

"I can understand your disappointment," Rob agreed, "so let's get right down to business." He cleared his throat and wiped sweaty hands on his jeans. "Well, uh, as you know, I *left* Paramount...."

"Yeah, I read the release where they fired your ass. I wish I could say I was sorry."

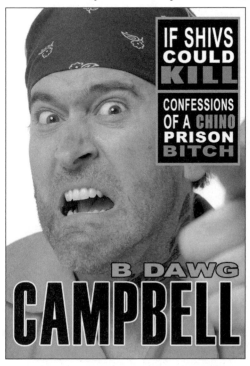

IF SHIVS COULD KILL

CONFESSIONS OF A CHINO PRISON BITCH

B DAWG CAMPBELL

"Oh, don't be, they gave me a first-look producing deal."

"Hey, I'm really impressed, but can you get to the point? I can only use free weights during certain hours."

"I just pitched a reality-based TV series, and Paramount bought thirteen on air. We'd like you to guest-star in an episode."

"What is it called?"

"*Celebrity Sing-Sing*," Rob said, barely able to contain his glee. "Each week, we do a bit on celebs that have either been in jail, or are currently serving.

We've got Bob Downey, Jr., Heidi Fleiss, Glen Campbell — it's a huge, ensemble cast."

"Thanks, but no thanks. I'll pass."

"Actually, Mr. Campbell, legally, you *can't*," Rob's previously silent partner said matter-of-factly.

"Okay, now who are *you*?" I asked, confused.

"I'm Eugene Glass, Paramount business affairs."

I rolled my eyes. "Look, you guys pulled the plug. I had a pay-or-play deal. I don't owe you anything —"

Eugene unfurled my signed *Let's Make Love!* contract. "In section three, paragraph nine, it implicitly states that in the event of a force majeure, which this production experienced, Paramount Studios has the right to recoup its pay-or-play investment by placing you, at their discretion, in a comparable piece."

"A guest shot on *Celebrity Sing-Sing* is comparable to costarring in a Mike Nichols film? How do you figure that, Clarence Darrow?"

"Paramount is prepared to vigorously defend its legal position," Eugene Glass said with a disturbing finality.

"Can I be the host instead?"

"That role has already been committed."

"To who, Pee-Wee Herman?" I asked bitterly.

"Lanny Sticks."

I exhaled and leaned back in my plastic chair, randomly studying the graffiti scrawled on the walls of the booth. Somehow, it was all fitting. "Let me talk to my people, Mr. Glass, and we'll get back to you."

Later that day, after listening to my cellmate, Buck, ruminate over whether Ten-G, in Block 3, was really interested in a long-term relationship or just shower sex, I suddenly had a revelation. It occurred to me that for the past several months, in the name of research for a movie, I had unwittingly attended nothing short of relationship boot camp. Having recently studied every aspect of men and women, from dating to divorce, I came out the other side with some valuable, *publishable* information.

I sharpened the tip of my No. 2 Fort Ticonderoga pencil on the concrete and pulled out a piece of scrap paper. I was going to get myself a job.

BARRY,

'SUP, SUCKA? B DAWG C HERE, CAN'T TALK LONG — HO CHECK SOON, KNOW WHA I'M SAYING? BEEN LONG TIME SINCE YOU BE MONKEY MOUTHIN BOUT A RELATIONSHIP BOOK, AN' THE OFFER. WORD UP, FOO — I BEEN THINKIN' (PLENTY TIME FO THAT INNA JOYNT) AN' I THINK IT WOULD BE COO TO DO A BOOK AN SHIT 'BOUT MEN AND THEY BITCHES.

WRITE TO ME HERE:
B DAWG C
PRISONER #22987
c/o CHINO MENS CORRECTIONAL INSTITUTE
P.O. BOX 00-3344
CHINO, CA 91710

P.S. FYI, YOU WANT TO THROW DOWN, MAKE A REAL DEAL, FOO — TALK WITH MY ACE BOON COON, RANDY, HE BEEN SPENDIN' TIME IN THE LAW LIBRARY AN SHIT, SO, DON'T FUCK ME OVER ON PAPER, DAWG, OR HE'LL STICK YOU WITH HIS BANGER.

GOTTA BOUNCE,

B D C

P.P.S. THE WHITE SHIRTS IS ASS HOLES

**25**

# Love Springs Eternal

I liken the *Let's Make Love!* experience to a forearm burn from a hot iron — it hurts like hell, and the scar takes forever to fade. Whenever I run into a member of the cast or crew at some function or on another film set, we shrug or laugh at the memory, but mostly we just change the subject.

I was on location in Hong Kong recently, strolling just outside the Central Market, and I noticed a DVD shop. The urge to buy a crappy Hong Kong kung fu movie in Hong Kong was too great, and I ducked inside. The cramped store was a shrine to older, crazier Jackie Chan films, the immortal Bruce Lee, and the new cool cat, Jet Li. But most surprising was a DVD I found in a bargain bin. Upon closer inspection, I recognized both Renée Zellweger and Richard Gere in various photos on the cover, but the film wasn't called *Let's Make Love!,* it was called *Love You to Death!* It sure as hell wasn't a romantic comedy, it was an over-the-top kung fu flick that had obviously cannibalized the action scenes from *Let's Make Love!*

*At least it finally got released,* I mused.

The *Love You to Death!* DVD makes for a great party favor at home, and an even better paperweight. It's also a fitting reminder that relationships in front of the camera aren't nearly as interesting as the ones in real life.

As for the "B-movie virus" I was accused of spreading, I've got news for you: the virus had already been active for years. What Hollywood considers A-list blockbusters are really just pumped-up, cheeseball, Saturday matinee serials: *Star Wars*, *Indiana Jones*, and *Pirates of the Caribbean* are all great examples of this.

B movies won a long time ago; the A movies just don't know it yet.

FADE OUT

# Acknowledgments

This is undoubtedly the most boring part of every book, but acknowledgments are included for a reason. In my case, it's to admit that *Make Love the Bruce Campbell Way!* wasn't a one-man operation.

I write the words, but there are very talented people who join in during the process to make sure they are in the right order, are spelled correctly, and that they all add up to something in the end.

First and foremost, I want to give a fat-ass shout to Barry Neville. To call him my editor would be a mockery of his contribution. Through this sometimes bewildering process, Barry helped immensely to shape the fabric of the *Love* story and to establish, not only its tone, but its point-of-view, which is all-important when you're pulling this stuff out of your butt. FYI, for those of you who thought the book blew, I'll provide you with Barry's home phone number and you can bitch him out personally.

Backing up Barry's invaluable assistance is the ever-loopy

Craig "Kif" Sanborn and his graphic design. I still have a dial-up internet connection in Oregon, so downloading preliminary images for the book was torture because it took forever, and I couldn't wait to see how he had spun the latest idea. I've known the little bastard long enough for him to start giving me lip. Good on ya, mate!

Mike Ditz has always been a quiet, steady source of cool ideas when it comes to photography. Mike shot the cover of the *Chins* book, and I knew he had to do the same for *Make Love*. He also shot gobs of reference photos used in those bizarre "morphed" images that appear throughout the book. I've known Mike for a hundred years, and I love the fact that we still work together. He's in Los Angeles — hire him.

Many thanks also to Melanie "Mel" Tooker. I not only stole her identity for the book without asking, I've taken advantage of her makeup talents for years. Thankfully, she's still willing to work around me.

Once the elements of a book start to come together, an author relies on the publishing house to finish the heavy lifting. Pete Wolverton, my editor and boss at St. Martin's Press, is one such laborer. Pete is a no-nonsense New Yorker with good insight into material and he keeps dizzy Oregonians like me on the right path. "Right away, sir!"

You can't have a successful book without sales, so I must belatedly recognize both Joe Rinaldi (PR) and Harriet Seltzer (author events queen) for their efforts on the tour and promotion for *Chins*, and for their hard work on *Bruce's Summer of Love Tour*. Getting an author to forty-five cities in three months — and letting people know how to find him — takes more effort than you might imagine.

Jodi Reamer is my literary agent. Having her around guarantees that deals will get made and important things will not be overlooked. Aside from actually reading the books she repre-sents, Jodi is a big overall help behind the scenes. Thanks for the attention span!

My wife, Ida, and I just celebrated fourteen years of marital bliss. She seems to think living with an actor is a good thing and I love her for it. Rebecca and Andy are two of the groovi-est kids a defacto gypsy dad could ever have, and although we have difficulty recognizing each other from time to time, they are my favorite people to come home to. See you at the swimmin' hole!

Joanne, my darling mother, started writing way before I ever did, just for the love of it, and I'm sure it had a positive influ-ence on me. She's been an unwavering rock of support (except the time I broke the neighbor's Christmas lights), and I love her dearly for it.

A general note to the real people portrayed in the book: I hope you're happy – you all come across way smarter than I do.

Finally, I dedicate this book to my old man, Charles Newton Campbell, who passed away on November 3rd, 2004. Charlie was the guy who inspired me to become an actor, and he put his money where his mouth was as the first investor of my first film, *Evil Dead*.

Everyone in the arts needs a patron and I will be eternally grateful to know that I had one in Charlie. Thanks, Chook.

Charles N. Campbell
1928-2004